The FORTUNE TELLER'S Daughter

T0125927

Diane Wood

Bella
BOOKS
2014

Bella Books, Inc.
P.O. Box 10543
Tallahassee, FL 32302

Printed in the United States of America on acid-free paper.

First Bella Books Edition 2014

Editor: Medora MacDougall
Cover Designer: Linda Callaghan

ISBN: 978-1-59493-393-6

Other Bella Books by Diane Wood

Web of Obsessions

About the Author

Diane Wood was raised by an English mother and Scottish father between New Zealand, England, Scotland and Australia. Leaving home just after her fifteenth birthday, she fled to far North Western Australia where, by falsifying her birth certificate and qualifications, she won a position with an outback mining company. Returning to the UK as a seventeen-year-old, Diane worked on the London buses, joined the Army, got kicked out of the Army for being a lesbian, joined the Prison Service and spent many years enjoying the *gay* life in London—before returning to Australia. Losing both parents within weeks of each other as a teenager and years later, her brother to murder, Diane found an outlet in writing, and shortly after her brother's death began the process of writing her first novel, *Web of Obsessions*, which was published in 2013.

Diane now lives on the Central Coast of New South Wales with her partner of thirty-one years, and is working toward the magical day when she can retire to full-time writing.

Dedication

To our beloved friends, Gerry and Anne
Your incredible generosity will stay in our hearts forever
Now, during this, the worst of times,
this book is dedicated to you and your battle
Fight the Fight
And always know that the force of our Love is with you

Acknowledgment

To my ever supportive and ever loving, Barb, who is there for me every step of the way—not just in my writing, but in all things that happen around it. I cannot thank you enough.

A special thanks to my editor, Medora MacDougall. You challenged me to do things differently, and because of your efforts the book is much improved. Best of all, I learned so much from you. My gratitude also to all at Bella—you took my dream and made it real, and now you're doing it again.

To all of those friends and readers who bought my first novel, *Web of Obsessions*—thank you for your feedback and support, and especially to Terry who bought multiple copies, gave them to her friends and then organised a BBQ where we could all meet. With support like that, how could I not keep on writing?

PROLOGUE

Already nervous, Christine swallowed hard as she watched Nathalie Duncan push open the wrought-iron gate and step back into the shadows—at the same time motioning for her to lead the way. She hesitated, trepidation causing her heart to skip a beat and her large green eyes to widen in alarm. Her every instinct screamed for her to leave. Yet her youthful innocence made her want to please.

"It's okay, Chris," Nat murmured, looking into the vine-and tree-covered walkway. "It's dark, but it's okay."

"I don't know, Nat," she whispered. "This is a bit weird. Why do we have to do this?"

"Because Mother wants to meet you," the dark girl responded automatically. "She's insisting on meeting you. Please, Christine… for me?" Desperation flowed from intense gray eyes.

Nodding reluctantly, Christine ducked to avoid overhanging branches as a hideous shriek rent the air. Screaming, she turned to flee, and crashed wildly into her girlfriend.

"Shit," mumbled Nat, hurriedly grabbing Christine's hand. "It's only a cat."

"Jesus," Chris hissed, angrily, a shiver passing down her spine. "Can't we just do it another time?"

Without replying, Nat used her free hand to hammer with the old-fashioned knocker.

"I thought you lived here. Don't you have a key?"

"I do," she replied with a shrug, reaching into the pocket of her jacket. "But Mother likes me to knock first." Pulling out a set of keys, she undid first one lock and then a second. Pushing the door with her elbow and stepping into the hallway, she indicated for Christine to join her.

Peering into the dimness, Chris felt overwhelmed. Having a lover, and a female one at that, was peculiar enough at her age without this strange ritual that Nat was insisting on.

To their right a large wooden staircase disappeared upward, and to the left the gloom of the corridor stretched endlessly before them. Moving down the hall, they made their way in single file toward another heavy wooden door. The light filtering underneath it appeared to be the only light in the house, and it occurred to Christine that it was strange that Nat hadn't turned on a hall light. Then she felt the warmth of Nat's hand touch her back, guiding her firmly forward.

Nathalie knocked lightly before pushing open the door. It looked like a door that would creak on rusty hinges. Instead it opened smoothly and silently. The light in the room was dim, but compared to the darkness in the hallway it appeared comforting. The room was empty except for several poodles sitting motionless—watching—their black eyes tracking every movement—their silence unnerving.

"Mother must be in the sunroom," Nathalie said, glancing around the room but making no comment about the dogs.

Suppressing a shudder, Christine looked around. The room had an open fireplace but no fire, and it felt even colder than outside. The furniture was old-fashioned but of good quality, and the wallpaper appeared colorless and mottled. She couldn't tell whether that was because of the way the light reflected from the two heavily covered lampshades or whether it really was stained and old.

Wordlessly, Nathalie guided Christine toward a door at the far end of the room. Still the dogs didn't move or make a sound—not that Christine would have heard them over the frantic pounding of her heart. Looking at Nathalie's face, she was concerned to see the iciness reflected back at her. Nat was every bit as scared as she was. This realization only worried her more.

Again Nathalie knocked lightly before pushing the door open. This room seemed even more dimly lit than the one they were leaving, but as Christine stepped down the single step into the room, it at least felt to her somewhat warmer.

"Hello, Mother," greeted Nat quietly into the large room. "I've brought Christine to meet you."

Squinting into the dimness, Christine made out the figure of a woman sitting at what appeared to be a card table. Her body was bent over the table, and the single bar electric heater at her feet cast an eerie red glow over her lower body.

"Welcome, my dear," replied the woman without looking up. "It's so nice to have you to my home. Do come in." The voice was low and smooth and the welcome almost sensual as the woman continued to look at the cards spread before her.

As Nathalie pushed her forward, Christine glanced around the room. It was quite a narrow room, but a long one and it opened out beyond where Nathalie's mother sat. All the windows were heavily curtained and every piece of furniture had something on it—books, charts, Tarot cards, crystals, candles and still more books.

Originally the room would have been a parlor, where years ago the ladies of the house entertained their guests in privacy. Now it was being used as a living room and study. Someone needed to replace the lightbulbs in the mock chandelier that hung directly over the card table. Its four small bulbs made everything in the room look dull and dingy. Swallowing a feeling of dread, Christine took a step toward Nathalie's mother.

Only now did the woman begin to rise from her table.

At first she thought that Nat's mother was very old and thin, but clearly the light had played tricks, because as she stood to receive the introduction, the woman before her appeared young, slim and stunningly beautiful.

"So pleased to meet you," the woman gushed, moving forward. "The cards are very auspicious for today's meeting," she said, indicating the spread of Tarot cards on the table beside her. Then, taking the surprised girl into her arms, she gave her a lingering—and very un-motherly—kiss.

The intimacy and passion of it took Christine aback, the overwhelming attractiveness and sensuality of this woman and the feel of her body against her own leaving her aroused and disgusted all at once. This was her lover's mother. This was all wrong.

"Pleased to meet you," she mumbled, trying to pull her eyes away from the intensity of the woman's gaze. Could the woman read her mind, sense her arousal? Suddenly Chris knew that she could—and that she was enjoying it. Her emotions in overdrive, Chris managed a glance toward Nathalie, expecting to see embarrassment or a look of apology. All she saw was open resentment aimed squarely at her mother. This time when she focused back on Nat's mother she saw triumph reflected in her eyes. Oddly she felt flattered by the attention.

"Can we move into the lounge?" Nat inquired quietly. "It would be more comfortable."

"No, I think the parlor will be fine," stated her mother, casting an impatient look at her. "I'd have to move my dogs if we used that room, and besides it's too formal."

Moving away from Christine, the woman began to walk toward the rear of the room, showing them both to an old-fashioned living area. The back part of the room was as packed with furniture and books as the study was, but here at least the seats were empty—as if awaiting the arrival of guests.

"Nathalie, do make us some coffee, won't you?" her mother demanded, gesturing toward a rear door.

For a moment Nathalie didn't move, her eyes flicking between Christine and her mother, her reluctance to leave obvious.

The hesitation hadn't gone unnoticed.

Glancing toward her daughter, her mother insisted, "Now, Nathalie. Goodness, girl, we'll all die of thirst waiting for you."

The voice was soft and gentle and at odds with the intensity of the demand.

Panic at being left alone with this strange woman flooded Chris, and she looked pleadingly at Nat, but her friend's focus was on her mother. Christine's heart sank as Nathalie turned and disappeared through the dark brown door.

"So, you're Nathalie's newest girlfriend?" the woman stated, sitting down in a rigid-backed chair and gesturing toward the ancient green sofa. "You're fourteen too, I presume? I must say that you're not like her usual friends."

Still embarrassed from the kiss and unsure what to say, Christine made a production of settling herself into her seat. As she did so, she took the opportunity to look around the room. It was as ill-lit as the others, and although there was a small lamp on a covered coffee table not far from them, most of the light seemed to come from the strange-looking chandelier near the card table. Suddenly she felt small and very much out of her depth.

"Thank you for inviting me, Mrs. Duncan," she said timidly. "Nathalie has spoken about you often."

"Oh, I doubt that, my dear," she challenged. Her eyes were flat and lifeless. "I truly don't think Nathalie is very fond of me. But then that's a mother's lot isn't it? Raising children, only to have them argue or rebel at the first opportunity."

The words held a hint of annoyance, but then she smiled, and the tension dissolved—to be replaced by a feeling of warm acceptance. It was as if a potent drug had just been released into the atmosphere, heightening Christine's awareness of her surroundings and of the attraction and fear she felt toward her lover's mother. Overwhelmed by guilt and confusion, Christine dragged her eyes away and again began looking around the room.

Every wall was covered in prints or paintings of esoteric beings—goblins, witches, angels, leprechauns, anything representing that *other* world. Nathalie had told her that her mother was heavily involved in the occult and that she read the fortunes of the wealthy for a living, but nothing had prepared Christine for this house or the feelings Nat's mother would evoke. "Your house is very interesting, Mrs. Duncan," she lied, desperate to break the silence. "Nathalie told me you're interested in the occult."

"Oh, not just *interested*, my dear," declared the woman with that flirtatious smile. "I live the occult and it lives through me." Then, pausing to adjust her long flowing skirt, she said, "But please, call me Charlotte…and my surname is Silver. I was never married to Nathalie's father. He only stayed around long enough to put his name on her birth certificate."

Something about the way she spoke reminded Christine of her grandparents, yet the woman couldn't have been more than about thirty-four, and she looked even younger. Her body was slim and supple, and although she gave the impression of being a "dark" woman, her coloring was actually very fair. Even as Christine tried to evaluate what it was about Charlotte that fascinated her so much, it occurred to her that her assessment hadn't gone unnoticed. The woman's smile had become blatantly sexual and her eyes deliciously inviting.

As Christine struggled to hide the blush spreading across her face, Nathalie entered the room with a tray in her hands. For a second she seemed to hesitate and Christine noted the flash of anger in her eyes and how the smooth dark skin crinkled around her mouth. She appeared tense and worried, but her eyes didn't meet those of either Christine or her mother. Instead she busied herself playing hostess. Had she sensed the electricity between them?

Laying the tray on a table, Nathalie handed her mother a black coffee and offered a plate of chocolate biscuits. Taking one with an acknowledging nod, Charlotte watched as Nathalie handed Christine her cup, extended the biscuits and then took a seat beside her.

"I hope Mother hasn't been asking too many awkward questions while I was gone," Nathalie said without any hint of humor. "You know what mothers can be like."

"Well, it isn't every day that a mother gets to meet her daughter's lover, is it now, Christine?" Then addressing Nathalie, "You are lovers, aren't you, darling?" she asked pointedly.

"Yes, Mother, we are," answered Nathalie quietly, glancing in Christine's direction. "But really that's our business."

"Oh, of course it is, my darling, of course it is," she murmured. "But you know how fascinated I am by anything perverse."

Stunned, Christine looked toward Nathalie, expecting her to be embarrassed or angry.

Instead she found Nathalie smiling at her mother, as if proud that she was doing something that had made her mother sit up and take notice.

For just an instant, Christine could see a likeness between mother and daughter. It wasn't a physical thing because Nat's athletic darkness was in complete contrast to her mother's delicate fairness. It was more in the strange challenging look that each wore and the coldness in their eyes. It sent a twinge of fear through her, as, with a start, she realized how little she truly knew about Nathalie Duncan.

* * *

They'd met at school a few months earlier, when Christine had moved to Sydney's inner city with her mother and older sister. It wasn't that they'd wanted to leave their large suburban home, but when her father had died, leaving them few resources, her mother had decided they needed a smaller, cheaper place that was closer to her work.

It had been traumatic for them all, but more so for a fourteen-year-old already suffering the disturbance of her emerging sexuality. For the longest time she made no effort to connect with anyone at her new school, but eventually her looks attracted a few. Still she was the outsider, groups and cliques having already formed in the earlier years of high school.

Then she'd met Nathalie. She had immediately been affected by the power of the strange dark girl with the very short hair. At times she seemed to blend perfectly into her surroundings, but at other times it was impossible not to notice her. In class she answered questions only when directly asked, but she always got them right, and when it came to tests or exams Nathalie never failed to earn top marks. Her classmates were in awe of her—but also envious, curious and discreetly disdainful.

The very strangeness of Nathalie attracted Christine and made her want to know more.

Theirs was a multiethnic school, yet Nathalie didn't seem to fit within any of the obvious social or racial groups. Her hair was black and spiky, her eyes were the lightest gray and she had skin the color of coffee latte, but her race was a complete mystery. At first she'd appeared to Christine as confident and aloof, but gradually it occurred to her that this was simply the way Nathalie dealt with being different.

And Nathalie was definitely different. She never wore the latest fashions of pretty skirts and dresses, makeup and accessories. She looked like a boy and dressed like a boy. Jeans, shirts and name-brand running shoes were her daily school uniform, her books and stationery thrown casually into an old army backpack.

Expecting Nathalie to be the target of taunting from her peers, Christine was fascinated to watch how deferential everyone was toward her—including the teachers. Behind her back there were whispers but never raised voices. It was as if she intimidated them—not overtly, but purely by her presence.

Nathalie paid Christine no attention at all for the first months. It was during the third month that she first spoke directly to her.

Missing her father and feeling particularly miserable and distracted, Christine had paid little attention during the lesson and had managed to miss the instructions regarding that night's assignment. Then as the final bell rang and everyone including the teacher exited the classroom, she'd found herself alone with Nathalie.

It was as if the girl knew she had a problem. "You seem so sad," Nathalie stated in her warm, smooth voice as Christine began slowly packing up her books and papers.

"What do you mean?" she heard herself reply, strangely affected by the intimacy of Nathalie speaking directly to her.

"You've been distracted all day and now you look puzzled."

Gathering her thoughts and stunned at her classmate's insight, she shrugged. "I missed what homework we had to do for tomorrow. Daydreaming, I guess."

"Do you do that often?" she asked casually. It had been said jokingly, but the look on Nathalie's face had been comforting and understanding, and Christine had felt herself warm to this strange creature. Perhaps it was loneliness or perhaps it was the way the girl looked at her, but suddenly Christine knew that she wanted to know Nathalie Duncan better. Wanted her to be her friend—wanted to tell her everything.

"Sometimes I like daydreaming," she stuttered slightly defensively. "I don't like being at a new school…and I miss my dad." Then without thinking, she added, "Not that my mother cares. She just thinks I need to pull myself together and settle down."

"Well, that's it then," the girl replied quietly. "After all, mothers are always right!" The tinge of bitterness that edged the girl's voice made Christine hesitate for a moment, but her expression hadn't changed, and straightaway she went on to write down the homework the teacher had set. Handing the neatly written paper over to her, Nathalie said, "I've got my mother's car if you want a lift home? You've probably missed your bus by now."

"You can't drive a car!" Christine laughed in surprise. "You're not old enough."

With a mocking shake of her head, Nathalie replied, "I don't need a bit of paper to tell me that I can drive. Besides, Mother maintains that if you can get away with something, then why not? I drive well and I enjoy it." Smiling slightly, Nathalie indicated for Christine to follow.

Without hesitation she did.

"So, do you trust me, Christine?" she asked over her shoulder as they exited the building. "To drive you home, that is," she finished.

Amused, Christine followed without replying. It wasn't really her nature to do anything remotely illicit, but she was sick of being obedient and law-abiding, and somehow this felt right.

Together they left the school grounds, heading for a small side street a short distance away.

"I can't let the teachers see me driving this," said Nathalie, indicating a late model Mercedes. "The secret of doing things you're not supposed to be doing is to make sure you don't flaunt it," she pointed out, unlocking the passenger door and holding it open. "People can turn a blind eye to wrongdoing while they're free to pretend it isn't happening, but if you insist on making them acknowledge it, then they'll feel they must act."

Inside the car the force of Nathalie's personality overpowered Christine, yet she felt comfortable, cared about and fascinated.

Without asking where she lived, Nathalie turned left and left again, heading along the main route to Christine's house. Nathalie was right—she *was* a good driver. But why should that surprise her? It seemed that everything Nathalie Duncan did, she did well. It was only when she stopped the car outside their flat that Christine thought to ask how she knew where she lived.

"Oh, I know everything," Nathalie acknowledged with a nod. "And what I don't know I'll find out."

"What does that mean?" Christine demanded, not sure whether to be worried or not.

"You interested me, so I followed you home one day." It was a statement with no hint of apology and no expectation that anyone would be upset.

Christine was speechless but also strangely flattered.

"I like you and I want us to be friends," Nathalie continued, "but you need to know that most people think I'm a lesbian. Therefore, if you become friends with me there's a good chance that you won't be accepted into any of the other groups around the school."

Her honesty took Christine's breath away. How could this girl, the same age as she was, be so open about such things with a virtual stranger? Was it that she didn't care, or was it some sort of defense mechanism?

"So, how do you feel about that?" Nathalie prompted, interrupting Christine's jumbled thoughts and emotions. "Do you want to be with me? Do you want to be friends?"

"I…I don't know," stuttered Christine, confused. "I…I mean… well, I like you. At least I think I do, but…"

"But…?"

Blushing madly, she asked the question that had been on her mind since she'd first noticed Nathalie Duncan and heard the schoolyard whispers. "*Are* you a lesbian?"

"I don't know…maybe," she replied nonchalantly. "I prefer having sex with girls than boys and I don't like girl's clothes much, but I'll do it with both." Pausing briefly, she asked, "Does it matter?"

"I don't know," Christine answered honestly. "But, I don't think I am…lesbian that is. I've never…well, I've never actually done it."

"So you haven't had sex. Is that what you're saying?"

Looking down at her skinny knees, Christine didn't answer.

Shrugging and indicating that it wasn't a problem, Nathalie said, "So what? Everyone has to start somewhere, but the first time would be much nicer with another girl than a man—believe me."

Looking up, it didn't surprise Christine to see the invitation reflected in Nathalie's serious gray eyes. It made her feel like a woman. This conversation wasn't like any other she'd had about sex. Those had always been secret, giggling, lurid discussions about a particular boy or boys and their anatomy, and although she'd experienced the same curiosity as her friends, the conversations had never made her feel like a sexual being. This conversation was personal and was taking place with someone she hardly knew, yet she was aware of a need building inside her that would have to be satisfied later in her small bedroom—secretly and silently, under the bed cover.

"I have to go," she muttered, trying to regain control of her burgeoning desire. "My sister will be home from university soon."

"Then I'll see you at school tomorrow?"

Christine was aware of Nathalie watching her as she gathered her books and began climbing out of the car. She didn't know if she wanted to continue with this friendship. It was strange, it was exciting, but she was also just a little afraid. When she failed to respond to her question, Nathalie added, "If you don't want to, that's okay too. Don't worry, I won't embarrass you."

Without waiting for a reply Nathalie leaned over and, pulling the door closed, headed back in the direction she'd just come.

That night, Christine slept very little. All night she was assailed by images of Nathalie—the intensity of her personality, the boyish attractiveness of the girl and the casualness with which she treated her sexuality. Did she want what Nathalie was offering? And if so, did that make her a lesbian? In the past, her erotic fantasies had always been about boys, yet at times many of these boys had appeared rather androgynous. It wasn't the first time that Christine had been confused by her own ambivalence, but it was the first time she'd had to actually confront it.

* * *

Their first time took place in a small flat that Nathalie said was owned by her mother. They'd let the friendship build over those first couple of weeks, spending every spare moment together but never again discussing sex.

Nathalie was intense, humorous and very intelligent, and for Christine it was such a relief to find a friend on the same wavelength as herself. It was hard to ignore the covert glances they received when they ate lunch together, and she felt the eyes of her fellow students burning into her back as she left school each afternoon with Nathalie. Yet while these things bothered her, Christine never doubted her decision to let the friendship take its course.

By the second week Christine had found herself lying to her mother and sister in order to spend time with Nat. Not that it was truly lies. She *was* going to a friend's place and they *were* studying together, but they both knew that it was much more than that. They both knew that inevitably they'd become lovers.

It started with a gentle kiss over coffee, and even now she couldn't remember who'd instigated it. Christine had kissed several boys and felt their hard young bodies against her own, but nothing they'd done had made her body respond with such desire—such unbridled passion.

Slowly and skillfully Nathalie began to undress her, each movement and touch sending thrills of excitement to places Christine didn't even know existed. Moving with her to the bedroom, Nathalie had laid her down and, stripping off her own clothes, had stretched out beside her on the huge bed. Only then did Christine begin to doubt.

Sensing her nervousness, Nathalie whispered, "It's going to be okay, Chris. I promise. You can't stay a virgin forever and this is the best way. Just trust me, I won't hurt you and I know you want it as much as me." Pressing herself against Christine, Nathalie kissed her lips, her neck, then down toward her tiny, young breasts. All the time her hands were wandering, playing a wonderful sensuous tune on every part of her body.

The feeling of flesh against flesh combined with those kisses made all doubt disappear, as Christine's body's demand for satisfaction increased.

Moving away slightly, Nathalie whispered, "I have something for you. Do you trust me?"

Barely able to control her need for completion, Christine nodded her agreement.

Reaching down and pulling out a drawer beneath the bed, Nathalie returned to their lovemaking. This time, though, instead of resuming her stroking and touching, she pressed something firmly between Christine's legs—the pressure making her moan and move to receive its hardness.

At first there was a little gentle pain, but Nathalie was touching her and it was exciting and made her want to open herself more. As she did so the hardness began to fill her and her movements against it became measured and rhythmic—the feeling so much more exciting than she'd ever experienced at her own hand.

Nathalie's movements mirrored her own, as did her breathing and the whimpers of enjoyment. Desperately they clung together in an erotic dance, allowing their need to dictate the pace. Finally, gasping and moaning at the intensity of her pleasure, Christine felt her passion reach its pinnacle—exquisitely releasing all of that glorious tension. Seconds later, Nathalie followed the same route, clinging to her and groaning her satisfaction.

It had been too exciting, too satisfying to turn away from. Doubts crept in at times, but her physical needs took over and Christine found herself almost permanently aroused when she was around Nat. It was like a drug—the more they had sex, the more Christine wanted it and the more exciting Nathalie made it.

Of course her mother and sister asked questions. They wanted to meet Christine's new friend—the one she studied with every afternoon after school. But they were busy with their own lives and didn't seem to notice that she never quite got round to bringing Nathalie home.

It wasn't the same for Nat. Early in their affair, Nathalie told her about her mother—that she lived in an expensive part of town and was independently wealthy, that Nat had never known her father and that her mother had always been happy to let Nat do whatever she wanted—sex, drugs, underage driving. All she demanded was that Nat bring her lovers home to meet her. When Nathalie spoke, Christine thought she detected a sliver of fear in the girl's voice. She dismissed it as her imagination.

* * *

"I think your young friend needs more than coffee," Charlotte whispered to Nathalie, as Christine sat with a stunned look on her face. "Please don't be offended, Christine. What's happening between you and my daughter is perfectly natural and rather lovely. I don't mean to embarrass you. But to the rest of society with its antiquated moral code, you would be seen as 'perverse' and perversity fascinates me."

Unable to formulate any kind of sensible response, Christine simply stared. This woman was so unlike anyone she'd ever met before—beautiful and delicate, but with a ferocious and blatant sexuality that took your breath away. It was hard to take offense at her words. In fact the more she spoke, the more Christine realized that this openness held a hidden promise, something that at once attracted and repulsed her.

"Let's have something stronger to drink," mumbled Nathalie, abruptly rising from her seat and heading toward the kitchen. Moments later she returned with a bottle of bourbon, glasses and an opened, half-full bottle of Coke.

Pouring the drinks, Nathalie said, "This will help us relax and enjoy the evening."

They discussed school and Christine's family and the fact that they didn't know about her "friendship." They spoke of boys and men, Nathalie admitting that her first sexual experience had been with one of her mother's male lovers. By then the alcohol and whatever they'd put into her drink had Christine in a blissful and erotic haze and nothing being said shocked her.

Eventually they ate, but while the food tasted lovely, Christine could not have guessed what it was she was eating. Her concentration was firmly on the feeling of being courted, flattered and given all the attention any normal fourteen-year-old could desire. The warmth of acceptance by this mother and daughter combination made her feel special. She wanted that feeling to last forever.

* * *

Christine's mouth felt dry, her body ached and the smell of the bedclothes was strange. Yet she didn't want to move. Moving was too painful. Slowly she turned her head, trying hard to peer through the gloom of the darkened room.

She was in a huge old-fashioned bed, and she was alone. But where was she? Vague memories flitted briefly through her brain, but as she tried to catch them and pin them down they evaporated, leaving behind only a disconcerting feeling of discomfort—of sadness. Sitting on the edge of the bed, she looked around. There was a strange musky smell that seemed familiar, yet not quite recognizable.

Suddenly, realizing her nakedness, Christine rolled back onto the bed, tears sliding silently down her face. Where was she? And why couldn't she remember? It was this that frightened her the most—the sheer terror of having no memory to draw from. And why was she so sore?

Then it hit her. The smell was sex—different from when she and Nathalie made love, but definitely sex.

Nathalie, something about Nathalie, Nathalie's mother's house? That was it. That was the last thing she remembered—meeting Charlotte Silver.

Rising tentatively and peering through the gloom, Christine found first her underwear, then her jeans and top. Moving slowly, she opened the heavy wooden door, listening for the slightest sound—nothing. The corridor stretched in both directions, but one end seemed to advertise the possibility of a doorway or stairwell, so treading carefully, she made her way toward it.

Questions flooded her brain, but she pushed them aside, hoping only to see an open door leading to the outside world, hoping that this was all a dream and that she would wake up in a moment, safe in the warmth and security of her own single bed.

"Sleeping Beauty awakes." The voice was deep and rich—and male. It came from behind her. Turning quickly, Christine stared. Standing before her was a young man not much older than herself. Tall and lean and startlingly handsome, he wore only underpants, a look of familiarity on his face and a shy smile in his eyes.

"Who are you?" she demanded with a gasp. "And where am I?"

"Well, you really did have a good night, didn't you," he replied nonchalantly. "I didn't think I'd be that forgettable."

Christine started moving toward the top of the stairwell. "I…I need to go home," she stuttered, panicked that once again her memory was failing her and disliking the inference that this boy/man was making about the night before.

"You were very good, you know," stated the boy evenly. "Lots of fun. Even Mother thought so."

She was on the first step now and ready to leap down the rest if he so much as made a move toward her. But he remained where he was.

Suddenly, from the doorway beside him, another figure emerged. She recognized Nathalie's mother, and the recognition made her feel somewhat calmer.

"Oh, good morning, Christine," Charlotte murmured, pulling her skimpy robe a little closer around herself. "How are you feeling this morning? Give me a minute and I'll get downstairs and make us all some breakfast." Reaching out to the half-naked boy, she pulled him into the room, nodding sweetly and closing the door behind them.

For a moment or two Christine stood staring at the door, unable to grasp why the boy, presumably Charlotte's son, would be in her room without his clothes. The whole scenario was too bizarre to contemplate. With the closing of the door, her burning need to leave this place returned. Quickly she moved down the stairs.

Making her way to the front door and turning the handle, she pulled, but the door did not move. Staring at it, she noted the two deadlocks above the handle. Neither came with a key. Pulling at the door in frustration, she began to cry. "Let me out," she begged quietly. "I want to go home. I want to go home."

"It's okay, Chris. It's okay." The voice was right beside her ear as the warm familiar body enveloped her, crushing into her, holding her firmly.

"Nat, thank God." Gasping, she tried to turn around, but the arms held her firmly.

"Ssssh," whispered the voice. "Mother rang your mother to let her know you were staying, so there's no need to rush off. Mother wouldn't like it. Let's have some breakfast and then I'll take you home."

"What happened…last night?" she mumbled, finally able to turn in Nathalie's arms. "Why did I end up in that bed and where were you?"

"Come," she answered, attempting to pull Christine by the arm. "Let's go through to the kitchen."

"No, I don't want to." Christine tried to shake her off. "Why can't I remember what happened? And why is this door locked? And who's the boy upstairs? You never said you had a brother."

"Chris, please—"

"What did you do to me? I want to go home."

"Oh, not yet surely," interrupted another voice from the bottom of the stairs. "That's very discourteous and would displease me immensely."

Both girls stopped in their tracks to look at Charlotte.

Now fully dressed, she stood, her head to one side and arms folded across her chest, a benign smile on her lips and ice in her eyes. "Please, let's at least have coffee before indulging in the guilty histrionics consistent with your conservative background," she demanded, indicating for the girls to move down the passage.

Silently, they made their way back through the room with the dogs, back past the card table and onward into a huge dining and kitchen area at the back of the house. Taking a seat at the large ancient table, Nathalie pulled Christine onto the seat beside her, all the time keeping a tight grip of her hand.

"Now, would everyone like orange juice?" asked Nathalie's mother, as if it were a normal family breakfast.

As Nat's mother moved toward the cooktops, Christine turned to Nathalie. The girl looked pale and her eyes wavered guiltily. "What's going on, Nat? I want to know."

"Nothing," she replied with a slight shrug. "You just got a little drunk last night and Mother phoned to check with your family if you could stay over."

"Then why am I so sore and why weren't you in bed with me when I woke up?"

"I was. I got up earlier, that's all." It wasn't true and they both knew it.

"That boy…the boy I met upstairs, is he your brother?"

"George? He's my half-brother. We had different fathers."

"So why didn't you tell me you had a brother, and where was he when I met your mother yesterday?"

"He didn't come in until later, after we all got drunk. We were having such fun, so he joined in. You didn't seem to mind."

"What?"

Nathalie's eyes were as hard as flint and her stare cut Christine to the bone, plunging her deeper into her nightmare.

"Oh, come on, Chris, don't pretend that you didn't enjoy it," she snapped. "You wanted something to spice up your life, that's why you wanted to be with me. I taught you to enjoy sex with a woman, and George showed you how it could be with a man."

"No…no…I…"

"And you were *very* good," muttered the young man as he entered the room and took a seat opposite. "But I didn't get too greedy. I shared you with Nat and Mother, didn't I, Nat?" Leaning across he reached out to touch Nathalie's face, but resentfully she pushed his hand away.

Laughing, he said, "Nat's just jealous. She'd have liked to keep you all to herself, but Mother insisted we share, didn't she, Nat?"

Staring at him in stunned silence, Christine was only vaguely aware of Charlotte putting down a plate of egg and bacon in front of each of them.

"George is right, of course," Charlotte said, standing behind him and running her hands down his neck and across his shoulders. "Life is only good when everyone is having their needs met, and you certainly seemed to be enjoying yourself last night." Smiling, she continued, "My daughter taught you well."

With that, the memories returned in volume, pouring into Christine's brain, flooding her senses. All of them naked on the huge bed she'd woken up in—Nathalie kissing her, touching her, George moving against her with Charlotte offering eager encouragement. The delicious desire and daring, the joy of feeling needed and the wild excitement of it all. It was fun, it was all about the moment, and she knew she wanted to experience this handsome boy inside her. Moving toward him, she guided him between her legs. There was the sense of Nathalie moving away, her eyes focused on some distant point on the wall, her face tense and miserable, but she wanted him—she wanted George.

"Oh God, oh God," Christine spluttered as the feelings that went with the memories began to intrude, forcing her to recognize her own participation in last night's events. But the memories continued—her awareness of Nathalie's unhappiness, but her own desire to continue what she'd started. "You must have drugged me," she accused, leaping up from the table and denying the crushing weight of her own guilt. "I'd never have done those things except if you drugged me."

"You only did what you wanted to do," answered Charlotte, still standing with her hands on George's shoulders. "It's nothing to be ashamed of. Sex is all a natural part of growing up. Experimenting teaches you how exciting it can be, and you did come back for more—several times."

"No, this isn't right. You're all mad," she mumbled, looking at Nathalie, who avoided her eyes. "I want to go home now. I'm going to tell what you did to me."

"And are you going to tell that you've been having sex with my daughter for weeks? Are you going to tell that you came here voluntarily? Drank alcohol and begged to join in the fun with your lover? And if you do, who's going to believe that you didn't want any of it?" Gasping as the words hit home, Christine ran toward the kitchen door, closely followed by Nathalie.

"Leave me alone," she screamed as Nat made a futile grab for her clothing.

"You haven't got your shoes or your bag, Chris," Nathalie pleaded. "Wait until we find them and I'll drive you home... please."

By now they were back in the hallway, but the front door was still just as locked as when she left it. Bursting into tears, Chris dropped to a crouch beside its formidable blackness. "Don't touch me. Let me out of here," she screamed, slapping at Nathalie's hands when they reached to help her up.

"I'll get your things," she said quietly, heading up the stairs toward the bedrooms. "And then I'll get Mother to let us out."

It was only a minute before she returned. Crouching in front of her, Nathalie whispered, "It will be okay, Chris. You liked George and he liked you. I was younger, but the first man who did it to me hurt me really badly and he didn't care. I didn't want it to happen to you like that."

"You brought me here deliberately so they could use me?"

"No, they wanted you to be part of the family. And you seemed to enjoy it."

"Oh God, you're sick," she spat, standing up. "I hate what you let me do, and I hate your fucking family."

"Now that's not very nice." It was Charlotte, standing slightly behind Nathalie and holding out a set of keys. "It's just your straitlaced upbringing making you believe you have something to feel guilty about. You'll feel much better later, when you come to remember how much you enjoyed yourself."

Snatching for the keys, Chris screamed, "Let me go."

But the hard-faced woman held them tightly and, moving closer to the angry young girl, she whispered into her face, "Don't ever threaten me or my family with disclosure. I have very powerful friends and you really wouldn't like to see me angry."

Then, stepping back a little, she softened her demeanor and, handing Nathalie the keys, she said, "Drive your little friend home, and make sure she's calmed down before you let her out of the car." Addressing Christine, she said, "You were very good, and we don't want Nathalie keeping you to herself. Anytime you want to, feel free to visit us. Believe me, it can be a mutually beneficial arrangement."

Too stunned to speak, Christine watched as Nathalie unlocked first one, then the second lock. As if sensing that she was ready to bolt the moment the door swung open, Nathalie took a firm hold of Christine's hand. "I'll drive you and we'll talk," she said strongly, before leading her like a small child to the plush car parked in the driveway. It was the middle of the morning, but the huge old house and its gardens appeared almost as dark and gloomy as they had last night.

Once in the car, Nathalie locked the doors and put the key in the ignition, making no attempt to start the engine. "We need to talk about this," she said, sounding completely rational. "What are you going to tell your family?"

Staring at her in stunned silence, Christine shook her head, she didn't know the answer. What *was* she going to tell her mother? Without warning the tears flowed. In one debauched night everything had changed. She wasn't Christine Martin, demure student, daughter of respected parents. Suddenly she was Christine Martin—the girl who would do anything for pleasure, including sleeping with her girlfriend's brother and mother. And yes, Charlotte Silver had been right, it had been pleasure, and she had enjoyed it, and she did want more. It had been satisfying and it had been exciting.

But, hanging above all of that, like the Sword of Damocles, was the guilt and the fear of being found out, and those emotions overwhelmed her. Her sobbing bordered on hysteria and nothing Nathalie said helped. She started the car and headed out. Vaguely Christine realized that she had no idea where Nat was taking her—nothing looked familiar—but lost in her own misery she didn't even question why she wasn't being driven home.

Arriving at Nathalie's mother's flat, Nathalie helped Chris from the car.

Only when she entered the flat did Chris ask why she was there. "I should be going home," she mumbled rather unconvincingly.

"I'm worried about you," Nathalie answered, putting her arm around the girl's shoulder and drawing her toward her. "I thought you'd like being part of the Silver family. Mother can be very generous when she's pleased, and you seemed to have a lot of fun when it was happening."

"Oh God, Nat, what am I going to do?" Her tears flowed, as she clung to her girlfriend, hoping she had the answers. "I did enjoy what we did, but people will hate me if they find out."

"It will be okay," Nathalie reassured her, gently touching her tear-stained face. "Nobody will hate you, and nothing has changed."

"Everything's changed," she muttered sadly. She wanted what Charlotte Silver's world offered—to live and be treated like an adult. She wanted to be taken seriously. She wanted to be wanted. Yet her mother would tell her it was wrong. Her sister would tell her it was wrong. They'd never understand.

Her sobbing escalated.

"You're really scaring me now," Nat said, pulling the girl nearer. "You'll make yourself sick. But it will be okay, Chris. I promise," she whispered soothingly, as she walked her toward the bedroom. "I've got something that will make you feel much better."

She heard Nat's words, but their meaning eluded her—the fear and confusion unremitting as Nat encouraged her to sit on the bed.

And then Nat was gone, disappearing into another room—leaving her alone with her pain and turmoil. The tension was unbearable now, as she tried to think logically, tried to calm the crippling thoughts that swirled and crashed inside her head.

When Nat returned, she was holding a belt and some sort of dish with what appeared to be a hypodermic needle in it. "What's that?" she asked, her tears easing slightly with her girlfriend's return. "Is that…" She didn't want to use the word "heroin," it was the ultimate taboo.

"It's just a little something I use occasionally when I have bad dreams or get scared," Nat replied quietly. "It makes you forget all the bad shit going through your head. It won't hurt you and it will make you relax."

"Okay," Chris mumbled, wanting only to feel better.

Sitting very still, she watched as Nathalie pushed up the sleeve of her filmy white top, brushed away the damp hair from her face, and tied off her arm with the narrow belt. She'd seen it in movies. She knew what it meant. And for a second Chris thought about stopping Nathalie…but only for a second.

Tapping out a vein, Nat seemed to hesitate, as if she was going to say something, but a moment later Chris felt the prick of the needle entering her vein and the rush of the sweet liquid washing away every frightening or confusing thought. The peace was instantaneous, and she allowed herself to slump back onto the bed.

A short time later she was being sick, and Nat was wiping her face. But even so, she felt so good, so totally relaxed, so unconcerned. For the moment, she didn't need Nathalie, she didn't need her mother or her sister, and she didn't care what anyone thought.

Releasing a satisfied sigh, Chris lay back down to enjoy the sensation.

She had no idea how long she'd been asleep when she woke and struggled to sit up.

Nat had been lying beside her, and she rolled toward Chris. "Are you okay?" Nat asked, the concern obvious in her voice.

"Sure. I feel…nice. But where are we?" Some of the confidence Chris had experienced earlier was leaving her now, and she was feeling just a little unsure.

"We're at the apartment. I brought you here because you were so upset. I only gave you a very small hit," she explained, "but you couldn't have gone home like that or your mother would have wanted to know what happened."

"I can't tell her, Nat," she whispered, taking hold of her hand. "She and my sister can't ever know. They'd hate me."

"They don't have to know. You can have a shower here, and once the smack wears off some more I'll take you home. It's not that bad really."

"I enjoyed it, Nat," she admitted, the drug allowing her to temporarily bypass the guilt. "I mean, your mother was right. I did want to do those things with you and her and George. It was fun and…God, it was so exciting. It was my fault."

"It was nobody's fault," mumbled Nat. "Mother says wanting sex is normal. She says that you shouldn't have to wait until a certain age, just because some old politician makes a law. She also says that her pills make it all the more enjoyable."

Slowly, very slowly, Nathalie's words sunk in through the delicious warmth of her hit. "What pill?" she asked. "What are you talking about?"

"Mother put it in our drinks. It's only herbal, but it seems to heighten the senses and relax us."

"So I was drugged?"

"No. Mother says it's a relaxant. We got drunk and relaxed. That's all. It hasn't changed anything between us, and Mother will forgive you for what you said before you left. Nobody has to know. It was just one night."

"Yes, you're right," she answered, touching Nathalie's face. "You don't hate me because I let George...and your mother... you know?"

Nathalie smiled. "Just so long as you still like me," she answered quietly, pulling Chris back down beside her.

"It's you I want, Nat," she replied, pressing herself into the dark girl's body and placing Nat's hand between her legs. She was mellow, she was carefree. How nice it would be to feel like this all the time.

It began with a kiss and escalated to warm tender loving, Chris reveling in the renewed enjoyment of her rising excitement and Nathalie's ability to satisfy her need. And yet a small part of her wondered if Charlotte and George would really still welcome her back after everything she'd said. And if so, how would Nat respond.

"Nat..."

"Mmmm..." she mumbled, dozy from the gentle lovemaking they'd just completed.

"The stuff you gave me earlier. It makes me feel really good. Can I have some more?"

CHAPTER ONE

Present Day

It was always the same—hands reaching out and pulling at her clothing, grabbing her wrists, touching her. Nothing she did would free her from their grasp. Then one of them would kiss her, his expensive aftershave and whiskey breath filling her nostrils and his harsh stubble tearing at her face. Then there was his weight crushing her and that excruciating pain as he forced his way into her. Then everything would freeze and she was in a different place, the pressure in her head and chest would start to build, so that drawing breath was difficult and painful. Her eyes wouldn't open, but she knew no one was holding her down. Instead there was the smell and feel of earth crushing her and a terrifying inability to move. Good Mother was watching her with sadness, seeing who she'd turned into and walking away.

They always ended the same way, these nightmares—two identical mothers, one ashamed and sad, turning her back and disappearing through a door, the other holding her down, letting them touch her, whispering words she couldn't hear, but that she knew started as cajoling and ended as threats. And still the paralysis and difficulty breathing, until gasping and sweating she woke—tears of fear and confusion fresh on her cheeks.

Afterward there was exhaustion and intense anger. She couldn't remember a time when they hadn't been part of her personality. Lately, though, they had been worse. Instead of once or twice a week, they were becoming almost nightly events and the breathing was more difficult, so that her lungs hurt and her head spun. When she did wake, it would be with a painful headache.

The clock showed two forty-five a.m., and she was exhausted, but the anger and sadness of the nightmare remained. Nathalie knew it was pointless trying to go back to sleep. Instead, wrapped in her ancient toweling robe, she made her way to the kitchen and turned on the electric kettle. Kick-starting the computer in her study, she returned to make herself a cup of tea.

"Good God, woman, what the hell are you doing?"

"Shit, you frightened me," she exclaimed, turning toward the sleepy male voice in the doorway. "I forgot you'd stayed the night."

"Another nightmare?" he asked, tucking his T-shirt into his baggy old track pants. "It's time you saw someone about those, you know." His voice, although tired, sounded genuinely caring, and once again Nat was saddened that she couldn't tolerate a relationship even with a loving, gentle man like Josh Dawson.

"Soon," she mumbled automatically. "I'll see a shrink soon, but that doesn't explain why you're awake."

Raising an eyebrow in her direction, the tall lean man indicated that it definitely did explain why he was awake. "Nat, you were growling and calling out. It sounded like you were having a major struggle with someone—even worse than usual."

"Sorry."

"So what are you working on?" he asked, indicating the computer through the open doorway. "Or aren't I supposed to know?"

"Just another custody case that nobody wants to handle," she replied vaguely. "An unemployed biracial mother with two kids fighting a wealthy manipulative Anglo husband. And all I can do is offer advice and write a few arguments."

"Aha, then it's probably good that you don't sleep well. You wouldn't have time to do volunteer work at the Women's Center as well as face the *challenges* of working in the prosecutor's office," he said with a grin, wondering if she'd pick up on his sarcasm.

She didn't respond.

"Speaking of which," he continued, "how is that going? I know you didn't give up working as a lawyer and join the police only to be back in lower courts running minor police cases."

"Do you really want to know about that now?" she said with a laugh. "It's three in the morning."

"Good point," he agreed with a wink, moving to lean on the kitchen counter.

Even after all this time it was hard for him to accept that they hadn't been able to make it. He'd loved her, and wanted to understand, wanted to know her better. But she'd never given herself emotionally, and in the long run, what she'd been offering—delicious as it was—hadn't been enough.

"Kathy's moving out today," he stated, running his hands through his dark brown, short-cropped hair. "So I'll take my gear with me and leave you in peace. I must admit it's been nice having your place to run to when things went sour…and nice to catch up."

"Anytime," she answered easily. "You've got the key, you're house-trained and you're used to someone screaming themselves awake in the middle of the night."

With a wave and a nod, he returned to his bedroom. His thoughts traveled to when they were working at the same police station five years ago. It had been love at first sight for him, but it had taken a long time to convince her to go out with him. All those *accidental* meetings and *friendly* cups of coffee before she'd finally agreed to a date. Things had moved quickly from there.

She wasn't his normal type. Not classically beautiful, nor even particularly feminine, but she was slim and sensual, and with a smile that disarmed and eyes that drew you like a magnet she was not to be ignored. And her voice had a cadence and timbre to it that reminded him of the lullabies his mother used to croon to him. It was easy to imagine how she could persuade a crusty old magistrate to see things her way.

Thinking of their time together was getting him aroused. It was the one area he believed they'd been totally compatible—sex. Whenever he was in the mood, she'd been willing, and she was able to satisfy him in a way exclusive to her. However, the lovemaking had been as brilliant as the emotional side had been poor, and eventually, after six exciting but emotionally frustrating months, he'd moved back to his own place. They remained friends and saw each other regularly. They spoke often on the phone and he'd introduced his new lovers for her approval. He suspected Nat had also had the occasional lover, but he never met any of them, and nobody else had ever moved into Nathalie's apartment. As a result, she'd allowed him to use the place whenever he needed to get away from one of his disastrous relationships. But she'd made it very clear the offer didn't include sex.

How he wished it did. Lying back on the bed and reaching downward, he allowed his imagination to take him back to how it used to be.

* * *

The police prosecutor's office was as chaotic as usual and Nathalie's head was pounding, but she had a stack of cases to review before court that simply wouldn't go away. That meant two more headache pills, a hot tea and an effort of will to shake off the feeling of loss and anger from the nightmare. From experience Nathalie knew the feeling would pass, as would the headache, but the frequency of the nightmares was becoming a worry. At this rate she would be too exhausted to do her job.

"Fuck! Police can be so lazy sometimes!"

The voice was loud and coarse and right behind her head.

"Oh God, Bella," Nat moaned, putting her hands to her ears. "It's not even eight o'clock and someone's already upset you?"

The woman was tall and skinny, and although only a few years older than Nathalie, she looked ten years older. "Take a look at some of these briefs," she complained, throwing a pile of files onto Nat's desk. "A six-year-old could do better. Some of them don't even attempt to meet the proofs of the crime, but they expect a successful outcome in court."

"Well, when you're commissioner you can sack them all," replied Nathalie, only half joking.

Bella Pittolo was ambitious and intended being the first Italian/Australian female commissioner of police. Like Nat, Bella was a fully qualified lawyer who'd chosen a career as a police officer. Both had ended up on loan to the Parramatta police prosecutor's office, prosecuting minor offenses in lower court. However, where Bella had a plan for her career, Nat was happy to transfer between any squads that the hierarchy decided needed her.

"So they're finally going to start transitioning out police prosecutors and replace us with civilians," Bella stated. "They're starting with our branch." Shaking her head, she continued. "Thank God they've finally realized that they can't afford to have experienced police tied up prosecuting minor criminals, when we already have the Department of Public Prosecutions set up for the more serious shit. A prosecution's a prosecution, for Christ sake. Anyway, we've got about three months. Can't say I'm heartbroken. I need something more high profile if I want to move up. What about you?"

"What about me…what?" mumbled Nathalie, trying to concentrate on the paperwork in front of her.

"Surely you must have a preference about where you want to transfer? You'll never get on if you let them hide you away in some obscure little cop shop."

"Don't really care."

"Strikes me," she said dramatically, "that you don't really care about anything. How long has it been since you got laid?"

"Fuck off, Bella! My head hurts, I'm very tired and I don't want to hear how you can set me up with one of your friends."

"Then have a drink with us after work tonight. I'm meeting Jackie at the Castle, having a meal and then heading home. You haven't got anything better to do."

"How the hell do you know?" She tried to sound indignant, but it didn't work.

"Just say yes, and I'll leave you alone."

"Yes."

Smiling, Bella picked up her files and returned to her office. She had only been in the force a short time and had already made sergeant. For Nathalie being a police officer was something she'd fallen into after two years of boredom in a prestigious law firm. The money had been excellent and there had been the promise of more to come, but it had been mind-numbing and emotionally draining to defend people who, for the most part, she loathed. The law degree and top marks at the police academy ensured she was on the fast track, but her lack of ambition over the last six years meant she'd never exploited her opportunities. Still, among numerous other police courses on offer, she'd completed the detective's course and worked briefly in the local police's detective's office before being rushed into police prosecutions. Idly it occurred to her that if transfers were imminent, it might be worth applying for a detective position in the inner western suburbs or Sydney central. At least that would be close to home.

* * *

Court took most of the day and then they were heading to the Castle.

Bella was hard to like—perhaps that was the very reason they'd formed a friendship. Neither woman shared emotions or cared what others thought of them, but in every other way they were opposites. Bella was pale, large-boned and awkward, with a plain, serious face, while Nat was dark, athletic and attractive. While Bella could be aggressive and demanding, Nat seemed able to command the same level of respect with a few simple words or one icy look. Intellectually they were equals, and it had taken only a short time for each to conclude that the other could be trusted.

Jackie was sitting at a table near the back of the room and waved as they entered. Every time she saw them, Nathalie wondered about how Jackie and Bella had got together. They seemed to have so little in common.

Bella never discussed her private life at work. People assumed from her physical appearance that she was lesbian, although they'd never mention it to her face. The only reason Nathalie knew about Bella's sexuality was because Bella had made the assumption that Nat was into women and had carried on a conversation accordingly.

Nat had told her about Josh and left it at that, but Bella insisted that at the very least Nathalie should open herself to the option of bisexuality. This wasn't a subject Nat wanted to discuss—even with Bella, whom she now considered a friend.

Jackie was short and slim with glasses and blond, curly hair that appeared to always be in her face. She seemed pleasant enough, although Nathalie sometimes got the impression she was flirting with her behind Bella's back. The two women had only been together a short time.

"So glad to see you again," Jackie greeted with a smile. "I was beginning to think you were avoiding us because of Bella's efforts to turn you into a dyke." The greeting came with a hug and a kiss that made Nathalie uncomfortable. She wasn't a tactile person and would prefer to shake someone's hand rather than embrace.

"It's good to see you too," she responded automatically, taking a seat opposite the two women. "How's your new job?"

"Don't ask," she said with a grimace, looking toward Bella for support. "Anyone who tells you being a waitress is easy has rocks in their head."

"Well, you could try staying in one job for more than a month and you might not have to lower yourself to serving other people meals," argued Bella, obviously not impressed with the girl's new job.

"She's right of course," agreed Jackie acceptingly. "But life's too short to stay in boring jobs that don't fulfill the soul."

"And being a waitress does?" snapped Bella in her usual aggressive manner.

There was silence while Bella threw back her whiskey and raised her hand toward the waiter for another. Again Nathalie wondered what these two women could possibly have in common. Yet Jackie never flinched, accepting Bella's comments with a giggle and a vapid smile.

They chatted for a while about mutual acquaintances, about the job and about Nat's social life or lack of it, and then Jackie asked about her work with the Women's Center.

"I don't do much," Nathalie explained. "I can't represent anyone in court because with me being in the police it could become a conflict of interest. But I can offer legal advice or suggest lawyers who might help. Sometimes it's just letting the women know their options."

"Sounds most altruistic," muttered Bella, who had little time for what she called "needy women." "But isn't that what their own lawyer is supposed to be doing?"

"Not everyone can afford a lawyer, as you well know, Bella," Nathalie reminded her. "And, as you also know, sometimes it's just a matter of writing a letter or pointing them in the right direction. Besides, I enjoy it."

"And it gives you an excuse not to have a social life," she responded dryly, slurring her words slightly from the whiskeys she'd poured down her throat.

"Bella, for heaven's sake, Nathalie doesn't look like she's pining for love. And I'm sure if she wants someone she'll have no trouble winning them. You're not her mother." The steely undertone in Jackie's voice drew Nathalie's attention, but all she saw was a smiling woman with a twinkle in her eye.

Forcing a smile, she replied, "Thanks, Jack. It's time someone told your girlfriend to get off my back about relationships. It's becoming an obsession."

Shaking her head, Bella just laughed.

While Bella was ambitious, Jackie was the opposite. Any job was a good job—for a while anyway. And her idea of a good book was a woman's magazine. Yet, she could be witty and funny and something about her left Nat with the impression she was far more intelligent and cunning than she wanted anyone to know. And that puzzled her. Still, Jackie did put up with Bella, who, although dismissive of her, seemed quite fond of the girl. And together they could be good company.

At the end of the evening, Nathalie dropped the two women back at Bella's house and headed home.

* * *

The nightmares continued the rest of the week. By Friday evening Nathalie was exhausted, but it didn't stop her going to the Women's Center.

The center consisted of an administration office, staff common room, large recreational area and five general offices. It provided medical and legal advice, a social worker, counseling and information services for women in difficulty. From time to time it also ran parenting, child health and basic money management workshops. Most importantly it provided a safe place for women to meet, share their experiences and support one another.

Established by Jordan MacKenzie and her partner, Danielle Veillard—wealthy ex-prison workers—the center continued partly through government funding, but largely because of a yearly grant provided by this couple.

While the center had numerous community contacts and a range of professionals who gave their time, they'd been missing the services of a psychologist. Recently they'd received information about a woman who might be able to help.

"We've decided that you should be the one to approach her," said Lenore Kingsley, the center's social worker and manager, addressing Nathalie.

"Me?" queried Nat, looking around the table at the faces of the other three volunteers. "Why me? I don't know her any more than you do."

"But you're the most persuasive," declared Rena, the jovial Pacific Islander who lent her nursing skills to the center two or three times a week. "You could convince anyone of anything or, alternately, scare them into submitting."

Stunned, Nat drew a deep breath. That wasn't how she saw herself, but it was how she thought of her mother. Was she really that much like her?

"Who is she?" she asked reluctantly. "And what makes you think she'd want to put in time at the center?"

"Her name's Alexandra Messner," replied Lenore, reading from the notes in front of her. "She's a clinical psychologist at the women's prison. A friend of mine works there as a social worker and recommended her because she's got an excellent reputation among the prisoners and the staff. She's straight down the line apparently and very good at getting her patients to acknowledge and find ways to deal with their problems."

"It definitely sounds like someone we could use here." Rena nodded amiably. "Some of these women have big problems."

So it was decided.

By the time she finished at the center, Nathalie was exhausted and grateful there was no work the next morning. Two glasses of port later, she sank into her first dreamless sleep for a week.

CHAPTER TWO

Offers Of Help

The noise wasn't her alarm clock. It was shriller and more demanding. Even so it took a long time to penetrate the wonderful haze of a good night's sleep. Moaning with annoyance and reaching out, she grabbed the offending handset.

"Hello," she growled, barely attempting to hide her irritability.

"Ms. Duncan…Nathalie Duncan?"

"Yes," she replied snappily, assuming it was someone selling something.

"My name's Alex Messner. A Lenore Kingsley gave your phone number to my answering service last night…regarding volunteering at the women's center," she finished hesitantly. "I'm sorry if I woke you."

"No…no," she mumbled, throwing her naked legs out of the bed and sitting up. "That's okay." Looking at the clock, Nathalie was stunned to see that it was ten fifteen. She never slept late.

"Then perhaps you can tell me what's involved?" the woman asked with a hint of humor, obviously aware that she *had* woken Nathalie.

"Yes…yes. I'm sorry. I'm not usually so vague," she mumbled. "I don't know what Lenore told you, but she's the manager of the Courtside Women's Crisis Center in Strathfield, and I volunteer a few hours a week there. What I'd like, if you've got the time, is to meet with you to discuss the center and what we do…to see if we could interest you in helping out."

For a moment there was silence and Nathalie assumed she was going to turn them down point-blank. Instead, she said, "I see. Help you out in what way?"

"To provide a counseling service for a few hours a week— many of our clients come with a range of emotional and personal issues."

"I see," she repeated.

"Look, it's a little difficult discussing this over the phone," Nathalie offered. "I was hoping you'd let me take you to lunch or at least buy you a cup of coffee…at your convenience. I realize you're probably very busy, but the center does some great work and we could really do with some help."

"Well, I suppose I've got nothing to lose by meeting with you," she replied thoughtfully. "But I must warn you that you may be wasting your time. Right now I've got a pretty hectic schedule."

"That's fine, I'll take my chances. When would you be free to meet?"

"What about lunch tomorrow at my house? I'll even provide the food. It's just that I'll be going out later and it makes it easier."

After she hung up, Nathalie couldn't shake the feeling that she knew this woman. There was a cadence to her voice that made her think of the past. Someone from university or the law firm maybe? The name meant nothing to her, but it made her curious.

* * *

The nightmares returned that night. The man with the rough hands had her on her stomach, penetrating her from behind. The pain was excruciating and his weight crushed the breath from her body. In the background a woman whispered instructions, her voice becoming more and more excited. Then there were the two mothers, one crying and turning away, the other leering and voiceless—her eyes promising untold horrors still to come.

She woke just after three a.m., the vivid memory of pain and terror producing gasping, body-shaking sobs. She sat up until dawn, every light in the flat blazing. That the nightmares were getting worse couldn't be denied, yet the idea of telling anyone the details of these hideous dreams frightened her more than the horror they evoked. Somehow she had to deal with them—had to make them go away or fade into insignificance. She'd done it as a child. Why was it so difficult now?

It was cloudy when Nat pulled up outside Alexandra Messner's large modern townhouse and found an attractive brunette pulling weeds from the small garden bed.

"You must be Nathalie Duncan," she said with a smile as she extended a soft, warm hand. "Please come in." She appeared to be several years older than Nathalie and was dressed for the garden in bike shorts and an old shirt—her suntanned shapely legs immediately catching Nathalie's attention. The woman seemed relaxed and her green eyes sparkled with warmth and intelligence.

Alex Messner was surprised. For some reason she'd expected Nathalie Duncan to be older and more motherly. Instead here was an attractive young woman of mixed race, dressed in a business suit, with the most startling gray eyes she'd ever seen. Instantly she knew this was someone she'd like. Indicating for Nat to have a seat, she threw herself into the chair opposite. "I'm sorry to have to ask you here," she said, assessing Nathalie's body language. "But as you can see, I'm not really into formalities, and I'm always more comfortable in my own setting."

"You're very honest," replied Nat, suddenly feeling nervous. "I appreciate you making the time to see me."

"Have you had to come far?" Alex asked, curiously.

"Not far," Nat answered. "I only live seven or eight kilometers from the crisis center at Strathfield."

"So what role do you play at the center?" asked Alex, keeping her eyes fixed on Nathalie's face.

"I give legal advice," she answered quietly, "and I do the occasional babysitting and paperwork."

"Babysitting?"

"It's optional," Nathalie replied with a laugh, enjoying the look of horror on the woman's face. "But it gives some of the mothers without family support an hour or so to themselves."

"So you're a lawyer?"

"I am a lawyer, but I'm also a police officer. Consequently, I never represent anyone in court, but I do offer legal advice and I'll sometimes write letters or make submissions for them."

"And you're looking for a psychologist?"

"Yes. Many of those we see, including the children, have suffered trauma. Often domestic violence or relationship breakdowns, sometimes sexual assault, sometimes it's simply a matter of not coping emotionally with what's happening in their lives. Most of them don't want anything to do with social services or the police, and they don't have the money to seek private counseling. We can't provide long-term fixes, but our aim is to provide them with coping mechanisms in the short term and some basic tools for the long term."

As she listened, Alex detected a hint of passion in Nathalie's voice. Obviously the center meant a lot to her. "Well, I'm a clinical psychologist," she stated thoughtfully. "So I imagine I could provide the service you want, but to be honest I'm not sure that I'd want to. The problem is that I work with traumatized and disturbed women all day in my job, and it can be quite exhausting."

"I understand," replied Nathalie reluctantly. "But that's exactly why you'd be ideal. You'd have a greater understanding of these women than anyone we could get from private practice. And perhaps if they get help in the early stages it might stop them from becoming clients of the prison."

Alex could see how Nathalie Duncan would be a good lawyer, something about the light in her eyes and her intensity made you listen—made you want to please her. And she certainly was attractive.

Standing, Alex indicated for Nathalie to join her. "I've made us a chicken salad," she said, moving toward the rear of the house and into a cozy dining area that opened onto a small patio. "If you're vegetarian, you'll just have to ditch the chicken," she finished with an accompanying laugh.

Moving to a seat, Nathalie looked around. The house was larger than she'd expected and tastefully and comfortably furnished. Everything was neat and tidy and seemed to mirror her own taste.

During lunch they discussed the center, the house, Nathalie's home, their jobs and general subjects that didn't intrude too far into the personal. Throughout, it niggled at Nathalie that Alex reminded her of someone and that she couldn't put her finger on it.

"You make an impressive argument," stated Alex seriously, as Nat finished explaining how her services would benefit the center's clients. "And I'm impressed by your own commitment. So how about you show me around, introduce me to the staff and some of the women and then I'll decide."

"Whenever you're available," responded Nathalie, sensing victory.

It was arranged for Wednesday, with Nathalie picking Alex up from her house.

Satisfied to have got this far, Nathalie left the house on a high. Alex's warmth and humor had raised her spirits and she knew that Alex would be the ideal recruit.

Alex was intrigued. Normally able to assess a person's sexuality and personality easily, she had found Nathalie Duncan an enigma. With her short-cropped black hair and somewhat androgynous appearance, she could appear either quite feminine or slightly masculine. Her manner was neutral to the extreme, as was her clothing, and she gave no indication by look or conversation that would indicate her sexual preference.

Glancing at her watch, Alex realized that she had only half an hour to get ready before her mother arrived and headed for the bathroom. As the water from the shower poured over her, she acknowledged to herself that if she decided to volunteer at the center, getting to know Ms. Nathalie Duncan could prove very interesting.

* * *

That night Nathalie received a phone call from her mother. It was their first contact in nearly twelve months. And the call did not come from overseas.

"So how's my only daughter?" she started, her cold, hard voice cutting through the phone line.

"Mother—" Nathalie gasped in shock.

"You could sound happier to hear from me," the woman interjected acerbically.

"It was a surprise, that's all," she mumbled, trying to stop the anxiety spreading through her body. "Of course I'm happy to hear from you."

"I'm home for a while and George has invited us to a get-together at the house. I trust you'll be there?"

Her soul shrieked, NO, but her voice asked where and when.

"Next weekend…you don't work weekends, so it shouldn't be a problem. George is keen to see you, since you don't keep in touch. And you wouldn't want to disappoint me, would you?"

Swamped by a dread that reached her bowels, she remained silent.

"Answer me, child," demanded Charlotte Silver. "You will be there, won't you?"

"Yes…of course, Mother," she stuttered by rote, the frightened child she thought gone forever returning in force.

"Then we'll expect you in time for tea on Friday."

"Friday…no…I work at a women's center Friday evening." It was out before she could stop herself. The less Mother knew about her life the better, but for some reason her brain seized when forced into confrontation with her.

"Then I expect you'll have to cancel it."

And Nathalie knew that's exactly what she'd do.

Staring blankly, she dropped into the lounge chair, her head threatening to explode. How could she go back now?

It had been years since she'd seen Mother or George and even longer since that unforgettable phone call in the middle of the night informing her that Christine Martin was dead.

"An overdose," Mother had said from Sydney. "Sometime in the early hours of the morning. George found her dead on the bathroom floor after a party with *friends*. I want you to give the police as little information as possible," she'd demanded. "They got your details from George. They want a statement from you because the flat is in your name and you're George's sister. They know you're in Armidale, at the university, so they're going to get local detectives to contact you."

The detectives had rung a few days later, requesting her attendance at the police station.

"So, how long had you known Christine Martin?" the middle-aged detective had asked when she'd presented for interview.

"Since we were fourteen," she'd answered quietly, remembering those early days together.

"What was your relationship with Ms. Martin?"

"She's...she *was* my brother's girlfriend."

"That was all?"

"She was a friend."

"Where did she live?"

"At the flat where she was found."

"You mean your flat!" It wasn't a question, it was more of an accusation.

"I own it, but I don't live there," she answered, trying not to show the annoyance she was feeling.

"Did you know she used heroin and other substances on a regular basis?"

Shrugging, Nathalie remained silent.

"It seems that nobody's willing to admit that they knew Ms. Martin had a serious drug problem, yet she must have been using daily."

"Is that a question?" she asked. "I don't live there, remember."

"Actually, Ms. Duncan," the older detective had answered, "it is a question. You see her family claims that it was your brother who introduced her to heroin and that your family encouraged her use. Is that true?"

"She made her own choices, just like we all do." Nathalie shrugged again. "My family gave her a place to stay after she got involved with my brother and left home. That's all."

"Your mother is Charlotte Silver, and her occupation is…" Now he made the pretense of looking at his paperwork, "fortune teller?"

"Yes."

"She has an impressive client list from what the Sydney detectives tell me."

"So?"

"Well, the family is claiming Christine was threatening to expose a crime committed by your mother. They claim the victim had intended taking her information to the police."

"Really, that's interesting, considering she hadn't seen her family for the last couple of years. She moved out of her home, dropped out of school and rarely contacted them."

As she'd said it, Nathalie remembered a strange conversation Christine had tried to have with her over the phone, about diaries and a murder and secrets that were too awful to talk about. Chris was obviously high and was rambling, and Nat remembered impatiently cutting her short—telling her that she'd talk to her the next time she was in Sydney.

That was the last time they'd spoken.

"So what are they trying to claim?" she asked angrily. "That her overdose wasn't an accident? That's ridiculous."

"Is George Silver…is your brother a regular drug user?"

"You'll have to ask him."

"What about you, Ms. Duncan, do you take drugs or were you ever present when Ms. Martin used drugs?"

"Of course not, Detective, they're illegal, and if I did anything illegal I wouldn't be able to apply to the bar once I complete my law degree."

The younger detective hadn't been able to disguise the grimace that crossed his face, but the older one had looked completely disinterested.

Nathalie realized that this was a routine inquiry brought about by the insistence of the Martin family. She also knew it wasn't going anywhere. She remembered feeling a strange sense of annoyance about this lack of interest.

The interview had lasted only a few minutes more and had included questions about where Nathalie had been on the night Christine died.

* * *

After Christine's death, even with the frantic pace of exam time, Nat found it hard to stop thinking about her. Her death had raised so many questions, things Nat had always refused to think about. Things Mother had always insisted didn't need thinking about.

At Mother's insistence, they'd gotten together after the interviews. Apparently Chris's mother had rung the house a few times, blaming them for luring Christine from her family and for encouraging her drug use. Nathalie had been upset by Chris's death, and George had seemed shocked, but it hadn't appeared to have worried Mother.

Nathalie had been so glad she'd moved away. At home she'd felt overpowered by Mother's personality and expectations, and she'd wanted it to stop. Yet somehow, while she lived there, she'd never found the courage to refuse. Life had been different at the university. For the first time, she'd actually seemed to blend in. It had meant dressing and acting more conservatively, but that had quickly become very comfortable. And she'd enjoyed the challenges of academic life without the feeling of being an outsider. Nobody there knew about her background or her past; it had been liberating.

By the end of the first year she'd excelled in all subjects, but best of all, because the university was nearly six hours away from Sydney, she'd spent the entirety of each semester without the obligation of bringing anyone home to meet the family. And for the first time since she could remember, she'd been under no obligation to sleep with anyone.

Of course she'd been expected to go home each Christmas, although she'd never been sure why. Mother didn't celebrate the holidays. It had only been Christine who'd made the effort to put up a tree and make a Christmas dinner.

Mother had been right. Christine wasn't like the other kids she'd brought home, yet she'd chosen to return to the house more and more often after that first night. For a while they'd continued to be together after school, but soon Chris made it obvious that she preferred being with George. That had hurt.

She'd really liked Christine, enjoyed being with her, and found her easy to talk to. But it wasn't surprising. George was as handsome as Mother was beautiful, and she'd never been able to compete with them in either looks or personality. It was how it always ended. Only this time it had actually mattered.

The more time Chris spent with Mother and George, the more her personality and attitude had changed, until a deep chasm formed between her and her own family. They'd fought it, of course, but in the end she'd cut them off. By then she'd thrown herself full tilt into the family business and had started doing her own recruiting for Mother.

Gradually they'd stopped noticing when Nat began spending more time at the flat, and less and less at the house, until eventually, Chris and George had stayed with Mother and Nat had moved to the flat.

On the weekends Chris had replaced Nat at the parties for Mother's rich clients. No one complained. Chris looked very young and was more beautiful and feminine than Nat.

It had been a relief to lose the obligation, although the money she'd saved over the years from this work was what had put her through university—certainly Mother had never offered to help.

That first Christmas, when Nathalie had returned at Mother's insistence, she found another young teenager in the house. Ari looked about fourteen, although he'd claimed to be eighteen. He was strikingly handsome in a very boyish way, and both Mother and George had doted on him.

Nathalie soon discovered that Mother's expectations of her hadn't changed. But *she* had. Although she'd participated, her role in this family's bizarre private life had become so loathsome she could only deal with it by the use of strong drugs. Whenever she'd thought of refusing, the permanent fear that had taken root in her soul would engulf her and turn her into Mother's submissive and obedient little girl.

The Christmas week hadn't gone well, to say the least. There was constant tension between Nat and her mother. At best Nat had only ever felt tolerated by her mother—now Charlotte didn't even attempt to hide her outright dislike of her daughter. In the end, the only way Nat had survived was to spend the whole time seriously high.

* * *

And so it had continued for the following three years—the comfort and challenges of university, independence and her studies, followed by the Christmas trip home and her almost childlike adherence to her mother's demands.

Until one day, just prior to her final exams, Mother had rung to say that she'd sold the house and was moving to California where she had numerous wealthy clients seeking her services. There was no explanation, other than she felt it was time to move on. George was to move to a large new home on the fringe of Sydney's inner city and continue Mother's business. The rich and debauched still wanted teenagers, still wanted to be entertained somewhere where they could be free to indulge their variety of perversities in a place of discretion, privacy and safety.

Nat didn't care. A benevolent force had finally released her from her dark obligations. She wouldn't be involved, and with Mother out of the country there would be the real chance to begin her life again.

Once settled in California, Mother had continued the lucrative business of supplying boys and girls to the jaded rich, only now she owned an impressive small estate in an expensive neighborhood and had developed a high profile as a clairvoyant. Privately, Charlotte Silver was the person to go to when you wanted your desires satisfied, no matter how perverse—confidentiality guaranteed.

After Mother had left, George had implored Nathalie to stay at his new home, but she'd avoided it. Then Mother provided tickets for them to visit in Los Angeles. It had been a demand. And it had been three weeks of hell.

From the moment their plane touched down in Los Angeles, it had been made clear that Mother expected Nat to help entertain at whatever parties Charlotte was catering to. Nathalie had refused, and Mother was furious. Twice during the stay George had forced his way into her bed, begging her to love him like she had when they were children, like she had when they'd been forced to perform for clients. Bitterly, she'd fought him, allowing him only the comfort of being held by her until he fell asleep. Nat had waited for retribution from Mother, but strangely, nothing happened.

After the trip, Nathalie had refused to see George and refused to give in to Mother's entreaties from America that they remain a close family. Now suddenly, with one phone call, she felt like she was right back where she started.

With a shock, Nathalie realized she was clinging to the sides of her chair—that her hands were white with the effort and her muscles aching. Stifling anger at her own cowardice, she rose, poured an almost full glass of brandy and swallowed it in consecutive gulps.

* * *

Alex Messner was ready when Nathalie arrived to pick her up on Wednesday. It took her only moments to recognize that Nathalie Duncan was severely stressed, the tension showing in her face and shoulders.

"So how has your week been?" Alex asked curiously.

"Okay, thanks." Nathalie shrugged vaguely.

For a while they traveled in silence.

Eventually Alex spoke. "So are you married…in a relationship?"

"No, I'm not. Are you?"

"No. I lost my partner to cancer two years ago. I've had the odd date, but can't really get interested."

"I'm sorry. It must be hard to lose someone you cared about."

"Loved…" she corrected. "I didn't just care about Lou…I loved her…she was my life."

"Of course, I'm sorry."

For the next three hours Alex sat in on various groups and spoke to the other volunteers who helped at the center. Nathalie noticed that she seemed to have a way of putting people at ease and making them feel included. And it was soon obvious that neither the women nor the other staff would have a problem working with her.

Later, on the drive home, Alex asked, "Are you always that quiet at the center?"

"I figure you'll either see the center as a worthwhile cause, or you'll decide you can't spare the time," Nathalie stated with a wry smile. "Either way, nothing I could say would change that."

"Aha, a fatalist," Alex commented drily. "I like that, although I don't necessarily agree with it. I do have a couple of things to sort out, but I imagine I can manage a few hours a week for the center. How about I ring you?"

"Thank you. That would be great, the others will be thrilled."

And what about you, Nathalie Duncan, Alex thought. *Will you be thrilled?* It was only a passing thought, but it irritated her. Instead, she asked, "Would you like a coffee…if it's not too late?"

"Thanks, but I'm very tired and I have a lot to do tomorrow, perhaps another time."

Disappointed, but not surprised, Alex arranged to ring Nathalie when she'd made her decision. Watching the car pull away, she wondered at the cause of Nathalie Duncan's distraction and the barely hidden anger in her eyes. Acknowledging it as none of her business, Alex entered the house. Tonight it seemed large and quiet and lonely.

After pouring herself a drink and flooding the room with the soulful voice of Aretha Franklin, Alex turned to look at the photo above the sound system. "God, Lou, I miss you so much," she said, raising her glass to the attractive woman smiling out at her. "You had no business leaving me like that."

By the time Miss Franklin was singing "I say a little prayer," Alex was on her third drink and the tears she'd been holding in check so bravely began to flow.

The ache never left, sometimes it eased, but mostly there was little relief from the crushing sense of loss and abandonment. Looking again at the photo, Alex was reminded of all they'd had together and all she'd lost, and this time her tears turned to sobs.

CHAPTER THREE

Catching Up On The Past

Nathalie had been irritable and short-tempered all week. Bella wondered briefly what was wrong, but Nat didn't mention anything and Bella didn't ask. Jackie had been nagging for a while to invite Nathalie over for a meal, but somehow the time never seemed right.

"So what's bugging you lately?" she asked, depositing her coffee on Nathalie's desk and pulling up a chair. "If I didn't know better, I'd think your lover had just walked out on you?"

Steely eyes glared back. "I'm really not in the mood," Nat snapped. "You know nothing about me, Bella, you just think you do. I could be sleeping with half the police force, for all you know."

It was the most emotion Bella had seen in two years, and she instantly recognized that her friend was in some sort of trouble. "You're right and I'm sorry," she said seriously. "But whatever is happening is eating you up. You look terrible and your personality is now officially a disaster."

The last comment made Nat laugh, despite her annoyance. "I'm sorry, Bella. It will get better, honest."

"You can talk to me, you know. That's what friends are for."

"I appreciate it, but it's nothing…really."

"If you say so," she muttered. "Anyway, what about dinner at my place next Tuesday. Jackie wants to try out a new recipe and I promised I'd ask."

"That would be great and I promise to be in a better mood."

The rest of the day went quickly, but by finish time the knot in Nathalie's stomach felt like a football. Facing Mother after all these years was turning out to be so much worse than she could ever have imagined.

* * *

George's house was large, modern, stood in its own grounds and was very different than their original home, yet hauntingly familiar. It was only thirty minutes away, but this was her first visit. Parking her Toyota Aurion alongside a Subaru and Mother's luxury hire car, she looked hesitantly toward the door. Its locked-down look, so similar to that of the old house, caused a shiver to run down her spine.

A biracial girl of fifteen or sixteen answered the door and silently led her toward the back of the house where Mother and George were sitting at a dining table. Even after all this time, Mother looked the same. George, however, though still very handsome, looked a little older, from alcohol and drugs, Nathalie presumed.

"Nathalie, darling," gushed Mother from her seat. "Do come and give me a kiss. It's been so long."

She moved toward the chair, and Charlotte stood, pulling Nathalie into a firm embrace. The kiss was lingering and designed to make her feel uncomfortable. When she let go, George was waiting to greet his sister.

"I've missed you, Nat," he whispered, holding her tightly. "You have no idea how much I've missed you."

Pulling away, Nat stood awkwardly. George visited Mother several times a year in Los Angeles, but to Nathalie both were now virtual strangers—just an occasional voice on the end of a telephone, calls that always left her feeling uncomfortable and fearful.

Pouring a drink, George called out to someone named Belinda. Within seconds the young girl who answered the door appeared beside him. "Nathalie, this is Belinda, my girlfriend," he said smugly. "I'm sure you two will get on like a house on fire. Mother thinks very highly of her." The girl blushed slightly but continued to look adoringly at George. "How about showing Nathalie to her room," he demanded, indicating for Belinda to take Nat's overnight bag. "Then when you've freshened up," he instructed Nathalie, "we'll meet in the lounge. Dinner will be in about an hour."

The room was big and well-furnished and the bed a large, well-sprung king. As she placed the bag on the floor, the dark young girl looked shyly at Nat. "You don't look like George," she said in a whispery childlike voice, "and you don't look like your mother. But you're very attractive anyway."

"Thank you," muttered Nathalie curtly, angry that Mother's expectation of her obviously hadn't changed.

"It's a comfortable bed," Belinda rambled on blindly, nodding toward it with a look of anticipation. "I'm sure you'll like it."

Glaring at the girl, Nathalie walked to the door and held it open. "Thank you, Belinda," she growled. "I'm sure you'd know."

Startled by Nathalie's animosity, the girl fled the room, the door slamming behind her.

* * *

It was beginning again. Nathalie felt overwhelmed and powerless. Yet there had to be another reason she'd been invited to the house for the weekend. Mother and George had a smorgasbord of young boys and girls to choose from, and she was no longer young enough to interest either of them or most of their clients. Besides, they had to know that she wouldn't participate any longer in their idea of family relations.

It was twenty minutes before she returned to the lounge, and the moment she entered, George rose from his seat and closed the solid-looking door.

"We have things to talk about, child," said Mother, taking a sip of her drink. "Important things that you need to be involved in. But before we discuss such serious matters, tell us what you're doing with your life. Obviously we know you're a police officer, but what about your love life?"

"My sex life, don't you mean, Mother?" she mumbled, struggling to control her fear of the woman in front of her.

"Actually, yes, you're right. I do mean your sex life." She smiled, but her hard eyes showed only scorn. "Are you living with someone and are they good in bed? That's really what I wanted to know, but you always were a secretive one, so I don't suppose you're going to tell me."

Shaking her head, Nathalie began to feel like a small child again. Mother was annoyed and that meant that she had to do something to please her. But she didn't really know what she wanted. Out of the corner of her eye she could see George watching her.

"Oh, I'm sure Nat's just a bit shy from not having seen us for so long," George offered from his seat opposite. He was a man now. Although he was still very slim, his shoulders had broadened and his face had a manly hardness. Dressed in expensive dark trousers and a white designer shirt—open at the collar—and with a single earring in his left ear, he looked roguish and powerful. Reluctantly, Nathalie admitted to herself that he was incredibly handsome.

"Nathalie is going to have to shed her shyness very quickly if she wants to fit back into this family," Mother pointed out emphatically. "Because families sometimes have to band together to survive and that requires a special closeness. Doesn't it, George?"

"What are you talking about?" asked Nathalie, experiencing a flood of emotions that she hadn't yet sorted. "I thought you were here for a holiday."

"And other business, but we'll discuss that after our meal. Perhaps George would like to show you the photos he has of his little daughter. She's going to be such a beauty."

"You've got a child?" she asked in a stunned voice, turning to George. "You never mentioned it on the phone."

"Why would he?" snapped Mother irritably. "You made it quite clear you didn't want to be part of the family, so I told him not to tell you. As it happens he has two children. Jeremy is six and Samantha nearly four. Different mothers, of course, but they're both as beautiful as him."

As the innocent, happy faces looked out at her from George's iPhone, Nathalie's heart sank and a sour taste flooded her mouth. They were certainly beautiful—too beautiful.

"Where are they now?" she asked, dreading the answer.

"Jeremy stays here," answered George proudly. "And Samantha is at her grandmother's. But Jeremy won't be home until tomorrow, he's visiting his mother down the coast. They—"

"The children are part of the business we'll discuss later," interrupted Charlotte, indicating that the subject of the children was now closed. "But in the meantime you must tell us all about your life."

Still struggling with the concept of George having children, Nathalie couldn't think straight. But Mother wanted answers, and she needed to create a reason why she shouldn't have to participate in what Mother obviously expected would be a *proper* family reunion. "I'm…I'm engaged to marry," Nat stuttered in panic. "He's another police officer, a detective sergeant."

"Really," declared Mother cynically. "You surprise me. always thought your preference would be women. After all y were never exactly a very feminine child and even now you se neither one thing nor the other." Stunned into silence, Nat stared blankly while George gave a comforting smile. But M had moved on. "So, what's his name…this fiancé of yours when do you plan to marry?"

"Josh…Joshua Dawson," she stuttered. "We live toge we haven't set a date."

Thankfully, at that moment Belinda returned to that dinner was ready.

The meal looked delicious, but Nathalie ate litt she did eat tasted like paper. Belinda spent her ti adoringly at everything George said, and the meal Mother spoke about America and the astronomi was making pandering to LA's rich and powerful.

For Nathalie, it was as if she were once again trapped in some hellish alternate universe that she believed she'd left behind. All she wanted to do was close her eyes and make it all disappear.

After the meal they retired to the lounge, where George handed them each a cognac.

"So what's the business you wish to discuss?" inquired Nathalie, trying to sound in control. "And how can I help?"

Mother and son caught each other's eyes—a furtive glance. "We want legal advice about the children," Charlotte stated without preamble.

"What sort of advice?"

"George is going to join me in America this year and he wants to take the children with him. However, Samantha's mother is in prison and won't allow George to put the child on his passport."

"So what do you want me to do?" she asked, suddenly afraid.

"Well, there has to be some legal loophole that will allow us to take her with us. Surely we don't have to resort to other means. George *is* the girl's father."

Wondering what "other means" Mother could be referring to, she replied, "So has Jeremy's mother agreed to him leaving Australia?"

"She will," snapped George quickly. "She's not the problem. Susan's the stubborn one, and we can't get to her," he finished lamely.

Charlotte glared at him.

"What do you mean, you can't get to her?"

"Because she's in prison…that's all he meant," stated Mother flatly, giving him another filthy look. "It's hard to negotiate with someone who won't allow you to visit."

Nathalie didn't believe her.

"From the little I know, I'd say that you only have one option, and that's to take Samantha's mother to court for full custody and let the court decide whether the child can leave Australia or not."

"Then we want you to start the proceedings."

"No. I can't do that," she answered quickly. "I don't know anything about family law, I don't deal with it," she lied.

Mother's face became hard, her eyes even harder. "Not even at that crisis center you say you work at? I would have thought that was nothing but family law?" Before Nat could answer, Charlotte Silver continued. "All that's required of you is for you to put the paperwork together and lodge the application. The rest will be taken care of by a friend of mine—a family court judge, a man who'll be very sympathetic."

"My God, you've got this all set up," she gasped. "But what about the child's mother?"

"We told you," she snapped again. "She's in prison—a useless junkie. The child will be much better off with us." Waving her hand in a dismissive gesture, she continued, "Anyway, it's getting late and we have all weekend to discuss it, so let's not bog ourselves down with boring details right now. It must be time to have some fun."

Nat's mind was spinning.

George has children and he actually wants to put them where Mother has access to them. Can't he see their young lives heading in the same direction Mother took ours? Doesn't he think there is anything wrong in that?

Flashes from the past hit her at once and she remembered a time, when she was a child, when, much as she despised what they were forced to do, she honestly thought this was how everyone lived. And then she remembered later times, when she knew better but wanted to please Mother, a time when she'd coldly lured other young teenagers into their lifestyle. A wave of utter exhaustion flooded her. Mumbling an excuse about needing to visit the bathroom, Nat stumbled from the room.

Lying on her bed, overwhelmed by a sense of defeat, Nat tried to close down her mind. But the thoughts of George's children in Mother's clutches allowed her no peace. Gradually, defeat turned to a need to protect. She didn't know how. She didn't know if she even had it in her. But she had to try.

It was close to forty minutes before she returned and when she did, she found Belinda, Mother and George doing lines of coke. Deciding that anything that got her through the weekend would do, Nathalie joined them at the coffee table, taking the straw George offered. They drank, did more coke and went to bed, but Mother never slept alone. On this occasion Belinda followed obediently to her room, while George and Nathalie went to their own rooms.

When Nathalie saw that her door didn't lock, her heart began to pound. She looked around, but there was nothing she could use to jam the door. Finally, after lying awake watching the door for over an hour, she began to drift into a troubled sleep. An hour later, she woke with George on top of her.

"I need you, Nat," he whispered, forcing his kisses onto her. "Mother said we could."

"No, George," she spat, struggling beneath his wiry body. "I'm not doing this anymore. Don't touch me."

"Only you understand what I need," he whispered, pulling away the bedclothes and tightening his grip on her wrists. "I need to be near you, please," he cajoled, holding her to him. "Like when we were kids. You loved me then, I know you did."

"We're not kids anymore," she growled, struggling to break free. "And we did it because Mother and her clients made us. I hated it then and I hate it now…and I will never do it again… ever. Now get off me."

"But it makes Mother happy, and I missed you so much," he moaned, continuing to hold her down. "I do love you, you know that."

That's when it hit—waves of nausea and revulsion—horror at what she knew she could not stop. There was no more fight in her. Helpless, she turned her face away, tears trickling down her cheek. "Take what you want, George. Mother will be proud of you."

"Oh God, Nat, I just want you to love me," he murmured imploringly.

But she didn't respond.

Rolling from her, he curled into a ball, his back to Nathalie, his arms around his own body. "I'm so sorry," he mumbled, rocking slightly. "I'm so sorry. I just needed to feel your arms around me. I just wanted you to hold me, to look after me, like you did when we were little. I hate it without you."

She lay staring at the ceiling, her mind in turmoil. "It can't go on," she whispered eventually. "I'll kill you if you ever try this again. You can't keep doing terrible things just to please Mother and because she says it's okay."

"She loves us," he mumbled without turning round. "That's why she wants us to be together. And I've missed you so much, Nat. You went away and left me."

"Does this lifestyle make you happy, George? Or do you feel like I do—like cowardly filth, like something that doesn't even deserve to draw breath?"

"She loves us," he repeated. "It's different for you, it's always been different for you, but I need her, and the only way she'll love us is if we're together and we make her happy."

For a long time they lay in silence, neither moving.

"I won't tell her what happened," he said eventually. "She can think we did it."

"I can't stay, George. I can't spend another night in this house. You know what she'll expect tomorrow night, and I just can't do it." She knew he was crying from his smothered gasps of indrawn breath. Turning, she curled her body into his muscular back— putting her arms around him and holding him—just like she had when they were children—after Mother and her friends had finished with them.

"You have to say no, George. If you go to America she'll own you forever and she'll ruin your children's lives, like she did ours."

"It's not that simple," he mumbled. "I've done things for her… bad things. Things I did to please her. I think she'd tell what I did if I tried to leave. And besides, where would I go? What would I do? The house is in my name, but Mother really owns it and the business. And she needs me."

"What are you talking about? What bad things did you do?" she asked quietly, not really wanting to know.

He didn't answer.

They stayed like that for hours, sometimes dozing, sometimes talking. Outwardly, he was a grown man, but emotionally he was a scared little boy, even more damaged than she was. Her heart ached for the two people they might have been.

* * *

In the morning Mother's look of triumph wasn't lost on Nathalie, but it changed swiftly when Nat announced that she would be returning home in the afternoon. George's son, Jeremy, was due to return from his mother's shortly and Nat wanted to meet him. Somehow knowing she had a niece and nephew in the world had made this visit a little more bearable.

Charlotte Silver wasn't happy. "So when do you propose getting information from George to put together the application for custody of Samantha?" she demanded harshly. "You're hardly going to be able to do it before you leave."

"I'm not doing it, Mother," she stated, as bravely as she could. "If Samantha's mother still has contact and doesn't want her going overseas, then I believe you should respect her wishes. Besides, as I said, I don't do family law."

"Then we'll find a lawyer who'll see things our way," stated Mother flatly. "I was giving you a chance to participate as part of this family, but quite obviously you can't overcome your need to be selfish—even for your own brother."

She'd gotten off lightly. Usually when Mother was opposed, it led to a tirade of vicious, cutting words that could flay the most hardened personality. And as children and teenagers, they had known it would also lead to further physical or emotional pain, sometime when they least expected it. Nobody displeased Mother and got away with it.

"You might as well leave now then," she snapped, after sending George to make coffee. "You haven't seen either of us for years, but you can only spare us one night. You always were an ungrateful bitch."

Suddenly, just for that moment, what Mother thought didn't matter.

"I'm staying to meet Jeremy, Mother," she said firmly. "I want to meet my nephew and I want you to leave him and Samantha alone." It was said.

Shoulders snapping back, the beautiful woman lunged and in one swift movement grabbed Nathalie by the throat, her slender frame belying the strength of her grip.

But it wasn't her physical strength that prevented Nathalie from fighting back. She was a lot more solid than Mother after all. It was all those years of Mother being in control.

"You will not demand anything of me, you ugly, frigid little bitch," Charlotte hissed into her face. "I am your mother and you owe me everything. The cards told me that you would betray me, but I will not allow it. Do you hear? You can stay to meet Jeremy, but when you leave you will have no further contact with any of us. You will not corrupt those children into feeling guilty about something that is natural and exciting."

Releasing her grip, but with her face only inches from Nathalie's, she sneered, "Now get away from me. You repulse me. You always have."

Charlotte sauntered back to her seat, rearranged her clothing and sat down as if nothing had happened, while Nathalie stood, her face drained of color, her mind trying to control the pain of her mother's words.

Nathalie didn't doubt when George returned that he was aware something had happened in his absence, but she knew the issue would never be raised. Fortunately, only moments later the door flew open and a small boy strolled into the room.

"Hello," he said, shyly looking at Nathalie, who was still standing. "You must be my aunty."

"Call me Nathalie or Nat," she replied, still trying to regain her composure. "And you must be Jeremy."

"And hello to you too, young man," interrupted Mother, obviously annoyed that the boy hadn't given her his immediate attention.

"Oh, hi, Grandmother," he said, moving toward his father.

"Charlotte," she snapped. "Remember, Jeremy, I told you to call me Charlotte."

His interest had moved on. "We went swimming at the beach yesterday," he gabbled exuberantly to anyone who would listen. "And we caught a fish and I brought back shells." Turning to Nathalie, he asked, "Do you like the beach? My dad takes me to the pool, but I go to the beach when I visit Mummy."

He had George's slim build and fair hair, but his eyes were the deepest brown and his skin the color of honey. One look into those happy, beautiful eyes told Nathalie that Jeremy had been loved and looked after and had not been used in George's business. At least not yet. Looking up, she saw George watching her, his face proud, his look conveying that she had nothing to worry about.

They spent the rest of the morning in the garden, she and Jeremy and George, the adults playing with the child and sitting on the swing seat talking. They even ate lunch together picnic style under the big tree. Not since their early teens had Nathalie and George spent this much time talking. It made Nat realize that she too missed the emotional closeness she and George had shared as children.

Mother remained indoors making overseas phone calls.

"How long have you had custody of Jeremy?" she asked quietly as the child climbed trees and ran around the garden.

"Technically I've always had joint custody, but I wasn't interested. Then he started spending time here when he was about two and a half. When he started school he came for the holidays and he just kind of grew on me."

"How does his mother feel about that?"

"Claire's okay, she was only fourteen when she had him and she struggled to look after him when he was small. I didn't help, except financially. I paid the bills and provided a house, but basically she was on her own. She loves him and is good to him, but she's happy for me to raise him for a while. She's started university now, doing nursing, but she has him every second weekend and during the holidays. We work it out between us."

"But will she let you take him to America?"

"She won't have a choice."

"What does that mean?" she asked softly.

Looking at her with sad, blue eyes, he replied, "I don't know exactly, but Mother has something in mind—possibly trying to pay her off."

"George—"

Putting his finger to her lips, he shook his head. "Don't, Nathalie. Just don't. You have to walk away now. You have to let it all go. I won't let her hurt my children, I promise."

Before she left, she held Jeremy's warm little body to her and he put his arms around her neck, snuggling his sweet-smelling face into hers. "I think you're very pretty, Aunty Nat," he said innocently. "You look just like my mummy, except she's not as brown."

The smell of him and the sound of his happy young voice stayed with her on the short journey home, and for the first time in a long time she felt attached to someone.

CHAPTER FOUR

Sandwiches and a New Woman

Bella noticed Nathalie's improved mood as soon as she returned to work on Monday, and she reminded her about dinner on Tuesday.

That evening Alexandra Messner rang and offered her services to the center, suggesting that she pop in on Wednesday to work out a schedule, get a copy of the center's protocols and meet those she hadn't already met.

"Thank you," replied Nathalie happily. "There'll be some paperwork and we'll have to sort out an office, but I'll pop in myself to get you settled."

"Terrific. Bring some sandwiches," Alex requested down the line.

"Sandwiches…?"

"I'll be coming straight from work," she said with a laugh. "I figure that's the least you can offer me."

"How about pasta instead?" Nathalie replied quickly, unsure if she was doing the right thing. "The center closes at eight thirty and there's a little Italian place around the corner that does the best pasta. I'm buying."

"Sounds great," Alex agreed eagerly, struggling to hide her surprise.

* * *

Bella's house was an older-style brick with four bedrooms and a small garden. It was neat and clean, but the fixtures and furnishings looked like she'd inherited them along with the house, and there was little color to be found inside. As usual, Jackie seemed cheerful and willing, and the meal, a simple baked dinner followed by apple pie and cream, was delicious.

"Just like Mother used to make," sighed Bella, finishing her last mouthful and pushing away the plate. "She's a good cook, my Jackie," she commented, unwrapping a cigar and putting it in her mouth.

After dinner they moved to the lounge room, where Nat felt the urge to talk about Jeremy and Samantha. It was the first time in her life that she'd ever wanted anyone to know anything about her family, and it felt strange.

"Can't see the fuss," mumbled Bella dourly. "I've got seven nieces and nephews and frankly, seeing them once a year is more than enough for me."

"And how does your brother feel about being a father?" Jackie asked, pointedly ignoring Bella's comment. "It's funny, but I don't remember you ever mentioning you had a brother—"

"Perhaps because Nat's like me—not into spilling her guts to anyone and everyone," interrupted Bella, puffing on the huge cigar. "We don't all twitter on endlessly. She probably didn't think it was important."

Expecting Jackie to react more stridently, Nat was stunned when she simply said, "Bella, you're so rude sometimes."

It was a mystery to Nat why Jackie put up with Bella's constant putdowns. Or why Bella would continue in a relationship where she had little obvious affection or respect for her partner.

They spoke about work, then about the center, and Nathalie told them about securing Alex Messner's services. But she didn't tell them about the meal she would be sharing with the woman tomorrow night.

"I might have met this Messner woman at a seminar last year," Bella commented, still puffing on her cigar. "She gave a lecture on personality disorders. We talked after the lecture and I remember she worked in the prisons. She was very impressive. And unless my gaydar was on the blink, I do believe the woman is a dyke."

"Well, I don't think that'll worry the clients at the center," muttered Nathalie, deciding she didn't want to discuss this anymore. "And that's all I'm interested in."

"I really must come down to this center one day and see if I can offer any help," Jackie proposed suddenly. "I've always wanted to do some sort of volunteer work."

"Since when?" spluttered Bella dramatically. "It's all you can do to concentrate on that sad little job of yours. Besides, what could you possibly do down there?"

"Oh, I'm sure Nathalie could find some use for my services," she said almost flirtatiously. "And I finish work early on Fridays. That's the day you volunteer, isn't it?"

Nathalie tried to be tactful. "That would be good," she agreed quietly. "But apart from needing a psychologist, I'm not sure what other sort of help they need at the moment." Something about Jackie worried Nat. Everything she did seemed to be an act—the dumb blonde with eyes of steel. And it didn't help that Jackie seemed to be flirting with her whenever they were alone.

* * *

The next evening, Nathalie was greeted at the center by a grinning Lenore Kingsley. "I knew you could convince Alex Messner to join us," she said happily. "I've already made a couple of appointments for her next Friday, but I didn't arrange anything for tonight."

Together they decided which room she'd use and set about trying to make it presentable. Twenty minutes later, Alex arrived.

"A coffee—urgently," she requested with a smile when they asked how they could help.

Nathalie glanced at Alex's casual attire of jeans, a white camisole and dark blue cotton shirt open at the front. It was neat and smart, but definitely not the corporate image. The only formal thing about her was her thick, well-worn leather briefcase.

Catching Nathalie's look, Alex smiled. "I like casual," she commented wryly. "I find it tends to put people at ease. I do hope you weren't expecting the formal look?" Alex's laughing green eyes bored into her.

Embarrassed that the woman had virtually read her mind, Nathalie shook her head and smiled.

The evening went quickly and, for Alex, included an official orientation with the center manager—during which Lenore explained the aims and protocols of the various programs. Part of this induction included providing a list of commonly used government and nongovernment agencies that the staff at the center had found offered a good level of assistance to the client group. Later, Lenore introduced her to a couple of their long-term clients.

"So, are you still available for dinner?" asked Alex when they'd finished everything. "I could eat a horse. All I've had is a couple of doughnuts."

The restaurant was quiet and the women were seated near the window. After ordering, they started on their basket of garlic bread and a spicy white.

"So, you're not a fan of psychology?" queried Alex with a twinkle in her eye.

"Why would you say that?" Nat asked, annoyed at how easily Alex seemed to be able to read her.

"Just a strong feeling..."

"I think it works for some—" Nathalie replied, deciding to be honest.

"But not for others," Alex finished for her.

Shrugging, Nat answered, "It just seems that some people spend years seeing psychologists or psychiatrists and end up just as messed up as when they started. Surely the prisons are full of them?"

"Yes, but that is the extreme end of mental health, and there's a difference between psychiatric illness and emotional or behavioral problems. Many people wouldn't be able to function in even a rudimentary way if it wasn't for counseling and medication. Many would give in to their pain or depression and simply end it all."

"Which makes counseling no more than a Band-Aid solution, good for a minor scratch, but useless for a deep wound," Nathalie argued.

Alex noted the acerbic tone. "I wouldn't say useless," she answered amiably. "But yes, the deeper the problem the more difficult to resolve. Psychology can't change what happened to bring about the problem, but it can help the client put mechanisms in place to deal with the effect…so that it doesn't escalate."

"For some that would take too long," Nat mumbled, challenging Alex to disagree.

Alex thought it likely that Nathalie was talking about herself, but she believed pushing the topic would cause the woman to stop talking completely. It was time to change the subject. Luckily the meal arrived, creating a natural break.

"So, do you enjoy your job?" Alex asked, studying the enigmatic woman opposite. "Was the police something you always wanted to do?"

"I'd love to claim it was my vocation," she replied with an easy smile, "but I joined because I found law boring and then ended up as a police prosecutor anyway."

"What would you like to do?"

"Detective…my ex, Josh, works in the Serious Crimes Squad and I'm envious." Nathalie found Alex's company pleasant and stimulating. She was forthright, but there was a warmth and kindness about her that made you feel important. The two women talked easily, and it was only when the waiter brought the bill that Nathalie realized they'd been there for over two hours.

"Will you be at the center on Friday?" Alex asked as they walked back to their cars.

"Unless something drastic happens," Nat answered casually, climbing into the sleek red Toyota. "I'll see you there."

Once again, Alex wondered about Nathalie's sexuality. She'd made a point of mentioning the ex-boyfriend, yet she couldn't picture this woman with a guy. She was attracted, but it felt like a betrayal of Lou. Perhaps it was just as well that she'd only see Nathalie Duncan at the center.

* * *

On Friday morning Nathalie phoned George from work. Mother was away on business and wouldn't return until the following week. It seemed strange talking to him after all the years of only sporadic conversation, but Nathalie acknowledged that, as twisted as the family dynamics were, she still loved and felt protective of the brother of their childhood.

Although George was older, Nathalie had always been stronger. It was George who wet the bed and cried himself to sleep. And when he was a teenager, George's fear of upsetting Mother was so extreme that Nathalie often thought he would literally jump off a cliff if she demanded it. Not that she was much better. Last weekend had proven that, but at least she'd managed to distance herself a little.

"How long is Mother staying?" Nathalie asked, hoping this was only a short visit.

"As long as she wants, I guess," he answered flatly. "You know Mother. She's not likely to let me know her plans."

"So how do you really feel about moving to the States?"

For a moment there was silence and Nathalie thought he wasn't going to answer.

"I have no choice, I have to go, so it doesn't matter how I feel."

"We need to talk...and I'd love to see Jeremy and meet Samantha."

"We have no plans for Saturday. Sam will be there."

"That'd be great. But I won't...it won't be..."

"I know," he said dully. "It's okay. But I have missed you...not the other stuff...I mean...you know...just you caring about me, I guess."

After she got off the phone a sense of excitement gripped her. Could she talk George into refusing to go to America— breaking with Mother? Would it be possible for the two of them to become friends, like a normal adult brother and sister? She wanted so badly to know that those children would *not* grow up the way they did, and deep down Nathalie believed that George wanted that too.

* * *

Bella had been in a bad mood for days. Jackie had been working overtime and Bella hated being on her own. "I only put up with the stupid girl because I want the company," she told Nathalie, only half-joking. "And now she's hardly ever there for me."

"Have you ever thought that if you were a bit nicer to Jack, she might stick around more?" asked Nat with a raised eyebrow.

"So now you're an expert on lesbian relationships, are you?" snapped Bella. "Funny, but you're the one without a partner."

Used to Bella's aggressive personality, Nathalie just shrugged. "Hey, you started this conversation," she reminded the woman. "My attitude is that relationships are all about sex and pretense and you're not too good at the pretense."

"Pretty cynical, Duncan," she said, wagging a finger in her face.

"Are you telling me you're happy in this relationship?"

"No, Nat, but someone like me has to make do, and it's still better than you've got."

"On that we'll have to disagree," Nathalie said with a shake of her head. "So how the hell did you ever get together anyway?" Finally, she asked the question she'd wondered about for ages.

"Lesbian club—a pick-up actually. I'd just been dumped and was feeling low. Jack was new to the scene and made a play for me. My ego needed a boost, so I went along with it. And she is very good in bed, by the way…very good." Sighing she said, "One night turned into two, then three and so on. Maybe it's just a habit that suits us both."

"It sounds charming!"

"It's what you do when you're lonely and not one of God's beautiful creatures," she said aggressively. "You settle for what's on offer because the ones you want don't want you. Not that your type would understand that, would you? Your type would be the one doing the impressing, stealing the ugly girl's boyfriend…or in my case, girlfriend."

"My type…?" Ice dripped from the words and Nathalie's eyes flashed.

"I'm sorry, I didn't mean that," Bella said, realizing she'd gone too far. "I'm just taking my resentment out on you because I think Jackie might be clubbing it and seeing someone else. It's not even that I care that much, but my ego does. And, well…I know that if I looked like you, I wouldn't have these problems."

Staff returned from court then, so the conversation ended. Afterward Nathalie thought about Bella's words. She'd only ever had two relationships, both very short-term. One was Christine Martin, who in the early days had lit a spark that had added a whole dimension to her life beyond the sex. The other was Josh Dawson.

Christine had been part of the life she told herself she had no control over, but there wasn't that excuse with Josh. He'd been mentally stimulating and had loved her openly and honestly. Yet it still hadn't worked beyond a sexual friendship. The thought depressed her.

It rained all day and the courts were busy. Bella's mood improved, but Nathalie didn't ask for an update on her relationship. One deep and meaningful conversation with Bella was enough for the week.

That evening she went home and, changing quickly, grabbed a piece of toast and some documents before heading to the center. Two women were waiting to see her and the next hour was spent offering advice on child maintenance and the rights of a foster parent.

Later, in the kitchen, she boiled the ancient jug and poured a large, strong coffee.

"Yes, please," said a voice from the doorway. "White, two sugars, and in return you can share my soggy sandwiches."

Alex was soaked through and clutching a dripping umbrella, but it didn't seem to dampen the warmth and good humor that shone from her sparkling green eyes. Nathalie felt herself warm.

"I must say, you really seem to have a thing about sandwiches." She laughed as Alex pulled out a squashed, clear plastic bag from her briefcase.

"When you've got sandwiches, you can survive anything," Alex replied with a wink. "Even this weather."

Placing the coffees on the table and sitting opposite, Nathalie watched as Alex peeled off her wet sweater and placed it on the back of the chair. The movement caused Alex to stretch upward and, unconsciously, Nathalie found herself admiring the lush contours of the woman's body.

Catching Nathalie watching, Alex smiled inwardly. But Nat's expression was blank and an immediate surge of disappointment brought her back to reality. Opening the plastic package and taking a seat, she pushed it across the table. "Please," she said indicating the neatly sliced sandwiches. "Cheese and pickles and cheese and ham. You can't let me dine alone; it'll ruin my reputation."

The sandwich reminded Nat of how hungry she was. Normally she'd have made something before coming to the center, but for some reason tonight she'd been keen to get here.

"So how was the rest of your week?" asked Alex, finishing the last of her sandwich. "No, don't tell me," she said before Nat could speak. "I've got a young woman waiting so I'd better make myself available before she gives up. But how about we meet here when we've both finished?" Already she was rising, ready to leave the room.

Nat just nodded. Why not? She wasn't in a rush and she enjoyed Alex's company. Besides it was only good manners to find out how the woman's first day went.

After attending a drop-in appointment, Nat made her way to the recreation area. There were about seven or eight women milling around, some talking to Rena about medical problems, their own or their children's, others sharing coffee and biscuits. After joining them briefly and doing some paperwork, she returned to the meal room.

It was nearly eight thirty before Alex emerged with a tearful young woman sporting a wide array of body piercings.

"You know, it's been a long day and I feel like a good stiff drink," Alex stated after returning from walking the girl to the door. "I don't suppose you'd like to join me?"

Nat hesitated before quietly replying, "Sounds good."

"Then let's make it my place," Alex suggested. "I've got a fully stocked bar, and you said when we first met that you lived quite close, so you won't have far to go afterward."

While Nathalie followed her home, Alex questioned the wisdom of her actions. Nathalie Duncan was supposed to be someone she saw at the center for a couple of hours a week. But it was too late now. She could hardly stop the car and tell her she'd changed her mind.

The rain was still pouring when she pulled into her garage and ran to the front door. Nat had parked beside the curb and was obviously contemplating the run from her car to the safety of the house. Or could it be she was contemplating the folly of going for a drink with a raving dyke? The thought brought a smile to Alex's face as she turned and waved Nathalie toward the house.

The home was warm and welcoming and Nat couldn't remember why she was initially going to turn down this woman's invitation. They spoke about the center, then gradually moved to more general subjects until eventually Nathalie asked, "Did you live here with your partner before she died?"

The question surprised Alex. Most people avoided the subject. "For the last three years," she answered thoughtfully. "Before that we lived in London. Lou was a doctor. We actually met over there."

"How long were you together?"

"Ten years," she replied, swallowing the force of her emotions.

"I can't imagine being in a relationship that long, let alone losing them after all that time. The hole left behind must be devastating."

Alex knew there was no expectation of an answer.

For a few moments they concentrated on their drinks, listening to Tracy Chapman singing about paper and ink. It was a comfortable silence and neither felt the need to talk.

"Are you in a relationship, Nathalie?" Alex asked eventually.

"No. I'm not good at relationships."

It was a light-hearted reply, but the shadow that clouded her eyes made Alex want to kiss the hurt away. "Have you ever been in love?"

This time Nathalie looked down at her drink as if the answer lay somewhere in the dark liquid. "I don't really think I understand the concept," she replied quietly. "It seems like love's just a word people use for all occasions." Then, as she looked up, "There was someone once, a really long time ago—a girl, actually. We were very young, but I really liked being with her. It felt good. I don't know if that was love, but she chose somebody else. So you move on."

Again there was silence.

"And of course there was Josh. I really did like him. He was good company and he's an intelligent, gentle man. But I don't know that I ever loved him," she admitted. "I wanted someone to care about. We lasted six months, but in the end I wore him down. Fortunately, we stayed friends. As I think I told you, he's also in the police."

"What do you mean you wore him down?"

"It's complicated." Nat shrugged, obviously not willing to discuss it.

As much as the psychologist in her wanted to pursue it, Alex knew this woman would only share so much, so she changed direction.

"Do you class yourself as bisexual?" Alex asked curiously, rising to pour more drinks and change the CD.

"I hadn't thought about it. But I didn't cope with the emotional demands of being in a relationship with Josh, and I can only imagine it would be worse with a woman. Besides, a woman would never put up with me." She'd said too much, Nat decided. Somehow Alex Messner made her want to talk—to share. But she couldn't do that or she risked being found out. "I have to go," she said, rising and taking Alex by surprise. "It's getting late."

Regretting her curiosity, Alex accepted that the evening had run its course, but she couldn't let it go. "I was wondering if you'd like to take in a movie or something on the weekend," she asked, trying to make it sound casual.

"Thanks, but I have plans." The reply was curt and halted further conversation.

It was obvious Alex was hurt by her dismissive attitude, but Nat knew it was how it had to be. Alex Messner was still grieving and vulnerable and would only end up hurt. Thanking her for the drink, Nathalie made her way to the front door. It had stopped raining.

"I don't apologize for asking you out, you know," Alex said as she reached in front of Nathalie to unlock the door. "And I'll probably do it again sometime, but apart from the fact that I want to get to know you better, I can still be a friend." Pulling the door open, she stood aside, her kind eyes serious and understanding.

"Believe me, Alex," Nathalie whispered as she climbed into her car. "You don't want to get to know me better."

* * *

That night when the hands grabbed at her in her sleep, when the man forced his tongue into her mouth and tore into her, when the pain and anger made her want to die, she heard a different voice.

Both mothers were there as usual and they both turned toward this voice. Still he was on her, but he couldn't drown out the voice. And it brought comfort. It was a familiar voice, but the words were indecipherable. The good mother, her face a picture of misery, reached toward the voice. But the bad mother turned back to Nathalie and, with hatred in her eyes, whispered threatening words, forcing her lips where the man's had been, her tongue where his had been. Nathalie was spinning out of control as the good mother lowered her eyes and walked away and the kind voice faded and disappeared. Now she was alone with the stifling presence of *Mother* and the man and a crushing inability to breathe properly.

Struggling and sobbing, she woke—that familiar overwhelming sense of loss filling her with despair. Gasping, Nathalie scrambled backward until her back was wedged against the wall, the bedclothes held close in defense, her head and body soaked in perspiration. "Oh God…Oh God," she cried, reaching out to throw on the light. "I can't do this anymore. Please, God, no more."

As the room grew brighter and her breathing evened out, Nathalie felt the pain of her nightmare—as if it had actually just happened—and she doubled over on the bed, tears coursing down her face. It was another minute or two before the horror ended and she was able to sit up properly.

Once again she walked through the house, turning on every light, pushing the button on the stereo to bring up loud pop music, anything to push those images away. It was four a.m. and the couch became her bed for what was left of the night.

CHAPTER FIVE

Dead Dykes

Peering from the doorway, Josh noted the two women lying naked and motionless on the bed, their bodies entwined in one last embrace. A dark stain had spread onto the pillowcase nearest him and sunlight was peeping through a crack in the curtains illuminating the scene and adding an eerie quality. Unconsciously he let out a sigh.

"Bloody dykes," grumbled Nigel beside him, nodding toward the bed.

Wincing, Josh moved inside the room, careful not to disturb anything. Once again he reminded himself that it was time to apply for another partner. Dismissing his animosity, he concentrated on the scene in front of him. Thanks to Josh's court appearance, Nigel had gotten here nearly an hour earlier. Josh hated it when he hadn't controlled a crime scene from the start. "I wonder if there's any connection between this and the woman killed near the lesbian club a week or so ago," he mentioned thoughtfully, pulling on his latex gloves. "That was a shooting."

"Jesus, Josh," responded Nigel sourly. "Just because all the victims were dykes doesn't mean they're connected."

Ignoring him, Josh stepped closer to the bed.

One woman looked to be in her midthirties, the other somewhat younger. Each had a single bullet wound to the side of the head. Even in death the older one seemed to be trying to protect her friend, her arm draped protectively around her lover's shoulder. They looked at peace to Josh, as if death had taken them in the middle of a pleasant dream. No sign of a struggle, no sign that either of them had any inkling it was their last moments on earth.

"Not bad," murmured Nigel, staring at the women, "I wouldn't have minded a taste of the younger one myself."

"Show some respect," snapped Josh irritably. "And concentrate on the job."

"Yes, sir, *Sergeant* Dawson," he growled sarcastically. "I'll check the rest of the house."

Returning his attention to the room, Josh noted that the women's clothing was nowhere in sight, but two sets of nightwear had been dropped messily onto either side of the bed, indicating the possibility that the women had stripped hurriedly, perhaps before or during lovemaking. The remains of a joint littered the otherwise clean ashtray and an iPod was switched on in the dock. Incongruously, even with the two murdered women still lying in their bed, the room had a peaceful feel to it, and it occurred to Josh that prior to the murder this had been a happy household.

Checking the bodies as carefully as he could without touching them, he saw no signs of a struggle. The room was neat and tidy and very ordinary. Moving carefully around the room, he opened the walk-in closet. The clothes came in different sizes, indicating the women were living together—otherwise, nothing unusual.

Covering the walls were paintings of women in a variety of sensual poses, as well as numerous family photos. The paintings were tasteful originals, and Josh surmised, for no particular reason, that they were either painted by one of these two women or by a friend. Somehow they seemed personal.

Walking into the bathroom, he carefully opened cupboards and drawers, noting the expensive soaps, bath oils and makeup. There were some pills in the cabinet above the spotlessly clean sink, but nothing looked like it had been disturbed.

It wasn't until he had a clear picture in his mind of the entire room, including the most likely position of the killer, that he left, closing the door behind him to preserve the scene.

The rest of the house appeared in order. It could have been any middle-class inner city home with a small dog waiting patiently in the lounge. Noting an address book and a pile of letters stacked on an entry table near the door, Josh used his phone to photograph the position of these items, before picking them up and leafing through the mail.

"Nothing unusual in the other bedrooms," interrupted Nigel, his voice cool and disinterested.

"Nor out here," replied Josh, still casually sorting the mail. "It looks like their names were Linda Djanksi and Stephanie Cameron, but we'll know more when we go through their handbags and purses. Have you spoken to neighbors?"

"Only the one who called it in," replied Nigel nonchalantly. "Uniforms are doing a door to door, but nothing so far."

"So what did she have to say?"

"Who…?"

"The neighbor," snapped Josh irritably.

"Oh, right. Well, she saw Djanski come home about five o'clock yesterday and heard Cameron's car go into the garage an hour or so later. Then she never saw them again."

"So why did she call the police?"

"Because the dog was barking continually, and that was unusual. She went over after trying to ring them and got no answer to the doorbell. That was when she used a key they'd given her, found the women and phoned us."

"Did you get a statement?"

"Fuck, Dawson, what do you take me for? I took it down in my notebook. She's coming to the station tomorrow to sign a statement."

Sighing, Josh said, "So, how did the killer or killers get in?"

"The security locks were intact," Nigel answered casually, indicating the door. "And there was no other signs of a break-in. I guess the killer was either let in or had a key."

"Okay, there's nothing more we can do here until scientific and fingerprints have finished and the place has been searched.

I'll bag and take the address book and once it's been fingerprinted we can start looking for next of kin, friends, that sort of thing."

Driving back to the station, they sat in silence, Josh remembering the peaceful look on the murdered women's faces. A strange darkness engulfed him and he knew instinctively that these deaths and the death of the other woman were connected, but he'd have to wait for ballistics. If it showed they were connected and they couldn't find a direct link between the victims, then these murders might be random lesbian killings. Tomorrow they'd begin sifting through the women's paperwork, contacting their place of work and personal friends, all the normal routines carried out after such a crime. Right now though, someone would have to contact the next of kin, confirm identification and hopefully find a home for the women's dog. Even though it was nearing the end of shift, Josh decided to organize that himself.

* * *

A week later they were no further forward. The door knock had turned up nothing. Djanski had lived at the house for ten years and Cameron had moved in a couple of years ago. Neighbors viewed them as respectable businesswomen. Many of them were not even aware they were a couple. The old lady next door knew and was fond of Linda Djanski, but not so fond of Cameron. According to her, Cameron could be very intense. Inquiries with work colleagues and friends turned up nothing. The bullets from the other homicide didn't match, and it now appeared the two killings might not be related.

Three weeks later Josh was called into the superintendent's office. "Anything new on the double murder at Glebe?" he'd asked casually, knowing from his daily briefings that there wasn't. Acknowledging Josh's frustrated shake of the head, the superintendent continued. "Unfortunately it's the same with the Oxford Street murder, so I've decided to amalgamate the two investigations and bring in an extra staff member. The lesbian and gay community is claiming there's a connection and people in high places are beginning to accuse us of dragging our feet. We need this sorted."

"Yes, we do," answered Josh thoughtfully. "And I must admit it's hard to believe that the murders aren't connected, but other than the victims being lesbian, we can't seem to find a link."

"Well, you'd better find something fast. We're putting you in as acting inspector in charge of the task force. I'll give you until the end of the week to select another staff member and I suggest it be a woman. A woman will have a better chance of getting information from the dyke community—and I want results."

* * *

Nathalie got his phone call on her mobile when she was at George's. Josh wouldn't say what it was about, but he arranged to visit on Sunday, coincidentally just in time for lunch.

The visit with George had been even better than she expected. It was as if, for the first time, he had something of his own to be genuinely proud of. Jeremy greeted her with a huge hug and shy smile and then proceeded to introduce his sister. The little girl was as beautiful as her half brother, except that she was fairer and her eyes were the clearest, brightest blue. It was obvious, as she shyly reached for Jeremy's hand, that she adored him.

They had morning tea together, Nathalie letting the children approach her in their own time. Gradually they relaxed with her and chatted, as children do, about anything and everything. She'd never seen George so smitten or so gentle with anyone and the children followed him everywhere.

Later they went to the playground, watching from a nearby seat as the children climbed and jumped and laughed together, Samantha's short little legs struggling to keep up with her brother's long ones.

"Thank you for letting me visit," she said quietly. "I know Mother doesn't want me around."

"I don't want to talk about her, Nat," he said, his eyes never leaving his children.

"You don't have a choice, George. She's here, staying at your house, being with your children."

"Yes, *my* house, *my* children. It has nothing to do with you. There's nothing to worry about." His face had grown serious, his eyes hardening, and Nathalie knew that if she pushed him he'd grow angry and cold.

"Thanks anyway," she finished lamely. "They're beautiful. How long have you got Samantha for?"

"A few days. Her grandmother's taking her to see her mother in prison on Tuesday."

She wanted to ask if he still intended trying for custody but decided against it.

After the park they went for a burger, the kids enjoying the attention of another adult and doing their fair share of showing off. Jeremy was the more outgoing and because he spent more time with his father, he was more relaxed. But Samantha showed she was a feisty little girl, well and truly putting Jeremy in his place when he teased her too much.

Back at the house, the children showed Nathalie their bedrooms, which were in an area totally separated from the main part of the house. Nat could see how George would be able to run his business without the children ever knowing what that business was—at least while they were so young.

It fascinated Nathalie to hear their childish chatter and fanciful make believe and to see how they related to each other and to their father. They seemed so secure and open. Nat couldn't remember a time when she and George were like that. She didn't really remember them being children, only very small adults with adult secrets and responsibilities. It made her glad that Jeremy and Samantha were so different.

She stayed for tea at George's request and it gave her more of a chance to find out about his life. He'd been really fond of Jeremy's mother and they had a good relationship, even after the split. But, according to George, Samantha's mother was a recovering addict who, while not able to look after the girl herself, would not agree to increased custody, preferring instead to leave the child with her own mother. It was the grandmother who, without her daughter's knowledge, allowed him access whenever he wanted. It went unsaid, but Nathalie presumed George was paying the grandmother for the privilege.

When Nat tried a second time to raise the issue of them going to America, George refused to discuss it.

As she left, the children gave her soft, warm kisses that remained on her face long after she'd left their company. It was then that Nat knew she couldn't let George put them under Mother's control. Somehow she *would* stop it.

* * *

Josh arrived at midday the next day. They spoke for a while about his new girlfriend and Nathalie could hear the warmth and happiness in his voice.

"Actually, I wanted to talk to you about work," he said, sipping his beer. "I want to know if you're interested in a transfer to Serious Crime—specifically to my task force."

In all the time they'd known each other, their working lives had rarely crossed, but it was Josh who'd encouraged her to work plainclothes and complete the detective's course.

"Why do you want me?" she asked, puzzled. "There are a lot more experienced detectives around who'd kill for the chance to work on a task force."

"But you've got the right look and you're one of the most intelligent people I know. Most importantly, I trust you."

"Got the right look? What does that mean?"

"Well, to put it bluntly, the murders we're investigating could turn out to be linked. But even if they're not, a lot of questions are going to have to be asked in the lesbian and gay community, and some of those women are going to respond much better to another woman than to some crusty bloke."

While Nat made steak and salad, Josh explained the structure of the task force and his theory that the deaths were connected.

"So, going back to me having the right look?" she said with a wry smile when he'd finished explaining. "Would you be saying that I could pass for a lesbian?"

"God, Nat," he answered with a grin. "That's not why I want you on the team, but…well…yes. I guess that is what I'm saying."

She burst out laughing. Their relationship had evolved into open friendship where they discussed anything—anything except Nathalie's past. But she had told him that as a young person she'd had female lovers. It didn't totally surprise him.

"So when would I start, if the transfer went through?" she asked, thinking that the timing was perfect.

"Monday week. We need to get going as soon as we can. If you want this, I need to know by tonight so that I can get the paperwork moving first thing tomorrow."

"I don't need to consider," she replied happily. "I'll do it."

They spent another hour talking about the murders and the implications if they were random lesbian killings. Then they talked about the alternatives.

* * *

Her nightmares came for her again that night. She was perhaps six or seven. He was Mother's rich boyfriend, and he liked children. The man had raped her and come back a second time, but this time she struggled harder, screamed louder and the man stopped—as if afraid to continue. And the bad mother was angry—whispering threats, hurting her. Still Nat resisted. Mother glared, but, smiling at the man, she led him to a beautiful boy. Mother gave George to the man and moved away. Nathalie wanted to wake—make it stop—but she couldn't move, and George looked at her in desperation, tears rolling down his cheeks. And he was begging and struggling as the man used him.

She covered her ears and closed her eyes, warding off her brother's plaintive cries—but she was too terrified that the man might turn to her again if she tried to help him. Fear for her brother and for herself, shame that she'd let it happen and relief that it wasn't her, overwhelmed her. But it was the shame of her cowardice that would stay forever.

This time there was no struggling or screaming when she woke, just tears of self-loathing and the knowledge that this was an actual memory. It was the first time Mother had offered her and George to her boyfriend—pretending to the children that it was part of a game.

The lights made no difference now, because the memories were still alive—right here, right now. Staggering to the kitchen, her body lathered in sweat, she ripped the cap from the bourbon and poured it down her throat, coughing and spluttering as it hit the spot.

It had been the beginning of a permanent arrangement involving both of them, and it was how she and George had come to find comfort with each other. Over the years, Mother had taught them to embrace a new reality—one that reconciled sex with fun, sex with love, sex with making money—a reality that espoused that society's attitudes were inhibiting and anachronistic. Most importantly, she'd enforced the reality that refusal to participate carried a very heavy and painful price.

The memories brought bitter anger—most of it self-directed. She'd not only participated, but as they got older, had, with George, actively recruited other young teens—but they'd never been involved with the children. They'd suspected there were others after them, but they couldn't know—didn't want to know.

Nausea washed over her and she only just made it to the bathroom. Slumped on the floor, her head inches from the bowl, Nathalie acknowledged that she needed help. Yet if she sought it she not only stood to lose her job but also would have to share with a stranger the vile and disgusting things she'd been involved in, including her culpability in recruiting other young people.

Cleaning her teeth and washing her face, Nathalie made her way back to the bedroom. Stripping off her soaking nightwear, she stood looking in the full-length mirror. Her body was slim and athletic, her breasts small and firm and her face dark and serious, but when she looked into those deep gray eyes all she could see was her guilt reflected back.

* * *

"Jesus Christ, girl, were you partying all weekend?" asked Bella worriedly, as she dropped into the chair in front of Nathalie's desk on Monday. "You look exhausted."

"And would I tell you if I was?" she responded defensively, hoping to change the subject.

"If you're not careful you'll end up looking older than me," Bella said with a smirk.

"And that's bad," they responded together. It was a routine they followed whenever Bella picked up on one of Nathalie's rough nights. It kept things nicely impersonal, but let Nat know that Bella had noticed.

"How's things with Jack?" Nat asked, not sure that she wanted to know.

Screwing up her face, Bella made a swishing movement with her hand, indicating not great. "She came over Sunday, but didn't stay the night," replied Bella, looking surprisingly upset. "We had lunch. I sometimes wonder if the girl's on drugs, she's so vague. But she did ask about you, and she's still on about doing some volunteer work at the center."

"I'm sorry—" began Nat, before Bella waved away her sympathy.

"Don't be. I really don't know why she made such a big play for me. I guess when she finally gets around to finishing with me I'll head back to the clubs. But there are worse fates."

Nathalie told Bella of Josh's offer.

"You're good detective material and you've been wasted tucked away here." Then with a sad smile, Bella said, "Looks like I'm going to lose you as well as Jackie, but it's you I'll miss the most. Now I'll really have to get my finger out and decide what I want to do and do some serious networking to get there."

* * *

It was Wednesday before Josh rang to say he'd got approval for her transfer and Thursday before she was notified officially. That night she and Bella went for a farewell drink, assuring each other they'd remain in touch.

When Nat got home there were two messages on her answer machine, one from George asking her to ring the house and the other from Alex Messner. It was nine o'clock, so she took a chance that it wasn't too late and rang Alex first.

"How have you been?" Nat asked quietly, remembering the cool way she'd treated Alex last time they met.

"Busy," she replied quickly. "But I went to the center for an hour on Wednesday and saw that young client I had last week. She's not good and I'm worried that she'll get herself into serious trouble."

"What sort of trouble?"

"Legal trouble for starters. I've recommended she talk to you, but I'm not sure she's listening."

"Okay. I'll talk to her tomorrow. I presume she'll be there tomorrow?"

"That's the plan."

The silence that followed was awkward, as if neither wanted to end the call, but the information had been passed and the purpose achieved.

"Look, I just wanted to apologize if I upset you when I asked you out last week," Alex said quickly. "I like you, and I don't want it to be awkward between us."

"It didn't upset me. And I do like you. It's just…"

"I know. You don't want to go out with a woman."

"No, that's not it," she replied slowly. "It's just that I'm not easy to be with, and I don't want you to end up hating me. I'm not a nice person."

"I'm a lot stronger than you think," replied Alex, relieved that Nathalie hadn't been offended by her approach. "And I'm willing to take my chances. If it doesn't work out, then it doesn't work out, but I'd like the opportunity to get to know you better."

"Does that mean you're asking me out again?"

Laughing, Alex replied, "I told you I would. So, how about joining me for a BBQ lunch with a couple of friends on Saturday… and see what happens after that."

"Okay, it's a date," Nat answered quietly, following her instincts. "I'll see you tomorrow and we can make the arrangements."

Nathalie tried not to think about what she'd just agreed to. There was danger in letting people get close, but she liked Alex a lot. She was attractive, intelligent and one of the warmest people she'd ever met. Perhaps having another interest would force the nightmares and memories back out of her life.

The second phone call, with George, was strange. He'd called to ask if she wanted to have lunch with him and Jeremy on Sunday, but he sounded distracted and the warmth they'd built up over the last couple of weeks had disappeared.

"Where's Mother?" she asked curiously.

"Out doing business. She's thinking of going back to the US in a few weeks and she's meeting friends on Sunday."

Gratefully she accepted, but George's strangeness worried her.

* * *

Alex and Nathalie met at the center the next evening and only had time for a very brief discussion before Alex's client arrived and both women retired to meet with her in one of the offices. After that the evening got more hectic and only at the end did they meet up again.

Alex invited Nathalie back to her house again for coffee.

While classical music played softly in the background they talked about their jobs. Nat told Alex about her transfer and that she would be part of the team investigating the recent lesbian murders. Then Alex spoke about her role in the prisons and the challenges that made the job worthwhile. Nathalie enjoyed hearing the passion and genuine empathy Alex displayed for her clients. It was obvious to Nat that Alex had genuinely found her calling as a psychologist. Later they discussed music and travel. Then Alex asked about Nat's family.

"I have a brother I see occasionally," she answered vaguely. "We lost touch for a long time, but we've actually seen a bit of each other over the last few weeks."

"What about your parents? Where are they?"

Nathalie's normal answer when people asked that question was to tell them her mother and father were dead, but for some reason she didn't want to lie to Alex.

"My mother lives in America, although she's on holiday here at the moment." Aware of Alex waiting for more information, she said as casually as she could, "We don't get on very well and we didn't have contact for many years. We met up again at my brother's recently, but it didn't work out. It's a long story."

"What about your father?"

"He left before I was born. Mother said he was a businessman who came from New Orleans. He didn't want a child."

"I'm sorry. It must have been hard not knowing him?"

"Not really. You don't miss what you never had, and obviously he didn't want to know me. What about you? Are your parents alive?" Nat asked, relaxing and enjoying the personal conversation.

"My mother is. She lives not far from me. My father died when I was nineteen."

"Did you like him?"

The question surprised Alex. "Yes, I liked him. He was gentle and fun and he looked after us. We were devastated when he died."

"Do you like your mother?"

Nodding, she said, "She's probably one of my best friends. We talk and laugh a lot, and there's not much she doesn't know about my life. I love her very much."

Now they were both quiet, Alex studying Nathalie and Nathalie studying her drink.

"Why don't you get on with your mother?" Alex asked eventually.

Nathalie didn't look up, but her eyes moved into the distance and her face became tense. For a long time she didn't speak, and when she did Alex detected a note of fear. "She's not a nice woman," she said, shaking her head and then looking up. "But hopefully she's out of my life now, so let's talk about something else."

It was obviously a very bad relationship. The psychologist in Alex wanted to investigate it further, while the friend wanted to heal Nat's pain. They spoke of movies they liked and actors and actresses, and eventually Nathalie asked what birth sign she was.

"You don't strike me as someone who'd believe in star signs," laughed Alex, taken by surprise. "Now me, I'm a born believer in things esoteric and spiritual."

"Well, there you go," Nat smiled. "I can surprise the psychologist. So what sign are you?"

"Leo. And you?"

"Scorpio," Nat replied with a grin.

"Oh, dear," Alex exclaimed. "According to the books we're not compatible—lots of obstacles." Then, smiling broadly, "But then obstacles are there to be overcome. So are you interested in the psychic as well?" Alex continued curiously.

"My mother's a clairvoyant," Nat answered reluctantly. "She's very popular among the rich and famous here and also in California." The easy company had loosened her tongue. "But hey, I don't want to talk about her. What's this BBQ tomorrow?"

"It's at the beachside house of a couple of friends, just a small gathering. I could pick you up about five o'clock. They've got a pool, so bring your swimwear."

The conversation had been lively and relaxed and Nathalie found herself wanting to linger in this woman's presence. Yet she was still unsure about letting Alex into her life and she wanted to take things slowly. "Well, I'll see you tomorrow then," she said, rising from her comfortable chair and writing her home address on a business card.

As they walked to the door, Alex longed to kiss Nat goodbye, but she didn't. She didn't want to move too fast too soon. Yet the moment Nat stepped over the threshold Alex regretted her decision. The attraction was definitely sexual, but she also wanted to reach her emotionally—to take away the darkness haunting those beautiful gray eyes.

Nathalie was scared. She longed to trust Alex, to confide in her. Yet while the secrets and lies were exhausting, Alex could never know the disgusting details of her past. And that was a problem, because the woman was on her mind all the time. She longed to be with her, to be held by her, to make love to her.

That night Nathalie didn't dream. In the morning, feeling better than she had for a long time, she decided to get caught up on her housework. Stripped to a T-shirt and shorts, she scrubbed and polished and vacuumed to the sounds of Cat Stevens and Tina Turner. It would be strange meeting Alex's friends, but she liked the idea of doing something with her that wasn't related to the center. Although Alex was only a few years older than she was, she seemed so grounded. There was a twinge of jealousy when Alex spoke of Lou. Not because of the relationship, but because she couldn't envisage inspiring such depth of emotion in anyone, and it made her feel cheated.

* * *

Alex arrived to pick her up just before five. Somewhere between Friday night and Saturday afternoon Alex had had her hair cut and styled and she looked stunning. Nat told her so.

"You look great too," Alex commented, as she waited for Nathalie to set her answer machine and hunt for her mobile phone. "But then with your coloring you'd look wonderful in a garbage sack." Without warning she moved to Nathalie, touching her face and kissing her tentatively.

Nat's response was passionate, searing and wonderful, but then she tensed.

Alex stopped. "Sorry," she whispered with a shrug, "I'm rushing things, I know, but I can't help it. When I want something, I want it yesterday."

They both laughed.

"Perhaps we should leave?" Alex suggested, moving away.

Nathalie didn't argue.

On the drive to the party, Nat thought about Josh. When he'd started asking her out she'd struggled. He was funny, intelligent and interesting, and she'd been very lonely. While she didn't want the obligation of a physical relationship with any man, she didn't want to lose the enjoyment of his company or the genuinely loving attention he paid her. So it became a compromise. Knowing she could offer him nothing emotionally, she'd put her energy and skill into giving him a highly satisfying sex life and making their home life pleasant.

But while he never questioned her commitment, he had known that what was missing was far greater than what they had, and it upset him. He loved her, was in love with her, but emotionally he'd felt locked out and alone in the relationship. Coupled with the terrible nightmares and a past she refused to discuss, he'd found the emotional gap just too wide to breach.

It scared Nathalie that this might happen with Alex.

The house was beautiful, with huge sweeping decks overlooking the ocean, and Trish and Jenny were lively, interesting, older dykes, who made Nathalie feel welcome.

Alex showed her through the house.

"It's beautiful," stated Nat as they wandered from room to room. "I could live here very easily."

"Trish is a retired surgeon, who spent a lot of her life working in various parts of Africa," Alex explained quietly. "She helped me look after Lou in the last couple of months of her life. Lou couldn't have stayed out of hospital without her and Jenny."

Squeezing her hand, Nat acknowledged the honor of being introduced to these people who were obviously very important to her.

As they talked, Nathalie found herself enjoying the easy conversation and friendly banter of her hostesses. Sometime later, several other couples arrived and were introduced to Nat. These included a male couple, one of whom seemed very familiar.

He was slim and dark and very handsome, and the recognition was mutual, but Nat couldn't place him. He said nothing during the introductions.

Conversation flowed freely to the rhythm of African music, and Nat found herself relaxing completely. Later they moved to the deck where Jenny busily cooked meat and seafood on an enormous built-in barbecue. It was while she leaned against the rail of the balcony staring mindlessly out to sea that the dark young man joined her.

"You're Nathalie Silver, aren't you—Charlotte Silver's daughter?" he asked quietly, as he leaned on the rail beside her.

Her throat tightened and her blood ran cold, but the man's attitude didn't seem malevolent as he placed his hand comfortingly on her own.

"It's okay," he whispered. "I don't want trouble. I'm Michael Anopolous, but you knew me as Ari or Aristotle...your mother's house many years ago?"

Swallowing hard, she continued to stare at him. "You were a boy then," she answered finally. "I wouldn't have recognized you."

"You weren't much older yourself. How is your mother?" he asked, unable to disguise the loathing in his eyes. "I actually loved her and George. At least I thought so at the time."

"She lives in America." Looking around, Nathalie was relieved to see Alex still deep in conversation with Trish.

Noticing her worried look, he said, "I've been with James for six years, but he doesn't know about my past, so you're in no danger from me."

"Ari—"

"Michael," he corrected quickly. "You know, you were always good to me and I liked you a lot, but you were no sooner at the house than you were gone. You weren't like Charlotte or George. You never seemed comfortable in that world."

"Like you said, you didn't know me very well. And my name's Nathalie Duncan. I never went under my mother's name."

"I was only thirteen when George and your mother seduced me," he stated unemotionally. "But I was having a lot of fun and finding out a lot about myself. Then all of a sudden…a few years on…it wasn't as much fun anymore and I couldn't wait to get out. I was lucky, my family took me back, sent me away to school and I got the chance to pull away from them and start again. But what about you? George told me a lot about growing up in that house. I can't imagine a childhood like that."

"No, you can't," she replied, unsure whether to trust this man or not. "But you don't get to choose your family, and in the end we all survive…don't we?"

"Yes, I guess we do," he said thoughtfully. Then his tone changed. "I want you to know that Alex is a good friend of ours. Do anything to harm her and I will come after you."

At that moment Alex arrived and stretching up, planted a warm kiss on Michael's cheek. "So, how's my Greek god," she laughed, touching his face lovingly.

"Much better for that kiss, my beloved Alexandra," he smiled gently. "And pleased to see you've finally found a new interest." As the words left his mouth, his eyes bored into Nat's, telling her in no uncertain terms that she was not to take Alex's interest lightly.

It scared her but also heartened her that Alex would inspire such loyalty.

"So what were you two talking about so intently when I walked up?"

"Horoscopes, my nosy friend," he replied a little too quickly. Then laughing, he added, "I was just telling your Nathalie that she'd better behave herself with you or she'd have James and me to deal with. I don't think she was intimidated, though."

"No, Michael," she said with a grin. "I seriously doubt she would be; you're just not mean enough." By now they'd been joined by James and were drifting back to where the food was being served.

Later, when it was dark and the lights had been dimmed, Alex asked Nat to dance. The music was slow and low, and Trish and Jenny were moving together in one corner of the vast lounge.

"I can't dance," she whispered in reply.

"Sure you can," she replied, pulling Nat to her feet. "You know how to hold a woman, don't you? After that the rest comes naturally."

And it did. Being in Alex's arms was warm and peaceful and sexy. She wanted to be close to her, to hold her forever, to be needed by her, to feel that soft, warm body against her own and to feel the pressure of her arms around her waist.

"You dance well," Alex whispered dreamily, as they moved in time to the music. "What else don't I know about you?"

Without answering, Nathalie moved closer, held her tighter and prayed that somehow she could make this work.

* * *

It was close to midnight when they left. Nathalie had enjoyed the company and the inclusion she felt with Alex's friends. Michael had seen her once more during the evening, but the discussion had been general, letting her know that, unless she raised it, the subject of the past was closed.

That Alex would come into her apartment for coffee was a foregone conclusion, and Nat knew that tonight they would sleep together. It was more about not wanting to let Alex out of her sight than it was about sex—at least that's how it started. But as they held and kissed and touched, Nat felt an excitement she'd never experienced before.

Somehow they ended up naked in the big warm bed, with Alex taking the initiative. Her passion had been obvious all evening and Nat could feel the tension and need pouring from her as she moved sensuously against her, tiny gasps escaping her lips as Nat moved with her.

"It's been so long," Alex whispered, as they kissed and stroked, exploring tentatively, then passionately. "I didn't think I'd ever want to do this with anyone again, but I want you so much."

"Oh God, yes," gasped Nat, as Alex shuddered and moved a little faster against her hand, her kisses becoming more demanding, her breathing more ragged.

Nat knew all the moves, but it wasn't like other times. It wasn't cold and mechanical. She wanted only to satisfy this woman, but now her body was assailing her with its own demands, and she didn't feel guilty, and her spirit and emotions participated in a way she'd never known.

Afterward, they lay in each other's arms, Nathalie feeling safe and loved for the first time in her life and Alex feeling a quiet joy and contentment and a certainty that Lou would not have minded.

"So tell me about your family," Alex said as they lay together talking. "What does your brother do for a living?"

"He works for Mother—looks after her business affairs over here," she answered vaguely, wondering what Alex would say if she told her that he ran an exclusive call service providing boys and girls to the wealthy or organized parties for the truly jaded.

"You don't like your mother much, do you?"

"It's mutual," Nat replied grimly. "I think she actually hates me."

"No," argued Alex, sadly. "She's your mother."

"I always seem to annoy her," mumbled Nat quietly. "But it's far more complicated than that." She grimaced, "I really don't want to talk about her. Instead I'd rather hear about your mother. What's she like?"

"I guess I'm very lucky. Mum and I have always been close. My biological father left when I was a baby. Mum remarried a couple of years later and I gained a new dad—a wonderful man who was always there for us. We had a terrific childhood."

"We—so you have brothers and sisters?"

"I had a younger sister, but she died a long time ago, a few years after our father."

"I'm sorry. You've had a lot of losses."

"I suppose so, but I tend to be grateful that I loved them and they loved me in return."

For a while they lay in silence, caressing one another, enjoying the closeness.

What Nat didn't say about her childhood indicated to Alex that her past contained a lot of pain. Hopefully one day she'd trust her enough to share.

"So does this mean we're seeing each other?" asked Nathalie tentatively. "Or was it just a fling?"

"I don't do flings, Nat," Alex replied gently. "You're the first person I've been with since Lou died, and I didn't sleep with you lightly."

Nat didn't know what to say. Even when she asked the question, it had sounded insecure and immature, but being with Alex was a whole new experience—a journey into emotions she'd only ever read or talked about or touched on briefly with Christine, and it left her scared and vulnerable.

Before long the holding and touching turned to kissing and the kissing to renewed passion. This time they spent time learning what the other liked, teasing and playing in ways that tantalized and delighted. It was as if they were striving to become one as they melded and clung together, moving in unison, desire engulfing them. The more they moved together the more demanding each became and the more urgent their need for completion. Finally, gasping and moaning, they reached that exquisite point of no return.

"Oh God, oh God," whispered Alex as her insides exploded in delicious spasms while she clung, shuddering and desperate to Nat, savoring her every movement, her every thrust. "I didn't think it could be this good…"

And then Nat was moaning her satisfaction, moving faster and faster until, with one last groan, her body collapsed onto Alex's. It had been like nothing Nathalie had ever experienced before, and she was left dizzy and totally sated, a warm glow replacing her usual feelings of guilt and disgust.

Afterward, snuggled together under the bedclothes, they had time for a few affectionate words before drifting peacefully to sleep.

* * *

It was five forty a.m. when Mother came to visit her dreams. At first Nat was able to push her away, telling her that she wouldn't give her what she wanted. But Mother just smiled and tried to kiss her on the lips, grabbing her wrists and holding her down. Then there was pressure and the weight of a man. Mother was on one side and the man on the other and they were both touching her and touching each other. And she was struggling, screaming at them that she wouldn't let them ruin everything.

"It won't hurt," he whispered, his body crushing her. "Your mother said I could."

"Nathalie...Nathalie...it will be okay. Nat, wake up. It's all right." The voice seemed far away. So calm, so soothingly familiar. But she was frightened, helpless, lashing out now, fighting to push them away. Sobbing and moaning, she rose to consciousness, struggling to back away. Then the lights were on and it wasn't Mother, wasn't the man. It was Alex—kneeling beside her, trying to grab her flailing wrists.

"Oh God...I'm so sorry," she gasped, trying to hide her face and pull away from Alex's strong grasp. "I'm so sorry. I shouldn't have let you stay."

"It's all right. It was just a nightmare," Alex soothed, trying to move closer to the dark woman huddled against the end wall. "It's over now."

Shaking her head and indicating she didn't want to be touched, Nat wrapped her arms around her body, attempting to back even further into the wall. How could she have been so stupid? Why would she expect that this relationship could be any different? It might take weeks, but eventually the nightmares scared away anyone she got close to. Now it had happened on their first night.

"I won't touch you, Nathalie," Alex promised as she pulled her discarded shirt around her naked torso. "But I want you to look at me."

When Nat turned her face away, Alex again implored her, "Please don't turn away, Nat," she said, moving back to sit on the chair a few feet from the bed. "It's just a nightmare, and it's over now. It doesn't matter."

"Doesn't it?" mumbled Nathalie, devastated and embarrassed. "You'd best leave."

"No. I don't think so," replied Alex, firmly, but gently. "What I will do is go and make us a cup of something, and I'll see you in the kitchen when you feel ready."

Pulling on underwear and buttoning the shirt, she quietly left the room.

* * *

It had been the mumbling and pushing that first brought Alex awake.

Nat was crying and sweating and struggling feebly against her. She'd tried to hold her, but she'd become more desperate—moaning incoherently and fighting, almost pushing her from the bed. Now she was curled into a ball, trying to defend herself, and although Alex couldn't make out the words, she knew Nat was begging someone—pleading for them not to do something.

Rather than being scared or repulsed, she wanted to protect Nat. Her studies had taught her that most people experienced nightmares sometime in their lives, but nightmares this intense and violent usually signified something far more serious—an horrific event or some form of abuse.

It was nearly ten minutes before Nat left the bedroom and wandered into the kitchen. She'd obviously washed her face. Physically she looked as if nothing had happened, but her eyes contained a mixture of embarrassment, anger and overwhelming sadness.

"I made a pot of tea," Alex said quietly. "It should be good and strong by now."

Taking a seat at the kitchen table opposite her, Nat looked defensive. "You don't have to stay," she murmured.

"I know I don't," she replied, pouring the dark brown liquid into two large mugs and adding milk and sugar. "But I want to." Pushing the cup toward Nat and indicating for her to drink, she said, "You'll feel better if you drink that."

It was more a command than a suggestion and Nat found herself obeying mindlessly—enjoying the feel of the hot sweet liquid sliding down her throat.

For a few moments they sipped silently on their tea, Alex watching Nat, and Nat looking downward.

"So, I presume this nightmare wasn't a one off?" Alex asked in her best psychologist voice. Nat didn't need a lover right now. She needed someone to talk to.

Still without looking at her, Nat shook her head.

"How often do you have them?"

"Often enough," she responded angrily. "But sometimes it's not too bad."

"Do you know what causes them?"

"Mostly," she laughed bitterly. "But knowing doesn't make them go away."

"Then you need to talk to someone."

"Yes, so Josh has been telling me for years. Who do you suggest—you?"

"You've had these nightmares for years?" she asked worriedly.

"They come and go. But they've been bad for a few weeks now."

"I don't want to be your psychologist, Nat," she volunteered gently, answering her earlier question. "I want to be your lover and your friend, and I'm emotionally involved. So apart from the ethics of it, I'd be useless to you. But I can recommend someone who's very good."

"I don't—"

"He's the best, Nat," she interrupted, raising a hand. "He helped my mother when she went through a bad time, and he was my mentor after university. There's no one better."

"He...?"

Alex made no comment, but barely nodded.

"I'll think about it."

Alex knew there was no point pushing. Only when Nat was ready would she be willing to talk to someone.

"So, what do you normally do when you're up in the early hours?" she asked, reaching for Nathalie's hand and taking it to her lips. "How about an early morning drive and stroll near the ocean?"

The sea was rough, but the crashing of the waves was peaceful and because it was overcast and gray they were virtually alone on the windswept beach.

"I want to go on seeing you," stated Alex, as she put her arms around Nathalie's waist and drew her into her.

Their faces were only inches apart and Nat felt herself drifting into Alex's warm, loving eyes. How she longed to stay like this forever. "I want that too. I'm just scared you'll end up hating me."

"Don't be. Maybe you're right and it won't work out, but maybe it will. You have to trust me, because it's too late for me to walk away now. Please give it a try."

Nat's answer was a kiss, tentative and gentle at first, then lingering and passionate. Quietly they held each other, oblivious to any questioning glances, enjoying the smell and sound of the ocean and the warmth of their embrace.

And in the distance a man adjusted his binoculars, picked up his long lens camera and began taking photos.

CHAPTER SIX

Disclosures from the Past

George seemed nervous and irritable when Nathalie arrived, but Jeremy was happy to see her as he led her back to his bedroom to show her his new soccer boots.

"Grandmother says I won't need soccer boots in America," he stated innocently. "But I really like soccer."

"Well, I'm sure you can play soccer there as well if you want," Nat said, her heart sinking at the thought of this child moving to live near Mother.

"Dad says that too," he agreed, his face lighting up.

"Do you want to go to America, Jeremy?" she asked. "Won't you miss your mother and your friends?"

Looking down and picking at some invisible lint on his shorts, he mumbled, "Grandmother says Mummy doesn't care, and she says I can go to a better school."

So it's beginning already, she thought. *Mother, reaching into this child's mind, twisting his thoughts, grooming him to think like her.* Taking hold of his small soft hands, she turned him around to face her and sat down on the bed. "But what do *you* think, darling?" she asked, looking into his deep brown eyes.

"I don't like Grandmother much," he whispered conspiratorially, glancing over his shoulder. "And neither does Sam. Grandmother tells Daddy off a lot. I wish she'd go away."

"That's no way to talk about your grandmother." George's voice made them both jump and the little boy's face fell, as if he'd been caught breaking something valuable. "Now, I don't want any more discussion. Wash your hands and go and get your lunch. We're eating on the patio."

As the child made his way past George, he mumbled, "I'm sorry, Daddy." But Nathalie noticed that there was no fear in it, just a genuine wish to take back what he thought might have hurt his father's feelings.

"It's none of your business, Nat," he said quickly, cutting off anything she might have been going to say. "And it's still not definite that we're going."

"So what have you and Mother been fighting about?" she asked, looking up into his handsome features. "Jeremy said—"

"He's a little boy," he snapped. "What would he know about anything? Now let's go out and have lunch. That's what you were invited for."

"How's your boyfriend…Josh, wasn't it?" George asked suddenly as they tucked into a chicken salad, presumably prepared by the invisible Belinda.

"Why?" she asked, looking into his eyes, which wavered and looked toward his son.

"Just general conversation," he muttered with a shrug. "That's the sort of thing most people talk about over lunch isn't it? And I just wondered if he was good in bed?"

"Well, we're not most people," she answered flatly, glancing at Jeremy who was working hard at cutting up a piece of chicken. "And your question reminds us of that. I am *not* going to discuss my sex life with you."

Pushing his plate away and giving Jeremy permission to play with his iPad, George lit a cigarette. "Nat, Mother's obsessed that you're out to hurt her in some way," he said, drawing the smoke into his lungs. "It's driving her crazy and it's all she can talk about."

"Why? I don't understand. It was she who told me she didn't want to see me again."

"Perhaps it's because you and your boyfriend are in the police. She's got this idea that you want to destroy her…and me. She says you've got secrets and that the Tarot cards have labeled you the enemy—the Tower of Destruction."

"All because I don't want to keep on doing what we did as children?" she asked, shaking her head. "She's my mother, you're my brother. I wouldn't do anything to hurt you."

"The cards tell her differently."

"Fuck the cards," she spat angrily. "Our lives were ruled by the cards and our lives were shit."

"No. That's not true. It's saying things like that, that would make Mother think…well, you know."

"What, George? What would Mother think—that I didn't like having sex with all those people…with her, with you? Well, she'd be right, I didn't. I hated every minute of it. Sometimes I just wanted to die, but I was too cowardly to even do that." Taking a deep breath, she added, "God, George, didn't you ever want a normal life? Don't you want one now?"

"It is normal to want sex," he answered defensively, "and people pay huge sums to get what they want. You were quite happy to take the money when you were younger. It put you through university and bought you the flat. Mother's been good to us. Look how I live, and all she's asking is for you to participate once in a while. It might make her realize that you're not out to destroy us."

"And if I don't?"

"I'm scared, Nat. You know what she's like. I used to hear her beat you until you were bloody when you were little, because you'd defied her. And in the end you learned it was easier to be nice to Mother. She's only here for a few months. How much could it hurt?"

"What beatings?" Nathalie demanded, looking at him in horror. "You're making that up," she accused. "Some of the men hurt me, but not Mother…"

He looked genuinely bewildered. "Why are you lying about it, Nat?" he said, shaking his head and staring at her as if seeing her for the first time. "She'd use a strap, sometimes a rope, and sometimes she'd leave bad marks on you and you couldn't leave the house. You must remember. That's how you got the scar across your bottom."

His face told her he wasn't lying, but she didn't remember. But then she didn't really remember much at all until a year or so before the men, before six or seven years of age. Now that he'd raised it, it occurred to her that there must be something wrong with her that she couldn't remember.

"I used to think she hit you because she was afraid of you," he said quietly, not really knowing why his mother would have been scared of a small child. "But it got better when you started doing what she wanted. Then she stopped hurting you so badly. Don't make her start hurting you again."

"Is that why you asked me here? To try and talk me into rejoining the family?" she asked sadly. "I thought—"

"I know we talked last time," he said with his hands raised to stop her talking. "But I still love you, Nat. And Mother wants us to be a family again while she's staying here. It's not that much further to work and it would prove you didn't want to hurt us."

Pushing back from the table, she moved toward the doorway, "I came to see Jeremy," she said, stopping to look at him. "Not to let you use me."

But he was on his feet and moving toward her, forcing her back against the wall of the house. "Just do it with me, Nat," he begged, holding her arms and pressing into her. "Mother needs to see that you're with us, not against us."

"Then you'll just have to lie to her again, won't you?" she spat, struggling against him. "Or are you going to force me?"

"She's watching," he whispered, moving his mouth near her ear, pretending to kiss her neck. "On the security cameras. We have to do this."

She struggled, but although lean, he was muscular and strong and she remained pinned to the wall.

"I'd never force you," he admitted. "But I'm begging you to just do it. If I can't convince her that you still love us, I don't know what she might do."

"She's here?"

"Of course. How else could she watch us on the cameras? She asked me to get you here, to get you upstairs."

"Oh God, George, I thought…I didn't think you'd betray me."

"Don't you understand?" he cajoled. "I'm doing this for us, for the family."

"What family?" she growled angrily, staring him in the face. "Families don't fuck each other, George. That's not love. It's sick and I won't do it anymore. I don't care what she does to me. Don't you understand? I don't even care if she kills me."

Letting go, he stepped back. The color had drained from his face, and suddenly the handsome, perfectly groomed young man looked twenty years older. Sitting back down at the table, he whispered, "I used to hold you sometimes when you were little and she'd been hurting you. You'd bury your face in my chest and cling to me. I wanted to protect you but I couldn't. And I can't now." He sounded exhausted.

"You were only a couple of years older than me," she stated flatly. "We were babies. You couldn't even protect yourself. It would be like Jeremy trying to protect Samantha against Mother or against her clients. He couldn't do it."

His head snapped up and anger returned to his eyes. "Jeremy won't ever have to protect Sam," he snapped. "I've told you. I'm keeping them right away from that."

"You were, George. You were until Mother came back. What is she doing here? Why did she come back?"

He didn't answer, just stared defiantly, shaking his head imperceptibly.

"Tell her to leave me alone, George, and tell her if she goes near those children I *will* destroy her. You're not a child anymore and neither am I, so there's no more excuses. We're all there is between her and your children. Don't ever forget that." Turning, she walked from the house. She wanted to see Jeremy again, but it was impossible while Mother was there.

She knew she'd lose any confrontation with Mother. Even now the woman terrified her.

* * *

Sitting on the sand, her hands between her knees, Nathalie stared unseeingly toward the ocean. Why was Mother back? It had to be George's children. Or was it simply that she wanted to regain control of her own children? But that made no sense—both she and George were far too old to be of any interest to Mother or her clients. They'd been too old at eighteen. But what could she do about it if it was George's children Mother wanted? Could she really take her on, with all her contacts and all her power, and win? And what if George gave in? What if he obeyed her and they disappeared with the children to America? Backward and forward her mind traveled until she recognized that it was like when they were children. Nobody had helped them then, and there was nobody to intercede now. She needed George to stand up with her. And, even if he did, she just wasn't sure either of them had what it would take.

Then she remembered George's description of the beatings Mother had administered. It explained why she had always felt Mother's dislike. But why would she forget that and remember the other stuff—the parties and the men? It made no sense.

In the end, she concluded that there was no explanation. That it was like everything else in her life—random, painful and unchangeable. It would pass. Mother would have her tantrum, she might even punish her, but afterward things would return to normal. She had to believe that.

It took her a long time to go to sleep, but once there she slept the night through. And that only created another puzzle. If the nightmares were caused by the past, then why did they come and go? Surely today's confrontation with George should have triggered one? But feeling happy and satisfied and content with Alex the previous night had. At least now she knew why she hadn't chosen psychology as her profession. How could anyone be expected to understand the sort of mess she carried in her head?

* * *

Nathalie arrived early for work in the morning and found Josh alone in the huge office they'd been allocated for the task force. Giving her a quick peck on the cheek, he said, "That's for taking the transfer and because it will be strictly business from now on. As far as I know, nobody knows that you and I used to live together, and I'd like to keep it that way."

"Of course," she replied with a smile.

"As soon as the others arrive I'll do the introductions and a briefing, but you already know the basics of the second killing. We still haven't found anything connecting the two, but we'll start today by collating what the two teams have got so far. Then if we still have nothing, we'll have to proceed by investigating them as separate crimes while sharing whatever the day's work has turned up."

While they waited for everyone to arrive, Nathalie began looking around the room. Several huge whiteboards had been set up, and numerous pin boards displayed photos of the two crime scenes, including photos of the dead women and everything that was known about each victim. Reading this information took her about twenty minutes, by which time people had begun to arrive and stand around.

Josh started with the introductions. There would be eight on the task force including himself and one civilian analyst. Each person gave his or her name, experience and where they'd come from. Other than the analyst and herself, everyone was an experienced detective, and all had met before. There was only one other woman in the group.

Lorna was about forty, chubby and bespectacled, but she had an air of authority that eighteen years in the force had given her and she was bright and articulate and friendly.

As they worked through the information they already had, they took it in turns trying to find connections between the dead women, their relationships, jobs, social lives, hobbies and deaths, but by lunchtime they were no further forward.

During the lunch break, Nathalie used Josh's office to ring Alex at work. She'd been thinking of her constantly and worried that perhaps, now that she'd had time to think, Alex wouldn't want them to continue. Perhaps the violence of the nightmare had scared her off.

The way Alex answered the phone made it obvious she was glad to hear from her, flooding Nathalie with unexpected relief. They spoke for nearly ten minutes, light, happy banter, before confirming arrangements for dinner at Alex's. "I'm missing you. Stay safe," Alex told her before hanging up.

"Me too," she answered softly, dropping the phone into the cradle.

"Me too, what?" asked Josh's familiar voice from the half-open doorway. "Me too I love you? Or me too for Chinese food?"

"Or me too for privacy," she responded irritably.

"My office," he replied with a shrug, looking around him. "So who is he? Do I know him?"

She didn't really know what to say. He knew she'd slept with women in the past, but she wasn't quite ready to share Alex with him yet. "No, you don't," she replied with a smile. "But I'm sure you will if it gets off the ground. In the meantime, it's none of your business."

At the end of the day, Nathalie felt tired but stimulated. Their hard work hadn't turned up any significant leads, other than it was possible that all three women had frequented the same lesbian club at times, but whether they'd ever met each other would have to be looked into. At least it was a link.

* * *

That evening she and Alex dined on lasagna, salad and garlic bread and discussed their day. Neither mentioned names or specifics, speaking instead of the questions and problems their day had presented. It seemed so easy to talk to Alex and so good to share things.

From the moment Nathalie arrived they'd struggled to keep their hands off one another. It was a challenge—pretending they weren't burning with desire, pretending they could last until after dinner. In the end, though, the lovemaking won, after a simple kiss had turned into so much more and they'd ended up in Alex's bedroom, throwing themselves into passionate lovemaking that left them gasping for breath and glowing with satisfaction.

Dinner was eaten late and afterward they returned to their lovemaking. This time, though, the urgency had been dulled a little.

"I love your body," whispered Alex as they lay wrapped together, their bodies gently moving against each other. First one, then the other, was on top, grinding and thrusting, kissing and licking and gently biting nipples and necks, gasping with desire and the burgeoning need that was slowly building between them.

The dull ache became a scream as Alex rode Nat's leg, kissing with dueling tongues and muffled moans, heated bodies clasped together as one. Then Nat was inside her, her thumb pressed against her distended mound, her fingers moving deeper and deeper, and Alex was bucking and moaning and riding wave after delicious wave of need and desire and finally—sweet release.

But Nat didn't stop immediately. Instead she gently moved her thumb around the now highly sensitive clitoris with barely a whisper of a touch, causing Alex to let loose with one final jarring orgasm at the exact moment that Nat herself moaned and clutched Alex to her.

For a long time they lay clasped together, slick with love, exhaustion and the need to be one.

"I love the texture and color of your skin and the way your body responds when we're making love," Alex whispered finally, touching Nat's face. "You're a beautiful lover."

Nathalie said nothing. That wasn't how she wanted Alex to think of her—seducing and satisfying people was something she was practiced at. This wasn't about that, it was different. It *had* to be different.

"You're very quiet," Alex murmured eventually. "You did enjoy it, didn't you? You're not having second thoughts?"

"About what?" she asked.

"Being with a woman?"

"I love being with you…but not just because of the sex."

"I would hope not." She laughed automatically before realizing that Nathalie was being serious. "I never thought it was just about the sex, Nat. Why would you?"

She wanted to say, "Because it's what everything comes back to in the end," but she didn't. It would mean nothing to Alex and would only open up a conversation she'd rather avoid. Ignoring the question, she said, "I'll go home tonight. I've got work in the morning."

Disappointed, Alex replied, "Just so long as you come back soon."

Nat didn't want to leave, but the fear of driving Alex away with a repeat of the previous night scared her, and it seemed easier to walk away.

* * *

By Wednesday, Josh had assigned Lorna and Nathalie to visit lesbian clubs on Friday and Saturday night with photos of the dead women. Until then the team would make inquiries around the murder scenes and talk to family and friends. It was a slow process, but necessary. This meant Nat changing her night at the center and rearranging appointments there, but she didn't mind. Working at the women's center wouldn't be as easy now that she'd be doing shift work.

Alex and Nathalie didn't see each other on Tuesday because Alex was having dinner with her mother, but on Wednesday they ate at Nathalie's.

The conversation flowed easily as they discussed the minutiae of daily life in a way that Nathalie had never done before. It was so new, yet felt so right. There'd been a suicide in the prison the night before, so Alex's day had been spent counseling other inmates and staff.

"Did you know the woman who killed herself?" Nat asked.

"Not well. She'd never been to me professionally, but she was a wing cleaner and would make passing conversation. Suicides in that environment affect everyone in some way."

"Do you know why she did it?"

"Apparently she'd received divorce papers from her husband. She left a note addressed to him, but the police aren't saying what was in it."

"Have you ever felt suicidal?" Nathalie asked. "I mean, really like you didn't want to keep going?"

"Only once for a little while. It was just after Lou died. I was scared and angry and couldn't see how I could go on without her. I just wanted so desperately to be with her."

"But you obviously didn't do anything."

"No. You just keep breathing and doing the daily tasks and bit by bit it becomes a little easier, but I was lucky. I had great support from friends. And Mum was brilliant."

"So your mother knows you're lesbian?"

"She's known since I was at university."

"How does she feel about it?"

"She'd have liked grandchildren, and I think she's a little sad that she didn't get any, but otherwise…well…she always said she just wanted us kids to be happy."

"You're young enough to still have a child."

"Sure," she admitted. "But it's not a burning need right now."

"Do you believe there are people who should never be allowed to have children?"

"Definitely," Alex replied emphatically. "People can be taught parenting skills, but if they don't have the moral and emotional desire to care for, protect and love their children, then they're almost certain to harm them emotionally, if not physically. Believe me, I work with a lot of deeply damaged people who are paying for the parents they started out with."

"Yet those people end up doing the same thing to their kids?" It was a question.

"Not always. It can depend on a lot of other variables, including what help they get along the way. That's where, in some cases, psychiatrists and psychologists come in."

"Mmm…I'm not convinced," Nat muttered. "And I certainly wouldn't take the chance." She knew she'd said too much, given too much away, the minute the words were out.

Alex wanted to ask her what she meant but caught the look on Nathalie's face and decided against it.

Rising from the chair, Nathalie said, "You know, you're very sexy when you're serious, but I'm sick of serious now. Let's eat."

"Wait," Alex said, grabbing Nathalie's hand as she moved past her chair. "You always run away when the conversation comes back to you. But I want to know about you—that's what people do in relationships."

"Which is why I'm no good at relationships," she replied lightheartedly, pulling Alex up from her seat. "Come on, our food is waiting."

Afterward they snuggled on Nat's lounge and watched television. It was warmth and contentment and a peace that Nat would not have believed existed. Later they made slow tender love.

"Can I stay tonight?" Alex whispered later. "I want to hold you all night."

"If you're willing to risk another disturbed night," Nathalie answered shyly.

But the nightmares stayed away.

* * *

Bella rang Nat at work the next morning to see if she was free for lunch. "I'm in your building for an interview for an inspector's position," she explained, "and I want to see a friendly face."

They met in the coffee shop downstairs and spoke about Nat's new job and Bella's interview. Then Nathalie asked about Jackie.

"Who knows." Bella shrugged disdainfully. "She comes around three or four times a week and stays and we screw and she cooks. Then she'll tell me she's working and disappear for a couple of days. It hasn't changed since you and I spoke last."

"I'm sorry. I kind of hoped you'd sorted things out."

"Well, I suppose we have really," she replied flatly. "I'm still getting laid and a decent meal every so often, and she gets to use my credit card and car during the day. That's a pretty fair deal when you think about it. But what about you? What's it like working for your ex-boyfriend?"

"That was a long time ago, Bella," she said quietly, looking around to see if anyone from the task force was nearby. "And it's not generally known that we lived together."

"Aha. Wise move," she whispered, giving an exaggerated wink and nod. "But you didn't answer the question."

"It's good, Bella," she answered with a smile. "Josh is organized and experienced and fair—just like you were. Actually, you can probably give us some help," she said suddenly. "Two of us have to make inquiries at lesbian clubs in town. It's about the women who were murdered—"

"Do they think they're lesbian-related?" interrupted Bella curiously.

"That's one possibility," she answered quietly. "But maybe you could fax me a list of the clubs women tend to hang out at, especially the more middle-class professional women. It might make it a bit simpler."

"Sure," she said with a grin. "I always knew I'd get you into a lesbian club one day."

If you only knew, thought Nathalie a little guiltily. But it was too early to tell her about Alex. There were still too many things that could go wrong.

* * *

The center was quiet that Thursday, and at seven o'clock, just after Nathalie finished her appointment, Alex knocked on the office door.

"I thought I could last until Saturday morning," she said with a grin. "But I was only fooling myself. And besides, you need sandwiches."

Leaning against the door, they held one another.

"This is bad," Alex mumbled when they'd finished kissing. "I can't get you out of my mind. You're intruding into everything I do."

"Ditto," nodded Nathalie happily. "I'm glad you came."

That night they slept at Alex's and the nightmares returned. This time she was in a dark place she'd never seen before. The room smelled musty and damp and she was very small and hiding behind some furniture. She knew she wasn't supposed to be there, but she'd heard shouting and they hadn't seen her enter.

One woman was hidden by the shadows, but Nathalie felt a sense of recognition. The other woman was Mother and she was very angry. Then, as the other woman tried to walk away from her, Mother hit her with something and she fell down, landing right where Nathalie was hiding. The woman was on the floor and looking at her, trying to say something, trying to reach out. There was blood over her face. Nat wanted to hear the woman's words, but she couldn't move. Then Mother was on the woman, hitting her over and over with some sort of hard object, screaming words that Nat could hear but couldn't understand.

Anger and terror fought for control, but terror won and she curled against the furniture covering her face—overwhelmed by the most frightening sense of loss.

Now Mother was pulling at her, hands covered in blood, and she was struggling, fighting Mother, trying to escape.

Slowly a voice penetrated her terror and she knew it was Alex. But still Mother had a grip on her. Then Alex was holding her, reassuring and soothing her into sobbing, gasping wakefulness.

The sense of loss and terror remained as she curled into Alex, clinging to her with all her strength. The bedside light was on, the bedclothes strewn across the bed and her head felt like it was going to explode. They lay like that for a while.

"You were whimpering and crying," Alex said eventually. "And then suddenly you were struggling and telling your mother you were sorry. Do you know what it was about?" she asked innocently.

Shuddering, Nathalie moved away slightly. "You can't be my shrink, Alex," she snapped. "You said so yourself. If I need an interpretation I'll buy a dream book."

The anger made Alex flinch. It had been there, mingled with the fear, on the first night she'd woken Nat from her nightmares, but the fact that she wasn't attempting to pull away further told her that the anger wasn't really directed at her.

"You're right," she replied slowly. "It's not something I need to know. I'm sorry."

Sitting up, Nat looked at the clock. It was two forty-five. "Shit," she said, moving to the edge of the bed. "It's a work day for you. You'll be exhausted. I'm so sorry."

"I don't care about that, Nat…honestly." Nathalie's back was to her, stiff and tense, but Alex knew she was crying. Kneeling behind her and encircling her with her arms, she held her gently, pressing her face against the wetness of Nat's cheek.

They stayed like that for a while until eventually Alex said, "You know I'm not going anywhere, don't you? I can manage without sleep, but I don't want to have to manage without you. Just trust me, Nat, please."

Turning, Nat clung to Alex as if her life depended on it as violent sobs wracked her body, until, still wrapped in Alex's arms, she eventually fell back to sleep.

But it wasn't that easy for Alex. Given the trauma these nightmares caused Nathalie, she knew that Nat was in a lot of trouble. She needed professional help, but Alex was at a loss how to convince her to seek it without risking alienating her in the process.

Alex had meant what she said. Nathalie was becoming more important to her than she ever thought someone could, but Nat was complicated and proud, and Alex's biggest fear was that she might walk away rather than risk being hurt. Even so, she couldn't just sit back and let Nathalie suffer without trying to help.

Sighing, she acknowledged that it could be a no-win situation.

* * *

When Nathalie arrived for work on Friday afternoon, there was a fax from Bella waiting on the desk she shared with Lorna, and Josh was waiting to brief them.

"I want you to do the rougher clubs in the early part of the evening, before the drugs and alcohol get too much of a hold," he said, ticking off the ones he was talking about. "Concentrate mainly on the bar staff and regulars. See if you can find any connection between these three women. Did they frequent the same clubs, were they seen with any of the same people? If we can establish even the most tenuous connection it will give us something to work on."

* * *

It was only seven thirty when they started club hopping. The first few were sparsely populated, but that gave them a chance to catch bar and door staff before they got too busy.

As a young person, Nathalie had frequented lesbian clubs, usually when she was stoned and in the company of clients who wanted the experience. That had stopped when she left home, and nothing she saw in most of them now would inspire her attendance in the future.

She was glad to be working with Lorna. She looked more like a spinster librarian, Nat thought, than an experienced police officer, but she appeared completely unfazed by the task ahead of them. It gave Nathalie confidence.

The reception was mixed, with some staff and patrons antagonistic and some keen to help. Most of the clubs were predominantly male, a few having a specific night put aside for lesbian patrons and these ranged between the rougher pub-style club to trendy bars. Only two were exclusively female. Both of these were well appointed with an air of exclusivity and executive-level clientele.

Several people recognized the photo of Renee Young—the first woman who had been killed—and could confirm that she was a frequent club user. There were descriptions of people Renee was seen with, but nobody had seen her the night she was killed or at least so they said. On the night of the killing, uniformed police had interviewed numerous people at the club near where Renee had been killed and had drawn a blank. Apparently nobody saw or heard anything.

By ten thirty the clubs were much busier and conversation was almost impossible. Lorna was excellent. She did the first couple of inquiries, allowing Nat to watch and listen. Her manner was quiet, respectful and unobtrusive, and she blended well in her jeans, T-shirt and black leather vest. It occurred to Nat that she knew nothing about Lorna. Was she straight, lesbian, married? Did she have kids? Not that it mattered. She was just a work colleague and Nat sensed they'd never really be friends.

The last club they visited was a cluster of rooms above a shopping mall. It was exclusively female, plush and well appointed. At first security refused them entry, but after the tough-looking woman at the door consulted with someone on a mobile phone, they were shown through to a small office.

Rising to greet them was a tall slim woman in an expensive business suit.

"Police officers?" she stated cautiously, indicating for them to have a seat. "We've never had any trouble here."

"It's in relation to the murders of three lesbians recently," Nathalie replied. "We have photos and we want to ask if any of your patrons knew the victims, if they'd ever seen them together, that sort of thing."

Extending her hand to take the photos, the woman laid them on her desk, rummaged in a drawer for glasses and examined them carefully.

"Renee something or other," she murmured, tapping the photo of the first woman killed.

"Young…Renee Young," clarified Lorna quietly. "You know her?"

"She is a member," she said carefully. "But I didn't know her well myself. She was a bit younger than many of our clientele."

"Did she have a friend or friends here?" asked Nathalie quickly.

"She would mix, but I don't remember seeing her with someone regularly. I'll introduce you to a couple of the women who seemed to talk to her, but you must be discreet. I don't want you upsetting people."

As the woman led them out of her office, Lorna promised that they weren't out to compromise anyone.

The first room was smaller and expensively furnished with a mixture of lounges and tables and chairs. It was obviously a retreat for people to have a quiet drink and socialize. The music here was subtle and relaxing. The room was nearly full and Nat noticed that everyone was very well dressed.

Taking Lorna and Nathalie over to a small group of thirty-plus women, the hostess quietly introduced them as police officers and explained their purpose. A couple of the women looked alarmed, but Lorna assured them of discretion and showed them the photos.

"Renee Young," said an older woman. "I know her from here. But I don't know anything about her."

"Is there anyone here who does know her well?" asked Nat quietly.

The woman looked embarrassed for having spoken out and started to shake her head.

"We all know her," said another woman, causing the others to look at her accusingly. "She provided a discreet service for members. Consequently she would often leave with someone when she was here."

"Unattached women?" queried Lorna.

"Mostly," the woman replied. "Married women who needed discretion, professionals who couldn't risk being outed. Sometimes she worked with couples as well. She was intelligent and attractive and, most importantly, very discreet. She would sometimes organize private parties."

"Did anyone ever see her with either of the other dead women?" asked Lorna.

The women looked at the pictures.

"The younger one was here once," said the same woman eventually. "She came as Renee's guest. We were introduced, but they spent the rest of the evening together."

"Would she have been a client?" asked Nathalie.

"Possibly…although they did a lot of talking and their body language was more that of friends than lovers. They danced together once or twice, but not particularly closely."

The woman with Renee had been Stephanie Cameron, but nobody remembered ever seeing Linda Djanski at the club. It wasn't much, but it was the first real lead they had.

Later the team met back at the office to go over what they knew. After discussion, Josh decided that he and a younger male detective would cover the mixed clubs tomorrow, while Lorna and Nat continued to ask questions at the female clubs. Different nights might provide different patrons, which might elicit different information. In the meantime they continued sifting through the phone and bank records of the dead women looking for any other connections.

"Fancy a drink after work, Duncan?" Josh asked quietly, as they packed up to go home. "I want to know about your latest squeeze."

They met at an out-of-the-way bar where no one from work would see them.

"So how are you finding the task force?" he asked when they were seated at a secluded table with their drinks.

"Good," she answered honestly. "A lot more interesting than prosecutions." Then, wanting to leave work behind, she asked, "How are you and Grace getting along?"

"The best," he grinned, his face lighting up. "I think I'm going to marry that woman and have lots of babies. Now, what about your love life? I know something's going on."

"Well, I've met someone, but you know me and relationships," she replied cryptically.

"Come off it, Nat. I usually know about them after the first date…which of course is usually the last date," he finished with a grin. "So, 'fess up—who is he?"

"Well, first of all, it's not a he, it's a she."

His head jerked back as if he'd been hit. "Shit, Nat," he muttered before he could stop himself. "A woman…bloody hell, what are you doing?"

Stunned, she flared back, "Why would you be surprised? I told you I'd slept with women when I was young."

"Sure, but…" he shook his head. "So who is she? Do I know her?"

His attitude stung. "Someone I met through the crisis center," she said coolly. "She's a psychologist…she's intelligent and gentle and sexy and I like being with her."

His sense of hurt and betrayal couldn't be hidden.

"I assume you're not happy for me," she said, her heart sinking at the thought of losing his friendship. "I never took you for a homophobe."

"You know better than that," he growled. "But you have to admit it's weird. When exactly did you decide you preferred women? Before or after we split?"

"Fuck you, Josh Dawson," she muttered, rising to leave. "I don't need this from you."

He wanted to apologize. Wanted to talk to her about the new person in her life, but his sense of betrayal ran deep and instead he watched her walk from the bar, her back straight and her head held high. The years had taken away much of the hurt and he was used to her occasionally dating other men, but even without her telling him, he knew this was different. And he hated it—hated that someone might get closer to her than he could. That it might be a woman had never occurred to him, and now, illogically, it felt like a huge threat.

It was only when she reached the car that Nathalie's shoulders slumped. She hadn't expected his response, but then she'd never before been aware on an emotional level of the depth of his feelings for her or the depth of his anguish when it hadn't worked out.

At home she poured another drink. She was tempted to ring Alex, but it was nearly midnight and she resisted. It wasn't really Josh she was mad at, it was herself. Her life was a graveyard of broken friendships and destructive relationships. Why would she think it would be different with Josh?

It took a long time to go to sleep, but at least the nightmares stayed away.

* * *

Saturday morning she drove to Alex's. There was another car in the driveway and for a moment she considered driving away. But Alex was expecting her for lunch.

"I've been digging in the garden," Alex beamed, answering the door in old jeans and a T-shirt. "Mum's here. She brought me over a beautiful rose bush that I just had to plant."

The older woman was small and neat and slightly round, with Alex's warm green eyes, and Nathalie knew from the moment she stepped into the room that she was being assessed.

"I'm so pleased to meet you," her mother said warmly, taking Nat's hand and squeezing it gently. "You're the woman who makes Alex blush when she talks about you."

Laughing, Alex said, "Thanks, Mum. That'll make Nat feel nice and comfortable."

"Give your mum a kiss and I'll leave you two to catch up," she said, reaching up to plant one on Alex's cheek. "And it really is lovely to meet you, Nathalie. Don't let my daughter bully you. She bullies me all the time."

The warmth and openness between the two women took Nat's breath away and brought home how different her own family life was. But she wasn't sad for herself, only happy for Alex.

"Sorry about that," Alex laughed on her return from watching her mother drive off. "I didn't know she was coming, but I'm glad you got to meet."

"So am I," replied Nathalie, unsure if she really was. Then they were in each other's arms, holding and kissing and simply enjoying the warmth of physical contact.

Later, when they were eating the pasta Alex had prepared, they spoke of their evenings apart. Alex told Nat about a young woman at the center who'd just been diagnosed HIV positive and wasn't coping. It hit home that the girl was so young.

Nathalie told her about her tour of the lesbian clubs and later about Josh's unexpected response to their relationship.

"It was probably a bit of a shock," Alex said realistically. "You were together six months, and he's only ever known you to date men. Most people don't expect their ex-partner to suddenly start a same-sex relationship out of the blue."

"God, you sound like you believe he has a right to be shitty about it. He's supposed to be a friend."

"So friends can't be taken by surprise? He's probably concerned about you."

"Or homophobic," she growled angrily.

"He means a lot to you, doesn't he?" she asked gently. "If he's the man you thought he was, then it's not homophobia talking, more like a good case of his nose being out of joint. Perhaps you just have to give him time to adjust."

Shaking her head, Nat left it at that. She wanted to believe Alex was right, but her tainted view of human nature wouldn't let her.

"What time do you have to be at work?" Alex asked with a twinkle in her eye.

The answer was a long passionate kiss.

Making love with Alex was wonderful. For the first time in her life it was something she looked forward to, something she could actually enjoy, physically and emotionally.

Afterward, as they showered together, Alex chatted happily about a new man in her mother's life. Nathalie listened, absorbing Alex's passion and happiness like a sponge, hoping that one day she could feel the sort of emotions that Alex experienced every day.

CHAPTER SEVEN

Seeking Help

Nat arrived for work that afternoon with only a minute to spare, and Josh made sure she knew of his disapproval. After the briefing she and Lorna discussed their own plan of action. Today, because they had the two men making inquiries, they decided to concentrate on the predominantly female clubs and spend more time mingling and less time asking formal questions. Perhaps someone would remember something about these three women.

It was obvious to Nathalie that Josh was sulking, but he was a professional and on the surface it would have appeared to colleagues that nothing had changed. Nathalie longed to talk to him, but work was not the appropriate place, and possibly Alex was right, perhaps all he needed was time to come to terms with the change.

The clubs were even busier when they returned, and their reappearance wasn't welcomed. A police presence in any drinking establishment could only be bad for business, but in a lesbian club it was considered even more intrusive. Consequently they got even less information than the day before.

The men did better, finding out that Renee Young had been seen at a mixed club shortly before she was killed. According to a male couple, Young had been dancing with someone they identified as Cameron when another woman had approached them. A few moments later an argument broke out between this woman and Young. Cameron tried to intervene, but the woman had stormed off and Young and Cameron had stayed.

Neither man could describe the woman, other than that she was an average-looking blonde in her mid-twenties and she'd been at the club before. Both men confirmed, though, that the third woman was not Linda Djanski.

This gave them new leads and added new headings to the whiteboard, so that by the end of shift they had a sense of something constructive having been gained.

* * *

Sunday and Monday were Nat's days off. Alex and Nathalie spent Sunday on the Central Coast. It was sunny and clear and magical as they chatted and laughed and watched the antics of the pelicans at feeding time. Every so often Alex would reach out and they'd wander hand in hand, not even noticing the curious glances from passersby. It all seemed so totally *normal* to Nathalie.

"The two women who sponsor the Crisis Center own the penthouse apartment overlooking the water here," pointed out Nathalie as they sat under a tree tucking into ice cream. "I think I could live here if I had to. Actually it would be a great place to bring my niece and nephew," she finished a little sadly.

"Do you see them often?"

"No. I've only met Samantha once and Jeremy twice, and now that my brother's angry with me, I don't suppose I'll have much future contact."

"Would you ever consider having a child?" Alex asked tentatively, not sure how she felt about it herself.

"No," she replied emphatically. "As you said a while ago, some people should never have children. I'm one, and George is another." Nathalie's shoulders were straight and rigid and her face almost blank.

"Why?" Alex asked gently, squeezing her hand.

"Because we're both too much like our mother," she responded quietly, her voice tinged with anger.

While Alex had a million questions, she knew better than to pursue the issue. "So what happened between you and your brother?" she asked.

For a moment there was silence.

"It's ongoing," she replied quietly. "I'm the black sheep because I pulled away from Mother. George sees her very differently than I do and the subject arises every time we meet." She shrugged. "It always ends badly." Her manner brooked no further discussion.

Whatever Nathalie decided to tell her about her past it had to be at her own pace. Push too far and she would close the door completely.

They stayed until dusk, wandering the shops and cafés at will, exploring the rocks, watching the ocean and sucking in the sunshine. Alex hadn't felt as at peace since before Lou received her fatal diagnosis.

Returning to Nathalie's, they made love before curling into each other and drifting into a dreamless sleep.

The doorbell woke Alex first and she glanced at the clock. It was one twenty-five and it was obvious that Nathalie hadn't heard it. A few seconds later the bell went again, this time more insistently, and Nathalie stirred.

"It's your door," mumbled Alex, trying to get a better response from Nat. "Do you want me to get it?"

"No," she mumbled, struggling into a pajama top. "Who the hell could it be at this hour?"

This time they knocked, strongly and loudly.

"Who is it?" growled Nat, fumbling with the door chain and trying to peer through the spy hole.

"Open the door, Nat. It's George," replied a muffled voice from the other side. "I need to see you."

Stunned, she opened the door.

George was dressed in a dinner suit and looked upset. "Can I come in?" he asked, staring into the apartment. "It's important."

"George, it's after one o'clock and I've got company. Besides, how did you know where I lived?"

"Just let me in, Nat, please."

Standing aside, she closed the door behind him. He used to do this after she'd moved to the old flat, before she went to university. Usually he was drunk or drugged and quite distressed. He'd climb into her bed and beg her to hold him. Then he'd cry himself to sleep. Next morning they wouldn't speak of his unhappiness.

"What do you want?" she demanded, trying to ascertain if he was sober.

"I want you to help me, Nat," he replied a little dreamily. "I want you to help me protect the kids from Mother. She wants us to take the kids on forged documents and go with her to California. I can't stop her, Nat."

She guessed heroin, but it was hard to tell with George.

At that moment, Alex appeared in the doorway, dressed in Nathalie's robe. "I'm sorry to interrupt," she said quietly, checking that Nat was okay with her visitor. "I thought I might head home, now that I'm up."

"Sorry to disturb you," George mumbled, taking in the rumpled look of the attractive brunette. "I'm George, Nathalie's brother."

He was tall and stunningly handsome with blond hair and blue eyes, and he looked nothing like Nat. Alex was overwhelmed by the feeling she'd met him before.

George was taken by surprise that Nathalie's company was a woman and confused by a strong sense of recognition.

"Pleased to meet you," Alex greeted, looking at him curiously.

Walking toward Alex, Nat said, "Make a drink, George, and I'll be right back."

"I'm so sorry," she said when they returned to the bedroom. "I have no idea what he wants, but he's upset and he wouldn't come here lightly, so I need to find out."

Assuring her it wasn't a problem, Alex slipped back into her clothes, hunted for her handbag and jacket and, kissing Nathalie warmly, told her she'd ring the next day. The presence of George Duncan unnerved her. There was a strange intensity about him that she'd seen in some of her patients. Yet he appeared intelligent and personable. And then there was the part of his conversation that she'd overheard—something about their mother trying to take the children to California. It was odd.

"So what happened to Josh, the fiancé?" George sneered, when Alex left.

"What do you want?" she asked, ignoring his question, "and how do you know where I live?"

"Mother's been having you followed. She had your address written down."

"She has no right…no fucking right," she spat. But she knew if Mother wanted something she got it, and if she wanted her address, she'd have it.

"Mother thinks I'm staying the night with a client I escorted to a charity party, but I saw to it that she went straight to sleep when we finished at her place. I had to see you because I just don't know what to do."

"It's very simple, George," she replied with a sigh. "You have to stop her."

"She's arranging forged documents, so the kids can go on my passport."

"Then don't allow it. She can't do it unless you agree."

His head was down, his eyes fixated on the brown liquid in his glass. But he said nothing.

"Only you can stop her," she pointed out angrily. "They're your children."

"I can't stand up to her, you know that," he mumbled. "Besides, she'll have me put in prison if I try to stop her."

"And how will that help her? She can't take the children to America if you're in prison and anything you and I did, we did for her, so she'd be implicated."

"Not the sex stuff, Nat," he mumbled. "There's nothing wrong with that. How often do we have to tell you?"

"Then what?" she asked impatiently.

"I can't say," he mumbled. "You're a cop, for fuck's sake."

The anger could no longer be suppressed as she hurled her half-full glass past his head. "Yes, George, I'm a police officer and a lawyer, one who's spent half her life being Mother's whore, who's pimped teenage kids for her—kids who had no idea what they were getting into. By doing nothing about it my whole life, I've condoned what she does and that makes me even more corrupt and filthy than her. So don't worry about me ever taking a stand and acting like a responsible human being, because I don't have the fucking guts. I'm Mother's puppet, just like you."

By now the tears were pouring down her face and she'd slumped into the chair opposite George, who was staring at her white-faced.

Eventually Nathalie said, "It doesn't matter what you did, George. I don't want to know. Both of us should be in prison for the things we've done, but we're not, and Mother has nothing to gain by putting you there. If she wants those children so desperately, then you have to know that there's only one reason."

"She says they're her grandchildren, and she wants them near."

"But you don't believe her!"

"I don't know, Nat. Sometimes I think she just wants us around her…you know…like most mothers would. Then sometimes I get scared for them—like tonight."

"Then you hit up, and by the time you get here it all goes away again? Is that how it is?"

"I know things, Nat, and sometimes I get scared that Mother will find out. I've got a book, a journal…" He stopped, staring into the distance.

It was obvious he'd popped something with his drink. He was getting vaguer by the minute and his last hit wouldn't have that effect.

"What are you talking about? What journal? And what's this got to do with the children?"

"The children?" he repeated, shaking his head. "No, it was Mother's. Christine stole it…Christine Martin."

"I know who Christine was," she answered irritably. "But what is it and how did you get it?"

"If she thought I had it, or even that I'd seen it…I don't know what she'd do," he mumbled to himself. "Chris told her she was going to the police with it unless Mother paid her off and let her go. Then she died."

Nat jumped up. "Are you saying Mother had something to do with that?"

"What?"

"Are you saying there's a connection between Christine threatening Mother and her death?"

"I don't know. But she made me search Chris's stuff and the flat for the journal. I didn't find it then, but I found it later, after Mother went overseas and sold the house. I was cleaning up and found a tear in the wallpaper behind a painting. Chris had hidden it in Mother's own house. I was going to tell Mother, but then I read it."

"What's in it?"

"I want to tell you, but I can't. I need it right now. If she doesn't back off wanting the kids, I'll threaten to hand it over to you or to the police. But I just wanted you to know that I will protect them. They're my kids and they'll never have to do what we did."

He was rambling and incoherent and no amount of questioning elicited sensible answers. He couldn't go home. No cab driver would take him. He couldn't drive, and she wasn't going near the house.

Staggering with him to the spare room she sat him on the bed, stripped off his jacket, tie and pants and rolled him under the quilt where he fell into a drug-induced sleep.

Even now at thirty-three, he looked innocent, and in repose she could still see the young boy who'd been her only comfort when Mother had begun to teach them about "love." She'd loved and hated him, needed and resented him, and he'd been good to her and vicious to her. But he was her brother, and gently she wiped away a tear that rolled slowly down his cheek, touched his hair and kissed him on the lips. Then climbing onto the bed, she curled into his back, holding him as a mother would her child.

* * *

"Something smells good," he said, joining her in the kitchen the next morning. "I could eat a horse."

There was never a "morning after" for George. No matter how much alcohol or drugs he consumed, he always woke refreshed and untouched. This morning, dressed in his pants and shirt and with his tousled hair and single earring he looked handsome and devilish with no telltale signs of the despairing, needy boy of last night.

Pouring coffee while he tucked into egg and bacon, she said, "What's in Mother's journal?"

Putting down his knife and fork slowly, he looked up.

"Terrible things," he said with a shudder. "It's an old journal, one she started when I was about five or six. It covers a couple of years after that and she wrote down everything."

"What sort of things?" she asked curiously.

Shaking his head firmly, he started back into his breakfast.

"Where is it?"

"Hidden," he mumbled with food in his mouth.

"And you plan to use this journal against Mother if she insists on trying to force you to take Jeremy and Samantha to America?"

"I don't know," he answered hesitantly. "Maybe. I just don't know what she'd do if she thought I'd even seen the journal, let alone if she thought I had it."

"What could she do? You're a grown man. She can hardly beat you, and if she cuts you off, then maybe that's for the best. You have to pull away sooner or later."

"You don't get it, do you?" he replied angrily. "You didn't *pull away* from Mother—she *let* you leave. You were no good to her at the time, so she put you on a rein and let you wander."

"Bullshit."

"Bullshit? Then why did you come running when she rang after returning from overseas? You knew what she'd want from you, but you still came back after years of being out of her clutches. She tugged the leash and you came to heel."

"She's still my mother and I wanted to see you again," she answered defensively. "But I refused to participate."

"Did you? Or did I cover for you—protect you like I've always tried to? I think she would have killed you when you were little except I kept getting in the way. I told her I could control you, so sometimes she'd leave you alone. But you don't remember any of that, do you, Nathalie?"

It was an accusation.

"You don't believe that I don't remember?"

"Do I believe anyone would forget being punched and beaten and terrorized, over and over, or being locked in a closet for hours, sometimes days at a time? No I don't!"

"Why? Why would I pretend I didn't remember?"

"Because you're just as cowardly as me," he spat, resentfully. "Even apart from the physical beatings, I know she tortured you mentally—taking you places in the middle of the night and doing terrible things that would make you sick for weeks after. Then when you got well, you'd pretend you didn't remember anything. She'd always ask what you remembered, and you'd always say, 'Nothing, Mother.' Then she'd be nice to you for a while and you'd continue to do whatever she demanded of you."

"You bastard," she shouted, launching herself onto him and knocking him backward—plates and cups falling on top of them.

He was nearly twice her size, but the ferocity of the attack took him by surprise and it was a moment or two before he could seize her wrists and hold her away, closing down her assault.

"Stop it, Nat, stop it," he said gently, as she continued to struggle. "I'm sorry, I'm sorry."

"She didn't hate me. She didn't." She was gasping now, tears pouring down her face. "I must have kept on upsetting her, that's all. But I don't remember any of it. I don't."

"Okay, I'm sorry. I believe you. Just calm down so that we can get off the floor."

They moved about the room, cleaning up the mess without speaking. Things were changing for both of them—suddenly the past was infiltrating the present, not just as nightmares and guilt and unspoken memories, but in a way that made them both feel threatened. For the first time in her life Nathalie believed she had something worth protecting from her past—her relationship with Alex and the promise of some happiness. And George had his children. And neither of them knew how to deal with any of it.

"You have to be careful," he said to her as he put on his shoes and socks and prepared to leave. "I don't know why Mother had you followed or even if she still is, but the cards are telling her things and it's got her mighty upset. I think it's the reason she came back here. And she's far more dangerous than you can ever know, Nat. Don't take her lightly."

"I'm no threat to her," she insisted. "And I have no control over her delusions. But you have to think seriously about how you can protect Samantha and Jeremy, because she's manipulative, and I fear for them if she doesn't leave soon. I'll help you in any way I can, but you have to tell me what you want me to do."

After he left, Nathalie showered, tidied the house and phoned Alex at work.

"I'm sorry about last night," she said. "That's the first time George has ever been to this flat. I didn't even know he knew where I lived, but apparently Mother did."

"It's not a problem, Nat," she responded gently. "It's good that you're having the contact. It might make it easier for you to see the children."

"I hope so," she replied without believing it. "But I missed you and I bet you were pretty tired when you got to work."

"I didn't come in until ten thirty," she admitted with a laugh. "I'm owed weeks of time in lieu, so I took a couple of hours and if you're going to be home, I might just take another couple this afternoon."

Alex arrived about three o'clock, carrying a bottle of wine and the movie *I Can't Think Straight*. It was just what Nathalie needed to take her mind off George, the children and Mother. Yet she kept drifting back to what George had said about Mother's abuse. She knew he wasn't lying, yet when she tried to remember, she'd feel physically ill and be forced to stop.

Alex knew as soon as she arrived that something had happened last night to upset Nathalie. Her eyes were troubled and her thoughts elsewhere, but Alex didn't ask questions, hoping instead that Nathalie would volunteer what was on her mind.

"Do you think it's possible to forget something terrible that happened to you as a child?" Nat asked casually, as they sipped coffee after the DVD.

"Yes," Alex replied. "It's quite common. Why?"

Ignoring the question, she said, "But not just one thing. What if a person doesn't remember anything before a certain age?"

"Well, it would depend on what age you're talking about. Some people can remember being two years old, others don't have any definite memories until they're much older."

Nathalie kept her head down, stirring her coffee, deep in thought.

Alex knew she was talking about herself and the only way she would continue would be if she set her own pace. Quietly she got up and replaced their coffees.

"What if the person had no memories before the age of six or seven? Would that be unusual? I mean...it would hardly be normal, would it?"

"It would be unusual. And it might indicate that the individual had experienced some sort of physical or mental trauma. Instead of blocking the specific incident, they block the whole time period."

"You mean pretend it didn't happen?" Nat continued to stare into her coffee.

"Not really," Alex answered gently. "Pretending something didn't happen is a conscious decision. Blocking a memory rarely is. It's the mind closing down to protect itself and allow the individual to keep functioning. Sooner or later though, those memories have to come out and be dealt with or they can trigger serious personality disorders, sometimes even psychiatric illness."

"How do they retrieve the memories?"

"Through psychotherapy and sometimes hypnosis—it can be a long process and it doesn't always work. When it does, there is still the original trauma and its repercussion to be dealt with, and that's the hardest part."

"Is that your job at the prison?"

"Yes, part of it."

Again Nathalie went quiet.

"Is this to do with your nightmares?" Alex asked eventually.

"Perhaps," she mumbled, without looking up. "I know what many of my nightmares are about, but with others it feels like I should, but I don't. And then George told me things about when we were little, and I don't remember any of it."

"Do you believe they happened?"

"Sort of...actually, I don't know," Nat finished with a forlorn shrug. She could feel Alex's warm green eyes bathing her and she needed to talk—wanted to know if she was insane.

Alex remained silent.

"I know why I have some of the nightmares," she continued, trying to put them into perspective. "But the events seem more terrible and frightening in the nightmares than I remember them being in reality. Then there are the nightmares that don't relate to anything that I know about. They're the worst. But none of them seem to relate to what is supposed to have happened to me before I was six or seven. It's just a mind fuck that makes no sense."

"There would be a connection," Alex said reassuringly. "But your mind is only releasing fragments at a time, so it appears confusing and senseless."

"So if I go to this guy you were talking about—this psychologist—what difference will it make? I already know where half the shit in the nightmares comes from and it doesn't stop me having them. How can he help?"

"He might be able to help you find ways of dealing with either the cause of the nightmares or the nightmares themselves."

"Then I suppose I don't have a choice," she said reluctantly. "They're getting worse and now George has told me stuff that makes me think I'm losing my mind. If I can't stop these nightmares, I know I'll end up losing you."

"Don't do it for me, Nat," Alex said firmly, "or for George. If you're going to do this, then do it for yourself...so that *you* can deal with the issues and find some peace."

Moving to the sofa, Nathalie snuggled into Alex, feeling her arms enclose her. "I think I love you," she whispered. "I think I finally know what that means."

* * *

On Tuesday, Nathalie was back on dayshift. Josh was still cool and distant.

Now that they'd found a connection between Cameron and Young, the task force could start a whole different avenue of inquiry starting with those they'd already interviewed.

Late in the afternoon, after everyone had left, Nathalie caught up with Josh in his office. He didn't look pleased to see her.

"I'm sorry I walked out," she said, taking a seat on the other side of his desk. "And I'm sorry you're not talking to me, but I want to know how this will affect our work."

"I don't let personal grievances affect work," he replied coolly. "And I hope you're professional enough to do the same."

"So why exactly do you have a grievance?" asked Nathalie with a puzzled shake of her head.

Pushing his chair away from the desk and walking to the doorway, he glanced around the outer office to confirm it was empty. Closing the door, he returned to his seat. "We've known each other for over five years," he said intently. "We were lovers for six months and now you drop it on me that you're lesbian. How do you expect me to react?"

"Not like this, Josh," she replied sadly. "And you already knew I was bisexual."

"Is that why we failed, Nat?" he asked, ignoring her comment. "Because you didn't want a normal relationship?"

"Normal?" she spluttered, shaking her head. "Jesus, Josh, since when was anything about me normal? We lived and slept together for six months. That was as normal as I'd ever been and it had nothing to do with sexual preference."

"Did you ever love me?"

"What's that got to do with your reaction now?" she responded in frustration. "Our affair was over years ago, but I never cheated on you or wished I was with a woman when we were together, if that's what you're asking."

"But you won't answer the question, will you?" he insisted angrily. "What did you always say? Ah, yes, that the word 'love' didn't mean anything. Well, I was in love with you."

"I didn't mean to hurt you," she whispered. "And I thought we'd got through that and become friends. You've never reacted like this to men I went out with."

The anger in his face dissipated and his shoulders dropped, then shaking his head, he said, "Let's be honest, Nat. You only ever went out with two or three guys in all these years and never a second time. They were never a threat. But when you spoke about this woman, it was like I was losing you all over again. I guess it brought home that I'd never stopped thinking of you as my lover, and it made me realize I'd wasted five years hoping we could work it out."

"I'm sorry."

"Don't be. It was my hang-up, not yours, and in a way it's made me appreciate what I have with Grace." Sighing, he continued, "Maybe this time we can both make our relationships work. Maybe it's a turning point."

"Does that mean that when Grace invites me to your place for dinner, Alex will be included in the invite?" she asked, almost shyly.

As he nodded, they moved to embrace, just a quick one, but enough to take away the hurt and confusion.

That evening Alex had to stay back at work, so they decided to take the evening to catch up with domestic chores, phone calls, bill paying—all the duties that continue even at the height of a new relationship.

* * *

On Wednesday Bella rang and they arranged to meet for a drink after work. Nathalie thought she sounded a little happier, but they were busy and didn't talk long on the phone.

The club was quiet as they took a seat in one of the lounges, well away from anyone else.

"I've had nobody to complain to since you left," moaned Bella when they sat down with their drinks and a bowl of chips. "But the good news is that I got the inspector's position I applied for."

"Congratulations," Nathalie said, raising her glass. "You deserve it."

"It's OIC of the Historical Crimes Unit," continued Bella with a shrug. "It's a new unit being set up to review serious unsolved cases before they're transferred to computer and archived. I start in head office on Monday, so we'll be in the same building. It's not exactly the prestigious position I had in mind," she said seriously. "But I'm not a people person, so pushing papers might be a better way to go for me. I'll have a sergeant and five detectives working for me."

"And how's things with Jackie?"

"Not bad actually," she said with a weak smile. "We've decided that we'll see each other three or four times a week and be free to do whatever we want for the rest of the time."

"And you're happy with that?"

"What can I do?" she said a little hesitantly. "She's still going to cook and fill my bed a few times a week and we have other things we like to do. It's better than nothing."

"Is she seeing someone else?"

"She says not, so I have to believe her."

"I'm seeing someone." It was out before Nat could change her mind.

"You're not back with Josh Dawson?"

"Why would you say that?"

"Because it's obvious he still loves you, and I thought that now that you were working together he might have sneaked back into your affections."

Nathalie shook her head. "I've been seeing a woman," she said, watching for Bella's reaction.

"Well, hallelujah," she declared, raising her glass. "The girl has seen the light. But the question is—if you were going to do it with a woman, why didn't you pick me?"

"Because you're too cranky and I'm too cranky, and two cranky people should never get together."

"Good answer," she replied, a strange light in her eyes. "So who is she, how did you meet? Tell me everything."

It came out slowly and concisely.

"Sounds serious," Bella stated quietly when Nat finished.

"I just feel good when I'm with her," she explained. "Alive and hopeful—do you know what I mean?"

Bella gave a gentle nod.

They spoke about work and the lesbian clubs Nathalie had visited, and they spoke of changes in the police service and the hierarchy. But at no time did they touch on childhood or family; Nathalie suspected that Bella's home life probably wasn't much better than her own.

* * *

Afterward she visited Alex.

Alex's warmth and affection was a whole new experience. It was the cuddle when they did the washing up, the sudden hug and kiss while they watched television or read and the way she'd touch her face or reach for her hand as they walked down a street or ate in a restaurant. The passion and desire were strong and a simple kiss or touch could easily turn to lovemaking, but it was the tender gentle gestures that Nathalie was so unused to, that felt so right.

Over the next few weeks they saw each other every night and when their days off coincided, they'd take drives to the ocean or mountains and go to movies or shows and eat romantic meals in out-of-the-way places.

A couple of times Alex's mother had popped in while Nat was there. Each time she included Nathalie in her brief conversations. Nat found her warm and friendly and accepting of her role in Alex's life.

As the days wore on, Nathalie came to trust Alex more and more, and the fear that she might leave if she found out about her past became less constant. At times there was even room for hope of a normal life. Gradually the nightmares decreased in frequency and intensity.

The work investigation was progressing slowly and Nathalie was enjoying the challenges and teamwork, especially when any minor breakthrough was made that gave them all a lift.

Eventually they got a good lead. It came from a lesbian work colleague of Stephanie Cameron's who'd been on holiday overseas during the first part of the investigation. She told them of a link between Cameron and the first victim and connected the two of them to the club scene.

According to her, Cameron and Young were ex-lovers, now friends, who clubbed together occasionally because Djanski didn't like the clubs. The colleague didn't believe, from the way Cameron spoke, that there was anything between the ex-lovers. Her experience of Cameron and Djanski was that their relationship was rock solid and that Djanski knew about and approved of the occasional clubbing arrangement.

This confirmed the connection between all three deaths and with the addition of the mystery woman from the Rubix Club it gave the team more to work with. One of the first tasks was to try and identify the fair-haired woman seen arguing with Young at the club. That task would begin again Thursday night.

Meanwhile, Bella invited Nathalie and Alex to dinner, with Jackie doing the cooking.

The meal was delicious, but things between Bella and Jackie were tense, and they bickered and snapped at one another constantly. It was obvious that Bella liked Alex and she was on her best behavior.

"So, Bella tells me you're investigating the killings of the lesbian couple and the other lesbian woman," said Jackie out of the blue. "What's happening with that?"

Nathalie's eyes shot to Bella, who had the good grace to look embarrassed.

"It's going well," she replied vaguely, wondering what Bella had said.

"So is it a vendetta against lesbians?" Jackie asked, her face blank, but her eyes alert.

"It's too early to tell," replied Nathalie evasively.

"And even if she knew, she wouldn't be able to discuss it," interrupted Bella pointedly. "I told you that when you asked me earlier."

"Sorry," Jackie said, addressing Nat. "But it makes us all fearful. I mean, if it is a serial killer any one of us could be next."

"We can only hope," muttered Bella under her breath.

This time Nathalie caught the flare of anger in Jackie's eyes, but the woman said nothing, instead, standing up, she offered to make coffee.

"I'll give you a hand," said Nat hurriedly, feeling a little sorry for her. Bella could be vicious when she was feeling aggressive.

The kitchen was as stuffy and old-fashioned as the rest of the house, and it occurred to Nat that Bella's taste in décor was as bland and dark as her personality at times.

"I really like Alex," said Jackie, taking cups from high shelves and setting them on the tiny piece of workbench. "So you decided to go with a woman in the end?"

"It wasn't planned," Nat replied with a shrug.

"Well, it's a shame you didn't let me know you'd changed your mind about women," she mumbled, throwing coffee into the plunger. "I did know you first."

"What do you mean?" asked Nathalie, confused.

"Oh, come on," she said, moving close and reaching up to touch Nat's face. "I just mean that we could have had some fun, but I didn't approach you because I thought you were straight."

"What!" She repelled backward as if pushed by an invisible hand.

"It's just that I like you very much," Jackie insisted, ignoring Nat's obvious shock, "and I'd have liked to show you a good time." Leaning forward, she clutched at Nathalie's waist, pulling her close and forcing her mouth over Nat's.

Pushing her away, Nathalie gasped, "Jesus, Jackie, don't."

"Don't be like that," she cajoled, moving forward again.

"Don't touch me, Jackie," threatened Nathalie, backing away. "Or I'll deck you."

"What's the matter?" she sneered, moving back to the coffee preparations. "Aren't I good enough for you? You're just like all those other stuck-up bitches that think they're special. Well, trust me," she muttered in a flat, dull tone, "I'll have the last laugh."

"You're supposed to be Bella's lover," whispered Nathalie angrily. "We're in her house, for heaven's sake."

"Oh God, surely you don't believe in all that monogamy bullshit?"

"Funnily enough I do," she said with a shake of her head.

"Well, maybe you won't if Alex ends up as boring in bed as Bella," she spat. "Or as obnoxious."

"You're a class act," snapped Nathalie, picking up the container of biscuits and moving as far away from Jackie as she could. "Bella's my friend, but I really don't like you, so please, just stay away from me in future."

"We'll see, won't we," she replied cryptically, picking up the drinks and moving past Nathalie with a superior look on her face.

Bella and Alex were chatting amiably, and Nathalie made a concerted effort to concentrate on that, rather than on what had happened in the kitchen. But she found it hard to keep her eyes off Jackie, wondering if Bella had any idea what she was really like.

While it troubled her, she knew it would serve no purpose to tell Bella.

As soon as the coffee was finished, Nathalie made their excuses and they left.

"Well, I haven't had so much fun since the last time I had a tooth pulled." Nat grimaced at Alex as they drove away. "I'm so sorry I got you into that."

"Not your fault," said Alex with a grin. "But it was certainly tense." Then a few seconds later, "They're such a mismatch and yet so strangely similar. How would they get together in the first place?"

"Mutual need would be my guess."

"How long have you known them?"

"Bella for a couple of years," Nathalie replied quietly. "But Jackie only came on the scene in the last few months. Why?"

"I think Jackie might resent your friendship with Bella, but that's just me doing my analyzing thing. It wasn't that she actually said anything."

Nathalie remained silent.

Their lovemaking was tender and gentle, but it was spoilt in the early hours by another nightmare.

This time she was struggling with someone, but there was something over her head so that she couldn't see and she was frightened, sobbing, asking them to leave her alone. Then there was whispering, followed by blows that hurt all over. And her hands were tied and Mother was angry—her voice cutting into her like a knife. Then more blows, followed by words that made no sense, and then silence. And the silence was worse. She was going to die—Mother told her so. Mother had thrown her down into some sort of hole and stuff was landing on her—getting heavier—and now it was difficult to breathe. Then the panic hit.

Alex was trying to calm Nathalie by talking to her gently when the fist caught her above the right eye. It stunned her, knocking her backward.

"It's okay, darling," she cajoled desperately a few seconds later, trying to hold Nat while blood poured from the cut. "You're safe. Just open your eyes, please, Nat. Just look at me."

Nathalie's eyes popped open, a shudder visibly passing through her. For a moment she attempted to back away, her face white and blank. Then her brain registered the blood.

"Oh God, I hurt you," she gasped finally. "You're bleeding."

"It's all right. I'm fine," said Alex, relieved to have brought her around.

But Nathalie jumped from the bed, shock written on her pale face.

Alex moved toward Nathalie, but she put her hands in the air as if to ward her off and, turning, moved swiftly toward the bathroom, while Alex dropped onto the bed.

Within moments Nathalie returned with a damp cloth, antiseptic and a large Band-Aid. With a shaking hand she gently tended the wound. "I'm so sorry," she said when finished. "I've never attacked anyone before."

"You didn't attack me," Alex assured her with a wince. "It was an accident and it's a tiny cut."

That was true, but like all cuts to the eye and head it bled profusely, covering Alex's T-shirt and the bedclothes and making it look like a massacre.

They had coffee with all the lights on, and it was three in the morning before Alex went back to sleep, believing that Nat had settled. Fifteen minutes later Nathalie climbed carefully from bed.

All she could think about was that she'd hurt Alex. Pouring a bourbon and Coke and curling into a chair in the lounge she deliberately tried to conjure any memory that might remotely relate to tonight's nightmare. Nothing came.

It couldn't go on. Apart from disturbed sleep, terrible headaches and the depression afterward, there was now Alex to consider. She knew that while Alex was strong and patient, the effects of these terrible nights would take a toll eventually. It was time to visit the psychotherapist before she drove Alex out of her life.

She rang the next day after Alex left for work and was surprised to find that she liked the sound of the man's voice. It conjured images of a gentle poet or writer and sounded open and friendly, and better still, he could fit her into his schedule on Monday. It scared her, but it had to be done.

* * *

On Thursday Nat and Lorna returned to the clubs, hoping that not too many people would know or remember them as police. Although the description of the woman seen arguing with Renee Young was vague, they were trying to blend with the crowd and watch for anyone who might fit it. Witnesses had confirmed that the mystery woman usually arrived alone and left with someone she'd picked up. By the end of the weekend they'd been hit on regularly, but were no nearer finding the woman. It was decided they would persist with the clubs as well as try to track down the mobile that phone records showed had rung Renee Young's home number on numerous occasions—a phone that did not seem to have an owner.

Alex's eye had blackened and looked worse than it was. She knew this depressed Nat, but she was pleased to learn that Nat had made an appointment with Dieter, the psychologist she'd recommended. She'd already spoken to Dieter about Nathalie and asked him to find an urgent spot for her, should she ring.

"I'll be happy to see your friend," he'd said with his faint German accent. "But you must neither brief me on her problems nor expect me to ever talk to you about those problems. That is why you are sending her to me in the first place. But rest assured I will treat her as I would you."

* * *

Sunday was spent listening to music, talking, laughingly playing Scrabble and Yahtzee and enjoying being together.

When they made love, it was slow and sensuous and satisfying, but afterward, Nathalie became depressed. What if tomorrow she woke up to find it was all a dream?

"You're becoming my world," Nat had whispered as their bodies moved against one another and their gentle affection turned to aching desire. "I can't imagine my life without you."

"And you never will," Alex had answered in short excited gasps while Nathalie probed and touched and stroked, turning desire into a desperate clinging need, destined to end in shuddering satisfaction.

But the darkness stayed with Nathalie, causing her stomach to knot, her heart to ache and a terrible fear to invade her soul.

* * *

Dieter, the psychologist, couldn't have been less like Nathalie expected. Instead of a chubby, wrinkled old gentleman in tweeds and spectacles, she found a slim, fit-looking man in his mid-forties who wore jeans and running shoes and a brightly colored vest over his denim shirt. His hair was short-cropped, almost military style, but he sported an earring in his left ear and wore a rope bracelet and wide homemade wedding band. His unlined, olive skin and clear blue eyes made him very attractive, and his smile would have melted an igloo.

The office was inviting and comfortable, and they were seated in lounge chairs facing each other. Dieter spoke first, introducing himself and telling her that Alex had spoken to him but that they hadn't discussed any issues relating to Nathalie's visit. Nathalie believed him.

"We'll begin by talking about your life in general, what you do for a living, the lifestyle you enjoy…and your views on psychology," he finished with a smile.

Nathalie warmed to him immediately.

"Then we'll get straight into the hard part—ascertaining the problem and probing those issues in ways that will very likely be uncomfortable. In fact, for a while you may feel worse than you do now, and that means you are going to have to learn to trust me."

The hour and a half flashed by, and Nat left with mixed feelings. On the one hand, she was comfortable talking to Dieter and she believed she could come to trust him, but on the other they had only just touched on her issues and that protective voice inside her head was telling her that she should be careful what she told him—careful that she didn't put them all in danger.

It was a frustrating week at work, but the team had three days off over the weekend and Nathalie was looking forward to being at the center on Friday evening, followed by a whole weekend with Alex.

On Saturday morning they bought groceries together. Later they planned to have coffee with Alex's mother. It would be her first visit to her mother's home.

The answer machine was flashing when they arrived at Nat's house, but she didn't check it straight away, choosing to unpack the groceries first instead. Just as they finished, the phone rang again. It was Mother.

"I rang earlier," she accused coldly. "I want to see you, Nathalie. George and I will be waiting for you."

Stunned, Nathalie flared. "I'm sorry, but I'm busy this weekend. Monday would be the earliest I could get over, but I'd need to know what it was about."

"Too busy for your own mother?" she mused. "Now what could possibly be more important than your family? Oh yes," she stated, answering her own question. "Perhaps your latest lover—a woman, I understand?"

"That's none of your business," snapped Nathalie. "And George had no business telling you anything about my life."

"Actually, I already knew," she gloated. "I know everything about you. Admittedly I didn't know who this woman was, but you're so wrong about it being none of my business. You see, George is convinced you really don't know who she is. But I don't believe that, and I'm not happy with you."

"What...what are you talking about?" stuttered Nathalie, scared by Mother's intensity and confused by her words.

"We shall expect you tomorrow, for lunch." The phone went dead.

"Not a good call?" asked Alex, as Nat slowly put the receiver back on the cradle.

The knot in her stomach tightened painfully. "My mother," she muttered eventually. "She wants to see me."

"Isn't that good?" Alex asked, concerned at the fear reflected in Nathalie's face.

She couldn't explain. All she could do was nod weakly, her mind spinning while a dark foreboding filled her. *What did Mother mean about not knowing who Alex was?* Nothing made sense, except her overwhelming urge to avoid seeing Mother at all cost.

CHAPTER EIGHT

The Awful Truth

The house was small and neat and welcoming. The lounge flowed out through double doors onto a paved patio and rear garden. It was the home of a gardener, with beautifully tended flowerbeds and bushes and neatly cut grass. Nat knew immediately that Alex's mother loved her home.

"I thought we might have Devonshire tea on the patio so that we can enjoy the warmth," her mother suggested, after welcoming them both with a kiss on the cheek. "I love the winter sun."

As they drank freshly brewed coffee and tucked into the lightest, most delicious scones, Nat complimented her on the food.

"Thank you, Nathalie, but it's not a chore. I love having time to spend in my garden and cooking up treats. Anyone who says they're bored in retirement mustn't have much imagination."

"What did you do when you worked, Mrs. Messner?" Nathalie asked, trying to imagine her in an office setting.

"Oh, that brings back memories," she laughed. "I haven't been Mrs. Messner since Alex was a baby. Norma, please," she insisted. "I remarried when Alex was tiny, but somehow we never got around to changing her name before my second husband died. We always thought we'd have plenty of time, and then life catches you out." Her voice reflected deep sadness.

After that they spoke about Norma's work as a bank teller and her retirement and the retired builder from the neighborhood center she'd had been out with a couple of times. It was light, easy conversation, and Norma was welcoming and inclusive.

It wasn't until they were about to leave that Nathalie spotted the photo. Alex had gone to the bathroom, and Norma was hunting for some magazines she wanted to give Alex. That was when Nathalie started looking at the collection of photos arranged on the telephone table.

It was between a wedding photo of Norma and a photo of Alex, and at first she didn't notice it. When she did, she was struck by an overwhelming feeling of unreality, followed by nausea and the burning desire to turn and run.

Looking out from an expensive gold frame was a picture of Christine Martin. It had been taken when she was about fourteen, and she was laughing and beautiful and innocent.

Snatching at the photo, Nathalie stared in disbelief, trying desperately to make it be someone else—someone who just looked like Christine.

"That was my beautiful daughter, Christine," Norma said from beside her. "We lost her only a few years after that photo was taken. It was a long time ago, but sometimes it seems like yesterday. She'd have been thirty now."

It was impossible to speak or swallow or take her eyes from the photo, and all the time a voice in her head was screaming in denial, telling her that this was impossible, that the implications would be too horrific. Then they were saying goodbye and climbing into the car and she knew she was talking, sounding perfectly normal, but the real Nathalie was somewhere else—somewhere in hell.

"Do you fancy a movie?" Alex asked as they drove back toward the city. "There's a good one in about an hour."

But Nathalie hadn't heard her. "What's your mother's surname?" she asked suddenly.

"Martin," replied Alex, concentrating on negotiating a right-hand turn. "Why?"

Again she didn't answer.

Looking at her carefully, Alex said, "Nat, what's wrong? Are you okay? You look awful."

"Stop the car," she gasped. "I'm going to be sick."

As the spasms wracked her body, her head spun and she kneeled on the grass verge clutching her stomach, unable to think a single coherent thought.

"My God, Nat, you need a doctor," said Alex, trying to support her lover, stunned by the sudden onset and violence of the illness.

Then, as suddenly as the sickness started it stopped and the emotional pain began to clear, allowing her brain to regain rational thought. "I'm okay," Nat said, wiping her mouth on the tissues Alex had given her. "It was just something I ate, I promise. I just need to go home." She felt empty and cold and alone.

"Sure," said Alex anxiously. "But it might be an idea to at least get something from the chemist on the way."

"No." It came out sharply and made Alex take a second look. But she said nothing and continued driving toward Nathalie's apartment.

By now Nathalie's head was pounding, her throat was sore from vomiting and she desperately craved a place to hide. Glancing at Alex, she saw that she appeared worried and upset, but there was nothing she could say. When she found out the truth, and she eventually would, Nathalie didn't want to imagine the look that would replace the warmth and love in this beautiful woman's eyes.

"I need to go to bed when I get home," she said coolly. "So there's no point in you coming in. There's no point you wasting your day."

"I'm not going to leave you while you're sick," Alex replied with a laugh, thinking that Nathalie was joking. But seeing the hard lines of her face and the cold glint in her eyes, her heart sank.

"I just want to sleep," she said flatly. "And I don't need you holding my hand to do that."

"I don't understand!" Nat's words were like a slap, and there was no getting her head around her sudden change of mood. "Have I done something to upset you? Did Mum say something?"

"Neither," she answered truthfully. "I don't feel well and I just want some time to myself. I'm sorry, but I did tell you from the start that I need my space and that I'm hard to live with."

"Yes, you did," replied Alex sadly. "And I'm sorry if I've moved too fast and made you feel pressured."

The silence that followed made Alex want to cry out. Made her want to grab Nathalie and force her to explain, but her training as a psychologist told her that if she backed off now and allowed Nat room, this coldness might only be temporary.

"Ring me later?" she asked desperately as Nat climbed out of the car. "When you wake up—just to let me know that you're okay."

Reaching back to touch Alex's face for what she assumed would be the last time, Nathalie nodded and without speaking left the car.

By the time she let herself into the apartment, the pain had taken over completely, causing her to sink to the carpet and curl into a ball—deep, heaving sobs crushing her chest and escaping her lips.

Pulling over to the side of the road in the next street, Alex began to shake. She had no idea what had just happened, but she knew it was serious. If she didn't know better, she'd suspect that Nathalie had a mental illness. That was how quickly her personality had changed. Everything had seemed okay until they got into the car. And no matter how hard she tried to understand, Alex couldn't relate that change to anything that had happened. There'd been the phone call from Nathalie's mother. She'd been a little quiet and distracted after that, yet she'd seemed fine at her mother's.

There was no point in going home. If she did that, Alex knew she'd end up returning within the hour. Instead she pulled out her mobile phone and dialed a number. A few minutes later she was back on the road.

* * *

The inner city house was small but luxurious and overlooked the water. Everything in it was classy and elegant and neat. She hadn't explained anything on the phone, only asked to come over, and the response had been instantaneous. Now as she stood looking out from the patio she felt a little foolish. Perhaps she was overreacting. Perhaps Nathalie really was just too sick to see her, too sick to want company.

"You look awful, girlfriend," Michael said as he walked up behind her and wrapped his arms around her. "What's happened?"

Turning and clinging to his strong, lean body, she lifted her head and said, "I think I've fucked up, Michael. I think I've fallen in love with someone who's terrified of the idea."

"Nathalie!" he stated flatly, continuing to hold her. "Have a stiff drink and tell us all about it."

Taking a seat opposite the two men who sat at either end of the huge modern couch, Alex took a sip of her drink. For some reason it tasted sour.

"I think I might have gone too quickly for her," she said sadly, looking down into her drink.

"So has she called it off?" asked James, dreading the answer. "Has she told you it's finished?"

Looking up with misty eyes, she replied, "Not exactly. But all the signs are there. It's just something I know."

Neither man argued with her. It would have been insulting. They'd known her for years and it had been Alex and Lou they'd turned to when James had been diagnosed HIV positive. Later they'd become firm friends and they'd never known her intuition about people to be wrong.

"Perhaps she's just not good at accepting help when she's sick," said Michael a little lamely, after Alex had explained what happened. "She's not exactly your run-of-the-mill girlfriend, is she?"

"No, she's not, but how do you know that? You only spoke to her for a few minutes at the party."

"Then I guess you'll have to put it down to my intuition," he said, regretting the comment.

"Are you telling me you didn't like Nathalie?" she asked quietly.

"Not at all, my darling," he said truthfully. It was their mutual past that was disturbing, not the woman herself. "But I didn't get the impression that being in a relationship with her would be very straightforward," he continued, glancing at James, who seemed to be looking at him strangely. "I just figured that if anyone could work it out, you could."

"Perhaps not," she sighed. "It's just that these last weeks have been wonderful and I really thought that she'd enjoyed them too. I don't know what I did."

The tears were welling in her eyes again, and Michael could feel his anger rising. They'd watched Alex go through the trauma of losing her partner through death and they'd seen her rebuild her life again. And now they were being forced to watch another unhappiness subverting all that effort.

"I'm being silly," she said, trying to put on a brave face. "All that's really happened is that she's told me she didn't want me to look after her while she was unwell. That's not exactly a sad farewell. I'm probably making a mountain out of a molehill."

"That's exactly what you're doing," replied James with an encouraging smile. Then, rising from his seat, "And you're not going to be allowed to dwell on it. We were talking of going to the movies, so that's exactly what we're going to do, and then we're going out for dinner."

"And if you're very lucky, Ms. Messner," Michael continued, "we'll succeed in getting you so stoned or drunk that by tomorrow you won't care if Nathalie's having a shitty, so long as someone takes away your hangover."

* * *

The apartment was dark by the time Nat got off the floor. Physically, she felt like she'd been hit by a truck. Emotionally she was drained and numb. Walking to the drink cabinet and pouring a bourbon, she threw it down her throat and refilled instantly. The flat seemed empty, bare and cold, and her mind told her that this is how it would remain.

Slowly her mother's words came back to her. "George is convinced you don't know who she is," she'd said during the phone call. So how did George know who Alex was? Presumably that was what Mother had meant? Or was it?

Stripping off her clothes and leaving them where they lay, she turned the shower to cold and then to full and climbed in. The icy water felt like needles ripping into her skin, but the pain wasn't enough to cleanse the disgust and guilt at what she and her family had done to Alex and her mother. Even the pain of losing Alex didn't override her self-hatred, and she knew exactly what her punishment should be.

* * *

Two cars were in the driveway when she pulled up the next day, and as usual Belinda opened the door. She looked surprised to see Nat and unsure what to do, but by the time she'd thought about it, Nat was inside and heading for the lounge.

Mother was at the dining table, her cards spread out in front of her. "So you decided to come, child," she said coolly, glancing up. "The cards told me you would."

"Then the cards win again," she retorted bitterly. "What do you want, Mother? I thought you didn't want to see me again."

"Now you're being silly, child," the beautiful woman replied with a cold smile. "What mother doesn't want to see her daughter? I was just a little angry at you last time, but I'm sure we can make things right."

"Where's George?" she demanded. "I want to know what he told you about my personal life."

"You mean your sex life," she retorted with a tilt of her head.

"Where is he, Mother?"

"You know, that job of yours really has turned you into an aggressive personality, Nathalie. You were raised to be a lover, not a fighter." Standing up, she moved toward the phone and, picking it up, dialed a number. "George," she said into the mouthpiece, "Your sister has decided to pay us a visit after all. I think perhaps you need to come home now."

Hanging up, she said, "He's not far away. He was just trying on a new suit I'm buying him."

There was a rage burning inside her, a bitter hatred that she desperately wanted to direct toward her mother, but she couldn't. Only cowards and those who couldn't face the truth blamed others for their own failings. The hatred was all hers. She was who she was, and it was what *she* did that invariably caused others pain. That was why Mother couldn't love her and it was why she had to return to the people who would at least tolerate her.

"I must say, Nathalie," said her mother, moving to one of the lounge chairs, "you always seem to be looking under the weather these days. Perhaps you need more vitamins…or perhaps an easier lifestyle?"

Looking around the room, Nathalie compared this house to Alex's home and that of Alex's mother. This place was luxurious with all the right furniture, floor coverings and decoration, but it wasn't warm or inviting. It wasn't a home. The only part of the house that seemed anything more than a show home was the section the children stayed in.

"Where are Jeremy and Samantha?" she asked, not sure if she hoped they were there or not.

"Samantha's at her grandmother's and Jeremy is spending time with his mother again. If you ask me, George is being very stupid allowing so much contact. He could have a fight on his hands when he wants to leave the country."

"But I doubt that will stop you, will it, Mother?" she answered sarcastically.

"Well, it never has in past, has it, my dear? You have to know by now that what Mother wants, Mother gets. But that's not a bad thing for you and George because I love my children and I can be very generous, as you know." Getting up to pour a drink for them both, she continued, "Then again, I can also get very mean when I'm crossed."

The conversation was making Nathalie's skin crawl, but in a perverse way that was good. It was what she deserved. It was letting her know that this was where she belonged.

Fifteen minutes later, George strode into the room, looking flushed and surprised. "I'm glad you came," he said as he bent down to kiss Nathalie on the lips. "We were hoping you would."

"Sit down, son," Mother demanded. "We have family business to discuss."

"And what business would that be, Mother," she asked flatly. "My business?"

"Nat, I—" began George, before Mother raised her hand, dismissing him.

"Yes, Nathalie darling, your business. You see the problem is that I can't help getting the feeling that you're plotting against me…against us. So I had to insure against it."

"Because I didn't want to participate in your sexual plans the last time I was here?"

"No. Because you're fucking the sister of Christine Martin, and because Christine Martin was an ungrateful little bitch who would have harmed this family if she could."

"What's that got to do with her sister? And for that matter, how did you know Alex was Christine Martin's sister? Because I didn't."

"I met her once," George answered, his face pale and tense. "We didn't talk, but she came to the flat looking for Chris, and I was there. She demanded that Chris leave with her and go into rehab—said that their mother was worried out of her mind. It was about six months before Chris died. I think the sister was home from university. I knew Chris and the sister had met once or twice for meals, but nobody expected her to turn up on the doorstep. Anyway, Chris was off her face and told her to leave— told her that she didn't want their straight, conservative lives and that she wanted to stay with us."

"So why didn't Alex recognize you when you came to the house?"

"It took *me* a while to remember where I'd seen *her* before, and she'd never spoken to me. She and Chris argued in the lounge and I stayed mostly in the kitchen, except for when I answered the door. But of course I was watching her through the door, so I was more likely to remember her."

"And you just had to tell Mother?"

His face blanched, but he didn't reply.

"But you see my dilemma, Nathalie," interjected Mother. "Here we have this woman who blames us for her sister's death, who suddenly turns up in your life and seduces you into her bed. Then you lie to us about having some male partner named Josh. I already knew that was a lie, by the way. I'd had you followed. I just didn't know who the female was that you were courting so lovingly. If you didn't know who she was and if you weren't part of some sordid plan to hurt us, why would you lie to us about who you were seeing? It's not as if we'd disapprove if you chose to sleep with a woman."

"Josh was my partner five years ago, and he's a good friend. I wasn't sleeping with Alex when I told you that. I just wanted you to think I had someone." It sounded pathetic and she was ashamed that she was even trying to explain. But if she wanted to return to them, then bridges had to be mended.

The knock on the door made her jump and made her realize how tense she was. It was Belinda, asking everyone if they wanted coffee. Mother decided they did.

"So are you trying to tell me that this woman—Christine Martin's sister—hasn't mentioned Christine to you once throughout this passionate affair?" Charlotte asked after the coffee had been delivered and served.

The anger was a painful knot now, burning viciously in her stomach. Discussing Alex with Mother was going to kill her, but she had no choice. It was her punishment.

"Alex told me she had a sister who'd died years ago," she answered, trying to control her voice. "But I don't remember her ever saying her name, and I had no reason to suspect anything because she doesn't have the same surname."

"Which also applies to you, I suppose," Charlotte mused. "If she knew George's surname, she would assume all his family would carry the Silver name. That's also possibly why she wouldn't have been able to place George when he came to your flat. She probably assumed he was George Duncan, if, of course, you are to be believed."

"Christine's mother knew my surname," George volunteered. "She was the one who lodged the complaint to the police about Christine's death. She even came to the flat once, just after Chris died, ranting and raving and crying, trying to blame us. I heard she had a breakdown after that."

Nat stumbled toward the bathroom, the nausea sweeping over her in waves. This was why she was here—Chris's mother's pain, Alex's pain. If she hadn't met Christine Martin at school, if she hadn't let Mother convince her to seduce her…But she had. And she'd killed her lover's sister and she had to pay.

It took a while to stop dry retching. Her stomach had been emptied too many times today, and there was nothing left. Just as there was nothing left emotionally.

George looked genuinely worried when she returned, but Mother looked triumphant.

"Of course, I'm still not totally convinced that this woman didn't come to you with a plan," Mother said, staring her in the face. "Christine Martin would have destroyed us if she could. Why would her sister be any different? But you're my daughter and I have to trust you. Of course we'd feel much happier if you moved back here for a while or at the very least stayed on your days off. And of course we assume you won't be seeing the Martin bitch anymore."

The invitation had been made, the olive branch extended.

"I want to do that, Mother," she replied. "I want to be here with you and George, but I need to be at my flat for work, so I'll stay on days off…if you'll have me. And I've already stopped seeing Alex. She was fun in bed, but she meant nothing to me."

They talked briefly about the children and Nathalie's work, and Mother did the Tarot endlessly, but it was tense and Nat felt ill. Then at ten o'clock, Mother indicated that she would like to retire. "I think we should celebrate Nathalie's return," she said to George. "I shall expect you in my room when you've had a chance to shower," she added, addressing Nathalie. "And of course you too, George."

* * *

The phone went unanswered all Sunday morning, the recorded voice inviting her to leave a message. It was the same when she tried the mobile. The first couple of times she spoke to the machine, but by lunchtime, Alex was getting desperate. The boys had done what they promised and kept her busy, but all she could think about was Nathalie—about what it was that had happened to so drastically change their relationship. It had only been a short time, and she knew that Nat had a lot in her life to sort out, but she'd believed Nat had come to love her, and she'd seemed happy and relaxed.

The ache in her heart vied for precedence over the pain and terrible fear that gnawed at her stomach. It couldn't be happening again. She couldn't lose another person she loved—and certainly not without a reason. But her intellect told her that Nathalie had backed away, and the unanswered phone calls told her that she would not be back. Yet she couldn't accept it.

Grabbing her bag and keys, Alex left the house. She would force Nathalie to face her. Force her to reveal what had caused her sudden change of heart. She had a right to know.

Nat's apartment was in a small, but luxurious block with a security intercom system that remained unanswered when she pressed it. Waiting patiently for someone to arrive or leave, Alex finally made her entrance when an elderly gentleman came out.

But Nathalie obviously wasn't home. There were no sounds from the flat even before she began pounding on the door. By now Alex was beginning to feel stupid and worried. What if this was all in her mind? What if Nathalie really had been too ill to want her company and was lying in a hospital bed somewhere while Alex was concentrating on her hurt feelings. This time her concern turned to panic.

Returning to the house, she phoned the local hospital, then two more within a reasonable distance. When Nathalie wasn't there, Alex wasn't sure if she was glad or not. How nice it would have been if there was a simple explanation.

The boys phoned in the evening and Michael hated hearing the pain in Alex's voice when she told him she'd heard nothing. At first, when he'd recognized Nathalie at the party, he'd believed that Alex didn't need someone with Nat's bad history in her life. He thought she deserved a lot better. But then over the weeks, he'd seen his friend come to life, watched as joy and laughter replaced the ever-present sadness in her eyes and listened to her speak of their relationship in a way that told him that Nathalie was making her happy.

Alex had spoken of Nathalie's nightmares and mentioned she and her family seemed to have some sort of unhappy history, but she'd been positive about it—the psychologist in her sure that in time Nathalie would sort it out. Michael wasn't so sure, but he couldn't say anything without risking his own past being known. Besides, he'd moved forward and so it would appear had Nathalie.

On Monday, Alex took time that was owed from work. She hadn't slept properly since Friday night and couldn't bring herself to eat. A terrible sadness filled her, and she felt a lot like she had after losing Louise. Work would have been a distraction, but she couldn't possibly concentrate on other people's problems right now. She had to know what was happening and why. Until then she clung to the slimmest hope that there was a reasonable explanation for Nathalie's lack of contact.

* * *

When Mother appeared at breakfast, she was buoyant, reliving the satisfaction she'd derived from asserting her authority over George and Nathalie the previous night—just as she had years ago. She'd particularly enjoyed exacting Nathalie's humiliation— no less than she deserved for her disloyalty.

George, on the other hand, appeared morose and depressed at breakfast, and this annoyed Mother. "What on earth are you sulking about?" she asked, before Nathalie arrived in the dining room. "I would have thought you'd be pleased your sister was back with the family."

"You didn't have to hurt her so much," he mumbled, rubbing his hands through his hair and avoiding her eyes. "She did what you wanted and came home."

"You disloyal little shit," she snarled. "Don't tell me my own son is plotting against me now? Your sister turned on us years ago by refusing to run the business with you, and now you defend her? She deserved to feel the pain of Mother's wrath."

"Like she did when she was little?" he muttered miserably. "I remember what you used to do to her. She couldn't have been any older than Samantha. What on earth could she have done to deserve that?"

"She defied me and questioned me and made me angry. Just like you're doing now," she retorted viciously, her euphoric mood disappearing instantly. "She needed to be shown who was in charge; she needed to learn obedience. I was protecting us both.

But I must say, George, while your stand on Nathalie's behalf is very admirable, it's a little late don't you think?"

When she appeared a few minutes later, Nathalie looked pale and tired and distant. Seating herself at the table, she didn't even notice the tension between mother and son. Her body was tender and sore and her mind numb—and that was how she wanted it.

"Do you have a key to the Martin woman's house?" Mother asked suddenly at the end of breakfast.

"Messner…her name is Alex Messner. Martin was her stepfather's name." Then seeing Mother's glare, "No, I don't have a key. Why?"

But the woman didn't answer and George gave her a look that said, "Don't pursue it. You're supposed to not care."

"I want your work and mobile phone numbers before you go home," Charlotte demanded. "A mother likes to know where her daughter is at all hours of the day and night. After all, it can be dangerous out there—especially for a police officer."

It was a threat to remain in line and it was hardly veiled.

Mother insisted she stay another night. She wanted to do Nathalie's cards again and she wanted them to have a meal out together. "As a celebration of Nathalie's return," she triumphed.

It didn't come as a surprise, and Nat knew what to expect again that night.

* * *

The messages queued up on the answer machine when Nathalie finally got home sounded desperate, and they brought with them a wave of anguish. Erasing them anyway, she made her way to the bar. That was another life, another Nathalie. Alex had to be relegated to the past like everyone else she'd slept with during her lifetime. But she'd have to finish it properly, otherwise Alex would keep persisting, keep hoping. And that wasn't fair. She'd do it this evening, so she could clear her mind for her job. It was the only thing she had left that didn't belong to Mother.

At four o'clock there was another phone call, and this time Nathalie answered it. The relief in Alex's voice was obvious and made her wince.

"Thank God," Alex muttered, "I thought something might have happened to you."

"I was out," she answered coolly. "You shouldn't have worried."

"Are you all right? Have you been sick? Tell me what's going on, Nat, please."

"I need to see you," Nat stated, trying to sound businesslike. "We need to talk. I'll come around now."

It sounded ominous, but this time Alex was prepared. Nathalie's voice had lost its warmth—that wonderful timbre that lifted her spirits. It could have been the voice of a telephone salesperson.

Just as the person standing at her door twenty minutes later, looking at her through flat, lifeless eyes, could have been someone she'd never met before.

"Would you like a drink?" she offered nervously, when Nathalie stepped into the lounge room. "I think I need one… or four."

"No, thank you," she replied politely. "I'm not staying."

"No, I didn't think you would…be staying, that is."

"So you know why I'm here?" she asked, wanting desperately to reach out and take away Alex's pain. But no matter how much pain she caused her now, it couldn't compare to what Alex would feel if she found out that her lover had slept with and ultimately been responsible for the death of her sister. And no matter how sadly, bitterly or angrily Alex looked at her now, that wouldn't compare to the expression she'd see in those eyes if she knew the truth.

"I imagine it's to tell me you don't intend seeing me again," she answered, her eyes defiant and tearful at the same time. "But I won't accept that without a reason…an explanation."

"Don't do this, Alex," she begged. "It's over. It just didn't work out. I told you, I'm no good at relationships."

"Not good enough," she stated angrily. "Not anywhere near good enough. Friday you make love to me, Saturday morning you're warm and kind and loving. Then on Saturday afternoon you're sick and suddenly you don't want to be with me again. It doesn't make sense. Are you ill? Is that it? Do you have some illness you don't want me to know about? Tell me, I'm not a child."

"It's nothing like that, I promise you—"

"Then what?" she shouted angrily, slamming her drink down on the cabinet. "What have I done to make you like this?"

"God, Alex, it's not you," she exclaimed gently, wanting to fall to her knees and have Alex hold her and never let her go. But all she could think of was the photo at Alex's mother's house and Norma's face when she spoke of Christine and how it would be if Alex found out the truth. "The truth is," she said, bracing herself, "I'm not comfortable having an affair with a woman, and I came to realize that the reason I feel this way is because I simply don't love you."

Alex looked as if someone had stabbed her, but her shoulders remained straight and her head high. "Then you're right," she said quietly, after a moment's silence. "There's nowhere to go from there. I'm just sorry that you didn't come to that conclusion sooner. It might have made it easier on both of us." Walking to the door and opening it, she said, "I'd like you to leave now."

The need to vomit had returned, and Nat wasn't sure if she could make it to the car, but she had to, had to walk straight and tall and convince this woman she didn't care.

Only when she got home and inside the door, did she let the emotions roll over her, and then she just sat in the chair, her head pounding, struggling with every ounce of energy not to set her emotions free. If she allowed that, she would never move again.

* * *

It wasn't true! It wasn't true! Alex's brain had kept on repeating the words even when she'd looked into Nathalie's eyes and found only a cold hardness staring back. But she'd had to accept that it was—that it had been an affair—a loving, warm, exciting, passionate, but unfortunate affair. Only now, with the door closed behind Nathalie, did Alex allow the tears to flow, but even as her emotions overwhelmed her, her brain continued its litany. *It isn't true, it isn't true*, it repeated over and over. *She's lying. Nathalie's lying.*

CHAPTER NINE

Protecting the Ones We Love

The alcohol and pills had knocked her out by eight o'clock and left no room for nightmares. It occurred to Nat that now she was living her nightmare and sleeping through the night.

"Christ, Nat, you look awful," Josh said worriedly when she arrived for work that day. "Are you ill?"

"I was," she answered quickly, "but now I'm fine—just a bad bout of gastric over the weekend."

"Just don't pass it on," he'd replied, laughing. "I can't afford to look that bad. Grace would throw me out."

At the morning meeting the team seemed subdued.

Accepting that the leads were drying up and that the likelihood of finding the mystery woman from the club were getting progressively slimmer, they'd begun to discuss other options and review the forensic evidence. The deeper they looked the more options they came up with and the more work it involved.

Nathalie was glad. If she had her way, she'd remain at work eighteen hours a day.

At least the raging pain inside her was under control. Stifling her emotions was something she'd learned from a young age. It had helped her cope with her return to the family and Mother's assaults on her. Now it would help her find a way to live without the only person she'd ever loved.

During lunch Nat rang the center and let Lenore Kingsley know that she'd now work Wednesday, rather than her normal Friday. Lenore sounded surprised, but she didn't ask any questions.

The week went in a haze. Several times, Josh asked her if she was okay. It was obvious to him that something was wrong, but as usual she wouldn't discuss it.

"Is it the new affair?" he'd asked her once, when they were in the coffee room together. "You're like a zombie."

"Are you complaining about my work?" she asked irritably.

"Not at all, you're doing twice the work of everyone else, but it's like you're not really here and I'm worried about you as a friend, Nat, not as your boss."

"Well, don't be," she'd responded coolly, walking away. "I don't need your concern."

* * *

Toward the end of the week, Bella popped into the office. She'd already met Lorna and Josh through Prosecutions and they offered to show her around. While they didn't go into details, Bella seemed interested in the exhibits and information they had up on whiteboards.

"Looks interesting," she commented, when she and Nathalie sat down for coffee. "Do you think you'll get them?"

"Them?" asked Nathalie automatically.

"Well, I just presumed there was more than one killer?" It was an odd statement, but not unusual for Bella, who often made obscure observations. Later Bella asked about Alex.

"It's off," Nathalie answered hastily. "It's not my cup of tea."

"Alex isn't your cup of tea or being in a relationship with a woman isn't your cup of tea?" she asked shrewdly.

"Both," Nathalie snapped. "And I don't want to discuss it."

"Well, I'd say I'm sorry," she laughed. "Except that you don't appear too upset about it." Her curiosity was aroused, but Bella knew it would be pointless to pursue the issue. "So how about coming home with me tonight then?" she suggested. "It will give us a chance to catch up and get drunk. I'll bring you back in here in the morning."

It was agreed.

Nathalie would do anything to avoid having spare time on her hands, and she knew Bella wouldn't harass her for information. Quite the reverse, in fact. By the time she fell into a drunken sleep in Bella's spare room, Nathalie had become aware of how bitter Bella was about her life and particularly her relationship with Jackie and a variety of other women over the years.

The next day at work was worse because of the hangover, but in a perverse way, Nathalie welcomed it. George rang twice in the week, apparently at Mother's insistence. The second time he rang, Mother wasn't home.

"Why are you doing this, Nat?" he asked. "You'd broken free and now you're back in her control?"

"I was back in her control the moment you told her who Alex Messner was," she replied coldly. "Why did you do that, George? Why didn't you just tell me?"

"I can't keep things from her, Nat," he replied sadly. "She already knew you were seeing a woman, she had photos. Later she found out I'd been to your place. She asked me about it, and that was when I remembered where I'd met Alex before. I was strung out...it just came out."

"Strung out? Not you, George! Are the drugs a regular habit now? Is that how she controls you?"

He didn't answer. Then tiredly he said, "She now thinks Christine's sister has the missing journal, that Christine might have given it to her before she died."

"Doesn't she realize that if that was the case, Alex would have used it against her long before now? From what you said, it would be very damning."

"I know," he answered with a sigh. "But Mother's convinced. The missing journal was one reason she came back. The cards told her she had to deal with outstanding problems from the past."

"What the fuck does that mean?"

"The missing journal and your defection, I think. But now that she knows about your friendship with Alex, she's even more convinced she's in danger."

"What *is* in the journal, George? Why is she so afraid of it?"

Again there was silence.

"Fuck you, George," she said flatly. "You're as bad as her, only more gutless. You have the means to set yourself free, and you don't use it. But I will tell you this, if either you or Mother ever go anywhere near Alex Messner, I'll go to the police myself, and even though I might not be able to prove most of it, it will start a major investigation."

"You love her, don't you?" he stated, the surprise obvious in his voice. "You came back to Mother…to us…to protect Alex?"

This time it was Nathalie who didn't answer.

"Don't hate me, Nat, please," he begged suddenly. "I couldn't bear it if you didn't love me. I'm sorry I told Mother about your friend. I didn't know you really cared for her."

"I'll see you Friday night," she replied with a sigh. "You're my brother, George. I can't hate you."

* * *

Alex didn't go to work until Thursday, and even then she only went because of pressing appointments. There were no more tears left, just an aching emptiness and the terrible feeling she'd somehow caused this. How many times had she picked up the phone to ring Nathalie but changed her mind? It would achieve nothing. Still that voice in her head kept repeating that Nathalie was lying. That something else had happened to force Nathalie's actions. Yet that made no sense. Ultimately she recognized that she'd have to accept that the woman really didn't love her.

When she arrived on Friday she wasn't surprised to find that Nathalie had changed her night at the center. Obviously she'd been in touch with Lenore and obviously Lenore realized that something had happened between them, but she made no comment.

Tomorrow she'd spend the day with Michael and James on their boat, but even the thought of a wonderful day on the harbor didn't make Alex feel better.

* * *

Mother was dark and angry when Nathalie arrived at the house after work. It was a side of her that her clients and wealthy friends never saw, but for George and Nathalie it was a constant. There was an obvious element of tension between George and Mother and it didn't take Nat long to find out why.

Nat had gone to shower shortly after arriving and came out to find Belinda in her room.

"What do you want?" she asked angrily. "Aren't I allowed any privacy?"

"You have a great body," the young girl said, staring at her wrapped only in a towel. "I think Mrs. Silver is going to let me join in tonight."

"And you had to come to my room to tell me this?"

"Your mother doesn't like you very much, does she?" the girl asked, ignoring Nat's comment.

"If you say so," she answered, wondering where this was going.

"Well, I don't like her much either," she said childishly. "Sometimes she hurts me and she treats me like a servant."

"How old are you, Belinda," Nathalie asked suddenly.

"Eighteen."

"That's what George told you to tell people, but how old are you really?"

"Sixteen," she answered shyly.

"And how long have you been with George?"

"One and a half years."

"So you were fourteen and a half when you came here? It's good to see nothing's changed."

"I love it here," she volunteered. "Well, I did until your mother came. I make tons of money doing the parties and we get the best drugs. George even got me a fake driver's license so I can drive his car sometimes. And one day I'm going to have his baby, he's promised." Sitting herself on the edge of the bed, she continued, "I came to tell you that she and George are fighting over the children. Charlotte wants them to go to America, but George told me he doesn't want them to."

"Has he told her that?" she asked curiously.

"Oh no, he's told her that their mothers' wouldn't give him permission to take them out of the country."

"So why tell me?"

"I just thought you should know."

Her face appeared guileless and genuine, and it occurred to Nathalie that this *child* really did love George and actually believed that the world they inhabited was exciting and fun.

Once again Mother asserted her authority on the weekend, endlessly doing their Tarot cards, forcing them to play card or board games with her and introducing an abundance of illegal drugs. Nathalie knew that it was all part of the control. But she didn't care. The drugs kept her numb and able to cope, and if she lost her job because of a random drug test, then life would go on. It always did. And if there was tension between Mother and George, then the drugs helped her remain oblivious.

Finally on Sunday afternoon Mother agreed to her going home to catch up with her household chores. There had been almost no opportunity to speak to George alone.

According to Belinda, George didn't have a habit, but certainly his drug use had increased since Mother's arrival, and so, according to her, had his anger. It stunned Nathalie to find out that since Mother's return he'd lost his temper twice, once kicking out at a prized autographed guitar and the second time accidentally hitting Belinda on the chin when he lashed out at his cup after spilling some sugar over the countertop. Until now, Nathalie had never known George to be in any way aggressive and Belinda had agreed.

When she arrived back at the flat, the answer machine had two messages from Josh inviting her and Alex to lunch on Sunday at Grace's house. She didn't call him back.

* * *

The boat was wonderful, the ocean and the clear blue skies were wonderful, and Michael and James were kind and attentive, but Alex was miserable. The grinding ache and the belief that there was so much more to Nathalie's decision wouldn't give her any peace.

"I just know there's something going on," she insisted to Michael for the tenth time. "Something happened, and I believe it had something to do with her family."

"That's the first time you've said that," he answered, sitting up and taking notice. "What do you mean?"

"Maybe I'm just clutching at straws," she sighed, taking a sip of the colorful cocktail James had prepared. "But she got a phone call from her mother just before we went out that day and she seemed confused by it. When I asked her what had happened, she just said that her mother wanted to see her."

"That doesn't sound too strange," commented James. "Mothers often ask to see their offspring."

But Michael wasn't so convinced. He knew that a call like that from Charlotte Silver would have been a demand, not an invitation, and he also knew that Charlotte Silver wasn't like any mother these two would ever have experienced.

"Why did you think it was so strange?" Michael asked, knowing that Alex was very astute when it came to reading between the lines.

"Well, I probably didn't at the time," she admitted. "I mean, it's not how Mum and I talk to each other on the phone, but I knew there was animosity between them. It was more that Nathalie seemed confused and worried when the conversation was over, and then she stayed a little distracted while we were at my mother's." Then shaking her head, she mumbled, "Oh shit, listen to me, I sound like Hercule Poirot. It's just…"

She couldn't finish for the tears choking her voice.

Seeing Alex this distressed was making Michael angry and James upset.

They spent the rest of the time trying to distract her.

On Sunday Alex woke knowing that today she'd have to bite the bullet and go and see her mother. She'd avoided her all week because she didn't feel up to telling her about Nathalie and because she knew that when she did, she'd probably fall apart.

When she let herself in, Norma was watching the football. "We're winning," she stated excitedly, indicating the television. "Come sit and watch." Then seeing her daughter's face, she switched off the TV. "I'll make us a hot drink," she said, leading Alex into the kitchen. "You look like you need it."

"It's a shame," Norma said quietly when Alex finished explaining. "I truly believe that she cared for you a great deal. It was written in her eyes. But whatever her reasons, you have no choice but to respect her wish to end it."

Sighing, Alex said, "I know, Mum, but there's no closure. It's like a book you never get to finish. It might not have ended how you wanted, but it was important to know what happened."

Later they ate and watched the replay of the football on pay television. That night Alex stayed in her mother's spare bedroom—the thought of returning to the house alone simply too daunting.

* * *

The investigation was turning up more questions than answers and the briefing on Monday examined everything they had to date. It was rare to have three people murdered and so little forensic evidence. Whoever was responsible must be intelligent enough to cover their tracks well, someone said. Especially in the case of the two victims who had died quietly in their own bed.

They were split into teams of two again and given a set of assignments. Josh didn't want the investigation at the lesbian clubs to cease because he believed the mystery woman to be an integral link, but the busy nights for the clubs were Friday and Saturday and few were opened Monday to Wednesday. This time, Josh took Nathalie as his partner and split up everyone else.

"Were you at Alex's all weekend?" he asked with a grin, when they were alone in his office. "I left you a message."

"I'm sorry," she said vaguely. "I got home late."

"What's going on, Nat?" he asked, gently.

"What makes you think anything's going on?" she replied sharply. "So I didn't check my messages. It happens."

"You look like shit, and suddenly you don't want to talk about Alex. Don't bullshit me, Duncan," he said, taking hold of her shoulders. "We're supposed to be friends."

Shrugging him off, she put up her hands in a defensive gesture. "Don't touch me, Josh," she hissed angrily. "I don't want to be touched."

He'd seen her like this sometimes after the nightmares. At first he'd tried to comfort her, but she'd shy away as if he were an attacker, and although hurt, he'd come to accept it. Invariably everything would return to normal the next day. But this was the first time he'd seen her react like this in broad daylight.

"I'm sorry, Nat," he said, putting up his hands and backing right away. "I'm just worried about you."

"In this office, you're my boss, not my friend, and I'm here to work, so when I'm not doing my job, that's when you have the right to be concerned. Otherwise it's none of your business."

"You're right," he said quickly. "And I apologize. But when you leave here, you'll revert to being my friend and I intend to find out what's happening to you, even if it means you have to slam your door in my face."

She didn't answer, returning instead to the documents she'd been sifting through. For the rest of the day Nathalie remained quiet, but professional.

At the end of the day, Josh invited her to join him for a drink. Knowing she couldn't keep the breakup from Josh any longer, she decided to get it over with.

"Why didn't you tell me?" he asked gently. "I know I didn't act well when you first told me about Alex, but...well...you're obviously upset that it's broken up, so why finish it? What's going on, Nat?"

"I didn't feel comfortable in a lesbian relationship," she offered with a shrug. "It was all wrong. The only reason I'm upset is because it's another failure. There's really nothing to worry about."

He didn't believe her, but there was no point pursuing it.

Later he discussed it with Grace and agreed that what Nathalie needed now was space.

* * *

The center was quiet on Wednesday. When Nathalie got home, the phone was ringing. It was George. Mother wasn't home.

"I've lived in this apartment for years, George," she stated impatiently. "And I've been in this job for a while. Why does Mother feel the need for you to keep checking on my whereabouts? It's becoming annoying."

"She's just nervous," he responded quietly. "It's the cards… you know. But I've got good news. Jeremy and Samantha will be at home this weekend. Jeremy's back with me until the next holidays, and I've got Sam for at least a week."

"What's happening with your business?" she asked, curious that there had been no activity at the house since she'd renewed the contact and apparently no parties.

"We've got one of the girls running the business from another house while Mother's here."

"In preparation for you leaving the country by any chance?" she asked irritably.

He was silent.

"When is it supposed to happen?"

"When she resolves certain problems she has over here."

"So she believes you're going with her?"

"Yes."

"And am I one of the problems she has to resolve? Or does she feel she's already done that?"

"How would I know, Nat?" he asked tiredly. "Since I tried to convince her that we don't need to take the children with us and since she found out I'd been to your flat that night and didn't immediately tell her about Alex, she doesn't tell me anything. Besides, the only reason Mother thinks she's got problems is because the fucking cards tell her so."

"I'll see you on Sunday, George," she replied flatly. "I want to go to bed now."

That night when she was getting changed, Nathalie found a T-shirt that Alex had worn the last night she'd stayed. Holding it to her face, she breathed in the precious sensual smell of this kind, beautiful woman—her lover. Memories flooded in. Curling into a ball she placed the T-shirt under her head, allowing the flashbacks of Alex's voice, her laughter, her warmth and affection to wash over her.

The nightmares still came, but their intensity was less. Or maybe it was just that in comparison to her life right now, they were having less effect.

* * *

On Thursday, Nathalie and Josh were out interviewing people when they heard the urgent call for a car to attend an intruder on premises at a location only one street away. Radio said the call had come from an elderly person inside the house and that the nearest uniform car was at least ten minutes away. Acknowledging the job, they headed for the address.

Knocking on the front door, their guns discreetly by their sides, and getting no answer, they pushed the unlocked door open. "Mrs. Landers, it's the police," Josh called out, carefully stepping into the hallway.

The house was deathly silent.

Identifying themselves again, they began moving from room to room. Finally, they moved toward the back area—Josh walking ahead of Nathalie into the enclosed sunroom. As his eyes focused on a movement at the other end of the room, he began to raise his gun.

That's when the baseball bat hit him across the chest and continued upward, smashing into his face and knocking him to his knees—his weapon flying from his hand.

Nathalie raised her gun and pointed it at the man with the baseball bat, shouting for him to put it down. But he had a partner further down the room.

"Drop the gun, bitch," he screamed, holding an elderly lady with one arm while he jammed a shortened rifle under her chin. "Drop it or I'll fucking kill her."

"No," she said, continuing to keep the gun trained on his partner. "Shoot her and I'll shoot your friend."

"Jesus, Luke," the man with the baseball bat whimpered. "She fucking means it." He was panicked, but the man with the gun was cooler—his eyes were vicious and mean.

"Let the lady go," Nathalie said, trying to keep her eyes on both men. "The place will be crawling with police in the next minute or two. You're not going anywhere."

"Drop the bat and move over here, Denny," the older man ordered. "She won't fucking shoot you if you're not armed."

Nervously the skinny young man dropped the bat and backed away from Josh, who was on his knees, watching in silence. Moving backward, Denny made his way to the man called Luke.

"Pick up the pig's gun," demanded the older man, indicating Josh's discarded weapon, but Denny hesitated. "Just do it," he ordered.

Bending down, but keeping his eyes on Nathalie, the skinny man held the gun in very shaky hands but made no attempt to point it at her.

Dropping the old lady into the chair beside him, Luke allowed the rifle to point toward Nathalie.

"That's two guns to one," he gloated. "Now what the fuck are you going to do?"

Stepping between the two men and Josh, so that her body shielded him, Nathalie pointed her gun directly at the older man's chest. "I'm going to arrest you. Straight after you put those weapons on the ground," she replied calmly.

Indecision replaced arrogance in the older man's eyes while the younger man just looked scared.

Still Nathalie kept moving slowly toward them.

"I'll blow your fucking head off if you keep coming," Luke threatened, pointing the gun directly at her head. "I swear I will."

"But I don't care, Luke," she said quietly, ensuring he was aware she knew his name. "And my Glock has a hair trigger, so the moment I'm hit, you're dead."

"Fuck, Luke, she's…she's nuts," stuttered the young man, dropping Josh's gun, raising his hands and staring at his companion. "Just…just do what she says."

The gunman wanted desperately to see a hint of fear or doubt in the police officer's gray eyes, but instead he saw a challenge— an invitation to shoot—and his resolve crumbled.

Putting his left hand in the air, he pointed the rifle upward, opening his hand and dangling it from the trigger guard. For a fleeting moment he thought he saw disappointment cross the woman's face.

Stumbling to his feet, Josh moved around Nathalie and carefully took the rifle from the shaking man's hand. Then he bent down and retrieved his own gun.

The whole incident seemed to take only a couple of minutes, but within moments other police arrived. As they removed the two men and tended the elderly woman, Nathalie helped Josh to a seat. "Are you all right?" she asked worriedly. "You're going to have one hell of a bruise on your face."

"It's my ribs that are killing me," he stated between gritted teeth. "The bastard took me by surprise and that pisses me off." Speaking quietly, he said, "What the fuck do you think you were doing?"

"Letting the good guys win for a change?" she said with a shrug.

"You could have been killed."

Again she shrugged.

"They hit me, you pointed your gun and they gave up their weapons. That's our story. Anything else and you're going to be spending the next six months having psych assessments," he whispered angrily.

Within minutes an ambulance crew had arrived, followed by senior police. Both Josh and the elderly resident had been transported to hospital and Nathalie had been driven back to the local police station.

Apparently the burglars had broken into the house thinking it was the home of a small-time drug dealer, which was why they were so heavily armed. The old lady had been in the back room and heard them moving around. That was when she'd phoned the police on her extension. Unlike the front of the house, the back room had been locked up like Fort Knox, so when Josh and Nathalie arrived the men had been unable to flee.

Josh had a bruised chest and ribs but no serious injury to his face, and the homeowner was treated for shock. Senior detectives spoke to Josh and Nathalie at length, took statements and then allowed them to return to their own office.

"I'll drive you home," Nathalie said as they left the area. "I've spoken to Grace at work and told her you were okay. She's going to meet you at your place."

"I could have got us all killed," he muttered angrily as they pulled up near the flat. "A fucking rookie wouldn't have stepped into that back room less cautiously than I did…and then to fall for the decoy trick. Shit."

"That's bullshit, Josh," she said gently. "I would have done the same thing. Neither of us expected to be ambushed. And no one got hurt."

By now they were heading toward his front door, which had swung open. In an instant Grace was in his arms.

"I'm okay," he assured her with a feeble smile as she clung to him—hurting his ribs even more.

"Oh well, that's okay then," she said, moving back into the flat angrily. "In that case I won't ever worry about you again."

Laughing, Josh said, "Hey, don't be mad. I wasn't in any danger. I had Nathalie watching my back. It was all over in seconds, honestly."

Then she was back in his arms, gently touching his face where a huge welt was beginning to swell. Then she was crushing Nathalie to her, thanking her and pulling them both into the flat. "Oh God," she said, wiping at stray tears. "I think I'd die if anything happened to you now, you stupid man."

"Then there's nothing for it," he said, a huge smile lighting his face. "I guess I'm just going to have to marry you."

Declining their invitation to stay, Nathalie returned to the office. It was way past the end of shift and she felt exhausted.

Later, over dinner, Josh and Grace talked. "I'm really worried about Nathalie," he said, looking up from his plate.

"Because of what happened this afternoon?"

"Not because of the incident," he replied, shaking his head. "She's a police officer and it goes with the job—even though you never expect it to happen to you. It's more than that, it's…"

For a moment he lapsed into silence, trying to translate a feeling into words. "It's just that…well, if I didn't know better, I'd have thought she actually wanted that piece of filth to shoot her."

"Why on earth would you think that?" she replied gently.

"She told him she didn't care when he said he'd blow her head off. The gun was pointing right at her and she said she didn't care."

"But surely she was just bluffing, trying to protect you and the woman…trying to do her job."

"You had to be there, darling," he stated carefully. "It was as if she was inviting him to shoot, and both of those men believed she meant it."

"But surely if he'd shot her, that would have left you unprotected. Surely she wouldn't have risked other people's lives…and why would she do that anyway?"

"No. She knew she'd get off a shot and take out the guy with the gun, even if he did fire. The other guy had put my gun down and backed off and he was too rattled to react anyway. She knew that she and the gunman were the only ones in danger."

"I don't know what you're trying to say," she answered, frightened at the implication. "Why would Nathalie want to die?"

"I can't answer that," he replied, putting down his cutlery and rubbing his swollen face. "Something terrible is happening with her right now, but she won't say what. I told you about the cock-and-bull story she gave me about calling it off with Alex, but it's far more than that. The life has gone out of her, it's like this empty shell is walking around pretending to be Nathalie Duncan…and I can't get through."

* * *

Friday and Saturday were late shifts and once again Nathalie was partnered with Lorna. Naturally, the conversation in the office at the start of shift was about yesterday's incident, but Josh played it down, forcing them to focus on their tasks. Barely able to move because of the rib injuries, he was on restricted duties for a few days, remaining in the office and directing the shift from there.

Before Nathalie went out, Josh took her aside. "We have to talk," he said quietly. "About yesterday and about what's going on with you. It's not a request. If you don't do this, I'll have you removed from the task force. I'm worried about you. You can come back to the office early and we'll talk then," he said firmly. "I'm serious, Nat."

"I'm sure you are," she snapped, walking away from him.

The clubs were particularly busy when they got there, but they made a breakthrough when a woman and her friend thought they might have seen the mystery woman.

"Do you know who she is?" Nathalie had asked eagerly.

"Said her name was Catherine, I think, but I didn't get a surname. But among other things she was complaining about her job, so I told her they were hiring at the hotel where I work. I don't know if she ever applied."

Taking her details, including her workplace address and phone number, Nathalie thanked the woman and returned to Lorna. It was more than they got for the rest of the evening.

Returning early, as instructed, Nat told Josh about her information. Josh decided to make inquiries at the hotel the next working day. Closing the office door and shuffling slowly toward the seat at his desk, he said, "Okay, Nathalie, I can make this official if you want, but I'd rather it didn't have to be. You deliberately put yourself in danger yesterday, and I want to know why."

"I was just doing my job," she stated. "Nobody got hurt. It was by the book."

"And telling him to go ahead and shoot you—was that by the book as well?"

"You must have misheard," she replied irritably. "You'd been hit around the head, remember."

"I don't want a suicidal member on my team," he said gently, "because sometimes it's only fear that keeps us alert out there. If you don't care, you'll be careless and just maybe it won't be you in the firing line next time."

"Are you sacking me from the team?" It was asked with no hint of emotion.

"I should be referring you to the Police Medical Officer for assessment," he said. "But, damn you, Nat, if I do that, your career will be shot, and you were prepared to protect me with your life. It's just that I'm so scared for you."

"Well, don't be," she responded dully. "Only the good die young."

People were starting to drift into the outer office and the conversation was getting Josh nowhere. "Please talk to someone, Nat," he begged. "If you don't trust me, then find someone you do—even a psych. Whatever's eating you up has to be dealt with or it will destroy you."

"Thanks for the advice," she replied, standing up. "Now if you don't mind, I've got some paperwork to finish."

* * *

It had been a hectic day at work and busy at the center and Alex was grateful to be home. Every day was a struggle, and she wondered if it might be an idea to take some long overdue leave.

It took a minute for the mess in her lounge room to register, and when it did, she just stood and stared. It never entered her head until much later that the intruders might still be in the house.

Every cupboard and drawer had been opened and the contents thrown onto the floors, cushions had been pulled from the lounge suite and the bedding from the beds. Even pictures hanging on walls had been moved. Every room was the same, even the bathrooms. It was a total mess. Yet only the laptop, jewelry and the DVD player appeared to be missing.

She phoned the police.

Pushing one of the cushions back onto a chair and dropping into it, Alex looked around. The sanctity of her home had been violated and with it her sense of safety. All of a sudden the last couple of weeks caught up with her and the tears began to flow, followed by heart-wrenching sobs that left her head aching and her chest heaving.

An hour later, when the police still hadn't arrived and she was feeling calmer, she rang Michael and James. The boys came immediately, busying themselves making coffee and taking it in turns to keep Alex's mind occupied. Finally the police arrived, took details and told her that the fingerprint unit would be out in the morning.

"Well, you can't stay here," they told her when the police finally left. "But we can take time off tomorrow and come back with you to clean up."

That night, after a hot bath, warm meal and sleeping tablet, Alex finally fell asleep.

"Cocksuckers," James spat as he helped wash up their dinner dishes. "I'd love to get my hands on whoever did this. It's all she needs right now, some prick trashing her house."

"It *was* trashed, wasn't it?" said Michael thoughtfully. "It was as if they were looking for something, rather than just robbing the place. Who turns coffee tables upside down and moves heavy furniture when they're robbing a house, for Christ sake? Or empties out kitchen cupboards? What would they possibly expect to find?"

"What are you getting at?" James asked quietly. "Do you think it might have been personal?"

Tiny suspicions were forming in Michael's mind, but he couldn't say anything to James. Tomorrow, he'd talk to Alex and find out if she kept anything of value in the house. It would surprise him if she did, but he needed to know.

* * *

It took most of the day to clean up after fingerprints had been taken, and Alex was even more subdued than usual. Several times, Michael noticed her wiping away tears and his anger grew by the minute. Alex had not been able to think of anything she had in the house that would interest burglars and certainly nothing she'd be likely to keep under coffee tables or in crockery cupboards. It left them all puzzled.

They didn't want to leave her alone, but Alex was starting to get angry at her own helplessness. "It's as if some unseen force is playing with my life," she'd explained when the boys had tried to get her to stay at their place again. "I've let losing Nathalie make me feel miserable and hopeless, and now this burglary has almost succeeded in driving me from my home. I've got to take a stand somewhere. Who knows, I might even find the courage to try and find out what really happened with Nat."

* * *

Although Nathalie was dreading seeing Mother again on Sunday, she was looking forward to seeing Jeremy and Samantha. Last night's nightmare had been particularly ugly, with images of children being buried alive in lonely graves. It had woken her at four in the morning. At daylight she'd opened all the curtains, flooded the room with light and snatched another three hours sleep on the lounge.

Samantha was still shy with her when she arrived on Sunday morning, but Jeremy wrapped his warm, soft arms around her neck and gave her a huge cuddle that made her want to hold him forever. Mother glared silently for a moment before dismissing the children to their area.

"Hard work chasing criminals is it, my dear?" Mother said sarcastically as Nathalie bent to kiss her on the cheek. "You're really looking your age."

"Thank you, Mother," she replied. "I'll try to take better care of myself."

"Good, because we're going to a party tonight, and I want you looking your best. I have a couple of women friends who want to try something different—an all-girl party. They want someone with experience."

"I'm not one of your prostitutes anymore," she retaliated quickly. "You'll have to use one of George's girls."

Standing up and moving toward her, Charlotte growled, "You need this family, Nathalie Duncan, but to be part of it you need to contribute to it. So you'll do what's expected and you'll do it well."

"And if I don't?"

"Then you'll disappoint me," she said, straightening to full height and reaching to touch Nat's face. "And I'll have to start worrying all over again about exactly what you and that Martin bitch were concocting behind my back."

Pulling her face away, Nathalie said, "Are you threatening me, Mother?"

"Oh no, my child," she said, moving even closer. "But it would be a shame if the woman you were fucking so lovingly should find out that you're Charlotte Silver's daughter...the same one who seduced her sister."

"You really do hate me, don't you?" she asked quietly, feeling small and helpless.

"Oh, I don't hate you, Nathalie," she said softly, leaning in again, grabbing her face and kissing her on the lips. "I don't know why you'd think that."

The rest of the day was spent with the children building sandcastles in the huge sandpit George had established in the back garden and having make-believe afternoon tea with Samantha at a tiny table she barely fitted into. Nathalie loved how patient Jeremy was with his little sister, who endlessly bossed him around. They were affectionate, open and happy children, and once again it occurred to Nathalie that despite everything, George was obviously a good father.

It wasn't until dinner that Nathalie saw George, and then it was noticeable that there was an underlying tension between him and Mother. That night, before going out, she tucked Samantha into her bed.

"You smell nice, like my mummy," she said innocently when Nathalie gave her a kiss goodnight. "But Mummy doesn't come home anymore," she finished sadly.

"She will one day, darling," replied Nat, holding her tiny hand in her own. "And I bet she's thinking of you every single day."

"I might draw Mummy another picture," she mumbled sleepily. "Daddy takes my pictures to Mummy, but he said I couldn't tell anyone." Then she was asleep and Nathalie was staring blankly at her. So George was either lying to the child or he did have contact with her mother in prison. Turning to leave the room, she saw George watching from the doorway.

"So you visit her mother in prison," she whispered as she pulled the door over. "I assume Mother doesn't know?"

Looking over his shoulder, he whispered back, "Susan's a good woman and Samantha's her life. I told her to refuse Mother's visit request, and I pretended I didn't have access either. That way I had an excuse not to take the children to America."

"How long is she in prison for?"

"She's got another three months to do."

"Is she a junkie?"

"No. That's what I told Mother. Sue was involved in embezzlement at the bank where she worked. She didn't do it, but she covered it up."

"You sound like you're very fond of her?"

"It didn't work out between us, because of what I do I guess. She's twenty-six and intelligent and kind, and she's never been involved with the business. When I wouldn't give it up, she finished with me."

"So it's not the grandmother who lets you have Samantha, it's her mother?"

"Yes. She won't give me custody while I run Mother's businesses, but she wants Sam to know Jeremy and she really doesn't restrict my access to Samantha at all."

"These children had better be safe while Mother's here," Nathalie murmured. "And you'd better sort out how you're going to tell her that they won't be going with you to America."

"I'm already doing that, Nat," he said tiredly. "I've told Susan to apply to the court to cut my access and I won't fight it. I'm providing her with a lawyer who will tell the court that Sam is in danger of being taken out of the country on false documentation."

"Then you won't be able to see her at all."

"Maybe that's best…at least while Mother's here."

"And Jeremy—how will you stop Mother's claim on him?"

"Claire's going to do the same. They should lodge their applications next week. It won't matter what false documentation Mother comes up with, the custody orders will take precedence, the children's photos will be on the system, and Customs and Immigration will be notified."

"God, George, I'm so sorry."

"It's not forever. Mother will have to go home soon, her business is over there now, and then there's her dogs, she's always talking about how much she misses them. When she's gone I can get you to help me reverse the custody orders."

Reaching up, she kissed him gently on the cheek. "Thank you, George," she said quietly. "Thank you for taking a stand."

The party was in a discreet and luxurious apartment, and the women were beautifully turned-out society hostesses in their forties. Both were married to prominent businessmen and looking for something to spice up their lives. There was alcohol and drugs, flirting and dancing and eventually bed, but not together. Strangely enough, when it came time to go beyond the kissing and petting, they wanted individual attention. Afterward they appeared ill at ease and desperate to get Nathalie out of the apartment. This suited her well.

On Monday she and George took the children to the movies and then to the kids' gymnasium. George didn't mention the previous night or ask Nathalie where Mother had sent her, but it was obvious he was aware of what she'd been ordered to do. While they both knew the situation couldn't remain as it was, neither seemed to have the power to change it.

"I want to know what's in the journal," Nathalie demanded as they sat watching the children play.

"It's about things she did years ago—people she hurt. It's hideous. It's almost as if she's bragging about them."

"What sort of things? Give me an example."

"No, Nat. I told you, I don't want to do that. You were only about four or five at the time. She's changed since then. I should have destroyed it, but—"

"But you thought you might need it one day. And now you do."

"I can't use it against her, Nat. She's my mother."

The children arrived back then, puffing and loud and full of laughter. It took Samantha only two minutes strapped into her car seat to fall asleep, a cloth doll she'd won at the gymnasium clutched in her hand.

* * *

Mother insisted Nat stay for tea. Nathalie desperately wanted to ask her when she was returning to America, but she knew Mother would take it as an insult and didn't have the energy to enter into another battle with her.

By the time she got home, Nathalie was exhausted.

Later, after a hot shower, she was surprised by the doorbell and stunned to find Ari on her doorstep.

"What do you want, Ari…" she began, "we really don't—"

But he barged past her and was in the lounge. "Shut the door, Nathalie," he demanded, making no move to leave. "And my name's Michael. Ari hasn't existed since I was sixteen."

His presence was imposing.

Closing the door, she said, "You're wasting your time. I don't have anything to say."

"Oh yes, you do," he responded coldly. "I told you I'd come after you if you hurt Alex and right now she's hurting very badly."

"I'm sorry," she mumbled. "I never wanted to hurt her, but it has nothing to do with you."

"Sit down," he instructed. "You actually look worse than Alex." Then, noticing the blanket and cushion left on the lounge from Friday night, he said, "Still having the nightmares, Nathalie?"

"What do you mean I look worse than Alex?" she asked, ignoring his last comment. "What's wrong with Alex?"

"You mean apart from having her heart ripped out?"

No answer was expected, so he continued. "Someone trashed her house on Friday," he stated frostily, watching her reaction. "And I think they were looking for something specific."

What little color she had in her face drained away and burning anger flooded her eyes. "Are you suggesting it was me?" she asked.

"I don't know, Nathalie. You tell me?"

"Get out," she spat, standing up. "I wouldn't do anything to harm Alex. You know nothing about me."

"Sit down," he commanded. "I know everything about you, and I'm not going anywhere until I get some answers. I couldn't care less about you, but James and I love Alex, and I know that there's more to this than you're telling her. Somehow your family is involved."

"Really?" she said angrily, dropping slowly into a chair. "You think you know a lot, don't you? But did you know that Alex Messner is Christine Martin's sister?"

"What...no...don't be ridiculous," he stuttered in shock, sitting on the edge of the seat opposite. Then, seeing the look on Nathalie's face, "God, you're serious." Then when she said nothing, "I had no idea. We met her and Lou at the HIV/AIDS Clinic when they were volunteering there. I've never spoken about my past. I knew she had a sister who overdosed, but she never talks about it."

"Did you meet Christine Martin?"

"Yes, she and George lived at the flat. I remember she had a pretty heavy heroin habit, but I only knew her for a few months before she died."

"Who seduced you into the family?" Nat asked dully.

"Why?"

"Who was it?" she demanded.

"George, Christine...your mother."

"Well, it was me who brought Christine Martin into Mother's web. We met at school and I seduced her and handed her over to Mother and George. Four years later she was dead. Do you still think I should continue seeing Alex?"

Shaking his head, as if trying to wake from a dream, he got up to pace the room. "Did you know who Alex was when you started seeing her?"

"Sure. I just thought it would be fun to fall in love with someone who would end up hating the sight of me." Her eyes were hard and her face full of pain.

"So, how did you find out?"

"When we had afternoon tea at her mother's—I saw the photo of Alex's sister and found out the stepfather's name was Martin."

"Jesus," he gasped. "What a fucking mess. I need a drink."

They both had one.

His heart went out to this woman now. Nothing in his life could match the pain of what her youth was going to cost her. He'd been able to put his past behind him and move on, and it had only been a few years out of his life. But knowing Charlotte Silver and having listened to George speak of their past, he knew that Nathalie's horror had begun when she was a small child. It would have been all she'd known. Yet she'd managed to leave it behind, only to find it irrevocably interwoven with the present.

"How did you get involved with my family?" she asked finally.

"I met George at a youth center when I was thirteen. I was confused about my sexuality and I wasn't getting on with my father. I hated the world. George took me home to the flat, and from there he introduced me to a lifestyle beyond my imagination. Then I met Charlotte. She took a fancy to me and basically bought me anything I wanted. Of course there was a price, but even then it seemed like fun."

"So why did you leave?"

For a moment she thought he wasn't going to answer.

"I wanted George, but I didn't want the rest of it. I guess maybe I was starting to grow up."

"And she just let you go?"

"I left when she was in America on business. I went home and my father sent me out of the state to a boarding school in Victoria. Then I went on to university."

For an age they sat staring into their drinks.

Finally, Michael said, "Alex is convinced there's more to you dumping her, and she's talking about trying to find out what."

"Then you have to stop her…discourage her. She can't ever know."

Shaking his head, he said, "I doubt she'd ever simply stumble onto your connection with her sister. My concern is that while she doesn't let go, she doesn't move on."

"Then you have to make her."

Again the silence until Nathalie finally asked, "What happened at her house? What was stolen?"

"Only jewelry, the DVD player and laptop, but the place was ransacked as if they were looking for something particular. Her top-of-the-range entertainment system was left, as was the iPad, desktop computer and an expensive leather jacket. It didn't make sense."

The anger was building, but she couldn't let Michael know that she thought her family might have been involved. That would only compound the harm and make Michael angrier.

"You know, you do look awful, Nathalie," he said finally, rising to leave. "You really do love her, don't you?"

The pain in her eyes answered his question, but she nodded. "She has to believe that I don't care. Please help her to find someone else."

"You know, it's been two years since Lou died, and it's taken her all that time to even date again. When Alex loves, she doesn't do it lightly."

"She was with Lou ten years, she was with me a matter of weeks," Nathalie said sadly. "It's not the same."

Pulling a business card from his jacket pocket and handing it to her, he said, "Use that if you need it. It's got my mobile number on it. James doesn't know I'm here, but I'll tell him I came to confront you about dumping Alex. I'll tell him that you've got someone else. Eventually, if Alex insists on continuing to try and find out what went wrong, that's what I'll tell her." He saw her wince, but she covered it quickly and nodded her agreement.

"How did you get my address?" she asked as he exited the flat.

"I went through Alex's handbag when I was at her house. She's old-fashioned enough to carry an address book," he said with a shrug.

After he left, Nathalie took a sleeping pill and, leaving all the lights on, headed straight to bed. Without doubt, George or Mother knew something about the break-in at Alex's flat, but she couldn't do anything about that now. Without sleep there wasn't any chance she could survive another week at work. Even without people telling her she looked awful, Nathalie knew she was on the brink of collapse and there were things to be done before she could give in to that.

* * *

Thanks in part to the effort put in by Michael and James, Alex's house was back to normal by Sunday morning. That afternoon her mother had come over and cooked her favorite meal—the smell of cooking and her mother's pottering beginning to make the home feel like her own again.

It had been easy to tell Michael and James that she wasn't going to give in to her misery, but after they left, the emptiness had overwhelmed her. The feelings of loss and devastation she'd experienced when Lou died were rekindled, only this time it wasn't caused by an act of God and therefore seemed somehow even more difficult to accept.

Something specific had caused Nathalie to pull away, of that she was certain, but no matter how often she went over that day, Alex couldn't come up with anything except the phone call Nathalie had got from her mother. Yet, even though Nat had seemed upset after that call, she'd still been warm and loving. Whatever happened came after that—at her mother's house.

Over dinner on Sunday, Alex had again asked her mother if she could think of anything unusual that might have happened during afternoon tea. Something she'd missed.

"I honestly can't think of anything," she'd answered patiently. "You were there for virtually all of it, except when you went to the bathroom before you left, and then Nathalie and I didn't really get the chance to talk because I was looking for something for you."

"The magazines," Alex reminded her.

"Yes, the magazines."

"So what was Nat doing during that time? Did she make a call on her mobile or anything like that?"

"Not unless it was very quick. She was just looking around… looking at the photos, that sort of thing." Sighing, Norma said, "Don't you think that perhaps you're clutching at straws, darling. Maybe she just wasn't the person you thought she was?"

"You're probably right," Alex replied with a shake of her head. "But I can't help feeling that something happened that neither of us is aware of." Then, embarrassed, "Well, it's a better explanation than that she just didn't like your house or my driving or the plans we had for the afternoon…I don't know…"

"You know, perhaps you have to ask her," Norma suggested reluctantly. "But if you do confront her, then you're going to have to be prepared to accept that it might go badly and perhaps Nathalie really just doesn't want to be with you."

CHAPTER TEN

Confessions

Josh looked considerably better when they started back at work, although the bruise on his face was now a mixture of blue and yellow.

The first thing they did was ring the personnel manager at the hotel where the mystery suspect may have been seeking work. Over the past three weeks thirty-five people had filled out job applications. Eighteen were men, leaving a list of seventeen women, only ten of whom were within the age range of the mystery woman from the club. The manager faxed copies of those applications.

One name caught Nathalie's eye straightaway—Jacqueline St. Clare.

"I know one of these women," Nathalie stated, looking up from the list. "She's lesbian and she could fit the description we've been given." She didn't mention Jackie's connection to Bella.

"A personal friend?" he asked seriously.

"More of an acquaintance," she answered vaguely. "A friend of a friend."

"Then we'll put her at the top of the list. But we still need to check everyone that fits the age range.

Detailing two more of the team, they split the list and began making phone calls. Nathalie rang Jackie, but the phone went unanswered. Her only address was a post office box. Obviously she was going to have to talk to Bella or let Josh know of the relationship at some point, but as all Jackie had done at this point was apply for a job, she decided not to mention it to Bella just yet.

Over the next two days Nathalie tried continually to get hold of Jackie, even trying Bella's number when she knew Bella would be at work. Other than Jackie, only two other women even vaguely fit the description of the woman seen at the club arguing with Renee Young and Stephanie Cameron. Both denied being anywhere near a lesbian club, but this still had to be investigated.

Nathalie knew that she couldn't postpone telling Josh about Bella's relationship with Jackie much longer. Before that, however, one of the other detectives accidentally spilled the beans to Bella.

As she often did, Bella popped in on Thursday morning to see Nathalie, who was out doing an interview. And also as usual, Bella asked one of the detectives how the investigation was going. Intimidated by her rank, he had updated the strange-looking inspector. Later, when Nathalie returned, Bella took her aside and asked why Jackie's name was on the list of people to be interviewed.

"We're checking all the women who applied for work at a certain hotel," Nat answered, annoyed at being ambushed. "It was a tip we got from someone at the clubs. It just happens that Jackie's name was on the list and she fits the description of someone seen arguing with one of the dead women at the club."

"Well, thanks for telling me," Bella responded sourly. "I thought you were supposed to be a friend."

"I am, Bella," Nathalie answered tiredly, thinking that all she needed was one more person being pissed off with her. "But it would have been irresponsible of me to divulge critical information to the partner of a person of interest. You know that as well as anyone. I haven't told Josh of your connection to Jackie yet. I planned on seeing you today to tell you and get you to come with me to talk to Josh."

"You don't really think Jack's involved, do you?" Bella asked, slumping into a seat near Nat's desk. "Christ, what's her connection to these people anyway?"

"Well, that's what we don't know, Bella," she said. "At the moment the only link we have is that, if it was her, she was seen arguing with Renee Young and Stephanie Cameron, a couple of days before Young was killed. It could be something or nothing. The problem is we haven't been able to get hold of her at either your place or hers. Do you have a mobile number, or know where she's working at the moment?"

"I haven't seen her since Saturday morning," Bella said flatly. "She was supposed to be staying for the weekend, but she changed her mind and went home after lunch. I tried ringing yesterday, both at home and on the mobile," she continued. "I got no answer, but I didn't try her job. To be honest, even I could figure out that the relationship is well on its way out."

"I'm sorry, Bella, but we need to see Josh," Nathalie said reluctantly. "Your connection with her needs to be made official, and it would be better coming from you."

Scowling, Bella followed Nathalie to Josh's office.

Josh wasn't happy. "You should have let me know immediately," he told Nathalie angrily, after she'd finished her explanation. "It could have compromised the investigation."

"Are you accusing me of something, Sergeant?" Bella demanded. "Because I only found out an hour ago that Jackie St. Clare was a person of interest, and it wasn't Nathalie who told me."

"I'm not accusing you of anything, Inspector," he replied evenly. "But Nathalie has known of the relationship between yourself and a person of interest for two days without making it official. A defense lawyer would have a field day with that if we ever had to charge Ms. St. Clare."

"Surely you can't seriously think she killed these people?" exploded Bella.

"That's the whole point, Inspector, at this time we don't have a clue if Ms. St. Clare was even the person at the club and if she was, whether there's any connection between that meeting and the deaths. But suddenly the woman is missing, which only makes it look worse."

"Well, I didn't know you were looking for her until an hour ago, and she's obviously been missing a few days. If you're suggesting the difficulty you're having contacting her is related to the crimes, how would she have known you were looking for her?"

"If that's the reason we can't find her, and we're not saying that it is, perhaps she was warned by someone we've questioned at the clubs," argued Nathalie. "We've probably given her description to a hundred people by now."

Josh took down the work and mobile number that Bella had for Jackie. "I'm going to tell my commander that you discovered we were looking for someone you'd had a *friendship* with and that you made that friendship known immediately," he stated. "Apart from supplying us with a list of anyone you know Ms. St. Clare is friendly with, or any place she might frequent, I must ask you not to visit this office again while this investigation is ongoing. And you will, of course, be given no further information about the case. You can supply the information we need to me directly, and please contact me immediately if Ms. St. Clare makes contact."

Bella looked stunned, but she said nothing as she left the office.

"So, did your inspector friend really only find out about the possibility of St. Clare's involvement an hour ago?" Josh demanded when she'd gone. "Or had you mentioned it to her before this?"

"What do you want me to say?" Nathalie answered, annoyed at his inference. "I'd hardly admit it if I did pass the information to her, so you're going to have to take my word for it that I didn't."

"Yes, I am," he said firmly. "Therefore I'm going to ask you again, officially—Detective Senior Constable Duncan, did you at any time, prior to this afternoon, inform Inspector Bella Pittolo that Jacqueline St. Clare was a person of interest in an investigation?"

"No, I did not," she answered truthfully.

"Good. Then let's get on with the job. I'll go and see the boss now, so that everything is covered. And I'll reallocate investigating St. Clare to Mark and Lorna. I want you right out of that side of it."

As it turned out, Jackie hadn't been at work since the previous Friday, failing to fill two shifts on the weekend and another on Monday. And nobody on the short list that Bella supplied had seen or heard from Jackie all week.

* * *

All day Friday, Nathalie was haunted by the knowledge that Alex would be at the center that night. It wasn't that her thoughts were ever far from her, but today seemed particularly bad.

It was past six o'clock before she left work, and instead of heading to her mother's, which had been the arrangement when she'd left on Monday, she drove slowly to the Courtside Women's Crisis Center. It wasn't a conscious decision—the car just seemed to lead her in that direction.

Parking opposite the entrance and noting that Alex's car wasn't already there, she sat and waited. Fifteen minutes later the charcoal Volvo pulled up on the other side of the road. For a moment or two Alex sat in the car, staring blankly ahead—as if trying to focus on the task in front of her. Then, straightening her hair and reaching for her briefcase, she climbed from the vehicle and made her way inside.

It hurt Nat to watch. Alex was thinner and the energetic bounce that was so much a part of her personality was gone. She'd caused this, and guilt flooded her, while anger at what she'd lost made her want to lash out and hurt someone. If there was one thing she struggled with as a police officer, it was the need of most criminals to blame others for their actions. Right now, though, Nathalie longed to find someone to blame—for Alex's sadness and her own bitter loss. Right now she wanted it to be anyone's fault but her own.

Starting the car as Alex disappeared inside the center, Nathalie drove home. Mother and George could go to hell. If she saw them now, she'd never be able to control her temper. Without doubt, they'd deny any knowledge of the break-in at Alex's and without doubt she wouldn't believe them. Perhaps tomorrow she could deal with the situation better, but right now all Nathalie wanted to do was get totally smashed and sleep for twelve hours.

Mother wasn't at home when she arrived at lunchtime the next day, but George was and he appeared miserable.

"Mother was expecting you last night," he said grimly. "She had a client here."

"I had to work," she lied.

"She made me ring your work," he said hurriedly. "And the house and mobile."

"I was exhausted, I turned them off. But I'm sure she coped."

"Jesus, Nat, you know she'll make you pay for that."

"And how will she do that?" she asked angrily. "By making me have sex with people of her choice or perhaps by telling me once again what a miserable specimen I am? Or will she send someone to wreck Alex Messner's house again?"

By the look on his face, she knew he was involved.

"Was it you, George, you bastard? Did you do that?"

"No," he replied, unable to look her in the eye.

"But you knew about it?"

"Only afterward—she's still convinced Christine passed the journal to someone. She's in a paranoid spin since she found out about you screwing the sister."

"And now—is she satisfied that she doesn't have it?"

"Not really," he answered, shaking his head. "The cards keep telling her that it's close by. She thinks perhaps with Christine Martin's mother," he finished lamely.

"Then you'll have to admit you have it."

"I can't do that" he spluttered, his eyes hardening.

"Can't you, George? I'm not offering you a choice."

"You don't understand," he said angrily. "You don't know what you're playing with."

"Then give her back the fucking diary, so she'll go home. Or go with her…I don't care. But Christine's family is not going to suffer any more because of us, and if I have to tell Mother you have it, then I will."

"Don't threaten me, Nathalie," he growled. "If you knew what was in that journal you wouldn't even suggest dropping me in it."

"Then find a way to ensure that she leaves Alex and her family alone. If one more thing happens to them, I guarantee she'll know exactly who's had the diary all this time."

As she attempted to leave the room, he grabbed her by the top of the arms. "You're choosing this woman and her family over me," he hissed. "I thought you were supposed to love me."

The look in his eyes stopped Nathalie dead. It was a mixture of anger and hurt and something else she couldn't put her finger on. It was a look she'd seen at times in Mother's eyes—an icy coldness that made her shudder.

"I came back here so that Alex would be left alone, but you didn't keep your part of the bargain," she snapped, trying to shrug him off. "Now I have nothing to lose."

"Mother's right," he sneered. "You have no loyalty."

"Is that what she said?" laughed Nathalie bitterly. "Is that why you won't let me see the journal—you don't trust me?"

Letting go of her arms, he said, "I've done what you wanted all along. By next week I won't have any access to the kids, unless it's supervised, and they'll be out of Mother's reach. I thought that would make you happy, but you still want more. What have I got to do to make you love me?"

"I thought you did that for the children," she said, staring at him in disgust. "I thought you wanted them to be safe."

Shaking his head as if to bring himself back to reality, he mumbled, "Yes…you're right. I did do it for them. I don't want to fight with you, Nat," he said almost sadly. "We're family. We have to stick together."

"Then keep Mother's thugs away from Alex Messner and her family. That's all I want, George. You know they don't have the journal, so do whatever it takes to stop anything else happening."

"I'll do it, I promise," he said desperately. "Just don't leave me again, please. I need you."

Nathalie left the room.

"So you decided to grace us with your presence," Mother said coldly when she arrived back at the house an hour later. "This isn't a hotel where you can come and go as you please. You have commitments to this family, you know."

"And I thought we had an understanding that you'd stay away from the Martins if I rejoined the family," she stated evenly.

"What are you talking about?" Mother snorted. "I haven't been near those people."

"But you had Alex's house burgled. Didn't you, Mother?"

Glaring at George, she turned to face Nathalie, "You seem to think I'm some sort of Ma Barker who sends her boys out to break the law. Why would I want to do that? What could that woman possibly have that I'd want?"

"I don't know, Mother," she lied, casting a quick glance at George, who was grim-faced and pale. "But I don't believe it was a coincidence."

"You know what, Nathalie," she replied. "I don't care what you believe. When the cards advise me to take a certain course of action, then that's what I do. But why would you care? Didn't you tell me it was just a fling between you and the Martin bitch?"

"I'm going home, Mother," Nathalie stated as calmly as she could. "We have an agreement. Please don't break it again, or I'll have every government agency I can think of onto you in seconds."

The blow came from behind, knocking her to the ground.

"Don't talk to Mother like that," George screamed down at her. "You are supposed to stay until you go back to work. That's what Mother wants."

"Thank you, George," said Mother, bemused by his attack. "But I don't need you to defend me. I'm sure she'll be able to give us her full attention on her next days off."

George's face was livid, his eyes blazing a strange mixture of fury and pain. This wasn't the boy who'd tried to protect her or the young man who'd covered for her with Mother. This was a frightening stranger on the brink of insanity.

"Get up," he demanded, making no move to help her. "You said you were staying. You're supposed to stay."

The blow had had more shock value than pain, and she was quickly on her feet.

"I won't be back," Nathalie stated emphatically. "If you harm Alex Messner or her family in any way, I'll destroy you by whatever means at hand. Leave me alone and leave them alone and you'll never hear from me again. Don't, and I won't be responsible for what happens."

"You ungrateful little bitch," Mother spat furiously as she moved directly in front of Nathalie. "I gave you a second chance to prove the cards wrong. All you had to do was be part of the family. But you couldn't…you're just like…" Instantly, she stopped herself, fear entering her eyes and turning swiftly to anger.

"Like whom, Mother?" snapped Nathalie, suddenly feeling brave. "Like my father? He scared you, didn't he?" she said, stunned at her own discovery. "I'm like someone who scared you and that's why you've never been able to cope with me. That's it, isn't it, Mother?" she finished, moving closer to the woman who'd terrified her all her life.

Just a hint of the fear remained in the beautiful woman's eyes, an uncertainty Nathalie had never seen before, and it gave her hope. But it was fleeting.

"You have no idea what you're talking about," Charlotte spat, pulling herself to her full height again. "If it wasn't for my generosity you wouldn't even be alive today. If you want to turn your back on this family, I won't stop you, but don't ever try to hold me to ransom again. Now get out."

"What do you mean, I wouldn't be alive today?"

"This discussion's over. I want you to leave my house now."

"No," interrupted George desperately. "It's not your house, Mother. It's mine and I want Nat to stay. We've got a deal," he said, turning to Nat. "You can't leave me again. I won't allow it."

"It's over, George," Nathalie said quietly. "I'm going to tell Alex who I am, so there's nothing else you can do to me. But you know what will happen if the Martin family are hurt in any way."

"What deal are you talking about, George?" spluttered Mother. "Are you betraying me as well…my own son?"

Ignoring his mother, George followed Nathalie as she made her way toward the front door. "But you love me," he said, grabbing her arm and pushing her against the hallway wall. "I had plans for us. We could even get married, bring up the children. We could really be a family."

"Let me go, George," she said, trying to shake free. "You're my brother, for Christ sake. Mother's got you so confused you don't even know how to think like a normal person anymore."

"George. Let her go now," demanded Mother from the doorway. "You're making a fool of yourself."

"You don't understand," he whispered into Nathalie's ear, attempting to ignore his mother. "You're not really my sister. We can love each other. We can marry."

"George!" The voice was close now—strong and desperate. Pushing between them, Charlotte hit George across the face, forcing him to let go of Nathalie. "Have you lost your mind?" she hissed at him. "Listen to yourself. Nathalie doesn't love you. She can't love anyone. It's in her blood. Now leave us."

Close to tears, he turned and strode back into the lounge room.

"What's he talking about?" demanded Nathalie, staring at her mother. "Why is he saying that?"

"Because he'll say anything to get you to stay," she snarled. "The fool thinks he's in love with you. I don't want you having any further contact with him. You don't deserve us and from now on you're on your own."

* * *

On Sunday, Nathalie got several calls where the caller hung up or remained silent when she answered. On each occasion the originating phone was listed as a private number. She assumed it was George. Then at four o'clock, it rang again. This time the silence only lasted a few moments before Alex's voice came on the line. She sounded businesslike but unsure.

"Hi, Nat," she said. "I know you don't want to hear from me, but I need to speak to you."

With a pounding heart, Nathalie asked, "What do you want?"

"I want to meet with you. I want you to tell me you don't love me and that what we had was all a figment of my imagination, because I don't believe it was."

"Alex, don't do this," she replied after a long pause. "This is how it has to be."

"Then tell me why. Tell me the truth."

"I met someone else, a man. I love him."

The silence seemed to go on forever. "I don't believe you," she said eventually. "And I need to see you. I need to be able to watch your face. You owe me that much."

"Yes, I suppose I do," Nat answered dully. "But not today. I can't do it today."

"Then when?"

How long could she put it off? How long before Mother or George told Alex that she was a member of the Silver family? Not long she suspected, given the mood George was in. Sighing, she surrendered. "If you can arrange for your mother to be there, I'll come over now."

"My mother...I don't understand."

"Please, Alex. I need her to be there. I can't do this twice."

By the time she arrived at Alex's house, her head was pounding and it took every ounce of will to force one foot in front of the other to reach Alex's door.

"Come in," Alex requested flatly as they moved into the lounge room.

"I don't want to sit down," Nat replied quickly when offered a seat on the sofa. "I'd rather do this standing up and then leave."

"And I'd rather you sat down," stated Norma Martin bluntly. "I would have thought this was between you and my daughter, but as you've asked me to come, I think the least you can do is take the time to explain yourself properly. Now please, sit down."

Recognizing Norma's protectiveness of her daughter, Nathalie did as requested and moved into one of the lounge chairs.

"So, what is this about?" Norma asked more gently.

They looked so unprepared for the blow she was about to deal them. But there was no easy way. "As you know, my name's Nathalie Duncan," she began, addressing Alex. "But what you don't know is that my mother's name is Charlotte Silver...and my brother is George Silver. Your sister Christine died while she was living with my brother."

Norma looked as if she'd been struck, but Alex looked confused.

"Silver?" she muttered, looking at her mother. "No. That doesn't make sense."

"You're...you're the Nathalie that Christine met at school?" stuttered Norma. "Nathalie Silver?"

"Silver was never my surname...but yes, that is who I am."

"Is this some kind of sick joke?" Norma continued while Alex sat stunned. "Your family destroyed my daughter and now you're sitting in my other daughter's lounge room bragging about who you are."

"I didn't know Alex was Christine's sister," she said, shaking her head. "I had no idea. I really had no idea."

"George Silver," gasped Alex, staring confusedly at Nathalie. "That was George Silver in your flat that night. That's where I knew him from. Why didn't you tell me?"

"I didn't know who you were until I went to your mother's house and saw the photo of Christine. It was the same day George remembered how he knew you. I ended our relationship as soon as I found out." Her voice had tapered to a virtual whisper.

"You have to be making this up," Alex muttered, shaking her head in denial.

"Your family killed my daughter," accused Norma angrily. "She was sweet and innocent and then she stopped going to school, stopped talking to us and stopped coming home. In four years we only saw her half a dozen times…and then she was dead." Her voice was stilted and tearful, and Alex moved closer to her mother.

"It's okay, Mum," she whispered, touching her hand. "We have to get to the bottom of this." Then turning to Nathalie, her face white, her eyes blazing, she said, "I want to know what happened to my sister. Your family shut us out and the police didn't tell us anything. George only gave us back her personal items when Mother turned up demanding them."

"I'll tell you whatever you want to know if I can," she replied flatly, unable to hold Alex's gaze. "But I was away at university when she died. I'm so sorry."

"That's it?" Alex demanded. "You're sorry? You were supposed to be her friend, but you helped her turn her back on *her* family and then *your* family destroyed her life."

"Yes," she muttered miserably.

"Why didn't you stop it…why?"

Alex looked furious. Her mother looked close to tears.

"I don't know what you want me to say," Nat replied quietly. "I didn't think it had anything to do with me. Christine made her

own decisions and back then I didn't think that what we were
doing was so wrong."

"But you knew she was using drugs?"

"We all used drugs."

"But you didn't become an addict, and neither it appears did
your brother," stated Alex evenly.

"No, we didn't."

"Why didn't your mother do anything to stop it?" Norma
asked suddenly. "You were living under her roof. Why would a
mother let that happen?"

"My mother isn't like you," Nathalie answered dully. "She
encouraged us to experiment. That's why young people wanted
to be around her."

"Experiment with drugs?"

Nathalie nodded. "And more."

"Then it should have been her child who died, not mine,"
Norma spat. "Christine should be here in Alex's house, instead
of you. And your mother should have been the one watching her
daughter buried. She should have been charged."

"Mum," interrupted Alex, trying to calm her mother. "We
need to know why this happened, so that we can let Chris rest in
peace." Turning back to Nathalie, she asked, "How did Chris get
caught up in prostitution? Was it for money for drugs?"

Pain coursed through Nat's body and her eyes closed, and for
a brief moment so did her mind. But it was short-lived.

"We read two of her diaries," continued Alex accusingly. "They
were among the personal items George threw into a box when
Mum harassed him. We know all about the sex at your mother's
house and the parties she went to and the fact that it continued
after she and George moved into the flat. But she never wrote
how it started or why she was a part of it."

"Does it matter now? It doesn't change anything," Nathalie
muttered.

"I want to know," gasped Norma. "I want to know why my
little girl would change so much. You said you would tell us
anything we wanted to know, so that's the least you owe us."

It took a minute to focus. But they were right, she did owe
them.

"When I met Chris she was sad," she began. "Her father was dead, she was at a new school and feeling isolated. She was lonely, vulnerable and sexually curious, and that's what we took advantage of." Pausing to gather her thoughts and rub her aching head, Nathalie forced herself to continue. "I think at first our lifestyle seemed fun and exciting, but Christine was decent and her background was decent and in the end it ate her up."

"So why didn't she just come home?" demanded Norma, tears forming in her eyes.

"Because she was ashamed and it was too late, she was in too deep with the drugs and too dependent on the family—especially George. It wasn't her fault. It is how Mother works."

They were staring at her as if she was from another planet.

"You mean she did this to other families…to other kids?" Alex looked exhausted, but her eyes still blazed pure fury.

Nathalie couldn't look. Dropping her eyes and standing up, she mumbled, "I have to go now. I don't expect you to understand, but if I could have died instead of Christine, I would. If I could take back your hurt, I would. I'm sorry."

Norma's voice stopped her in her tracks halfway to the door. "All I hope is that one day you know the pain of having someone you love snatched from your life, so that you can suffer the way Alex and I did."

"Oh, trust me, I already do," she mumbled without turning around.

By the time she'd closed the door behind her and reached the car, Nathalie could barely walk. The journey home seemed to take only moments. Then she was curled on the couch, her mind blank and her emotions numb. Somewhere in the misty distance she could see Good Mother's face and she was crying—reaching out to her with tears in her eyes. Opening her own eyes, Nathalie made the image disappear. There was no Good Mother and this numbness was her reality. The thought brought some measure of comfort.

* * *

At first Alex was worried about her mother. When Christine died, Norma had been eaten up with guilt and recriminations and in the end she'd broken down. That was when Alex had met Dieter. He'd been her mother's counselor and had helped her to understand and deal with her grief. As a result Alex had changed courses at university to study psychology.

This time though, it was different. This time her mother seemed to be the strong one and it was she who was struggling to cope. The conflict of hating Nathalie for what she and her family had done warred with memories of the love they'd shared. But right now bitterness and anger had the upper hand.

Norma stayed the night—both of them feeling the need to talk. And in the morning Alex rang work and was granted two weeks' leave. Nobody questioned it. Nobody doubted that something very serious had been troubling Alex Messner recently.

"I'm sorry this has cost you your relationship," her mother said at breakfast when her daughter finally emerged from the bedroom looking as if she hadn't slept a wink. "I know you love her."

"Some psychologist," Alex stated morosely. "I can't even tell the good guys from the bad anymore."

"It's never that simple, is it?" Norma responded, dropping some toast onto Alex's plate. "When Chris died I wanted so much to find someone to blame, but the one thing I learned from Dieter was that even when you do, it doesn't make the pain go away."

"You sound almost as if you forgive Nathalie for what she and her family did!"

"I suppose I'm confused," Norma answered, sitting down with a coffee in her hand. "In my mind I saw them all as monsters and I still feel that way about the mother, but I look at Nathalie and she's this attractive, intelligent person in a stable job and I wonder, if Christine had lived, would she have worked that hard to move away from her past?"

"We'll never know, will we? Because thanks to Nathalie and her family, Chris never got the chance to have a future, never got the chance to meet someone decent, maybe have a career or kids. And they didn't even go to her funeral—that's how much they cared about her."

For a long time, Norma remained silent.

"I wouldn't let them," she said finally. "Nathalie and George both asked. I refused to let them. I was very angry."

"I didn't know," Alex mumbled. "But I'm glad they weren't there."

Again there was a long silence, while they concentrated on buttering toast and sugaring coffee. Eventually, Alex said, "I feel like such a fool. I knew Nat had terrible secrets in her past, what with the nightmares all the time and the evasiveness when I asked about her family or her childhood. But to find that she was responsible for what happened to Chris—it's too bizarre—too awful. It's like I betrayed Chris somehow."

"Do you believe that Nathalie didn't know you were Christine's sister?"

"God!" she answered, holding her head in her hands. "I really want to, but then I wonder if she didn't break it off because she thought she'd been discovered when George came to the flat unexpectedly. What if being with me was all part of some horrible game? Everything else that family did was hateful and immoral. Who's to say Nat wasn't up to her eyeballs in it?"

"Are you really that bad a judge of character?"

"Obviously I am," Alex finished weakly. "Not that it matters now." She said with a sigh. "It's over and she's gone for good. Now we can forget the Silver family and hope they rot in hell."

Somehow Norma didn't think it was going to be that simple. And her heart ached for her oldest daughter and the pain of her latest loss.

CHAPTER ELEVEN

Piecing It Together

The team had only been at work an hour when they got a call about a body in a Dumpster behind an abandoned warehouse in an outer suburb. When detectives from the local area investigated, they'd found identification in the name of Jacqueline St. Clare. Finding the missing person's warning on the system, they immediately notified Josh.

"We need to get down there and see what they've got," Josh told the team. "If it is St. Clare then we need find out where she's been in the last week and her body may tell us something."

"I can identify her," volunteered Nathalie quietly. "Otherwise you'll only have the description to go on."

Reluctantly Josh agreed.

It took only a minute to identify the body as that of Jacqueline St. Clare. Even though she didn't like the girl, Nat felt a twinge of regret that she'd end up dead in a Dumpster. According to forensics at the scene, Jacqueline had been dead about a week. The cause of death was presumed to be the bullet wound to the chest. Until an autopsy could be carried out, they would know very little else. An anonymous tip to the local police had alerted them to the existence of the body. The call hadn't come through the triple zero emergency line, so there was no recording and the police officer taking the call couldn't tell if the caller was male or female, young or old.

"Do you want to tell Inspector Pittolo about this?" asked Josh after they'd finished talking to the attending detectives. "Uniform will inform the parents, once we find out where they are."

* * *

"Stupid bitch," Bella gasped when Nathalie told her about Jackie. "Stupid, stupid bitch. Why couldn't she just have stayed home and made a go of it with me? Instead she's out picking up some stranger who shoots her."

They were in the coffee room on the fifth floor and the door was shut. Bella looked pale, and her eyes showed a mixture of anger and pain.

"We don't know what happened yet," Nathalie said quietly. "But obviously we believe there's a connection between Jackie's death and the others. Hopefully we'll know more after the autopsy."

"Surely you don't still believe she killed the other three women?"

"We don't know," she answered carefully. "All we know is that she was shot in the chest, which is different to the other three, but at this stage we've got no idea with what."

Bella nodded.

"Bella, did she have anything at your house…you know, personal effects?"

"Not much. Perhaps some toiletries, underwear, that sort of thing. Why?"

"We'll need anything you've got," Nat replied. "The small things are all we have to go on right now. Jackie's flat has been sealed and a search team will be going through it. We desperately need to find something other than the argument in the club, to connect the three…now four…of them."

"Do you still think they could be random lesbian killings?" Bella asked quietly.

"Possibly, but we don't really know."

"Do you want me to take you home?" Nat asked after she'd made Bella a coffee and they'd talked some more.

"No," she replied quickly. "I don't see any point in doing that. There's nothing there for me. I'd rather be around to see if they find out anything new."

It was awkward, but it had to be said. "Bella, Josh isn't going to allow any information that comes out of the investigation to be passed on to you. I'm sorry."

"Why?" she spluttered. "I thought that was because I might pass on information to a suspect? I can hardly do that now."

Without answering, Nathalie reached out and touched Bella's hand.

"Jumped-up little germ," she spat. "Who does he think he is? I outrank him and I should be kept informed."

"He's an acting inspector, Bella," Nathalie reminded her gently. "And if you go over his head, the bosses will know it wasn't just a friendship between you and Jackie. And they still won't give you what you want because you're personally involved."

"But you will, won't you, Nat?" she begged. "She was my girlfriend."

Again Nat shook her head. "Go home, Bella," she suggested. "Take some time off. When you've had a chance to get over the shock, you'll recognize that none of us have a choice. We have to cut you out of the loop. Technically, you could be a suspect. We don't know for sure it's the same murderer."

When she left, Bella insisted on taking her own car, and in a strange way, Nat was relieved. Things had obviously been bad between Bella and Jackie, but she didn't doubt that Bella was upset. Once the initial shock wore off, Bella would need a friend. But right now, Nathalie was barely managing to get through the day herself.

After Bella left, Nathalie made her way to Jacqueline St. Clare's flat, where Josh and Nigel were carrying out a search. It was small and messy and only furnished with the basic necessities, but there were a variety of family photos above the small television and even more in her bedroom. Some were obviously of her parents and siblings, but others appeared to be of grandparents, cousins, uncles and aunts, and it dawned on Nathalie that even though Jackie had lived poorly, she obviously had a lot of family support—a lot of people who would mourn her. Nowhere in the flat was there a photo of Bella.

The search turned up a small amount of marijuana, Jackie's address book and a letter from a credit company demanding immediate payment on an outstanding debt. Pinned to her rusty fridge by magnets were a variety of overdue unpaid bills, including telephone and electricity.

At the end of the day, they'd learned that Jackie was heavily in debt and that those bills that did get paid had been done so on Bella's credit card. Obviously Bella would now have to be interviewed and as Bella outranked Josh, a more senior officer would need to be involved. Bella would not be happy.

By the time she got home, Nat was exhausted, her sense of loss and loneliness enveloping her. Heating a can of baked beans, Nathalie ate in the lounge room, sipping bourbon and Coke and listening to her *Crossing Jordan* CD. It was the first meal she'd eaten all day and although she had to force herself to bother, the warmth of it in her stomach felt good.

She curled onto the lounge, her mind traveling to Alex—to the warmth of her smile, the intelligence and humor in her eyes and to the peace Nat had felt when she was near. She'd experienced nothing like it before, not even with Christine in the early days.

As devastated as she felt, her anguish didn't translate to tears. Instead it coldly highlighted the worthlessness of her life. While George had produced two beautiful children, who, if left alone by Mother, might just go on to live normal, ordinary lives, she had done nothing—produced nothing of any worth or value to anyone. That thought left her bitter and despairing.

How tempting to go to sleep and never wake up.

At some point while she lay staring blankly into the distance, Nathalie fell asleep.

* * *

The voice was loud and accusing but the words seemed meaningless. Then she was being lifted and held by her throat, and she knew she was very small, but still she struggled. It was so hard to breathe, and Mother's face was so close, so vicious and angry. And still she couldn't understand the words.

Then she was on the floor and the floor was slippery with blood. She tried to scramble away, but slithered instead in the gory mess as the voice continued to ramble and rant. That was why she couldn't understand the words—they were angry and garbled. The smell of blood was everywhere. Then suddenly she was having her clothes ripped from her body and someone was kissing her face, holding her close—sobbing. And she was even more frightened.

"I loved her," the voice was repeating in words she understood. "I loved her, but she was going to betray me again, so I had to do it. But I have you and you're part of her, so I'll let you live. But you must do everything I say…you must never tell…you must never betray me."

It was Mother's voice and her grip was painful and cold.

Then she was in a forest, naked, cold, dirty and very scared, but the smell of the damp earth was better than the smell of blood. Still the fear remained. There was Bad Mother's voice and pain—so much pain—and her own voice, childlike and small, screaming and begging, and the overwhelming horror of it all.

The screaming woke her—her own voice, adult and large, and the pain and terror, and her breathing in desperate, lung-bursting gasps, her arms protecting her face. Even with her eyes open and the lights blazing, the terror remained, causing her to bring her knees to her chest, the sofa cushion clutched protectively in front of her. "Oh God, Oh God," she gasped aloud. "Please make it stop."

* * *

The rest of the week went quickly as the investigation plodded on. Bella had taken time off work and Nathalie contacted her daily by phone. Outwardly Bella appeared untroubled by her lover's death, but then she'd never have shown it if she'd been devastated.

In Jackie's address book they found Renee Young's phone number and address and it was then that Nathalie remembered that they'd never found any kind of organizer, address book or contact list among Renee Young's personal effects or in her home.

"That's very strange," she commented to the team at the next morning's meeting. "I don't know of anybody who doesn't keep some kind of record of people's phone numbers and addresses, even if it's only in an old notebook. She didn't have any addresses on her computer, and her mobile lists only phone numbers, but no addresses."

"So what are you thinking?" asked Josh seriously.

"What if the killer knew Renee Young, but the other victims were drawn from her address book? After all, we found Young's address and her phone number in Cameron and Djanski's address book and Young's in St. Clare's. So it stands to reason that both of them would have been in Young's as well."

"Random lesbian killings taken from one woman's address book?" replied Josh thoughtfully. "That could make sense. If we can find the address book, we might find the killer."

* * *

On Friday night, Nathalie had a meal with Josh and Grace. She didn't feel like it and didn't stay long, but she liked Grace and knew that Josh was worried about her.

The meal was delicious and Grace was funny and warm and obviously just as concerned as Josh, but even so, Nathalie was struggling. Watching them together and feeling the love between them only made her feel even more isolated and alone. She would have loved a hit of something to make her feel better, but in the end she decided to stop at the Liquor Barn instead.

* * *

Saturday was bright and sunny and Alex was lunching with the boys. The break from work gave her time to spend in her garden and spring clean the house and when that was done she'd started on her mother's house and garden, until eventually Norma had told her to find somewhere else to channel her energies. In the end she spent more time at the center, making sure she avoided Wednesday.

On Friday, Alex had got the news that one of the clients she'd seen quite regularly had committed suicide. She felt a huge sense of responsibility. That night, instead of heading straight home, she drove around aimlessly. Twice she passed Nathalie's apartment block, slowing to look up at her window. How she longed to be with her. But Nathalie's past had killed her sister and she couldn't forgive that—especially the pain it had caused her mother. So she kept on driving, wishing deeply that she'd never met Nathalie Duncan.

Alex told Michael and James that she'd seen Nathalie.

Assuming that Nathalie would have told Alex she was seeing someone else, Michael was stunned to find out she'd told her the truth.

"Why didn't you tell us about your sister?" James had asked gently. "About the circumstances?"

Shrugging, she said, "Her death and Mum's breakdown had such an impact that I didn't want to dredge it up again."

"So Christine lived with Nathalie's brother," James stated. "But was Nathalie there when she died?"

"She claims she was at university, but she admits she introduced Chris into the family…was Chris's lover." Alex hesitated for a moment, looking down at her hands. Then looking up. "They let her become a drug addict and then kept her isolated from us."

"But surely your sister made her own decisions?" Michael stated quietly. "After all, she was nearly nineteen when she died."

James looked puzzled but remained quiet.

"Why are you defending them?" asked Alex, annoyed. "She wasn't even fifteen when they seduced her into their awful way of life."

"Do you think Nathalie knew who you were when you got involved?" James asked, trying to deflect Alex's ire.

"My mother asked the same thing," she admitted. It was a question she'd asked herself a hundred times since, but even now she wasn't sure what she thought. In the end, her anger answered.

"Given her family's moral values it wouldn't surprise me if she did know," she said quietly. "Maybe she thought it would be fun to seduce Christine Martin's sister."

Irrationally, Michael felt the need to continue defending Nathalie. "You know, Alex," he said slowly, "it was you who chased Nat, not the other way around. And you didn't know who she was, so how would she know you? Did she seem like she was gloating when she told you why she'd finished it with you?"

Irritation and confusion showed on her face

"Well, did she?" he persisted quietly.

"Michael, for heaven's sake…" stated James, "What are you doing?"

"No, James," he retorted, raising his hand. "It's important Alex ask herself these questions, because it seems she's trying to talk herself into hating Nathalie—blaming her for things way beyond her control."

"Thanks for the support, Michael," mumbled Alex, stung by his words.

He was getting in too deep, but it had to be said. "It's just that you said that at fifteen your sister didn't understand what she was getting into, but wasn't Nathalie also only fourteen or fifteen at the time?"

"So?" she asked, shaking her head.

"Well, we know Nathalie didn't have the stable, supportive upbringing that Christine had."

"What does that mean?"

"I guess it means that while your sister may have been lured into that lifestyle, she had alternatives. What you have to ask yourself is how much choice Nathalie Duncan had about anything in her life at that time."

They were looking at him as if he were an alien.

"I'm sorry, Alex," he continued, unable to stop. "I'm not used to you being so judgmental, and it saddens me to see you this way—especially about someone I know you love."

"Loved," she murmured irritably. "All I feel now is disgust and regret that I ever met her."

"Do you feel that way about your sister as well?"

"What the hell is that supposed to mean?" interjected James angrily.

Without looking at him and directing his conversation to Alex, he said, "It's just that Christine stayed with Nat's family for more than four years, so the presumption has to be that she did the same things—the drugs, the sex, the parties. For all you know, maybe your sister did what Nat did and recruited others into the family."

"How dare you? You have no idea what my sister was like," Alex spat angrily, rising to her feet. "Even Nathalie admitted Chris was decent. Why are you taking her side?"

"Yes, why would you?" snapped James, rising to stand beside Alex. "You know nothing about what happened in that family, except what Alex has told us, and you hardly know Nathalie Duncan. What's going on?"

Michael was trapped by his own words. "I know how it sounds," he mumbled anxiously, "but thing are rarely as black and white as they seem. Someone has to play devil's advocate."

It was weak, and the look in James's eyes told him he had a lot of explaining to do.

"I don't understand what you want from me," Alex said quietly when James had renewed their drinks. "Do you think I should just forget the role Nathalie and her family played in my sister's death?"

"Alex, I'm sorry," he began, glancing at James, who glared back. "I'm just worried that you're reacting how you think you should, how you think your mother would expect you to. Rather than how you actually feel." Sighing, he continued. "You're my friend and I love you, but I think you're making a mistake."

For the longest time she looked at him with a mixture of hurt and suspicion.

"It must be time to drop in on Trish and Jenny," James declared, breaking the uncomfortable silence. "They're expecting us for afternoon tea."

"Let's do it," replied Alex pointedly. "Suddenly I feel like a change of scene."

They didn't get home until after ten. The visit with Trish and Jenny had been a success and the tension had eased gradually, but Alex had remained cool toward Michael, and Michael felt awkward and disloyal. Later they dropped her home, before continuing the drive in silence.

"You've hardly spoken to me all afternoon," Michael said finally as he and James sat with a joint and a cappuccino. "Are you still mad about what I said to Alex?"

"I guess I'm waiting for you to explain," James replied caustically.

"Explain what?"

"Well, for starters, why you suddenly appointed yourself Nathalie Duncan's advocate? But even more importantly, how you knew what age Christine Martin was when she died?"

"Alex must have mentioned it at some time," he replied with a racing heart and dry throat.

"No, Michael," James stated, shaking his head, his eyes never leaving his lover's face. "That's not true and you know it."

A wave of anxiety rolled over Michael. He'd never lied to James nor cheated on him, now he felt like he'd done both and was about to be found out. "Oh God, James, it's so complicated," he muttered with a sigh. "So hard to explain."

"But you're going to try, right? After all, we've got all night."

* * *

On Saturday, Nathalie rose late, sporting a bad hangover. The nightmares had returned to the way they'd always been and it was almost a relief. At least they related to something tangible in her life, whereas the more recent ones were full of pain and terror and emotions that belonged to someone else.

After a hot shower, toast and lots of coffee, she went rummaging among her personal papers until she found the crumpled copy of her birth certificate that Mother first had given her when she'd applied for her driver's license. Since then it had been used for numerous purposes.

The document was registered in Sydney, Australia, stamped and witnessed and appeared to be genuine. Certainly the passport office thought so, because they'd issued her a passport. But if it was genuine, what did George mean when he said she wasn't his sister?

George definitely wasn't adopted. He looked too much like Mother, whereas she and Mother didn't bear the slightest resemblance. She'd always explained that by her mixed race. Now suddenly this lack of resemblance took on huge significance. It wasn't that she believed George. In his present fixated state he'd say anything to get her to stay, but why didn't she have any memory of her early childhood and of the beatings George said Mother gave her?

It was time to find some answers.

The birth certificate listed Charlotte Silver as her mother and Abraham Duncan, birthplace New Orleans, as her father. It was dated the same week she was born. According to the birth certificate, Charlotte had been eighteen and Abraham Duncan twenty-six at the time of her birth. Her obvious first step would be to check the authenticity of the birth certificate with the Registrar of Birth, Deaths and Marriages on Monday—her additional day off.

In the meantime she needed to talk to George, but after all that had happened, she could hardly ring the house.

In the end Nathalie rented a car that wouldn't be recognized and parked near the house. Nobody came or went during Saturday evening, and both cars remained in the open garage. By ten o'clock she figured they weren't going anywhere and returned home to bed.

Sunday was another bright, sunny day, but it didn't make Nathalie feel any better. The ache of missing Alex hadn't decreased and neither had the effort it took just to get through a day. Constantly she'd find herself drifting into memories of Alex's warm, gentle smile or her quick, open laugh. Then she'd remember how it felt to be in her arms, the smell of her skin and the feeling of safety when Alex held her after one of the nightmares.

With these thoughts came burning anger that fate would allow her to fall in love with Christine Martin's sister. Perhaps this was God's idea of perfect revenge? Then she would force these emotions away, an act of sheer will practiced over a lifetime of burying feelings that served no purpose. You did what you had to and moved on. That was all there was.

It wasn't until nearly lunchtime on Sunday that anyone emerged from the house and then it was George's girlfriend, Belinda. Driving George's car, the young girl took off down the road. Nathalie followed.

When Belinda alighted at the shopping mall, Nathalie approached her.

"What are you doing here?" she asked nervously, looking like a startled deer.

"I want to see George, but I can't ring the house, so I want you to give him a message."

"He was very upset when you left and so was your mother," she accused. "She yelled at him a lot for something he said to you. Maybe it's better if you don't have contact."

"I'm his sister, Belinda," she argued. "How can we not have contact?"

"And she's your mother, but you don't seem to care for her much."

"Will you give him the message?" she said, ignoring the girl's comment. "I need the chance to talk to him again, to sort out our differences."

Reluctantly she nodded. "But you must never tell your mother. She frightens me."

"With good reason" were the words that flashed through Nat's mind as she walked away.

On Monday, Nathalie went to the Registrar of Births, Deaths and Marriages with her passport, driver's license and police identification card to apply for a copy of her birth certificate. But there was no record of the birth. Nor was there a record of George Malcolm Silver. She could only conclude that someone in the Passport Office had been paid by Mother to issue Australian passports to her and George.

It would make sense, if she were illegally adopted, that Mother would lie about where *she* was born, but why would she lie about George's birth? The physical resemblance was too extraordinary for him to be anything but her biological son, so why the false documentation? And where did she go from here? Confront Mother? The thought invoked a dark terror that made her shudder.

Perhaps George would finally tell her what he knew and it would be enough to continue her own investigation without Mother knowing. Silently she hoped he'd contact her.

* * *

Later that afternoon, Bella rang and invited her for dinner. It was hard to refuse. The woman had lost her lover in a terrible way and she'd made no effort to offer comfort other than by phone.

Bella looked awful and Nathalie suspected she'd been drinking heavily. The house was a mess, with leftover pizza and other takeaway cartons littering the kitchen and dining area, rubbish overflowing the bin and dishes piled in the sink.

"I thought we'd just order out," Bella said when she arrived. "I can't be bothered cooking. Hope you don't mind."

Nat didn't. Her appetite had decreased considerably since the split with Alex, and it took a conscious effort to bother eating at all.

"So, how are you coping?" she asked after Bella poured them both a drink and placed a CD of seventies' music into her ancient stereo.

"Fine," she replied with a shrug. "I'm not going to get my knickers in a twist about someone who didn't love me and was cheating on me at every turn."

The bitterness took Nathalie by surprise. "You don't know that for sure," she told her. "Just because she was going to the clubs didn't mean she was having an affair."

"Well, it doesn't matter now anyway. If she was cheating, then she paid a heavy price, and if she wasn't, then it was probably only due to lack of opportunity."

"Do you miss her?" Nathalie asked, thinking about the pain of losing Alex.

Sighing heavily and finishing the remains of her drink, Bella mumbled, "I'm pretty used to being on my own, even when I'm in a relationship. And I don't think you'll argue that Jackie and I were hardly suited. I can't think of one meaningful conversation we ever had. Mostly we just argued."

"That didn't answer the question."

"You're letting the lawyer in you take over," Bella muttered, glaring. Then shaking her head, "Yes, I miss her, but I knew that one way or the other she was going to leave me."

"I'm sorry, Bella…that it had to happen that way."

"But are you any closer to finding out who's behind these killings?" she asked flatly. Then raising a hand palm outward, she indicated for Nathalie not to answer. "I know," she stated. "You can't talk about it."

For some time they continued to drink. Nathalie asked about Bella's immediate plans. Surprisingly, Bella indicated that she was considering leaving the police.

"Why?" asked Nat, stunned. "You're such a career person and you love the job."

"Do I, Nat? Sometimes I wonder if I don't cling to the job because there's nothing else in my life. Anyway, I haven't made up my mind yet. I'll see how things go over the next few weeks, but what about you? Now that you've experienced being with a woman and didn't like it, what are you going to do?"

The look on Nathalie's face told Bella she'd struck a nerve.

"God, Nat, you're still in love with Alex, aren't you?" she uttered in genuine surprise.

Nathalie made no comment.

"Then why the hell did you split up?" Bella asked after a moment.

"Circumstances," Nathalie answered evasively.

Again there was silence as Bella looked at her questioningly.

"Things that couldn't be overcome," she offered in further explanation. "Stuff neither of us could ignore. It was complicated."

"And how does she feel about the breakup?"

"Relieved, I imagine. I'm not her favorite person." Then feeling guilty that she was shutting Bella out, Nat added, "I can't explain, Bella. I'm sorry, but I just can't."

"That's okay," she shrugged. "Ultimately the reasons don't change anything. It's still over and the only thing to do is pick up and start again. Problem is it gets harder each time. Sometimes I wonder why I even bother."

Later, Nathalie told Bella what she'd discovered about her and George's birth certificates, explaining only that it had started because of an argument and George's comment that she wasn't really his sister. The revelation came from a need to talk about this huge discovery in her life.

"So what are you going to do now?" Bella asked, guessing that there was more to the story.

"I'm going to see what else my brother knows. Assuming he'll contact me. We didn't part on the best of terms."

"I take it you don't get on with your mother and brother?"

"It's—"

"Complicated?" interrupted Bella with a grin.

"Very," she answered with a nod of her head. Then relenting, she said, "I love George because he looked after me when we were small and things weren't good. We were very close then… because we only had each other. And I guess Charlotte's the only mother I've got, so I should love her, but it's always seemed to me that she couldn't stand the sight of me."

"Why would you think that?"

"I believe you always know when someone doesn't like you, even when they're trying really hard not to show it. And believe me, Mother never made too much effort to hide her feelings, especially when we were alone."

"Surely if it were true, there'd be a reason?"

"I often thought it was because I was mixed race," Nathalie admitted quietly, taking another swig of her drink. It was the first time she'd ever articulated it, even to herself, and it hurt badly. "Mother and George are so stunning looking and I'm like the ugly duckling—the ugly *brown* duckling."

"Jesus, Nat. That's a big call. Your mother obviously slept with a black guy, so why would she dislike you because of it? And if the birth certificate is a forgery and she adopted or fostered you, then she could hardly have failed to notice you weren't white before making that decision."

"I don't know." Nat shrugged. "Sometimes when I was growing up I felt like I'd come from another dimension. I didn't look like George or Mother, I didn't think like them and they didn't seem to understand me. I'd see people looking at me and wondering what race I was, and I didn't even have the solace of being secure in my own identity."

"Did you ever ask your mother about all of this?"

"Many times when I was younger, but all it ever got me was more punishment."

"What sort of punishment?" Bella asked suspiciously.

Nathalie didn't answer. Instead, her eyes were focused into the distance, filled with memories and a terrible sadness that even the insensitive Bella could recognize.

"Why don't you let me investigate for you?" Bella said suddenly. "I've got plenty of spare time at work, and because my team is reviewing historical cases, I've got access to interdepartmental and interstate computers and archives and I have a liaison in Interpol. I can access immigration records and try and track down when your father entered Australia and what address he gave when he departed. If that doesn't work, I'll try to track your mother. Once I've established where they lived around the time of your birth or George's, we might be able to track your original birth certificates."

Nathalie was staring at her with a mixture of concern and hope.

"Come on, Nat. It could take you years to track down that information through normal channels, especially if your mother doesn't part with any information."

"And you could get the sack for accessing those computers unlawfully," she said, shaking her head. "It's not worth it."

"For God's sake, Nat," she said, bouncing up from her seat. "They'd have no reason to audit my use of the computers. Nobody's interested in all these old files, so long as they get written off. And if necessary I'll create a fictitious file to cover myself. Please let me do this. At least I'd be doing something interesting and useful."

Her friend's enthusiasm was catching. It was the most animated Nathalie had seen Bella since before Jackie's death. Bella was right, if her mother didn't tell her about her father or why her birth certificate was a forgery, it could take years to track down who she really was or where she was born, assuming she managed it at all.

"Okay," she said tentatively. "But only if I can't get anywhere with George or Mother and if you still want to do it when you're sober."

Within minutes, Bella's demeanor had changed from depressed futility to excitement. At least this was giving her something to distract her from Jackie and her loss.

Meanwhile Nathalie prayed that George would make the effort to contact her soon.

* * *

The conversation with Michael had occupied Alex's mind all the following day. Nothing about it was right. She arranged for them to meet.

Michael had had no choice but to tell James the truth. James had known from the moment Michael defended Nathalie that he was hiding something, and he wouldn't let it go. The friendship with Alex might depend on it, and their relationship certainly did.

"It's your past, Michael," he'd said gently after hearing it all. "You were a kid. Most of us have done worse. Now you have to tell Alex why you said what you did. She needs our friendship and can't be left thinking that you're blindly taking Nathalie's side."

"So you're telling me you knew about Nathalie but didn't think to tell me?" Alex murmured angrily when he'd finished explaining.

"Yes," he replied guiltily. "But it was the past and I'd never told James about that period of my life, so I saw no reason to tell you. I had no idea of your connection to the family."

"Did you know Christine?"

"Yes…but only for a few months before she died."

"All these years I've known you," she whispered, tears welling. "And I had no idea you were there…with that family. Were you there when Chris died?"

"No," he replied sadly. "I wasn't at the flat, George told me about it later."

The look on Alex's face tore at Michael's heart.

"And was Nathalie there…at the flat?"

"No, she wasn't. She was away at university. I didn't meet her until after Christine's death. George talked about her a lot. He was like a puppy waiting for her to come home. It was obvious he worshipped her…but not always in a good way."

"What does that mean?"

"It doesn't matter," he replied quietly, looking toward James for support.

But James shook his head. "You have to tell her everything," he said strongly. "No more secrets."

"God," he murmured. "This is so hard." But James was right. It had to be told.

"George and Nathalie grew up in an abusive and incestuous home," he began quietly. "Charlotte Silver and her partners slept with them both from when they were small children, and they were forced to *sleep* with each other for the entertainment of wealthy customers. For a price these customers could do whatever they wanted with them." Sighing deeply, he continued slowly. "They grew up believing this was normal family life. Later, as teenagers, they were sent out to seduce other teenagers into the family—the younger the better, but age didn't really matter so long as they looked young. Charlotte Silver is pure evil."

Her face white, her eyes a mixture of shock, anger and sorrow, Alex whispered almost to herself, "Chris looked much younger than she was."

For some moments nobody spoke.

"George just told you all this?" she asked eventually.

"Not all at once. I lived with them for nearly two years and was George's *special* friend. The story dribbled out over time, usually when George was depressed and seriously stoned. He obsessed about Nathalie and how much he missed her and how things were when she lived there. I doubt he even remembered what he said."

"How old were they?" she eventually asked. Then when he looked puzzled, "When she first did this to them?" she continued.

"I don't really know, Alex," he replied gently. "But I gather about six or eight…"

"I think we all need another drink," interrupted James suddenly, rising from the sofa, obviously upset.

"So was Christine involved in this…in recruiting other kids? Were you?" Alex continued. She needed to know everything.

"Yes." It was barely audible.

More silence.

"How many kids were at the house at any one time? How old were they?"

"Most of us were recruited at about fourteen or fifteen, but only a couple of us stayed at the house at any one time. Charlotte called us her favorites. The others would stay in apartments or houses that she owned."

"Was Christine involved in recruiting you?"

"Alex…"

"Was she?" she demanded.

"George recruited me, but they were both—"

Her hand was up, indicating for him to stop. And Alex was stepping out onto the balcony drawing in deep gasps of fresh air.

When James returned, Michael took his drink gratefully, swallowing it in one swift movement. He was going to follow Alex outside, but James indicated for him to stay. "She needs a few minutes," he said quietly. "It's a lot for her to take in."

It seemed like hours before Alex returned, but it was only ten minutes. Taking the drink offered by James, she also swallowed rapidly, holding out the glass for a refill and dropping back into the seat she'd occupied.

"Why did you stay? I'm trying to figure out why Christine would want that life?"

"Charlotte targeted troubled or lonely kids—"

"Christine wasn't troubled," she interrupted, cutting him off.

"Perhaps you just weren't aware of it," he answered kindly. "Didn't you say you'd lost your father and moved from your home not long before? Your mother worked and you were at university…"

Alex didn't respond.

"I didn't get on with my father," he continued. "He was a typical old-style Greek male. I wasn't tough enough for him, and on top of that I was confused about my sexuality. I'd run away from home and was ripe to be recruited."

"That doesn't explain why you stayed."

"We were in young person's heaven, Alex. Charlotte supplied a place with few rules, no school unless we wanted to go, parties and sex, drugs and alcohol. We even had cars we could use and money in our pockets. She was stunningly beautiful and knew the psychology of kids. She made you feel special, loved, understood—until she had total control of you. Then if for any reason you rebelled she would use the psychology of fear. And she was even better at that."

"You were a runaway, but Christine wasn't."

"You have no idea the power that woman had over all of us. Those who wanted out and didn't conform just seemed to disappear. As an adult I realize that they probably just ran away, but she would let us believe that something more sinister had happened and enforce that if we didn't participate, it could happen to us too. Worse, she'd find your weak spot, the person or thing you really cared about and threaten that or she'd know your needs and ensure they were always met. Nothing was overt. It was all psychological warfare and the occult."

"The occult?" asked James.

"Tarot cards, crystal balls, strange potions. She used superstition and fear to maintain total control. And of course there was George. Those kids that weren't in love with Charlotte were in love with him. Perhaps Christine was too."

They talked into the evening about Michael's life with the Silvers and his struggles to adapt to the real world after he left. Alex asked numerous questions. From these she realized that when an individual was in favor, Charlotte could be very generous, paying for nights at exclusive hotels, name-brand clothing, tickets and backstage access to concerts and sporting events—everything teenagers loved but couldn't afford. The kids also had the camaraderie and support of each other through their shared experiences and secrecy—a cult-like family environment. It was obvious to her that everything Charlotte did was designed to keep the kids emotionally immature and under control—a fairytale world with lots of adult fun and no responsibilities, except the sexual ones.

Alex didn't know if any of this changed how she felt about Nathalie. Intellectually she knew that Nathalie and George were even more the victims of Charlotte Silver than Christine or any of the other kids who were recruited. Yet the Nathalie she knew was intelligent, educated and independent. Her mind didn't want to equate that person to the abused and brainwashed young child. If she did that, then she'd have to look elsewhere for someone to blame for Christine's death.

* * *

The detectives on the task force had rung everyone in Jacqueline St. Clare's address book. They'd spoken to her parents and found the connection between St. Clare and Young. It dated back to high school when the two girls were in the same class. The source, a cousin of the same age, told them it was obvious St. Clare worshipped the more sophisticated and openly lesbian Young. She knew it hadn't been reciprocated, but she didn't know if they'd kept in touch.

"So we have to presume they did meet up again," said Josh, adding this information to the board. "And that St. Clare was definitely in Young's phone book. It gives us a connection between all the victims and reinforces the importance of Young's missing address book."

At the very least it opened new avenues of inquiry.

* * *

Through everything that had happened Nathalie continued her sessions with Dieter, the psychologist. Although he was friends with Alex, Nathalie trusted him and found she could be honest about her childhood and family life. There was no mention of Alex or what had happened to her sister. Dieter asked questions but made no judgments. Instead, he forced her to delve and question and confront her own feelings and memories, both about the actualities of her life in the Silver household and her nightmares.

"At our next appointment," he told her during session three, "we'll explore whatever it is that's happening in your life at the moment that's disturbing you so much."

"No, that's got nothing to—"

Putting his hand up to stop her objection, he continued, "I need to know about it...because it's greatly affecting the judgments you're making about yourself. There's a marked difference between our first session and the last two."

"I'm not here for that, Dieter," she insisted. "I want to know about the nightmares and lost memories."

"It's a process, Nathalie," he said gently. "And when you're ready, I'll look at hypnosis as an option, but I don't believe you're ready, and whatever is going on right now is going to interfere with that process."

How close she'd come to not continuing. Yet she needed to talk, and ultimately she wanted to know her own secrets—wanted to understand why going to sleep was so painful and dangerous.

* * *

A week after Nathalie had seen Belinda, George rang. "I thought you'd finished with us," he stated coldly without introduction.

"I want to know what you meant when you said you weren't my brother."

"Then you'll have to meet me." His voice was cold and flat, but she could feel the tension.

They met at a club, taking seats in a quiet corner away from everyone. George's handsome face looked tired, his eyes betraying his fragile emotional state. She'd never seen George anything but immaculately groomed, now his clothing looked less than perfect and there was just a trace of stubble on his chin.

"So, talk to me, George," Nathalie said, sipping bourbon. "What did you mean about me not being your sister?"

"Mother's very angry," he stated, ignoring her question. "The cards are telling her that she's being betrayed by someone close, that she'll be forced to defend herself."

"So what else is new? Isn't that the supposed reason she came back here?" asked Nathalie impatiently. "If it wasn't the persecution delusion, it would be some other event that the cards predict. But I don't care. I want to read Mother's journal."

"I'm scared of her, Nat. Really scared."

"Our birth certificates are forged."

There was no surprise in his eyes, no questions, just a calm acceptance.

"You knew?" she accused.

"I think we were both born in America," he answered quietly. "I remember leaving what I think was the US a while before you started school."

"Why do you think this?"

"I have memories of being in California, I think. Then we traveled on a plane, I believe to the UK. Then we came here a bit later and moved into the old house. And for a long time Mother never let anyone come to the house. But I didn't know why then."

"And you do now?"

"It's in the journal."

"Have you brought the journal with you?" She knew he hadn't, unless it was in his car.

"I'll tell you about some of it," he said quietly. "But it's too dangerous. If Mother was sure you'd read it, she might…"

"Might what?" Nat asked when he trailed off into silence.

"Nat, she's so much worse than…maybe it's not true, but the things she says she's done…" He was rambling and pale, his eyes darting around the room as if expecting Mother to walk in at any moment. Then he'd focus back on her and try again. "The journal's hidden," he declared, watching her face. "But I know you're not my sister. She kept you after your mother died. That's why she left America and went into hiding in that terrible house we grew up in."

"What…what do you mean she kept me?" Shaking her head, she said, "George, you have to show me this journal. Does it say that in there? Are you saying she's definitely not my mother?"

"Yes," he muttered.

Disbelief, relief, confusion, bitterness all fought for priority. "Is she yours…your mother?"

Nodding yes, he added, "I think she might have been your mother's friend. The journal says she loved someone, it rambles a bit, but I presume it was your father. So she kept you after…when your mother died."

"Why? Where was my father, why didn't he look after me and why would she leave the country?"

"He was also dead. Sometimes the journal is hard to understand; it's like she was having a breakdown. Also a lot of what she refers to obviously happened before she started writing this particular journal."

"Then I have to read it!"

"Never, Nat—you can't ever read it, ever. I'll destroy it first."

"Why?"

"Because she's my mother and it's my job to protect her…and to protect you."

"Protect her from what? You just finished saying you were afraid of her."

He wouldn't answer, and she wanted to hurt him—somehow force him to tell her. But it wouldn't work. Nothing scared him more than Charlotte Silver—except perhaps losing Charlotte Silver.

"Then tell me what you know about me, George. I want to know who I am—who my mother was? Suddenly I'm not Nathalie Duncan, you're not my brother and Charlotte isn't my mother. I know who I'm not, but I need to know who I am."

"The journal doesn't really say," he conceded. "A lot of it is her feelings about people…things."

"Why did she leave America?"

"I think she was running away. I don't think she was supposed to take you out of the country. She called this person…I assume your father…the love of her life."

"Was he her lover?"

"I don't know. Sometimes it sounds like it, other times not."

"Did she mention either of their names?"

"Olivia was your mother."

"Olivia," she repeated quietly as if trying to invoke her presence. Sadness and a sense of overwhelming loss flooded her, making it difficult to focus. But she showed none of it.

"Mother only ever referred to him by his surname—Duncan." George continued with a shake of his head. "There were rambling declarations of love and jealousy, followed by anger and bitterness. A lot of it didn't make sense."

"Where did we live in America? Did she mention that?" It was obvious there was so much he wasn't telling her.

"No, but she did mention London—things that happened in London."

"So, couldn't we have come from England instead of America?" she asked desperately. "If you remember flying here, it could have been from England?"

"Maybe," he answered carelessly as if bored with the subject. "But I don't think so. It's good though, isn't it?"

"What is?" she replied, trying to keep up with him.

"That we're not brother and sister?"

"God, George—"

"It means we weren't doing anything wrong all these years," he offered eagerly.

Shaking her head, she tried again. "If you won't let me read the journal and won't tell me what I need to know, then I'll have to confront Mother," she responded angrily. "I have to know who I am…who my parents were, and I don't have time to play mind games with you."

"I'm trying to help you," he whispered aggressively. "But you don't seem very grateful. Mother always said you were ungrateful and she's right."

"So remind me, George—what is it I should be grateful for again?"

"She saved you," he said defensively. "She said so in the journal and she brought you up as her daughter."

"Saved me from what?"

"I don't know," he admitted sullenly. "She doesn't say."

"What does she say?"

"That she was risking everything to save you and keep you with her."

"This is useless," snapped Nathalie, getting more frustrated by the minute. "I need to read the journal for myself. All of it."

"I can't let you, Nathalie," he said, standing. "You'd take it to the police and we'd all be finished. And nobody would understand. While she doesn't know where it is we're all safe, that's the way it is. I'm protecting you, so don't make me out to be the bad one here."

"Don't you want to know who you are?" she asked, trying to keep him talking. "Your name's not George Silver. What if she's not your mother either?"

"Jesus, Nat, I know I'm not as bright as you, but even I can see how much I look like Mother and how she treated me so much better than you."

"Better! She abused us both and worse, let everyone else do it as well. She's a monster."

"I'm...I've got to go," he finished. "It's just better that you don't know what was in the journal. Christine read it and...and then she died."

"What does that mean," she demanded, following him to the car park.

"She's after you, Nat," he mumbled, turning and pulling her toward him. "She's scared of you, and I'm scared for you, but with the journal I can make her leave you alone. I'm going to tell her I've got it and that it will end up in the hands of the police if anything happens to you or me. I'll try to protect you."

Without another word, George stepped into his car and slamming the door, pulled onto the street.

* * *

It didn't matter how hard she tried, Alex couldn't get Nathalie out of her mind. She took her mother away for a week to the South Coast, and they walked and talked and visited old churches and plant nurseries, but the ghost of Nathalie was as constant as that of her sister.

"I just don't understand it," she divulged to her mother one evening after a quiet meal and plentiful wine. "I want to be with her so much, I want to talk to her and find out what was happening during those years...what she's thinking now. I want her to tell me that she was beaten and forced to do what she did, so that I can find a reason to forgive her. But why do I even care?"

"Only you can answer that," Norma replied quietly. "If you weren't emotionally involved and this was a scenario a patient came to you with, what would you suggest?"

"Talking to her, I suppose…or leaving the country. God, Mum," she confessed after a moment's silence, "I've tried to be detached and think about it logically, but I'm all over the place. I want Chris's death to be someone else's fault because it stops me thinking that there was something I could have done. Then I revert to not having a clue how I feel."

"You know, for a long time I blamed myself for Chris leaving home," Norma stated in a small, flat voice. "And I still think I could have paid her more attention. I know she was devastated by her father's death and me returning to work. I know she hated leaving the old neighborhood, yet I know that other kids go through much more without coming off the rails."

"But how could we have missed those early changes?" Alex queried. "If we'd have acted early on, she might never have stayed with the Silvers."

"Chris was always good at deception and sometimes quite willful." Norma shrugged. "Because she looked so young and innocent, we forgot she was a teenager with teenage desires and a teenage need for acceptance. I believe that we didn't see the early changes in Chris because basically she was happy with the freedom and acceptance she got in that house. By the time the decline was noticeable she'd moved right out of our lives and turned her back. All the fighting to win her back was a waste until it was what *she* wanted. If she had lived, maybe she'd have cleaned up and forged a life, but we can't know that."

"How could she clean up?" muttered Alex angrily. "She was kept drug dependent to serve the Silver family's purposes."

"Perhaps…although Michael, Nathalie and George didn't take that route," Norma argued. "Michael got away when he'd had enough, and to an extent so did Nathalie."

"Oh God, Mum, don't do this," whispered Alex. "It sounds like you're blaming Chris for her own death."

"You mean instead of Charlotte, George, Nathalie or you and me?" she questioned.

The silence gave them time to absorb the thoughts they'd both finally verbalized.

"Perhaps Dieter was right," Norma said eventually, "when he said during one of my sessions that maybe Chris died because of how she chose to live or because of an accident or because she had the type of personality that chose to run away and chose drugs. Maybe we weren't the perfect family for Christine, but does that make us responsible? Because she was living with George and living that horrible lifestyle, does that make them responsible? I've thought a lot about that over the years. Now perhaps you need to as well."

* * *

Nathalie waited fifteen minutes after George left, unsure what to do. And then she left too, assuming he was returning home.

Did George really expect her to just accept his decision about the journal? She had to know what it said, who she really was and what happened all those years ago. When she arrived at the house, though, the garage was open and George's car wasn't there. Mother's hire car was also missing and the frustration threatened to boil over.

It was late and there was work tomorrow, but instead of going home Nathalie rang Bella.

"Come over," Bella invited when Nat let her frustration pour down the telephone line. "I've got a drink with your name on it."

The house seemed even gloomier tonight and something about it reminded her of the awful place she grew up. An unpleasant feeling of déjà vu settled over her, but Nathalie shrugged it off. It was irrelevant to everything that was happening in her life.

"So you still don't know much more," Bella commented when Nathalie relayed her conversation with George. "Except that your mother's name was probably Olivia. Did he say how she died or when? Perhaps we could find a death certificate."

"I have no choice but to confront Mother…Charlotte," she corrected, momentarily confused. "I have the right to know what happened. Why I ended up with her."

"What you need is the diary," remarked Bella. "Then you'd have something more to base your questions on. But your broth…George obviously isn't going to part with it easily."

They talked at length with Bella assuring Nat that she'd put a rush on her Immigration inquiries, but now it was going to be more difficult because it was highly unlikely Charlotte Silver brought them into the country in her own name—if her name was even Silver.

At the end of the conversation, Nathalie was even more convinced that the only way she was going to find anything out was through George, the journal or by a direct confrontation with Charlotte, none of which offered a great deal of hope.

Having had a few drinks, Nat stayed the night. The spare room comprised a single bed with stale sheets that smelled unused, a single ancient bedside table and a very ugly old lamp. Homemaking definitely wasn't Bella's forte.

There were no nightmares that night, because not even the alcohol could put her to sleep. The revelation that Charlotte wasn't her mother or George her brother had left her reeling. Everything that had been her life, bad as it was, was suddenly gone and with it came a thousand questions. If Charlotte had lied about her origins and George being her brother, what else was a lie? Was Abraham Duncan, whoever he was, really her father? And was he still alive? Presumably Charlotte hadn't legally adopted her, or if she had, why flee? There were too many questions and too many possibilities.

At three in the morning she decided a hot drink might help and wandered to the kitchen.

Bella's house was set out with the main bedroom opposite the lounge in the front of the house, and the other two bedrooms, a study, kitchen and dining room at the back. All the rooms were small with a door between the front and back areas. Nat shut this door, hoping she could avoid waking Bella.

With hot black tea in hand, Nat started mindlessly wandering the back rooms where the doors were open. The third bedroom was actually larger than the one she was in, but it was full to the brim with a double bed, two old wardrobes and a large chest of drawers. Piled on the drawers and on top of the wardrobes were boxes of all different shapes.

The study was the only room that had been modernized, and although small, it contained a state-of-the-art computer, good quality desk and chair, a bookcase full of law books and law articles and a lockable filing cabinet. Down-lights had replaced the old open light shades and, incongruously, on the computer table sat a pile of soapy-style women's magazines.

Lifting one to take back to bed with her, Nat accidentally bumped the pile, causing the lot to tumble and slide to the floor. Annoyed at her clumsiness and embarrassed that she might be found scrounging around in Bella's personal areas, she hurriedly tried to gather them up, only to spread them even wider across the floor.

As she made her second attempt to pick them up a small slim-line address book slid from the pile. Picking it up and automatically replacing it on the computer table, she finished piling the magazines beside it—only then glancing at the intertwining initials RY embossed in gold on the black cover.

For a moment it didn't register. Then, curious that they weren't Bella's initials, she picked it up and opened it to the first page. The words were written in red ink—*Property of Renee Young. Please return by phoning 0402 671 379.*

The words flashed in her brain. They meant something important. Suddenly she was ice-cold and unable to think. Was this another nightmare that she'd wake up from at any moment?

"What's up?" The voice sounded sleepy and concerned, but that quickly changed when Nat turned around with the address book open in her hand.

"Jesus, Nat," Bella gasped. "What the fuck have you done?"

The words wouldn't come. How do you ask a friend what she's doing with a murder victim's missing address book? For what seemed an age, but was only seconds, Nat stared at the awkward-looking woman in the flannel pajamas.

"This is Renee Young's," she accused quietly, shaking her head in confusion.

The color drained from Bella's face, but she was wide-awake now and the tension poured from her. "You need to pretend you never saw that," she whispered, straightening her shoulders and taking a defensive stance. "You need to put that back, go back to bed and never mention it again."

"What are you talking about?" whispered Nat, still holding the offending book in front of her. "What does this mean?"

"Just do what I tell you, Nat, or I'll be destroyed. It's not what you think."

Speechless, but shaking her head, Nathalie felt an overwhelming sadness. This could have no happy ending.

"You're not going to leave it alone, are you?" Bella asked wearily, her shoulders slumping. "I just want you to…shit, Nat…please…please let's get a drink and I'll explain."

There was no threat in her voice, just total resignation.

Bella led the way and Nat followed dutifully but cautiously—aware that if Bella was responsible for the deaths of four women, she could be in danger herself.

Sitting so that she could move quickly if she had to, Nathalie watched Bella's every move.

"It was Jackie," Bella explained, seating herself opposite Nat. "It was Jackie who killed Young, Djanski and Cameron. When I found out, she tried to kill me, but I overpowered her and the gun went off and shot her in the chest."

"That's a nice, neat explanation," replied Nat, moving into interview mode. "And, of course, Jackie's not here to deny it."

"That's exactly how she planned it, only she didn't expect to die," Bella stated desperately. "She was setting it up to make me look like the killer. That's the truth, Nat, I swear."

"Why, Bella, why would she do that? Why would she kill all those women just to make you look bad?" The sarcasm came from emotional exhaustion; she regretted it immediately.

But Bella was too rattled to notice. "No," she replied intently. "Pinning it on me was probably an afterthought. She hated them, hated us all, but mostly she hated me."

"Start from the beginning," demanded Nathalie. "How did you find out Jackie was the killer?"

"I came home early one day and decided to try and sort some of the stuff in that spare room. I hadn't seen Jackie for days and suspected she might have dumped me for good. I started with the boxes on the floor and then decided to sort the wardrobe. I pulled out some old coats and a heavy object wrapped in cloth dropped from the pocket of one of them. It was a handgun. I've never owned a gun in my life, other than my issue one. So I was stunned."

"How did you think it got there?"

"I didn't know. I couldn't figure it out. Some of the stuff in the wardrobe had been there for years. I never went in there. I just kept looking at it and trying to imagine where it had come from. Then I decided to see what else was in there. It only took me a couple of minutes to find the address book. It was in the pocket of another jacket and with it was my police ID. Even then, my mind couldn't take in what I'd found. That was when Jackie walked in."

"So you hadn't seen Jackie for days, but she just happened to walk in when you'd found the stash?" Nat couldn't help but articulate her disbelief.

"She assumed I was at work because it was lunchtime, and my car was out of sight in the garage. I'm telling you the truth, Nat. She was like a different person. She looked and sounded different, as if she'd only been pretending to be the dumb blonde waitress. She was…attractive."

"Did you know your ID was missing?"

"Yes, of course, but not immediately. I thought I'd misplaced it somewhere in the house, which was partly what inspired the cleanup. In the middle of that I won the inspector's position. I planned to report it missing once I was confirmed."

"Jesus, Bella, what were you thinking?"

"I wanted a career, Nat," she replied tiredly. "I didn't want an Internal Affairs inquiry over the missing ID to interfere with this promotion. Surely you can understand that?"

Nathalie didn't answer.

"So then what happened?" she asked finally, after trying to absorb what she'd been told.

"Jackie started laughing," Bella recalled. "She stood in the doorway and laughed. Suddenly she looked quite insane, but I didn't know what she was laughing at because I still hadn't opened the address book. At that stage, I didn't know the connection. She asked me what I was doing home, and I actually answered her."

Bella looked exhausted, puzzled and beaten, and a part of Nathalie wanted desperately to believe her story. But it would be too easy.

"I was sitting on a corner of the bed," Bella continued slowly. "Jackie walked over and picked up the gun and then took the address book from my hands. I didn't even attempt to stop her. Then she was pointing the gun at me. 'So much for the great police inspector,' she said, grinning. I asked her what she'd done and she held out the book. 'It's the fabulous Renee Young's address book,' she bragged. 'Full of all the names and addresses of the stuck-up tarts she'd been screwing since she left me behind in nowhere town.'

"She explained then that she'd followed Renee to the city, followed her to let her know that she wasn't the dull, boring little girl she knew at school. She found her in the club with the Cameron woman, but when she approached her, Renee told her that she should move on and make her own type of friends."

"Jackie was so angry," Bella continued. "I hardly recognized her. Then she started repeating the words 'my own type of friends,' over and over, like some sort of chant. Then just as quickly she calmed down. But she still held the gun pointed at me. I asked her what she'd done, and she sat down on one of the boxes facing me."

Bella shook her head. "She'd waited for Renee for years, she told me, sounding very bitter. Since they were at school together. She'd always loved her, but Renee acted like she was so much better than her. She'd thought it was because they were just kids, only it wasn't that, she decided. Renee just didn't like her, didn't think she was up to her high standards. So Jackie had decided to show her that her standards meant nothing."

Sighing, Bella continued. "She told me that she'd waited for Young to return to the club. Then waiting outside until she left, she'd walked up to her as she took the road back to her car. She supposedly told Young that she was returning home and wanted to say goodbye. Then she pulled the gun and held it to Young's head. She told me that she wanted her to know what it felt like to be disposed of like rubbish. Then she shot her. She found the address book when she went through Young's pockets for a memento."

"She told you all this?"

"She didn't intend for me to leave the house alive, so she wasn't worried about what I knew," answered Bella quietly. Pouring herself another drink, she continued. "I don't know when she decided to go after Cameron, but she said that Young had introduced her to someone called Stephanie in the club the night they argued. When she started looking through the address book she found Stephanie Cameron and decided she should be taught a lesson as well. Jesus, Nat, she was actually gloating about it."

"Cameron wasn't having an affair with Young, they were just old friends," stated Nathalie, remembering the interviews she'd done with friends of the couple. Then thinking about their investigation so far, she asked, "Did she say how she got into Cameron's house or why she killed Stephanie's partner, Linda Djanski?"

"She bragged about using my police ID to gain entry when Djanski was home alone. She thought Cameron might remember her from the club, so she waited until it was just Djanski. She used the pretext of asking questions about Renee Young. Djanski let her in and arranged for her to come back the following evening to see Cameron. At some stage she went to the bathroom and I gather she unlocked a door or window and jammed it so that it would close but not lock. Apparently they locked automatically if fully closed. She let herself back in during the early hours and shot them while they slept. She actually told me that she wanted to wake them first, but lost her nerve.

"When she left after the killings, she did so by the same way she came in, but removed the obstacle so that when the window shut. It automatically locked, leaving the house locked from the inside."

"Bella—"

"I know it's unbelievable," she interrupted. "I know how it looks, but it's the truth. I kept thinking that she was lying, that the gun was some sort of replica and that she hated me enough to want to scare me. But I couldn't move—I guess deep down I knew she was telling the truth."

Nathalie's head throbbed with the exertion of trying to assimilate Bella's words.

"Nathalie, she was going to kill you and then set it up to look like it was me," Bella stated emphatically.

"Kill me? Why? Surely she didn't think you and I were…"

"She said you'd treated her the same way Young had—like she was garbage. She kept asking me what Alex had that she didn't, but I didn't understand what she was talking about. Then she started ranting about educated idiots and how snobbish we all were. Apparently she hated me so much that she wanted me to live but to lose everything. She wanted me to go to prison. That was how coldly she'd planned it. You were going to be her next victim and I was going to be the suspect."

"But then you found the gun, ID and address book?" Nathalie murmured, deep in thought.

"Nathalie, I knew she was going to kill me. Suddenly I just knew she was going to pull the trigger…and I lost it. She must have seen something in my face because she went to move away, but she tripped, and then we were struggling. Suddenly the gun discharged and she moaned. She didn't move. She just stood there looking at her chest where the blood was seeping through her top. Then she started crying and she held out her arms to me. 'I don't want to die, Bella,' she cried. 'Help me.'"

Bella was visibly shaking as she spoke.

"I grabbed hold of her and she collapsed. Then she closed her eyes and was gone. I was so horrified I didn't know what to do."

"Why didn't you call an ambulance or the police?" queried Nathalie, unable to hide her skepticism. "It was self-defense and you're a trained officer."

"I went to, Nat, I swear. But it looked so bad. I didn't know what else she might have been keeping at my house to incriminate me and I just panicked. I took her body out of the house late that night and dumped it and then came home and cleaned up. I assumed you'd think it was part of the killings."

Somehow Nathalie couldn't imagine Bella panicking, but did that make her story a lie? Trying to clear her head, she began moving around the small room. Something was missing from the account, but she couldn't put her finger on it. "We have to call this in now," Nat stated assertively. "I can call Josh so that it's dealt with as discreetly as possible, but you know I have to do this."

"I'll go straight into custody, Nat," she begged. "They have to charge me with Jackie's death, and because of suspicion regarding the other murders they'll never give me bail. Please don't do this. It was a bloody accident and the murders have been resolved. There's nothing to be gained by me going to prison or being humiliated and losing my job. It's all I have, you know that."

"Bella, you killed someone, disposed of her body and hid evidence relating to other crimes. I'm sorry, but you know we don't have a choice."

Bella just kept staring at Nathalie, shaking her head. "You know, if I did kill all of them, then I only have to kill you as well to keep my involvement secret. And it would hardly be difficult. You've left yourself very vulnerable. You haven't even asked what I did with the gun." It was just a statement of fact.

"Is that what you plan to do?" Nat responded as calmly as she could.

"I want until lunchtime to sort out my finances and to organize someone to look after the house, then I'll hand myself in and do it with some dignity. I don't want to be led from here and into the station in handcuffs."

"I can't give you that time, Bella, but I can phone Josh and ask him to meet us at the office. Then you and I can go there together with no fuss."

"But it won't just be Josh, will it?" she asked needlessly. "Internal Affairs will be involved at a senior level and everyone will know within twenty-four hours."

"Bella—"

"No, it's all right," she declared, raising her hand. "I know…I know…that's my problem."

Again there was silence.

"Then that will have to do," she stated coolly, rising from the chair. "I guess I've run out of choices, and so have you. But I want to shower. It will be hours before I get another one."

"Where did you put the gun?"

"The river. I'll show the divers. You ring Josh and I'll be ready in five minutes."

Nat knew she should go with her—watch her. But she couldn't be the one to inflict that first indignity. After this, Bella would be searched, booked in, questioned, charged, fingerprinted, put in a cell and then sent to a place where nobody on the planet hated police more. Even if Jackie's death was found to be accidental, Bella would have lost everything. She couldn't bring herself to be the one to start that process.

* * *

Josh was worried. When Nathalie called and told him the story, he ordered her to remain in sight of Bella Pittolo at all times. He wasn't convinced that the gun had been disposed of—after all, the incriminating address book hadn't been. He desperately wanted to send a car around to the house immediately, but Nathalie begged him.

"Please, let her do this," she argued. "If she's got the gun and wanted to hurt me she would have done it before I rang you. I gave her my word. We're leaving in a few minutes, and we'll be in the office ten minutes later. I don't want mob-handed cops coming to the house."

She'd hung up and was on her way to the bedroom she'd been using when she heard the shot. For a split second she expected pain. Then she knew—and in an instant was bounding toward Bella's bedroom. Pushing open the door she flicked on the light—everything her police training had taught her not to do. But the room was empty.

She found Bella on the bathroom floor, clothed in her dress uniform. She'd started out with her back against the bathtub but had toppled sideways in death. The gun was lying loosely in her hand and blood was seeping from the wound in her forehead.

That's when the world crashed in on her and Nathalie sunk to the floor opposite her dead friend. Strangely, she was feeling nothing except overwhelming exhaustion.

Josh waited fifteen minutes after he arrived at work before he rang Nathalie. The superintendent from Internal Affairs was forty minutes away, but the uniformed duty officer had joined him to receive Bella. When he got no reply, they dispatched uniforms to the house urgently. It was the worst five minutes of his life before the radio crackled into life, conveying the information that Nathalie was safe.

She'd refused to go in the ambulance. The numbness had worn off and weary resignation had taken its place. It was too soon to analyze what she'd done wrong, but deep down she knew that the final outcome for Bella would have been the same no matter what. Bella would never have survived the humiliation.

* * *

When the death of a female commissioned officer and the involvement of a second officer were reported on the TV and radio the next morning, Bella eventually was named, but not Nathalie. However, there was a media clip of Nat leaving the house with Josh's arm around her waist.

Alex knew instinctively she'd been involved and a terrible fear gripped her. What if it had been Nathalie in the body bag?

When the press found out Bella was a lesbian, they immediately began connecting her death to the other lesbian killings, inventing wilder and wilder scenarios. However, the police statement told them only that "a senior police officer, Inspector Bella Pittolo, has died in her house as a result of a gunshot wound, and a second female officer was present at the death. Until police have the opportunity to investigate further, no statements will be forthcoming."

"I have to go to her," Alex told her mother tentatively, when she rang that morning. "I can't let her go through this alone. But I don't want to upset you."

"You won't," her mother said quietly. "But you should be prepared that Nathalie might not welcome you with open arms. She might see it as pity."

"I love her," Alex confessed. "And I have to let her know I'm there for her, even if she rejects me."

It took a lot of phone calls before she got put through to Josh's office, and in the end she had to leave a message. Meanwhile she'd tried Nathalie's home and mobile, but she got answer machines both times. For now, all she could do was wait.

CHAPTER TWELVE

Reconciliations

The questions went on forever. Josh had been forced to remove himself from any part of the investigation into Bella's death. He and his team had been mustered into a conference room and instructed that nothing was to be spoken about outside that room until official statements had been issued. His team was in shock—unable to comprehend that perhaps a senior police officer had been responsible for four murders.

Nathalie was making a statement to Internal Affairs. She'd been dusted for gunshot residue and forced to hand over all of her clothing, changing into a tracksuit she kept in her locker. When she finally emerged white-faced and exhausted, Josh guided her straight to his office.

"I'm taking you home, and you're on leave from now," he told her gently. "And while I'm sorry about Bella, I have to ask if you think she was telling the truth?"

"I don't know, Josh," Nat answered flatly. "I really wanted to believe her. Jackie was strange, but then so was Bella." For a moment there was tense silence before Nat offered, "I think there's a possibility they were in it together and then fell out. I'm just too drained to think about it now."

"Internal Affairs will deal with Bella's death, but we'll continue our investigation into the other four. Hopefully we can clear Pittolo, but it doesn't look good."

Josh hadn't wanted to leave Nathalie on her own after he drove her to the apartment, but she insisted that all she wanted was to sleep. It wasn't until after he'd returned to the office that he saw the messages from Alex. Curious, he dialed her number.

The phone was answered immediately.

Their conversation took a while, with Josh reluctant to pass on any information, believing that Nathalie had finished the affair with Alex.

So she gave him the abridged version of their relationship and its unhappy ending.

Josh knew Alex was telling the truth because it answered so many questions about his own relationship with Nathalie. Eventually, he told her that Nat was at home and that she was emotionally and physically exhausted and probably asleep by now.

"I have to go to her," Alex told him. "I don't know if she'll want me. I said some terrible things to her. But I love her and I don't want her to do this alone."

"Good luck," he replied, actually meaning it. "In case she's asleep…she keeps a spare key taped at the back of the potted plant near her door." He knew it was a breach of Nathalie's privacy, but he also knew Nathalie needed someone and Alex had all the qualifications.

Alex knocked gently when she got to the apartment, then she pressed the bell, but when she got no response, she used the hidden key.

Nat was on the lounge with all the lights on, still in her tracksuit. A glass and packet of tablets were on the coffee table and she was curled in a tense ball facing the back of the lounge.

Alex moved toward the sleeping figure, calling her name. She didn't stir. Looking down at this woman she'd so readily abandoned, Alex felt an overwhelming love and protectiveness. Touching her gently, she turned Nat toward her.

As she opened her eyes, Nat's face crumpled—every emotion stored within her over the last few weeks bubbling to the surface in the presence of this mirage. Tears of anguish flowed down her face, and as Alex slid in beside her and held her close, gasping sobs broke from her lips.

Alex silently held her while Nathalie clung to her with all her strength. Eventually the wracking sobs subsided, Nat's body gradually relaxing, until exhaustion, comfort and the pills won out.

Alex waited nearly half an hour before disentangling herself from the thin warm body. It shocked her how much weight Nathalie had lost since she'd left—her once athletic body was now skin and bone.

Nat slept for ten hours, occasionally moaning or crying out in her sleep but never waking. When she did, it was groggily—slowly. Memory of a wonderful dream rose to the surface. Alex had come to her—still loved her.

The side lamp was on, casting a gentle yellow light over the lounge room, and for a moment she was puzzled. The voice from the lounge chair made her sit bolt upright.

"How are you feeling?" it asked gently. "You seemed to get a good rest."

Alex had been reading and was still holding her book, and there was a look in her eyes that conveyed warmth and love and understanding.

"So you weren't a dream," Nathalie stated quietly, her heart pounding with the joy of being in this woman's presence. "But what are you doing here? How did you get in?"

"You need to hide your key in a more original place," she replied vaguely, hoping that Nathalie wasn't about to ask her to leave.

For a moment they looked at each other, each trying to assimilate the myriad emotions that were swirling in their consciousness. It was Alex who spoke first.

"I saw the news," she stated kindly. "I'm so sorry about Bella."

"Why did you come?" Nat asked, watching Alex's face for any signs of pity. "I thought you hated me."

"I thought I did," Alex replied slowly. "It was easier to hate you and your family than to take any responsibility for what happened to Christine. But I don't have the right to judge you and I know now that I could never hate you. I love you too much."

Then they were in each other's arms, touching and kissing and clinging together.

Initially their lovemaking was fevered and desperate, as a mutual need to be inside each other—part of each other—overwhelmed them. Afterward, as they continued to move against each other gently, they built to a second delicate, more passionate climax that seemed to cleanse and heal. Their only words had been of the moment, of their love for each other and the ache of separation, but they both knew that the pain of reality was only a whisper away.

Later, as they ate the bread rolls and broth Alex had prepared, Nathalie told her about Bella.

Inevitably, Alex asked the question that was foremost in everyone's mind.

"I really don't know if she was telling the truth," answered Nathalie, better able after her sleep to give the nightmare of the last twenty-four hours some serious thought. "I know that I wanted desperately to believe her. That may have clouded my judgment. There are questions I knew would have to be asked, but that's not possible now." As she thought of Bella's last moments, tears welled and she dropped her head.

"You couldn't have prevented this, you know," stated Alex gently. "It may not have happened the same way, but I believe it would still have happened. I think you know that."

"Yes, I do, but if I hadn't found the address book it might have been different. Mother's right when she says I cause trouble and bring pain. Look at what I did to your family—to Chris."

Mentioning Mother brought home with clear recollection George's revelation prior to all this starting. Suddenly Nat wanted to tell Alex everything—wanted her to know the full extent of her culpability and of Charlotte's role in their mysterious beginnings.

Alex let Nathalie tell her story, only stopping her at times to clarify something.

The events of Nat's life were told in a monotone that excluded revealing the emotions involved. But Alex knew the supreme effort it took for someone like Nat to disclose what she did. At the end, Alex made coffee.

"I have to see George again," Nathalie declared. "But I think he's too scared to tell me any more. I also need to see Charlotte's journal because whatever is in it has George scared out of his wits."

"What she's done to you both and to the other kids who became involved with your family is a form of brainwashing— the alternate use of rewards and fear," stated Alex seriously. "The younger and more dependent a child is when this technique is applied, the more compliant they are throughout their lives. You got away by going to university, while George remained under her control. What I'm surprised about is that she allowed you to leave."

"I've wondered about that from time to time, but I think she hated me more than she needed to control me, and anyway, she still has…had…an enormous amount of control over me. I can't let that happen to George's children, though."

It was after two in the morning and they were both spent and exhausted.

"May I stay the night?" Alex asked tentatively, wrapping her arms around Nat from behind. "I don't want to let you out of my sight."

Showering together turned into another delicious session of gentle and passionate lovemaking with both women reveling in the touch and closeness of the other. Eventually they fell asleep wrapped in a warm cocoon of togetherness.

CHAPTER THIRTEEN

Deathly Discoveries

Nathalie was instructed to do a walk-through of the events leading up to Bella's death, and the house was examined with a fine-tooth comb by scientific. No more incriminating evidence was found to link Bella to the murder of the other three women, but neither was there any evidence to link Jacqueline St. Clare.

Blood traces that didn't belong to Bella were found in the spare bedroom, which if they proved to be St. Clare's would substantiate Bella's story that Jackie had died there. And while there was no blood found in Bella's car, Bella would have known enough to wrap St. Clare's body in something before dumping her at the industrial estate where she was found.

The department had put Nathalie on indefinite leave until they had more answers. They'd also offered counseling and welfare services, all of which she'd declined.

For the next couple of days she and Alex hardly left the apartment. During that time, Nat talked more than she'd ever talked in her life, and the more she talked, the angrier Alex became.

"Have you thought about making an official report?" Alex asked at some stage. "Charlotte Silver obviously heads up a significant pedophile and prostitution ring with connections to other countries. What she's done to you and George alone would be enough to jail her for years. And then there's Michael—I'm sure he'd give evidence."

"I've thought about it," she replied. "But you have to understand that George and I would also be charged. We never reported what she did, even after we were adults. And George has been actively involved in recruiting teenagers to feed to these monsters right up until now. Besides, if I do that," she explained, "I may never find out who I really am. I have to try and get George to hand over the journal. Because the only other option is to confront Mother and…and I guess that terrifies me," she admitted with a gesture of exasperation.

"I want to come with you," Alex responded seriously. "I don't believe you should have anything more to do with that woman or your brother on your own."

For a moment Nathalie was stunned by the proposal. "Alex, I can't let you do that. As it is, Charlotte's paranoia has convinced her that you and your mother are out to get her. Unless George has already told her otherwise, she even suspects that one of you has the journal."

"Then all the more reason for me to be there. Let her see a united front and recognize that her victims are finally fighting back—that she might have something to lose if she doesn't tell you what you want to know."

"It's too dangerous," she replied automatically. "You don't understand what she's like if you cross her. I wouldn't be able to protect you."

"I'm not underestimating her, Nathalie, but she has to be stopped from ruining any more lives, and she has to let you get on with yours. I'm part of your life now and I want to be there."

It was a minefield. The thought of having Alex in support buoyed Nathalie greatly but warred with her desire to protect her from Mother's sordid world.

"I won't take no for an answer," Alex stated quickly, cutting off any further objections. "Until you find out about your past, we can't move forward. And I'm not about to let my future slip through my fingers again. I love you."

They were in each other arms. Nathalie hadn't known such tenderness or comfort existed until she gave herself over to Alex. It wasn't just the all-consuming passion of their lovemaking. It was the joy of having someone to live for, someone who loved her and someone to love equally.

* * *

Josh had been in touch to let Nathalie know how the investigation was going. The gun Bella had used on herself was the same one used to kill Jacqueline St. Clare, but they were unable to trace its origins. They also found no other weapons at Bella's house. What worried Josh was why St. Clare would have disposed of the guns she used to kill the other women, when, according to Bella, Jackie hadn't finished her killing spree. And if Jackie's idea was to incriminate Bella, then why not leave those weapons with the address book? Why a new gun that couldn't be traced to the previous crimes?

"Do you mean that you think Bella was lying?" Nathalie asked during one of these conversations. "Do you think she was the killer?"

"It's still too early to tell," he replied vaguely. "We really haven't come up with a motive for either St. Clare or Pittolo. It's one thing to feel resentful by perceived disrespect, but would that be enough to send someone…two people…on a murder spree? We desperately need more physical evidence linking one or both women to the crimes."

Nathalie was glad to be out of the investigation. At the moment it all seemed too hard. She wanted Bella to be the innocent she claimed, but she couldn't shake the terrible suspicion that Bella and St. Clare were involved in the killings together—that St. Clare's death was some kind of falling out. She had nothing on which to base these terrible thoughts, though, and she didn't want to dwell on them.

* * *

George wasn't answering his mobile, so Nathalie decided to try the house. She got Belinda, who said that George had been acting very strangely and hadn't been home or in contact for two days. She confided that Charlotte was furious, but she didn't really know what was going on.

"Please, Belinda," Nat pleaded. "I need to talk to George urgently. If he gets in touch, please ring me." Passing on her mobile number, even though she knew he had it, Nathalie hung up. Did Mother know he'd read the journal? Was that why he was in hiding? Or was it to do with the children? *God, George,* she thought bitterly, *why do you have to choose now to disappear?*

That night her frustration got the better of her. "I have to speak directly to Mother," she stated to Alex irritably. "George has disappeared, so I have no choice."

"There might be another way you can find out more about your past," Alex suggested quietly. "It's a long shot and not the best way of doing things, but you could approach Dieter to do a hypnotherapy session with you—taking you back to your early childhood."

"Would that work?" she asked excitedly. "Could I find out who I am?"

"It probably won't be that simple," Alex replied gently. "But it may give you some insight into your nightmares. You need to see Dieter again anyway, especially with what's just happened."

Alex phoned Dieter, and they went to see him together that evening. He had a lot of reservations, but he agreed to listen to what they had to say.

At the end of Nathalie's explanation, Dieter said, "Under normal circumstances I wouldn't even consider it. As Alex is aware, we do a lot of preparation with a client before entering into hypnotherapy. Your mind has suppressed those memories for a reason, so to bring them to the surface without the proper preparation could be very traumatic and detrimental."

"It can't be any more horrific than the nightmares," Nathalie retaliated, "nor living with not knowing why I ended up in this situation in the first place. Please, Dieter, I'll sign a waiver removing you from any responsibility. Anything, but please, let me do this."

"I really believe Nathalie's ready to confront whatever comes out of this," stated Alex quietly. Then looking toward Nathalie, she added, "I've seen her when she has these nightmares, Dieter, and she's right—she can't keep going like this. Whatever happened is destroying her. At least if she finds out what it is she has the chance to deal with it."

"If I do this," Dieter asked, addressing Nathalie, "will you agree to Alex remaining in the room?"

"Yes, of course. I don't want any more secrets between us."

* * *

Alex sat in a chair in a corner of the darkened room, while Nathalie stretched out on Dieter's couch. Dieter had explained the process at length and had laid down the ground rules. "If at any time I think you're showing signs of too much distress, I will stop the session. If Alex thinks that it has gone far enough, she will also have the option of telling me to bring you out of it. That's the only way this will work."

Twenty minutes later, Nathalie was in a hypnotized state.

At first Dieter worked with the memories Nathalie did have of her childhood, taking her back until she came to the edge of her recollection. At that point he asked her to explain where she was and what she was doing. Nathalie said she was six years old.

"It's George's birthday," she said in childlike language. "And George wants a bicycle because we had to leave his last one at the old place."

"What country are you in now?" Dieter asked gently. "Do you know?"

"London," replied the young voice.

"And where did you come from?"

"We came on the airplane from…"

Then there was silence.

"From where, Nathalie?" prompted Dieter gently. "Do you remember?"

"Mother says we mustn't tell." There was a slight agitation in the voice as she attempted to push past the edge of her memory.

"Did your mother say why you mustn't tell, Nathalie?"

"She'll hurt me if I tell. George says I must do what she says or she'll keep hurting me and then she'll send me away."

"Who is George?" Dieter asked, testing her response.

"He's my brother. He said Mother doesn't want me to remember. She'll put me in the woods if I remember." Now the childlike voice sounded truly scared.

"Nobody can harm you now, Nathalie," Dieter crooned gently. "Not your mother or anyone else. You're in a safe place and you are allowed to remember. Do you understand?"

"She'll put me in the ground again!" The voice was struck through with terror and Dieter immediately changed course.

"It's all right, Nathalie. Let's talk about something else. You said George had a bicycle in the old place. Did you have a bike?"

"No."

"Did you like the old place?"

Her face reflected conflicting emotions. "I think…I think I liked it with my old mummy," she replied carefully. "But she went away. Aunty Charl…my new mother…made her go away."

Both Alex and Dieter noticed the alternating terms of "mother" and "mummy" for the two individuals. When she spoke of "mummy" there was warmth. When she spoke of "mother" there was only fear.

"Nathalie, do you remember what the place was called that you lived in with your old mummy?"

"My address is 1110 National Boulevard, San Diego. Mummy said I must remember that in case I was ever lost."

There was a small intake of breath from Alex. This was better than Nathalie could possibly have hoped for.

"Nathalie, do you know what your full name is?"

"Nathalie Olivia Duncan, and I live at 1110 National Boulevard, San Diego," she stated by rote.

"Who lives with you?"

"Mummy and George, Aunty Charlotte, sometimes a man."

"Does the man have a name?" Dieter persisted.

"Mummy doesn't like the man, and I don't like the man, and George doesn't like the man. Once he hurt George, and Mummy got really mad at him and he hit Mummy."

"Nathalie, do you know what George's last name is?"

"Um…Green—he says it's like the grass."

"Is that Aunty Charlotte's name as well?"

A shrug and hands raised palms upward in a childish gesture. "I don't know."

"Nathalie, do you remember that I told you that nobody can hurt you any more, that you are completely safe and that you are allowed to remember anything at all and say anything you want?"

"Mmm…"

"Do you believe me?"

"I…but Mother said…" It was obvious that Nathalie, the child, was torn, her face worried, yet somehow trusting. In the end she replied in a rather unconvincing voice, "I guess so."

"Nathalie, you said that the bad mother made your good mummy go away. Can you think about that time now?"

"No! No!" she whimpered desperately. "Mother will put me in the dirt again." Nathalie was squirming on the sofa now.

"But your good mummy wants you to tell me everything you can remember," he tried, hoping this didn't bring repercussions. "I won't let anyone hurt you. I promise."

She went quiet.

Dieter also remained quiet.

"I don't like it here," she whispered eventually.

"Where are you, Nathalie?" he asked tentatively.

"Downstairs."

"How old are you, Nathalie?"

"I don't like it down here. It's dark and cold and I want my mummy."

"Why are you down the stairs, Nathalie?" he prodded gently.

"Aunty put me here. She said I had to hide and then Mummy would find me. But she put stuff on my hands and my mouth."

"What sort of stuff," he asked.

"It's sticky and too tight and it hurts. I can't get out. I can't get out!" Her voice had become a little louder and laced with panic, and now her arms were crossed at the wrist, emulating them being tied together. Tears trickled from her eyes.

Alex was worried. At the moment Nathalie seemed to be handling the journey, but what was being revealed exceeded anything she'd imagined, and she knew just by the sequence of events that it was going to get worse. Catching Dieter's eye, she nodded. If she stopped it now, Nathalie would still have too many unanswered questions. Her eyes relayed her fears but acknowledged that Dieter should continue.

"What is happening now, Nathalie?" he asked as she seemed to stop struggling, her body tense and listening.

"Mummy," she replied excitedly. "I can hear Mummy. She's talking to Aunty. I think she's coming down the stairs. It hurts my mouth and I can't tell Mummy I'm here."

"Can you see your mummy?"

"Yes, she's calling me, but she can't see me. Now the man is here too. I don't like the man. He's touching Mummy funny. They're fighting and Aunty is watching, and she keeps looking at me. No! No! Don't hurt Mummy…" The child was mumbling, struggling madly on Dieter's sofa. This was followed by more stifled, mumbled moans.

"Are you all right, Nathalie?" Dieter asked worriedly. "Is the man hurting you?"

"Aunty is hurting Mummy. Mummy's seen me, Mummy's seen me! But they won't let her come to me. Aunty is saying lots of things. She's yelling at Mummy—she's saying lots of words. She's very angry with Mummy."

Now Nathalie's struggles seemed to become more desperate, although only her hands and arms moved. Then she was very still, tears pouring down her face, anguish and pain etched across her features.

"What's happening now?" Dieter asked carefully.

And for a long time there was no answer.

Alex sat bolt upright in her seat, but Dieter indicated for her not to move.

"Can you hear me, Nathalie?" he asked. "Remember what I told you about nobody being able to hurt you. Not Aunty. Not the man."

There was a low, keening sound deep in the back of Nathalie's throat and a quiet sob or two. Then she went limp.

Alex's and Dieter's eyes met in mutual agreement that the session should end. Nathalie hadn't moved, and both were worried.

Quietly, Dieter said, "Can you hear me, Nathalie?" But he got no response. "Nathalie, it's Dieter, and you're back in my office now. I'm going to count back from ten and when you hear the number one, you will slowly wake up. You will remember everything that happened, but you will remember it as if it was a movie you were watching and you will not be frightened any more. You also have permission to remember anything you want. Nobody can hurt you now."

Nathalie came out of it with a small gasp and sat up immediately—her eyes wide and her body tense.

"Are you all right?" Dieter asked gently, encouraging her to lie back down for a moment.

"I think so," she mumbled a little shakily, "although I've got a headache."

Alex was watching her every move.

"Oh God," she said suddenly, standing up. "I remember things...my mother...my real mother." Then she sat back down, sadness reflected in her face, tears in her eyes. "It's really strange," she whispered intently. "She was my mother, yet I hardly knew her."

Pouring a brandy for each of them, Dieter moved them to lounge chairs beside a low coffee table. "How do you feel now?" he asked her as they took their seats. "It's important to debrief as soon as possible after a hypnotherapy session, but I don't want to push you."

"She was so different to Charlotte, Alex," she said, tears welling again. "She was dark like me and so beautiful...and...I miss her so much." A sob escaped as Alex reached out and took her hand.

For a short while they sat in silence.

"Can you tell us what you remember?" Dieter asked after a few minutes. "I know it will be traumatic, but you need to acknowledge what you experienced."

"Surely, she doesn't—"

Dieter cut Alex off. "You're here as an observer, Alex," he said firmly. "Nat is my patient and if she wants to move on in her life, then she needs to deal with her memories."

"It is okay, Alex, I want to do this," Nathalie responded. "I know you're only trying to protect me, but I *need* to do this."

"Do you remember what you told me your name was?" Dieter asked.

"Nathalie Olivia Duncan," she answered slowly. "I really am Nathalie Duncan."

"Good, now tell me what you know from this session. Anything will do."

"Well, I seemed to be quite young," she began, closing her eyes and sitting back. "Maybe four or five…I don't really know. I was very scared because I was in some sort of basement. I think my hands were tied together and then tied to a post or something. I had tape over my mouth, which hurt and made it hard to breathe. It was dark and cold. Charlotte put me there," she remembered. "Even that small I knew that she hated me."

She took a sip of brandy. "I think I was down there for a long time, but I'm not sure."

"You gave an address during the session," Dieter stated. "Do you think this cellar was at the house you lived in?"

"No, it wasn't. The house we lived in didn't have a cellar, I don't know why, but I remember that. I don't know where we were."

"What happened next?" Alex asked carefully, aware not to step on Dieter's toes.

"I remember hearing my mother's voice at the top of the stairs, she was calling my name and she sounded frantic. I remember trying to answer her, but I couldn't because of the gag. I remember being really scared that if I couldn't call out to her, she'd never find me. Then the door opened and both mothers… oh, God," she exclaimed suddenly. "That's why my nightmares always had two mothers—Good Mother and Bad Mother." Looking at Dieter, she whispered, "Now I understand that much at least." Then continuing with a sigh, "I think they were arguing as they came down the stairs. And the man was there."

"Do you know who this man was?" Dieter asked. "Or what his relationship was to either your mother or Charlotte?"

"No," she replied, trying hard to remember. "But I know that he used to be mean to George, and I don't know how I know that."

"What happened when your mother went into the cellar?" he asked, moving her on.

"She started calling my name, and I tried to struggle and call out, but I couldn't. It was a big area and I was behind a box or something. Then the man grabbed her by the hair and was forcing her to kiss him."

"What was Charlotte doing?"

"Looking at me and laughing. My mother pulled away and she saw where Charlotte was looking and tried to come to me. But they held on to her."

Nathalie was on her feet now, her eyes wide. Then just as quickly she dropped back onto the seat, her head between her hands, staring into the distance, struggling to remember.

"Oh God," she muttered finally, staring at the floor and becoming agitated. "Charlotte was yelling at her, she was so angry, and my mother was arguing back and trying to reach me. That's when Charlotte lashed out. She had something in her hand…maybe a hammer. My mother fell. The man was laughing, but then Charlotte was crying and holding my mother, begging her to wake up. When she didn't move, she started screaming at her that it was her fault, all her fault. While she was screaming, she was hitting her with the hammer, again and again. I'd closed my eyes, but then it went quiet and I opened them. Charlotte was coming toward me, and she was covered in blood. And then it all went black."

Now Nathalie was rocking back and forth on the chair, her hands running through her hair, tears pouring down her face. "Oh my God, I watched her kill my mother."

Alex was beside her in a shot, but Nathalie moved away.

"Leave her for a moment," Dieter said assertively. "Her mind and emotions are on overload. She needs to work through this herself."

Alex glared at him, but the psychologist in her knew he was right. What had come out of this session was enough to destroy anyone, and Nathalie had been fragile over Bella's death to begin with.

"You need to go home now, Nathalie," Dieter directed. "And you need to take strong sleeping tablets. You need time to rest and absorb the changes that have taken place. You had three or four years of lost memory that obviously involved terrible events, and bit by bit, much of that will start coming back to you. Because you were very young, some of it will only be impressions, but you need to be strong to deal with all of this. You need rest."

She'd stopped rocking now and was sitting back in her chair looking totally drained. "Are you saying I'll remember everything now?" she asked tonelessly.

"That's unlikely and what you do remember will probably come in bits and pieces and might not immediately make sense," he said, shaking his head. "We need to talk more and you'll need more hypnotherapy. In the meantime you might experience flashbacks or something totally unrelated may trigger a memory that you're not sure about. What we've done today is open up the opportunity for you to remember. We've taken away some of the fear Charlotte instilled to close off your memory. Some things that come back to you may not mean much, but that's normal for childhood memories. There will still be constraints, because you were so young, and Charlotte did a very good job of brainwashing you. That's where Alex will be able to help and support you. You need to tell her every time you remember something. She can help you expand on that memory and deal with any emotions they invoke. I want to see you again in two days."

* * *

On the way home, Nathalie remained deep in thought. The image of her mother was burned into her consciousness, yet she was terrified that if she didn't concentrate—didn't keep it at the forefront of her mind—it might fade away, never to be retrieved.

Olivia had been young, with light brown skin and straight jet black hair cut into the nape of her neck. Her eyes had been the warmest brown and her features fine and delicate. But it was the light in her mother's eyes when she'd spotted Nathalie in that cellar that lit her memory. It emanated a protective all-encompassing love unlike anything Nat had ever experienced. And then it was gone—snuffed out with a single blow. White-hot rage, so violent that she couldn't sit still, flooded every fiber of her being. She wanted to kill Charlotte and the man who'd taken her mother from her.

Suddenly, of its own volition a mournful groan escaped her lips and she was screaming at Alex to stop the car.

Alex stopped dead.

Instantly, Nathalie was out of the car and running full tilt across the open park.

Alex tried to follow, but she knew she could never outrun Nathalie and besides within a few paces Nat had disappeared into the darkness of the night.

"Oh God, Nat," Alex moaned, climbing back into the still-running car. "What the fuck have we done?"

Not sure what to do next, Alex sat in the car trying to peer into the darkness. Nat was in pain and confused. It was unforgivable that Alex should underestimate that, but all she could do now was cruise the exits and hope she'd calm down enough to get back into the car.

That didn't work. An hour later there was still no sign of her. While Alex's instincts informed her that Nat would be okay and would make her own way home when she was able, a lover's protectiveness was making it hard to accept that.

Eventually, returning to Nathalie's flat, she poured a large drink and, using every ounce of willpower at her disposal, sat in the semidarkened room to wait.

* * *

Nathalie ran and ran, stumbling and falling in the dark. Picking herself up, she plunged onward—oblivious to the scrapes and bruises she was collecting. Bitterness and anger drove her forward, kept her legs pumping. Her utter sense of loss caused her to sob and cry out as she staggered and weaved through bushes and trees and over tufted grass. Each time she hit a tree or bush she lashed out at it, punching and kicking and screaming her pain, until eventually there was no more power to drive the broken engine, and she fell to the ground moaning and sobbing, wet with sweat and bloody from dozens of cuts and bruises.

There she stayed, welcoming the pain in her lungs and legs, welcoming the coldness of the night as the sweat coated her in an icy layer. If only it could all end here and she could just go to sleep and never wake up.

And then a bitter certainty came over her—if she died tonight, Charlotte and all her evil would escape justice, and her pain and George's pain and her mother's death would all go unavenged. Even worse, Charlotte would be free to take George's children and start the whole cycle all over again. That was not going to happen.

It was four a.m. before Alex heard Nathalie at the door. By then she was terrified. But when Nathalie staggered in declaring, "I have to know what happened and why," she knew that at least mentally, Nathalie would survive. Physically she was a wreck, with blood smeared over her head, arms and hands.

Alex flew to embrace her. "God, Nat," she said desperately, kissing and touching her bloodied face. "I've been so worried."

"I'm sorry…I don't know…"

"Sssh," Alex whispered, gently touching her face. "It's okay. You're safe and that's all that counts, but you're freezing," she stated, stripping her of her damp clothing. "You need a warm bath before we do anything else." With tears in her eyes, she gently guided Nathalie toward the bathroom.

After the bath Alex gave Nat sleeping pills, dressed her wounds and made a hot drink. Most of the cuts were superficial, but Alex knew that there'd be extensive bruising, particularly on Nat's hands, feet and legs.

When they climbed into bed there was no discussion of the evening's events.

"Make love to me, Alex," Nathalie whispered as she clung to her. "I want to feel you inside me. I want you to love me."

Alex knew it had nothing to do with sex, as she gently touched and stroked her lover. It was all about reassurance and affection and comfort. Within moments Nat gave a gentle shudder and drifted into a dreamless sleep in the safe, warm cocoon of Alex's arms.

It took Alex considerably longer to fall asleep. Nathalie's session with Dieter played over and over in her mind. From what had come out, it seemed very likely that Charlotte Silver had killed Nat's mother and that Nat had witnessed the whole thing. Alex doubted that Charlotte would have had to work too hard on a four- or five-year-old child to force her to bury that sort of memory. Recovering from that memory would take a whole lot more effort.

CHAPTER FOURTEEN

Confrontation and Confession

The next morning, Nathalie and Alex each contacted their workplaces to extend their leave. Josh was happy for Nathalie to remain off. He told her that very little had developed with the murders but that Internal Affairs had been in contact and had cleared Nathalie of any wrongdoing in the death of Bella Pittolo.

Later that morning Alex rang her mother and told her what had been happening with Nathalie.

"I hope Nathalie can find out more about her childhood from that woman," Norma said. "But I doubt she'll admit to anything Nathalie has remembered through hypnosis. Please, just promise me you won't put yourself in danger. Charlotte Silver, or whoever she really is, is obviously ruthless and won't hesitate to hurt you both if you become a threat."

"I won't be taking any chances," Alex agreed. "But it appears to be the only way Nathalie will get to the truth." Alex parted with the promise that she'd keep in touch every couple of days.

* * *

Stiff and sore and with her myriad cuts and scratches stinging furiously, Nathalie was trying to focus on how to approach George. Quickly she placed another call to the house. Again Belinda answered, telling her that she really didn't know where George was, but she would leave some more messages for him.

It was only a couple of hours later that Belinda rang back. She sounded scared. "George rang here," she whispered. "I gave him your message and he said I could tell you where he was. I think he's hiding from your mother, so he didn't want to use his mobile." Passing on the address of a flat in the warehouse district, she said he'd expect Nat about eight o'clock and that he'd have something she wanted.

Nat wondered if he was finally going to give her the journal.

* * *

The area was made up of a combination of abandoned warehouses and warehouses developed into apartments. Eventually the whole area would be residential and probably quite expensive. The address was one of the better apartments with a sophisticated video intercom system.

"Why is *she* here?" George demanded when he finally answered the intercom. "She's not your friend, Nathalie," he stated. "I won't let her up."

"Then I'm not coming either," Nathalie responded, taking the risk that he actually wanted to see her. "Alex is part of my life, so you might as well get used to it."

It was a standoff, but it was only moments before his cold voice came back through the intercom. "Top floor," he spat before the door buzzed and they were on their way to the lift.

The lift was glass, modern and speedy. Each of the five floors appeared to house only one apartment and there was no sign of other occupants.

George ushered them in, staring in surprise at Nat's badly scratched and bruised face. But he made no comment, instead moving directly to the drink cart. Nathalie thought he looked awful. His shoulders slumped, his face pale and unshaven and his clothes rumpled.

"Do you want a drink?" he asked, addressing them both.

"No," Nat replied curtly. "I'm not here to socialize. I want answers about our childhood, and I'm not leaving without reading Mother's journal."

"I told you—"

"I know—you're protecting me," she cut in sarcastically. "But I'm not accepting that this time, George. I know that Charlotte killed my real mother. So you can't protect her anymore."

"Oh God, Nat," he moaned, putting down the decanter. "You don't know what you've done."

"He's right, you know," Charlotte said, stepping through the doorway.

"Mother!" Nathalie exclaimed, spinning to face her, then looking at George. "You told her I was coming?"

"He didn't need to," she interjected. "The cards told me betrayal was afoot and I knew you'd go for the weakest one."

"She made me ask you here," George stated flatly, refusing to look her in the eye. "We need to work this out."

"So you told her you had the journal? Which doubtless means it no longer exists?" Nathalie replied bitterly.

"So, you're Christine Martin's sister and my daughter's lover?" Charlotte declared, ignoring Nathalie and focusing her attention on Alex. "You don't look a bit like Christine. Much more attractive, although nowhere near as sexual. I think it's ironic that you end up with my daughter, given that it was Nathalie who seduced Christine in the first place."

"If I'm supposed to be shocked, you're wasting your time," Alex replied pointedly, trying hard to hide her revulsion for the woman before her. "Nathalie told me all about my sister and how she ended up with your family. We don't have any secrets."

"Well, well, so forgiving," Charlotte smirked. "But then Nathalie always did have a way with the women. Even I found her a pleasure to bed. Or could it be that you're just using her to get your revenge on our family?"

"You really are a piece of work, aren't you?" Alex responded icily. "I doubt you've ever experienced a human emotion."

"But I'm very rich and very powerful, so please don't think you can lord it over me, you overeducated little bitch. Now what do you want with George?" she asked, turning back toward Nathalie.

"I want to know why you killed my mother. I want to know who she was and why you didn't kill me when you had the chance." The words tumbled out angrily, yet even now Alex detected the inner fear.

"How dramatic…and uncivilized," Charlotte replied calmly. "You want to discuss matters of life and death, and yet you won't even take a drink from our host. Do sit down, child, so that we can talk rationally."

"I don't want to sit down, and I'm not your child. I want answers."

"Then there will be no discussion," she said turning away. "I will not be defied."

"Do what she wants," Alex suggested, gesturing toward the large sofa. "What's she going to do, Nat—attack us? I left the address we were coming to with my mother, so we're quite safe."

"Aha, yes, your mother," Charlotte said cryptically as she took a seat opposite the women. "Now there's a paragon of virtue. But we'll discuss her later. Right now we need to sort out why you would make the preposterous claim that I killed your mother. Given that I am your mother that statement would seem quite insane."

"No, it's you that's insane. I had hypnosis and I remember the house in America and the cellar. I know my real name and I know that you're *not* my mother. So let's stop fucking around," Nathalie retaliated angrily.

"Well then, you obviously have me cold," she retorted with a shrug, appearing totally unfazed by the revelation. "If the information came from hypnosis, then it must be true. Although… somehow I don't think you can use it in court. So I guess you're back at square one. And if you think I'm going to discuss this with you without George searching you first, then you really are quite delusional. Well, George," she snapped suddenly, making him start. "What are you waiting for, search them and be thorough."

At first Alex wanted to refuse, but she knew if she did, Charlotte would disappear without ever speaking to Nathalie.

When George finished, Charlotte indicated for them to sit down again. The whole scenario had a surreal quality to it.

It scared Alex how attractive and charismatic the woman appeared and yet how vicious and evil she truly was. One minute she was charming and sweet and just as suddenly ruthless and cold. It was easy to see how people, especially young people, could so easily fall under her spell. She would be anything you wanted her to be—a chameleon offering generosity, sexuality and acceptance—until you were trapped in the mire of her true personality.

"Why should I tell you anything?" she questioned, sipping on a drink. "I owe you nothing. I raised you as my own when your mother left, and you lived well."

"Left?" Nathalie spluttered. "You killed her. You abused me, you lied to me and you sold me to anyone who wanted me—to make money? What I want—"

"What *you* want?" Charlotte spat through clenched teeth. "What you want? Who cares what you want? You're so like her. She thought she had the right to be ungrateful, the right to treat me as if everything I'd done for her was nothing. But she found out differently, and so will you." Then, very softly, "I loved her though…I loved her so much…but she thought she could leave me."

Nathalie was stunned. "What do you mean you loved her?"

"She was my lover," Charlotte responded triumphantly. "We were lovers for years."

Nathalie turned to George, confused. "You told me the journal said that Charlotte was jealous of my mother because Charlotte had loved my father?"

"I—" George stuttered.

"What would George know?" Charlotte cut in coldly. "George wouldn't have the brains to understand my journal."

Glancing at George, Alex noted that with each comment directed at him by Charlotte, he shrunk into his seat—the picture of a beaten man.

"So what's the true story?" Alex challenged. "Nathalie's regaining her memory, so she's eventually going to remember anyway. Why not tell her your version? You know how memories can distort things."

Charlotte glared, but she lifted her head and shoulders defensively.

"If you loved Nathalie's mother, why did you kill her?" Alex persisted gently.

"That…that was an accident," she answered, looking into the distance. "She was leaving me again. She was going to the police…and I couldn't have any of that."

"Going to the police about what?" Alex asked, glancing at Nathalie, who acknowledged that she should continue asking the questions.

"We were in the same foster home, you see," Charlotte explained, focusing on the distant past. "It was an awful place, dark and fetid. I was twelve when Olivia arrived and she was a year younger and so beautiful. Dark and exotic and intelligent. Her father was Native American, and her mother was white. Both of them were useless junkies who died or disappeared. She'd been in and out of care for years. Just like me." Again she stared into the distance, her face hard and cold. "There were six kids at the home," she continued. "And the old man took turns with each of us, but at least we got fed and were pretty much allowed to do whatever we wanted. Sometimes he'd entertain friends and they'd pay to use us, and at those times we got extra money to buy clothes or go to movies. It didn't worry me, but Olivia hated it and wanted to run away. After a while we became lovers and eventually we left together."

"How old were you?" asked Alex, reverting to the psychologist role.

"Thirteen or fourteen…"

Alex knew Nathalie wanted to ask a thousand questions, but she discouraged her with a look that said, "If you stop her, she may not continue."

"We did men for money and got our own cheap little flat. I was so happy. She made me so happy. Then some of them started to pay us for being together with them, they liked the contrast of my fairness and Olivia's darkness. Word spread, and a lot of businessmen who were into young girls started using us. The money was excellent and we lived very well." Sighing, she continued with her recollections. "I thought it was exciting, but Olivia hated it. She wanted to go back to school. When she went to school she was always top of the class. We argued about it a lot, but in the end I gave in—and that was my biggest mistake. The cards told me not to let her, but I did anyway. That was the last time I didn't listen to the cards. They don't lie."

For a moment she stopped talking, and Nathalie thought she wasn't going to continue.

"She was spoilt, you see," she said eventually, directing the comment at Alex. "She had me, she had plenty of money, but she wanted more. She wanted to be a nurse and eventually maybe a doctor."

"Why was school such a bad thing?" Alex asked, trying to keep her talking.

"It was okay for a year or so," she acknowledged. "We still worked together when the clients wanted doubles, but otherwise she studied and I worked. She was very clever and finished high school in twelve months. But then she went to college and that's when she met him."

"Him?" questioned Alex.

"Andre Abraham, Nathalie's father."

George rose quietly and poured four drinks, handing one to each of them. Then just as silently, he sat back down.

Nathalie shook her head at Alex to warn her not to drink. She knew that the drink could be laced with anything. It was a favorite party trick of Charlotte's. She noted that neither George nor Charlotte took a drink either.

"What was he like?" Nathalie asked, unable to stop herself.

Looking directly at her for the first time in a while, Charlotte curled her lip in a sneer, "What do you think your father would be like? He was as ugly as you with gray eyes. It was bad enough that Olivia had dark blood. I forgave her for that, because I loved her, and she was beautiful. But to screw some New York Jew boy without getting paid—it couldn't be allowed. Of course, I didn't know about it then," she said, her eyes focusing on the distance again. "He was another student, and they started having coffee together. At least that's what she said when I finally found out about it." She moved into silence, deep in her own thoughts.

And it seemed to stretch to minutes.

Alex didn't know whether to say something but decided against it.

Eventually, Charlotte sighed, pulled herself a little more upright in the chair and began again. "But before I found out about them the cards told me I was being betrayed, so I decided to test her. I told her that she needed to go back to work. She refused. It was the first time she'd ever defied me. That was when I fell pregnant with George. Olivia was thrilled and wanted me to keep the baby, but I didn't want some squalling brat, so I was going to get rid of it…"

Alex looked at George and saw the pain on his face as he stared at his mother.

"Then she told me she'd go back to work if I kept him. She promised she'd stop going to college," she continued. "She said she'd look after the baby. And I could see the value in using the baby to keep her around, even if I had to sell it later. People pay a lot of money for white, healthy babies on the black market. It was worth the risk."

"My God," Nathalie blurted, looking at George, who was on his feet and pacing behind his chair. "He's your son."

"You are so much your mother's daughter," she snarled. "So completely crippled by your pathetic emotions and society's rules. Anyone can spawn brats, even people like my drunken useless mother and your drug-addled grandparents. Animals rut and babies are born. It's meaningless. It is how you turn that nothingness into something of value that counts."

"I'm going to the bathroom," George mumbled as he headed from the room. "Please feel free to carry on without me, Mother."

"Don't be long," she demanded. "It's your fault that we have to rehash all this old history, so you *will* be here to hear it."

She didn't speak again until he returned a few minutes later. Somehow, George seemed more buoyant than when he left.

Nathalie assumed he'd popped or snorted something while he was gone.

"Anyway," Charlotte continued, glaring at George. "George was born and it became very annoying. Everything was for the baby. It took all of her time and attention, and then she'd be tired and not want sex. She expected to drop out of our business— supposedly because she didn't want to leave George, but I suspected otherwise, and naturally I wasn't going to tolerate that for too long. So I decided to bring the clients to her. I told her that if she didn't buck up her ideas, I'd take the baby and find it another home. That brought her into line."

"Yes, I suppose it would," Alex commented dryly.

For a second Charlotte wasn't sure if Alex was being sarcastic, but she decided to ignore it, because she was actually enjoying telling her story. After all, it wasn't as if these two women would ever get the chance to tell anyone else. She had that covered nicely.

"So, how did Olivia—"

"Have Nathalie?" interrupted Charlotte. "That stupid Abraham bastard just couldn't leave things alone. He tracked her down through college records and made contact. I knew nothing about it, because the bitch didn't tell me. She told me later that she'd confessed to him how we made a living. She wanted him to go away because she was afraid of losing George. But he wasn't put off and declared his love…and she fell for it. Of course they kept their relationship hidden, but the cards told me about it and I started watching her whenever she left the house. Eventually I saw them together. She would take George with her when she went to meet him."

At this point her face was like stone, her eyes burning with hatred.

"I watched them for weeks," she continued viciously. "Because I wanted them to feel nice and safe before I taught them not to cross me. They were like stupid children—wandering in parks or taking George to the beach. Playing happy families with *my* son. He'd carry George around on his back. He'd even change his nappy. Pathetic! Of course I knew she was sleeping with him."

"Did you confront her?" asked Alex, glancing at Nathalie and George, both of whom appeared mesmerized.

"Don't be ridiculous. The cards told me that I had to do something much more permanent." At this point Charlotte began gently rubbing her forehead, deep in thought and seemingly oblivious to her horrified audience.

For a while she didn't speak.

Alex indicated with a shake of the head for Nathalie and George not to say anything. She wanted to believe that Charlotte telling the story was her way of getting it off her conscience, but she knew otherwise. This was Charlotte bragging about her actions. Promoting how clever and powerful she was. It occurred to Alex that Charlotte was the consummate sociopath.

"She left me," she suddenly stated. "Before I could decide what to do, they disappeared. I was doing readings all day at some society luncheon. When I got home she was gone, and so was George. I went around to Abraham's apartment, but it was empty."

Now she looked at Nathalie. "She stole my son from me. That's why I kept you after she died. I wanted her to know there was a price for stealing from me."

"But that must have been years later, and my mother was dead. How was that going to punish her?" Nathalie asked in disgust.

"The dead see everything," Charlotte answered matter-of-factly. "Every time I punished you I made you more and more mine. I knew she'd be crying and I wanted her to cry. She was supposed to be with me. We could have been rich and powerful together, but the cards said she'd betray me and she did."

"When did you see Olivia again?" Alex asked, trying to divert Charlotte back to the story.

"It took me eighteen months to track her down. By then I had important contacts in the police—men who enjoyed my favors. They were living in another city. She told me later that he came from a wealthy family and that they were angry that he'd gotten involved with someone with a young baby, a woman who wasn't Jewish and who had seemingly appeared from nowhere. They assumed she was after his money. Of course they would have been even more against it if they'd known her background. Apparently they cut him off financially until he came to his senses. So they never knew they were to have a grandchild. Of course Olivia could have made good money, but he wouldn't let her." Charlotte shook her head to indicate her lack of understanding about that decision. Then she continued, "He got some menial casual job and continued studying. Olivia studied with him, looked after George and got pregnant. I gather you were an accident," she said, staring at Nathalie. "But of course there was no way they would consider an abortion. So here you are."

"So Nathalie's mother raised me?" George interrupted. "I remember some of it." He was addressing Nathalie now. "I remember a time when I was happy and safe, when I felt like someone loved me. I remember the lovely smell and softness of a woman who would cuddle me, talk to me kindly, tuck me up in bed and read me stories. I thought it was her," he said, looking at his mother, "and that she'd changed later on. But it was never you, was it, Mother?" he asked in a defeated tone. "It was never you. And to think I used to cling to the idea that if you loved me in the past, and if I was very good, then maybe one day you'd care for me like that again. As much as I hated it, I was even grateful when we shared a bed, because I thought that meant you loved me."

"You sound pathetic," she snapped. "I've let you be part of my relationships and part of the business and you're not even grateful. She made you soft and demanding in those early years. When she went, you were clingy and pathetic. I thought of getting rid of you, but you had my looks and I knew that with Nathalie and you together—dark and light, we could make a lot of money. I gave you a good life. You could have sex anytime you wanted, with anyone you wanted. You had money, clothes, jewelry and good cars, and I never tried to keep you for myself. It would have been any young boy's dream."

George appeared cowed and lost, while Charlotte reveled in her ability to strip away the last remnants of his self-esteem.

Nathalie wanted to scream that what she made him do, what she made them both do, had nothing to do with love. She wanted to attack her and scream her outrage for all the pain of those abusive years. But she didn't want her to stop talking about her mother, and so with a huge effort of will she forced herself to sit still, looking only at her knees in case her disgust and anger communicated itself.

Alex was feeling the pain of both of them. She could see that Nathalie was struggling to maintain control, while George was reduced to being a small boy again, totally under his mother's control. Like Nathalie, she knew that one wrong word or signal would stop this woman from continuing.

"How did Olivia end up back with you?" Alex asked quietly. "You said she was with Nathalie's father, so what happened to change that?"

"It was brilliant," she enthused. "Olivia had Nathalie and George to look after and no car, so it was difficult to get around. I used to watch them, and I saw that the Jew would pick up their shopping after work each Monday and Thursday. It was dark by the time he came out of the shops and he had to cross to the other side of the road. I hired a powerful SUV, used a disguise and obscured the license plate, and when he stepped off the pavement, I stepped on the gas. He didn't stand a chance," she said joyfully. "Any witnesses wouldn't have had time to take the number, even if it hadn't been obscured, and I was dressed like a guy with a baseball cap and glasses. I knew they'd never trace who did it."

"My God, you killed him too," exclaimed Nathalie. "Why?"

"He took something from me. He took Olivia, he took my son and, worse, he gave her a baby."

"But I still don't understand why my mother would return to you," Nathalie stated, struggling with her anger. "She would have to suspect you killed my father."

"She would have if I'd suddenly shown up. But I didn't. I left her to sweat it out with two small children and no income. She got kicked out of the house they had and ended up in a couple of rooms. I didn't come back into her life until about six months later, and then I pretended that I'd only just managed to track her down through Social Security. Remember, she believed that I didn't even know about Andre Abraham, so she didn't suspect his death was anything more than a random hit-and-run."

"So you went there as her savior," stated Alex in an understanding voice.

"That was the idea, but she refused to come back. Can you believe that? Living in terrible rooms with two brats and she turned down all that I could offer. But her stubbornness didn't last long when I told her that I was taking George. He was three by then, and she kept bleating that she was the only mother he'd ever known…God, how she begged. In the end she decided to return with me, providing she could continue to raise the children as siblings."

"You agreed?"

"Of course. They were exactly what I needed to keep control of her. I intended to make sure there would never be another Abraham, and the threat of losing George would ensure she helped in the business and earned her keep. It was supposed to be perfect."

Even in the prison, Alex knew that she'd never met anyone as vicious or calculating as Charlotte Silver. There wasn't the slightest hint of human emotion.

"So what went wrong?" Alex asked carefully.

Now, for the first time, Alex thought the woman actually looked agitated.

For a few moments she stared off into the distance again. "The bloody journals," she muttered quietly. "The cards told me I shouldn't keep journals, but I like to see things in writing. When it's written down it means that it's real. You understand what I mean, don't you?" she asked, addressing Alex. "Otherwise, when you're dead people will forget what you did."

"Yes, I do understand," Alex replied, astounded at the blind arrogance of the woman. "It's important to be remembered as someone who takes charge."

"Exactly," she exclaimed, strangely pleased. "Anyway," she continued with a sigh, "Olivia had often seen me writing my journals, but she never asked what was in them, so I suppose I got complacent."

"How did you get on after Olivia returned?" asked Alex, trying to understand the dynamics of the relationship at the time.

"Not very well," she admitted in an annoyed voice. "She couldn't get it into her head that we had to do certain things to build the business and keep our reputation for being discreet. She was constantly arguing with my decisions. But the real problems came when Vladimir moved in. She hated him."

"Who was Vladimir?" asked Alex, suspecting he was the other person in the cellar when Olivia died.

"I took him on as security, but he was so handsome and powerful in bed that I let him stay at the house. Both male and female clients loved him, and he loved the business. Olivia wouldn't let him touch her and her refusal was getting out of hand. He was threatening to start up a business for himself. She always kept the kids out of our way, but one day George did something to upset Vlad, and he punished him." A small vindictive smile contorted her lips as if the memory brought a moment's pleasure. "Anyway, Olivia heard George screaming and attacked Vlad. Of course he got the better of her and finally took what he'd wanted all along."

"You saw it happening?" gasped Nathalie, jumping to her feet and leaning over Charlotte. "I thought you were supposed to have loved her?"

Alex was beside her in a second, fearing that she'd attack Charlotte physically.

Charlotte hardly blinked. "Don't take me on, child," she stated coldly, rising to her feet. "You lose every time."

"I'm not a child anymore," Nathalie replied, trying to get past Alex. "I'm not afraid of you now."

"Really?" retaliated Charlotte. "Remember the forest."

A cloak of fear enveloped Nathalie, causing the blood to drain from her face and her feet to root to the spot.

Alex saw the change immediately, as did Charlotte.

"Don't ever forget the forest," she repeated viciously. "How many times did you mess yourself in the forest, but you soon learned not to take me on."

Nat was shaking now, yet making no attempt to move. Alex didn't know if it was rage or fear.

"What forest?" Alex asked, still standing in front of Nathalie. "What are you talking about?"

"I don't have to discuss this with you. It was something between us. In fact, I don't have to discuss any of it. I was trying to help Nathalie understand why my actions were necessary, but obviously all she wants to do is blame. This conversation is over."

Now George was on his feet, looking at his mother expectantly.

"Make the call," she snapped at him. "It's time these two found out exactly how it's going to be."

For a moment he hesitated, then he disappeared into another area.

"I'm sure Nathalie didn't mean anything." Alex tried to placate Charlotte. "Please, let's all sit down and finish what we started."

"Oh, I intend to," Charlotte said, raising her head high and straightening her shoulders. "But I have no intention of telling you anything more. You will have to spend the rest of your life wondering." This was aimed at Nathalie, who stared back, anger emanating from every pore.

"Then we'll have no option but to go to the police with what we know," Alex replied. "And we'll leave them to investigate."

"Either you're stupid, or you think I am. Did you really think I would have told you anything you could use against me? You have no idea where any of this took place, not even what country. And if you think I used people's correct names, then you really are naïve—"

"Except that I remember things now," Nathalie interrupted. "I remember my full name and I know my mother's name was Olivia Duncan, so I know you were telling the truth—"

"No, you know what your mother called herself," she said with a vicious smile. "Duncan was the name she used after running away from the foster home. I made her change her name because the police were looking for us. She stupidly thought it was because she was fourteen when we'd run away, but it was because I went back and set fire to the house the next day. I knew the police would suspect us…be looking for us."

"God," muttered Nathalie.

"I don't know why but she didn't give you your father's surname, which wasn't Abraham by the way," she gloated, impressed by her own cleverness. "I guess she never wanted him having a claim on you."

"Or she was trying to protect him from you," snapped Nathalie. "I know my mother died in San Diego," she continued. "I know from the memories I retrieved."

"No, you know that that was where you once lived. You have no idea where your mother died…assuming she's even dead."

"What…?" Nathalie's mind spun.

"She knows her mother's dead," interjected Alex angrily, "because if she wasn't, she would never have let you take Nathalie or George from her. Even now you want to play with Nathalie's head?"

"*Olivia wouldn't let me?*" Charlotte almost screamed. "Nobody *lets* me do anything. I do what I want. But the reality is that Olivia wasn't there for them. She abandoned them and she abandoned me. *I* raised them and they owe *me*. But instead of being grateful they want to betray me."

"Come on, Nat," Alex said, moving away slightly. "She's obviously not going to tell you anything more and it looks like she's not letting George out of her sight. We'll start an inquiry and get to the bottom of this that way."

"That's an option," Charlotte replied smugly. "And who knows, you might even uncover some information, but if you do that, then you'll never see your mother again."

Nathalie assumed this was directed at her, but strangely it seemed to be Alex she was talking to. For a moment confusion showed on both their faces.

"I have your mother," Charlotte stated coldly, now obviously addressing Alex. "I'm quite happy to let you talk to her."

"What…?"

"My friends pretended to be the police and told her you'd been in an accident and that they'd take her to you. She got quite upset I gather, but nowhere near as upset as she is now. I don't think she likes me very much."

"If you've harmed her—"

"She won't be harmed if you two do exactly as you're told. Otherwise…"

The sentence was left hanging.

"You're bluffing," Nathalie declared defiantly.

"George, bring me the phone."

Dutifully George handed Charlotte his mobile phone, which she passed on to Alex.

"Mum?" Alex asked tentatively into the mouthpiece. Then listening for a moment, "Mum, where are you?" Alex demanded. "Are you okay? Have they hurt you?"

"That's enough," snapped Charlotte, indicating for George to take the phone from Alex.

"Mum, I love you," she managed before George took the phone from her hand.

"What the hell are you doing?" she demanded, pushing George away and turning on Charlotte. "Why are you doing this?"

"A little insurance, my dear," Charlotte replied. "I'm leaving the country tonight on a private charter, and I want to retire in comfort. I've started arranging the transfer of my assets and cash to a place with no extradition and lots of sunny beaches, and I want to ensure that I get there without any problems. But in case I ever want to return to the States, I wanted my missing journal returned."

"Why are you helping her with this?" Nathalie asked bitterly, addressing George. "After everything she's done to us. After what you heard today."

"She's my mother," he said flatly. "She's my flesh and blood— you're not."

"We have a deal," Charlotte stated gloatingly, overriding him. "He's helping me to convert my assets and he's returned my journal. In return, I've guaranteed to return the children to their mothers."

"You have the children?" Nathalie challenged, trying to grab Charlotte. But she was expecting it and moved quickly away as George stepped between them.

"She's in trouble in the States," George said. "Some of her regular clients got caught in a pedophile investigation and rolled over on her. She came here to give herself enough time for me to transfer her money and assets and to have new passports and identity documents created. I don't want to help her," he finished desperately. "I love you and I wanted you to have the journal, but I can't let her hurt the children. So I've had to help her. If I don't do this the animals that have the kids will hand them over to some of her friends…and you know what will happen to them. It's you or them," he finished quietly.

His face was stony, but Alex recognized it hid deep anguish.

"You don't have to explain to her," snarled Charlotte. "Just do what you have to." Then turning to Nathalie, she said, "Norma Martin will be fine and so will the kids, providing you keep your mouth shut and that includes after I'm gone. Remember that I have powerful friends and I can get to her or those children anytime. I want to leave here cleanly, so if you do what I say, you'll have nothing to worry about."

"There's no end to your evil, is there?" stated Alex, at a loss as to what to do.

"If you harm Norma Martin or those children," Nathalie said, moving closer to Charlotte, "I'll find you and you will wish for death. Just remember how much I learned from you."

The steel in Nathalie's voice made Charlotte take a step back. Then recovering, she said, "You two will contact nobody until you hear from George. When we're safely at our destination, George will tell you where the Martin woman and the kids are. If our friends don't hear from us within thirty-six hours you will never see them again. The choice is yours."

"Please, Nat, just do what she says," George begged. "I'll make sure she keeps her word. Then the children can go to their mums and you two can get on with your lives. You'll never have to see us again. You can't change the past, but you and the kids have a chance to move on. Please."

"We don't have a choice, do we?" snapped Alex angrily.

Charlotte stared at Nathalie. "And you? Will you do what I want? Will you obey Mother?"

Nathalie nodded, hatred pouring from her soul.

"Stay in the flat for at least another hour," Charlotte demanded. "And then you're free to go. George will call your mobile within twenty-four hours."

Turning and marching to the door with George in her wake, the woman entered the hallway. Glancing back as they exited, George nodded and, pointing to the back of the flat, nodded again, before following Charlotte out.

Both women glanced behind them after George left, expecting to see someone, but there were only the empty rear living areas. Nathalie was angry, but Alex was panic-stricken.

"Oh God," she muttered after the door closed. "How do we know she'll keep her word? What if something happens to Mum?"

Nathalie didn't know what to say. She didn't trust Charlotte either.

"There has to be some record of a property she or George owns," Nathalie stated, going into detective mode. "The records would be at George's house. We need to start searching."

"That could take days," Alex answered desperately. "What if we don't get the phone call?"

Taking Alex in her arms, Nat said, "It's in her interest to do what she said, otherwise she knows we'll go to the police. If your mother and two children are missing, it would become a major investigation involving Interpol. She also knows that if she returns them safely the police won't follow up in another country—especially one without extradition."

"Oh God, I hope you're right."

"The first thing we need to do is check out this apartment," Nathalie stated. "I don't know what George was pointing at when he left, but it's worth a look."

The apartment was a very large three-bedroom, with walk-in closets and their own bathrooms. When they attempted to walk into the third closet they found the door locked.

"Why would you lock a closet door unless you had something to hide?" Alex asked. "There might be a clue to where Mum is."

It took a few attempts at kicking the lock, but eventually the door splintered and they fell inside. It was a big room, but instead of the expected boxes of personal items they assumed would be in there, it was set up with video recording equipment. The shelves and hangers had been removed and a ledge containing monitors installed instead. In total there were two cameras hidden somewhere in each of the rooms. The equipment was high-quality digital.

"What does this mean?" Alex asked, trying to fathom some of the equipment.

"They've been recording all the activity in this apartment," Nathalie stated thoughtfully. "She used to do that with high-profile clients. She called it her protection."

"So is it recording now?" she asked. "It's set on the area we were in."

"It looks like it," answered Nathalie, a little puzzled. "But why would she record us? With what she was confessing, she'd leave herself wide open to being charged."

"Unless she didn't know," replied Alex suddenly. "Remember George leaving to go to the bathroom? I must admit he looked a whole lot better when he returned. And he did indicate for us to check this back area. He'd know the equipment like the back of his hand, because he would have been the one using it all the time."

"Let me see if I can get this stuff to playback," Nat said, moving to the workbench and fiddling with the equipment.

Suddenly one of the screens covering the lounge area went blank. Pressing "Play" on the equipment, they watched as the discussion in that room, complete with sound, played out for them.

"George obviously wanted us to have this," Alex said as they watched Charlotte telling her story. "I guess he wants to help you after all," she said quietly.

"Then he wouldn't have helped her take your mother," Nathalie said bitterly. "She couldn't have done this without his help."

"Maybe he didn't know the full story. He seemed upset when she was talking about how your mother raised him, especially when she made it very clear that, but for your mother's interference, she would have gotten rid of him."

"Then all he had to do was stand up to her and tell us where your mother and the children are being held."

"Unless he genuinely doesn't know where they are. If he doesn't know where she's holding the children then he's as much over a barrel as you and I." Glancing over at the equipment, she asked, "What about these other monitors? Switch them on and see what areas they cover."

When they lit up they appeared to be looking at another lounge area and three other bedrooms, although two of the bedrooms were in darkness. The women looked at each other questioningly.

"It has to be one of the other apartments in this building," suggested Alex. "The layout is the same. What if George owns the other apartments? They'd be ideal for his business—very discreet. Perfect for the parties we know he runs."

"I wonder why those two bedrooms are in darkness," Nat said, staring at the two dark monitors. "What if your mother and the kids are there?"

"So what do we do?" Alex asked.

"We knock on the door. I'll make out that George sent me. If we get a response we could be onto something."

"Then what? They're bound to be armed?"

"Or maybe there is no *them*," Nathalie suggested. "I can't see any movement at all on the monitors. Maybe everyone's tied up in those darkened rooms, and whoever brought them there has gone. We have to try."

"But which flat?" asked Alex worriedly. "We don't know where these cameras are set up."

"I think the next floor down," replied Nathalie. "It makes sense that this bank of monitors would cover this flat and the closest flat to it. We have to give it a try."

The foyer area on the fourth level looked exactly like the one above, as did the front door of the flat. Knocking tentatively, the two women waited. Nothing happened. This time they knocked much louder, still nothing. The third knock included a loud shout of "Hello," but the result was the same.

"I'm going to break in," Nathalie said finally. "I'm willing to bet that George or Charlotte own all of these. There was only the one locked mailbox when we came in, instead of five separate boxes. And this setup is too perfect for the business. Even if there's nobody in there, there might be information that would be useful. I just have to go back upstairs and get something to fiddle with the lock."

A minute later she returned with an assortment of items including a tiny ice pick, paperclips and her credit card. "I learned a whole array of skills at Mother's hands," Nat commented dryly. "Now maybe they'll be useful. It's a fairly flimsy lock, because all the security is concentrated on the outside doors and windows— another reason I think they're all owned by the same person."

It was nowhere as simple as it looked in the movies and after ten minutes of fiddling Alex was growing impatient.

"Just trust me," Nat said gently, recognizing Alex's fear for her mother. "We will get into the flat, even if we have to batter the door down."

Suddenly there was a click and the lock sprung open. For a second they both smiled, then, remembering the seriousness of their task, they carefully entered the empty lounge.

It was a replica of the one above, only untidy. Bottles of beer and food wrappers cluttered the expensive coffee table, cushions were disturbed and *Playboy* magazines were left on chairs or on the floor.

Moving slowly, the women made their way toward the rear of the apartment and began opening bedroom doors. The first bedroom was the one that was lit and it was obvious at first glance that it was empty, even the walk-in closet was open to view. The next room was darkened by shades and curtains but was also empty—although someone had recently used the bed, which was unmade and messy.

It was in the third bedroom that they found Norma Martin.

At first Alex thought her mother was dead. She was lying on the bed with her hands and feet bound. Her arms were behind her and tape was plastered across her mouth. When the light went on, she didn't move. "Oh God, Mum," moaned Alex, moving straight to her. "Mum…Mum…can you hear me?"

Still there was no movement.

While Alex tore pointlessly at the rope binding her mother's arms, Nathalie felt for a pulse. Norma was warm and the pulse was quite discernible.

"She's alive," she told Alex. "Get a serrated knife with a thin blade from the kitchen. She's obviously drugged, but she's going to be okay."

"We have to call an ambulance," Alex argued.

"Just get the knife," demanded Nathalie, aware that they hadn't yet found the children. "Then we'll decide what to do."

When Alex returned moments later with a steak knife, they cut the ropes on Norma's wrists and ankles. All the time Alex was talking to her, begging her to respond.

Collecting a cold washcloth, Nathalie began gently wiping the sleeping woman's face. At first she only moaned, but finally she opened her eyes.

Drowsy and disoriented, she was helped to sit up.

"Oh, Alex…darling," Norma muttered, pulling Alex into her embrace. "Thank God, you're okay."

"Thank God, I'm okay?" questioned Alex in disbelief. "You're the one they drugged and tied up."

"They told me you'd been in a car accident," Norma said, attempting to sit on the side of the bed. "They said you were critical. They had police ID and offered to take me to the hospital."

"Oh, Mum," cried Alex, wrapping her mother in a huge bear hug. "I thought they'd killed you." The tears were pouring down her face now, but she didn't know whether to laugh or cry. The relief was unbelievable.

"I don't remember anything after I got into the car," she said. "Maybe just a sting on my hand. I actually thought I'd been bitten by something, and then everything went black. I woke up here once, and somebody came into the room and shoved the phone to my mouth to talk to you. Then there was another sting, this time on my neck, and that was the last thing I remember."

"What about the children?" Nathalie interrupted. "What did they do with the children?"

"What children?"

"My niece and nephew were supposed to be here. Charlotte supposedly grabbed them at the same time as she grabbed you."

"I'm sorry, Nathalie," she said slowly. "I never saw the children. What is this all about?"

"It's too complicated to explain fully," Alex said gently. "But Charlotte was holding you and the children so that we couldn't stop her leaving the country. If we went to the police, she threatened to harm you all."

"So, how did you find me?"

"Just luck," mumbled Nathalie distractedly. "But we still can't go to the police because we don't know if the children are safe or not."

"Surely she wouldn't hurt her own grandchildren?" Norma asked, her head still spinning from the drugs.

Alex and Nathalie exchanged glances but said nothing.

"So we have to wait for her call," muttered Nathalie, the frustration bringing tears to her eyes. "I just don't trust her."

Leaving her mother, Alex went to Nat and, taking her in her arms, wiped the tears from her face. "They'll be all right, darling," she whispered, not sure if she believed it herself. "George wouldn't let her harm them. I really believe that."

"But, as you said, I don't think he knows where they are. I'm so scared for them," she whispered back. "I'm so scared they'll end up…" She couldn't bring herself to finish the thought.

"I think we have to wait for the call now," Alex said, helping her mother toward the lounge room. "But in the meantime we can have a look in the other couple of apartments downstairs, just in case."

They were empty—no sign of occupancy and no children.

Returning to the fifth-floor apartment, they collected the digital recordings of Charlotte's conversation and then took Norma home. She was feeling better and insisted she didn't need medical care.

When they each had a hot drink and a sandwich in front of them, Alex told Norma the story.

"I'm so sorry, Nathalie," Norma said at the end. "I'd already come to believe that you and George were her victims, but I really had no idea how bad it was."

In the end they dozed off. The phone call might not come for hours, but Nathalie wasn't willing to risk the children. She knew how vicious Charlotte could be if crossed and she didn't want to force her hand. She just had to trust that ultimately George would protect his family.

CHAPTER FIFTEEN

Taking a Stand

When Nathalie's mobile went off, it woke them with a fright.

"Nathalie Duncan?" asked the slightly accented voice on the other end.

"Yes," she mumbled, knowing this was the call, but wondering why it had come so early.

"Ms. Duncan, it's Detective Sergeant Michael Russo, from the Federal Police attached to Sydney Airport," the voice explained unexpectedly. "Do you have a brother named George Silver?"

"Yes," she stuttered, wondering what was happening.

"It's my understanding that you're a serving police officer in the New South Wales Police Force and also a lawyer. Is that true?"

"Yes…yes," she stated impatiently. "What's going on?"

"Ms. Duncan, we have your brother, George Silver, in custody at Mascot Police Station. He's given me your number and asked me to contact you. He won't give us any kind of statement or even speak to us until you're present."

"Why is he there?" she asked, completely confused.

"I think we need to talk to you about that at the station, but it's not good news, I'm afraid," he finished on a more kindly note.

"Please, we're both in the job," she begged. "Just tell me what's happened for him to be in custody."

For a moment or two he hesitated. "I'm afraid there's been a shooting at the airport. We have no real idea what happened. But the pilot of their private plane told us that your brother got into an argument with your mother when she tried to take two small children onto the plane with them. It seems your brother pulled a gun, forced the pilot to leave the hangar and take the children with him. He also told him to call the police when he got to safety. A few moments later the pilot heard two shots. When airport police arrived, your brother was sitting beside the body of your mother and a Smith and Wesson revolver was on the floor. Police arrested your brother, but he refused to say anything, except to give them your phone number and the phone numbers for the children's families."

Numerous scenarios flooded her brain. Charlotte was dead, the children were safe and George…

"Ms. Duncan, are you there?" The detective's voice was worried now. Had he overstepped the mark telling a relative that her family was in serious trouble over the phone?

"Yes. I understand. I'll come straight over to the station," she managed finally. "And thank you for letting me know what was happening."

Norma insisted that Alex go with Nathalie. "I'm fine," she said. "Just a little groggy, but I fully intend to sleep that off. At least we know the children are safe and that will help me rest."

* * *

They were expecting her, and as soon as she showed her ID at the counter they ushered both women into the detectives' office.

Michael Russo was a big middle-aged man dressed in an immaculate suit. He had a highly professional and disciplined attitude, yet Alex could imagine him with a lap full of laughing grandchildren. After introducing himself and his subordinate, he asked who Alex was.

"She's my partner," Nathalie answered openly, "but she's also a clinical psychologist and knows all about the situation."

"And what situation would that be?" Russo asked in his best interrogation voice.

"I need to speak to my brother first, please," she insisted, looking him squarely in the eyes.

They'd spoken about it on the way to the station—how much to tell, how much to keep back. Nathalie decided it was pointless to tell anyone the full story. Charlotte was dead, the children were safe and George was in custody. Besides, who would believe it if she started from the beginning? So they'd decided on an abridged version and hoped that they could get that message to George.

"I can't let you do that," Russo replied. "You of all people should know that."

"Then I guess I'm wasting my time," she answered stubbornly. "Because until I can speak to him privately I won't be telling you anything, and as a lawyer, I'll be recommending that George Silver doesn't say anything either."

"That's a conflict of interest," he stated firmly. "You're putting your job on the line. If you have information in your mother's death, then you need to pass it on now."

"Charlotte Silver wasn't my mother," she explained coolly. "She was George's mother. I don't know what happened, but, providing I can have time alone with him, I will encourage George to tell you what happened. Obviously he's not denying killing her."

"No," he replied reluctantly. "He said he did it to keep you and the children safe—whatever that means. Then he refused to give us further information. The pilot had lodged a flight plan for Darwin and then another for Indonesia, supposedly with a cargo of children's clothes. There was no manifest for passengers, so whatever your family was doing, it was obviously illegal."

Nathalie didn't say a word but continued the eye contact.

There was frustration on Russo's face as well as reluctant respect, but he continued to be professional. "I don't have the authority to let you speak to him," he insisted. "But I can put it upstairs. If they agree, I'll give you ten minutes alone. No sound, but visual observation."

It was agreed, providing Alex could monitor the observation.

It was more than thirty minutes before Russo returned. "It was a fight," he said. "But they're willing to let you see him, provided we get a full statement, from both Silver and you."

* * *

George didn't look too bad. In fact he seemed to have grown straighter—the cowed look he left the flat with, gone. "I killed her," he said, reaching out to touch her hand.

"We only have a short time," she stated deliberately. "So I need to know what happened."

"She was going to take the children. She lied to me," he said, his eyes glistening with anger. "I suspected as much when she had the children in a different place to Alex's mother, but I didn't know where they were, so I couldn't do anything earlier."

"So you just killed her?"

"I tried to talk to her, but she laughed at me," he sighed. "I think I knew I'd have to kill her even back at the flat. You see, while she was talking about Olivia I was remembering. I remembered Olivia's smell and how safe and loved I felt with her, how she'd play with me and talk to me—how affectionate she was. I even have vague memories of your father—his kindness, his gentleness. Then they were gone and everything changed. And I never felt safe again…except with you."

For a moment he was deep in thought.

"If I hadn't killed her, Jeremy and Samantha would never have been safe," he continued, unapologetically. "It would have been you and me all over again."

"So you just pulled the gun and shot her?"

"No. After the pilot left with the children I asked her if, even for one moment, she'd ever loved me. That's when I shot her."

"What did she say?"

"She told me that of course she did. She told me that I was better in bed than anyone else." Now the tears were streaming down his face. "That's what she said to me—that I was a good lover. All I could think about was what you once said about us being the only ones standing between the children and Mother. Suddenly she wasn't my mother, she was just this woman who used us and controlled us and hurt us our whole lives. If it wasn't my children, Nat, it would have been someone else's. If I'd let her live, she'd go on destroying innocent lives. I had no choice."

Now she moved her hands to his. "I don't want you to do an interview until I get you a decent lawyer," she said quietly. "Russo will be mad as hell, but that's his problem, and don't admit to anything else. We'll use the abuse—"

"No," he interjected, shaking his head. "No more, Nat. No more excuses. I don't want the world to know what she made us do. It would serve no purpose except to lose you your job and self-respect and taint us both as victims or perverts. The press would have a field day, and the kids would be tainted for years. I want them to have a normal life—some happiness."

"But—"

"No, Nat," he said adamantly. "I'll tell them that she was planning to abduct the children because she was a domineering grandmother, that we fought and I lost my temper and shot her. They can accept that explanation or not, but it has to end here. I know I'll go to prison for a very long time, even life. But I don't care. It's not like I don't deserve it, and I'll do it easy knowing that you and the kids are finally safe."

Now it was Nat's face wet with tears. "Oh God, George," she said. "I'm so sorry. I should have done something years ago."

"You have nothing to be sorry for," he assured her. "Her evil controlled us both. I just want you to look out for Jeremy and Sam. I want you to sell up all the properties in my name and put the money in trust for the kids. I'd been converting her properties to my name for years. She might have been a genius at corruption, but she was useless at business. The kids should be well taken care of. Both of their mothers can do well with a bit of help, and they won't have to struggle financially. And with you as their aunty, I know they'll be okay. But I don't ever want them to know about what we did for her...not ever."

"George, what happened to Mother's journal?"

"She forced me to give it to her when she took the kids. She destroyed it. I'm so sorry," he said quietly. "It told how she killed Olivia and your father. She wrote about how she and Vladimir took you and your mother's body to a forest somewhere to bury. Vlad dug the hole and then Mother threw you in with Olivia's body, and they caved the earth in around you. But then, for some reason, she changed her mind and decided to keep you. When she'd left you buried long enough, they pulled you out and told you that you would forget everything or she'd put you back in the earth. She bragged about how you'd soiled yourself in terror."

He paused to glance around the room.

"Please tell me it all," she insisted. "It's too late for secrets."

Nodding, he continued, "According to the journal, after that, every time you rebelled, or referred to Olivia or your previous life, she and Vlad would take you somewhere, dig a hole and bury you alive, before pulling you out." He hung his head. "She said it was exciting to see whether you'd survived or not. In the end, of course, you became Charlotte Silver's obedient daughter."

"And what about Christine Martin, how was she involved?"

"I think she intended giving you the journal. She spoke to me about it, but she wouldn't let me see it or even tell me what was in it. She just said that it was awful, but that it was stuff you needed to know. I don't know what happened or why she didn't take it to you, but then she overdosed."

"Did she, George? Or was Mother's hand in that as well?"

He shook his head. "I don't know, Nat, I really don't. I suppose Mother could have given her some pure. I warned Chris that Mother was dangerous, but she didn't seem to care. Chris had a bad drug problem, and if anything it got worse around that time. The only reason Mother let her stay was because, despite the drugs, she still had her young girl looks and she made Mother a lot of money. I was out of it myself that night and I honestly don't know what happened."

Suddenly the door of the interview room opened. "I think you've both had enough time," stated the big detective. "We need to get on with the interview. Are you willing to give a recorded statement?" he asked George, indicating the video equipment.

"Yes," nodded George, looking at Nat. "It's time. Let's get it done."

"Are you sure you don't want a lawyer?" Nat asked, standing and moving toward the handsome man. "It's not too late."

"Yes, it is, Nat," he answered, moving to embrace her. "It's over now. And I feel better than I've ever felt before. Please don't worry about me."

* * *

After they'd taken George away, Russo said, "I need to know what he told you and I'll need a statement about the family situation. That was our deal…right?"

"Yes, it was," she admitted. "But you'll find it very uninteresting. All he spoke about was the children and looking after them. He argued violently with his mother when he found out she intended smuggling them out of the country. Immigration had a warning on the children and his mother's access to them had been a bone of contention for some time. His mother was very volatile and he assumed the pilot was working for her, that's why he had the gun. From what he said, the gun went off during a violent argument."

"He shot her in the head…twice. Did you know that?"

"Like I said, the gun went off when she attacked him. You know what anger and fear can do—you see it all the time. And, you'd know as well as I do that it's easy to fire off two shots in quick succession in a struggle."

"Right," he said, his eyes betraying his disbelief, but also his compassion. "Anyway, that will be up to Mr. Silver to tell us, but we will be denying bail until his court appearance."

"I doubt he'll seek bail," she responded quietly. "But I'll get him a lawyer for his court appearance."

They agreed to Nathalie returning to give her statement the next day and told her that her commander would have to be notified of the charges against her brother. Afterward they returned to Norma's. She was fine, having slept most of the time they were away.

Later, they spoke to the Department of Family & Community Services, who had been brought in by the police to take custody of the children when George was arrested. The children had seen nothing and were aware of nothing and had been returned to their families.

They'd decided to go to Alex's to shower, sleep and determine on their next course of action. Strangely Nathalie felt nothing at the death of Charlotte Silver—the woman she had believed to be her mother for almost her entire life. There wasn't happiness or relief or even sadness—just a strange lack of emotion. Her concern was for George, and yet a part of her knew that George was going to be okay—he'd vindicated himself and finally made things right. He'd find his own peace.

The children would be well taken care of. Emotionally they'd be supported by their own loving mothers and she'd do all she could to maintain contact.

Suddenly she was exhausted, but she still needed to contact Josh. There was a strong probability that there would be repercussions from George's charges and her consequent refusal to make a statement immediately. Depending on Russo's report to his superiors, the NSW Police Force could view it as obstructive. While she didn't care, she wanted Josh to know some of the circumstances.

After a fifteen-minute explanation, he told her to take a hot bath and go to bed, checking first that Alex would remain with her.

They showered together and, even as mentally and physically exhausted as they were, brought each other to completion while the steaming water poured over them. To touch and be touched was reassuring and provided both women with a sense of belonging, while their gasping, thrusting climaxes released the mountain of built-up tension and confusion.

Afterward they tumbled into bed and, clinging together, drifted into dreamless sleep.

EPILOGUE

Detective Russo never lodged a complaint about Nathalie, and she was cleared to return to work with no blemishes on her record.

After agreeing to a pre-sentence psychological assessment, George was eventually charged with manslaughter and received an eight-year sentence, with a six-year non-parole period. The psychologist, hired by George's barrister, was Dieter, and, though he didn't mention the sexual abuse, his conclusion to the court was that George had spent a lifetime emotionally intimidated by his mother and that the threat of losing his children to her caused him to panic and threaten her with the gun. He reported that, in the circumstances, George would have seen no other way to deal with her. George's barrister claimed that the gun had accidentally discharged when Charlotte had struggled to take it away from him.

Nathalie continued to see Dieter. There were still the occasional sweating, gasping awakenings, but now at least they related to something substantial. Slivers of memory returned intermittently, many of them unpleasant, but each memory provided another piece of the puzzle, which helped fill the gaps in her childhood.

There were no new leads in the murder investigation and no new killings. Reluctantly the task force closed the case and concluded that Jacqueline St. Clare had killed all three women as some sort of revenge for her perceived rejections. They also concluded that Bella Pittolo had killed St. Clare in self-defense when she'd discovered her girlfriend was the killer. A lack of forensic or other evidence and Bella's suicide precluded any other conclusion. Privately, however, the detectives believed that Bella Pittolo had been involved in the murders with Jacqueline St. Clare. Two embittered women living on the fringe, never quite accepted and often openly rejected—who'd taken their revenge on an uncaring and, as they saw it, hostile lesbian community. In the end the outcome would make little difference to the families of the dead women and with both Bella and Jackie dead there was no further danger.

* * *

Six months after reuniting, Alex and Nathalie took a long holiday. George had awarded Nathalie power of attorney over the children's trusts, and part of the reason for the trip was to amalgamate Charlotte's estate in the US with her Australian estate. There were no further journals among Charlotte's property and it looked as if everything personal had been destroyed prior to her fleeing America. Nor could Nathalie trace any record of her father or mother. They'd visited the address in San Diego that Nathalie had provided during her hypnosis, but disappointingly, the house had changed hands numerous times, and nobody remembered the young mixed-race woman and her two small children who had rented briefly all those years ago.

George wasn't giving up, though, and was now financing a highly reputable private detection agency to continue the investigation. To him, Olivia Duncan was the mother who'd shown him what a parent should be. She'd made him capable of loving his own children that way, and he wanted Nathalie to know all she could about her parents' families.

George had done what she couldn't do, but what she'd wanted to do since childhood. How many times, in her imagination, had she killed Charlotte? Seen all the horror and poison behind the beautiful façade and coldly pulled that trigger.

But Mother had been right, she was weak. She'd let the circumstances have control and she'd followed blindly, fearfully, into an abyss of corruption and destruction that had impacted so many.

Were there other children like her and George? Of course there were. That was where the real money lay. But because, as teenagers, she and George didn't ever see it—didn't want to see it—it didn't exist. How many children had Mother been allowed to destroy because she and George were too scared to fight her—too indoctrinated to tell anyone what she'd done?

Dieter brought her focus back to his rooms, his couch. And his words told her that she had to learn to forgive herself. And she listened—really listened. And her mind absorbed his sentiments, because she longed to believe him. But that part of her that she knew as *the inner truth*, that kernel right down near her soul, continued to scream denial.

You let it happen. Even after you'd experienced hell and survived, you turned your back and left those unidentified children to fend for themselves. You told yourself that no one would believe you. A child's word, a teenager's word against powerful, wealthy adults. And anyway, you'd brought it on yourself, so perhaps those other children had done so too. And you'd continued to help her right into your teens. Then as an adult the cowardice had lingered, and you'd asked yourself why you should attack the viper's nest now, when the viper had finally stopped biting you?

Justifications, excuses, cowardice, culpability—those were the words that reverberated and simply wouldn't go away. Yet she couldn't admit to how those demons haunted her, because then they'd worry endlessly—Dieter and Alex—without understanding that nothing they could do, nothing they could say, would ever erase the truth of those accusations.

She had to find a way to make it right. She couldn't change what she'd done or failed to do, so she had to spend the rest of her life making reparation. She had to spend it hunting down these evil creatures that tore away the hearts and souls of little children and poisoned their futures—simply to satisfy their own perverse needs. She had to become their destroyer. If necessary, she had to become the children's avenger.

In the end, though, no matter what she did, or how much therapy she undertook, only she could know what it had been like to be the fortune teller's daughter. And only Alex could help her forget.

Bella Books, Inc.

Women. Books. Even Better Together.

P.O. Box 10543
Tallahassee, FL 32302

Phone: 800-729-4992
www.bellabooks.com